Adam's Unorthodox, Unnatural Law Practice

By Lynn Marron

An Adam Martin Paranormal

Book Designer: Leonard J. Bloom, Jr.

Published by Kear Press
            Stratford, CT

LIBRARY OF CONGRESS: 2016931833
Print ISBN: 978-1-942888-09-3
E-Book ISBN: 978-1-942888-10-9
                    Rev 1 7/18

To contact Lynn Marron, or see more of her work, go to www.lynnmarron.com

This book is dedicated to

Karen Asard-Moreland

Who as a lawyer has always

sought to work

her own kind of magic

to help others.

It Began...

"Adam inherited Quentin's property and his weird law practice? "
said the shocked woman. "Have you told him?"

"No."

Unlike her twin brother's hair which was silver with age, Jereusila kept hers honey blonde. Now as the tall man sat down behind his chambers' desk, she settled in front of it.

"It's nearly a year since his great-uncle's death. Why hasn't Quentin's will been probated?"

"The executor is keeping it out of court."

"Who is the executor?"

"Me."

Her blue eyes brightened. "An inheritance. This is wonderful! You'll have to tell Adam and probate the will immediately!" Pronounced Federal judge, Jereusila Martin Obermeyer.

"Thank you, your honor." Her twin brother and Missouri State Court judge acidly commented. "What if our idiot nephew decides to continue Quentin's supernatural law practice?"

His sister stopped, obviously conflicted. "There were all those rumors about vampires and zombies. That can't have been true."

"Quentin enjoyed making fools out of the rest of us! I don't want another Martin tarred with all that superstitious claptrap!"

Jereusila seemed to be parsing it all out. "Why leave it to Adam? Uncle Quentin barely knew him. Quentin never dealt much with any of us..." She weighed it more. "I thought everything would go to that strange secretary of his, that woman he lived with."

"He didn't 'live' with Wynoma–she lives on the

property in one of the three guesthouses. She has a life interest in that house. That and the other tenant's rights will complicate the sale."

"Other tenant?"

"One André Duclair, a silver-haired black man who speaks with a French accent. He lives in a small cottage on the property and handles the farming end. André shared the farm profits with Quentin, and the will states that the arrangement is to continue. I may make a cash offer to buy out his life interest."

"You talked with André?"

Jeremiah shrugged. "If you can call it that. It was kind of like trying to cross-examine a bucket of wet cement."

"He's playing you! You can't farm successfully and be brain dead."

"That so? Try talking with André," her brother finished tartly.

"What does Quentin's estate entail?"

Jeremiah stretched his long frame back in his chair. "Lots of acreage, including most of a lake. There's the main mansion, three guesthouses. Barns. A few head of cattle, chickens. Some farmland and a decent orchard kept up by André. Forest acreage."

"Cash?"

Jeremiah shook his head. "Should've been a lot but, hell, I can't find any of it."

"Did you contact all the banks?"

"Everything in Missouri, but after the Great Depression, Quentin never really trusted banks."

She frowned. "How old was he anyhow?"

"The birth certificate I found said Quentin was thirty-one years younger than Grandfather Frank."

"That can't be right," Jereusila objected. "Grandpa Frank always referred to Quentin as his older 'uncle,' as the senior member of the Martin family."

"I'm pretty sure the birth certificate is phony. There were rumors about Quentin's connections and convenient paperwork."

His twin sister looked away. "Quentin was always showing me his silver dollars and ancient doubloons. He had collected stacks of antique coins. Do you think the secretary or someone else grabbed it?"

"Nope. It's all probably buried on the property somewhere. God, that Queen Anne main house has sixteen rooms, all crammed with stuffed bears, canoes, and monkey idols. I found a secret passageway in the Game room and another hidden room in the basement. I bet there's more. It's a spook house alright—Quentin made it that way, to push the 'odd' reputation."

"But if there is money there, Adam's got to search..."

"I don't want him anywhere near that house! Everything has got to be liquidated as soon as possible! Hell, being in that damned mansion I even started getting strange feelings."

"Could the practice be sold?"

"To who, some young lawyer specializing in werewolves? C'mon, Jereusie, there is nothing there!"

"Adam's passed his bar exam." Jereusila rose and looked down at her taller twin brother. "We're having a party for him, and since you're the closest thing he has to a father, you've got to come."

He glared at her. "We're celebrating that he was the lowest in his class? That he took an extra year to graduate? That he had to take the bar exam three times?"

"The first time he was nervous. The second, his friend was out of town when his wife went into premature labor, and Adam couldn't just dump her in the emergency room and run."

Jeremiah shook his head. "His cousin Franklin graduated Summa Cum Laude from Yale. He's now a respected Connecticut judge."

"Adam's younger."

"Not by much."

"Adam's bright–you've admitted that." Jereusie sat down again, to appeal to him.

Her brother grimly shook his head. "But he's always going off on some fool quest!"

Jereusila's face looked older, tired. "Adam lost his parents so young, and he constantly has such hard luck. I'm wondering if this inheritance will only make things worse for him."

"He's just got to shape up!"

"If you sold the estate, would he have enough money to buy into a decent law practice and get a house?"

"If he didn't invest it all in another phony 'electricity from fermented pickles' scheme. Or pay for some waitress' trip to France."

"That was to Lourdes because her cancer was advancing." Jereusila sighed. "Our nephew George is doing very well in the prosecutor's office, maybe he could get Adam a job?"

Her brother tightened his lips. "Adam Martin, a prosecutor? The kid who is always feeling sorry for everyone? Always trying to fix everything?"

"I think I can get him a starter position at Fenner, Chambers & Cockburne." She sounded unsure.

"You're attaching your reputation to a lazy, do nothing–what if he washes out?"

"Since mother died, he has nobody but us! Jere, he's our nephew, we have to do something. Paying for his college was fine,

but now he needs a start in life."

"He needs a kick in the..."

"Jere!" She stood up to her full six-foot height, signaling the end of negotiations. "The licensing party will be a barbeque at my house this Saturday at four p.m. We'll tell him of the inheritance at the party, and then it will be up to him."

Jeremiah rubbed his forehead, as if in pain. "Yhep. It's his decision, and the one thing I know Adam has inherited from the Martins is a streak of pure, hard rock bull-headedness!"

Summoned by the Resurrection Sisters

Since he inherited his Great Uncle Quentin's law practice, Adam Martin hadn't defended a succubus or bailed out a werewolf. That looked like it was about to change.

"It's all in Mr. Quentin's special clients' file cabinet," said the six-foot two-inch tall Wynoma as she strode down the darkened hall to the back of his offices in the Queen Anne mansion. Adam still couldn't believe he had inherited the house with the apartment upstairs, the law practice, farm, and Wynoma. Yeah, a great inheritance, but Adam wished his secretary didn't tower over him so much.

She stopped before a green-painted steel, legal-sized filing cabinet with five very solid looking drawers, each with an individual lock. Adam eyed them. In the three months since he had taken over this museum of a house, he never paid any attention to this cabinet.

Wynoma Poxcow's long cheeked, dark reddish face was unlined, youthful looking and the funny thing was that Adam remembered she looked just as youngish the few times he had come here as a boy. Those were kind of funny, scary visits, probably because his father always seemed so nervous, but usually those visits ended with kindly Uncle Quentin giving Adam a huge bag of root-beer
barrel candies for his ride back home.

Still, Adam hadn't seen his Great Uncle in years so with all the closer relations and prominent cousins in the law, why had Quentin chosen him to inherit everything? In Missouri, actually throughout the United States, the Martin family of lawyers and judges were renowned, but within the family, Great Uncle Quentin's practice was only discussed in whispers. In fact, the only times his father had brought Adam to Quentin's mansion had been for "special" cases, ones that could only be discussed behind closed doors. Of course, he had to admit, in the Martin family circle Adam's own legal work wasn't discussed too openly either.

Wynoma shifted through a ring of keys with some sort of a small, yellow feather fetish hanging off of them. Not the regular office ring, definitely not one he had seen before. When the lock popped out, she pulled out the third drawer. Nodding her head, she muttered. "Yes, green sticker. The Resurrection Sisters' Foundation. The Marie Pancoff Estate." With difficulty, she pulled out a thick folder from the overstuffed drawer, and then a second one, equally as thick.

As she handed him the two special, extension files, Adam noted that in the drawer there was another manila folder with a black sticker, marked "Poxcow, Wynoma." He would have to look at that when Wynoma wasn't around. But where did she keep those keys?

Wynoma looked at him as if reciting to a small not very bright boy. "Marie Pancoff was extremely wealthy but had never gotten around to producing an heir or making a will. Her greedy nephew and niece were eagerly waiting for her to die, but she had a number of friends at her Revivalists' City. There she formed what Marie called her 'little family,' and she wanted all her money to go to them."

"A simple will?"

Wynoma frowned. "The problem was that while some of these women were above reproach, an ex-school principal, a former women's jail warden..."

"Sounds good..."

"There were others not so pure. A convicted con woman, ex-vaudevillian stripper, and an illegal alien."

"Undocumented," Adam corrected without thinking.

"The correct judicial term is illegal," Wynoma returned frostily. "At Marie Pancoff's request, your uncle set up the Resurrection Sisters' Foundation."

Adam turned through pages of legal work and newspaper clippings. "The estate closed seven, nearly eight years ago, why are the Pancoffs questioning this now?"

"Apparently developers are very interested in the land Revivalist City is on."

"Why is called Revivalist City?"

"In the 1840's a charismatic, traveling preacher named Jacob Stoneman bought several farms around Lake Crystal, where he built a revivalist's parade ground. First, there was a big tent, and then as the crowds increased, he built permanent wooden buildings. Besides revivalist meetings, they had church cookouts, tenting, fishing, boating–it became a sort of church summer camp. Almost an amusement park with games and pony rides.

"It was active until 1876. During a meeting, with hundreds hallelujahing, lightning struck the central meeting hall and fire swept through, killing over fifty, including the Reverend Stoneman. His wife and children rebuilt some cabins and kept Revivalist City going as a religious-themed camping ground until it was sold in the Great Depression to Marie Pancoff's father. Marie was born in one of the old cottages and actually believed she might be the reincarnation of the Reverend Stoneman."

Adam could never really understand where Wynoma stood on an issue from her emotionless voice, so he was rapidly reading court papers. "So my Uncle Quentin set up this Resurrection Sisters Foundation. The named women would take care of Revivalist City until Marie was reborn into this life, and then take care of her?" He looked up at Wynoma. "The court accepted reincarnation as the basis of a trust?'

"Your uncle was a very persuasive man."

"The high priests of Tibet have been given signs to guide them to the next reincarnation of the Dalai Lama. How does the Foundation find the next life of Marie?"

"Your uncle left that to the Foundation's Board to figure out."

"Currently, there are three women in charge. Hildey Mountbattan. Georgia Peach, and Alison Brenner..." Adam glanced at a newspaper clipping. "She's the convicted con woman?"

"Peach and Brenner have crossed over, and they were replaced by ex-nuns, Reverend Mother Rose and Sister Josey. Under the Foundation's rules, they manage things with your uncle's oversight. Now yours. "

"You said there was a land offer?"

"Many times over the years the Directors have been contacted by developers, but the Foundation has always firmly refused to sell or even discuss relocation. Recently one of the more enterprising developers apparently contacted the Pancoffs, and now they've hired a lawyer."

"Who?" Adam asked.

"John O'Brien."

"Shit. Wenddal, O'Brien, and Morgan? They only work on contingency, and they never take a case, unless they know it's for big bucks and they're gonna win. They won't even discuss a settlement."

"Perhaps you might wish to consult with your Cousin Franklin, or maybe even your uncle, Judge Jeremiah?"

No–he did not! "Actually, I did manage to get through law school without my family's intervention." Much to the absolute surprise of the senior members of the Martin family, and even Adam himself. "Who is our client?"

Wynoma tilted her head to one side. "Of course the Resurrection Sisters personally don't have any money, but the Foundation is fairly solid. We can be paid out of that."

He looked at a colorful handbill. "There's a fortune teller there? Madame Terri? Is anyone still overseeing their finances?"

"Monthly I go over to the Foundation and look at all their bills, and they are supposed to consult me on any unusual upcoming purchases. Occasionally, I would have to send Mr. Quentin over to speak with them and point out that they must leave the principal to grow and not kill the goose laying the golden eggs."

"Do they listen?"

It was hard to read Wynoma's face. "They've all known what it is to go without food and shelter."

"If we have to show the Foundations books in court?"

She sighed. "The balance sheet is strong, but things like facelifts, imported wine for banquets, and group trips to Italy may be frowned upon."

"Does it get any better?" asked Adam bitterly.

"You have a court date next week before Judge Kustanick. He is a well know practical man, if a bit impatient."

"Respect a nun?"

"I believe he's an atheist."

"Any good news?"

"I don't think he will be too sympathetic to either side."

As she walked away, Adam wished he had taken a phone photo of that set of keys. He wanted a private look at this cabinet some time because he wanted to know more about his uncle's reputation for eccentric clients without Wynoma supervision.

*   *   *

'**Revivalist City**' read the wrought iron sign arching over the road between two substantial brick posts. As Adam stopped his car, he smelled freshly mown grass, and he saw spacious lawns stretched before clumps of trees. He got out and took a few photos with his cell phone. He had to build some sort of case to prove the Foundation was solid financially and functioning properly. Adam photographed two distant lines of white cottages, set on either side of a wide, central green space. Before the fire, that central area was probably Stoneman's revivalist sanctuary. Adam did not photograph the crudely hand-lettered sign duck-taped to the gate that said, '**NO TRESPASSING! THAT MEANS YOU!**'

Parking before the first cabin, Adam got out and

snapped a picture of an elderly, angular-faced man–no woman–
-on a riding lawn mower. Presumably one of his clients. He
walked onto a baseball field sized clearing before the sun
sparkling lake, studying two strings of one story, Victorian
style gingerbread cottages. He counted twelve on each side,
and behind the trees closer to the lake, he could make out two
larger white buildings.

As he stood lining up another shot, a woman in a
flaming red kimono screamed, "THIS IS PRIVATE
PROPERTY! NO PICTURES ALLOWED!" Arms waving
like some avenging fury, she advanced
on him. That flapping kimono had a fiery red face, brassy
blonde hair and a voice that could blister house paint. "GET
OFF THIS PROPERTY!"

Behind the obnoxious fury, a tall woman, in a heather-
brown jersey sweater and matching pants hurried towards him.
The brown lady said in a calming voice, "Hildey, please. We
don't even know the gentleman's name."

"HE'S TAKING PICTURES!"

Adam nodded. "Yes, ma'am, I am. I'm Adam Martin,
and I'm taking them because as your lawyer, I may want to
present them in court." Coming from the cottages several other
ladies were joining them as fast as walkers, canes, and
wheelchairs would allow.

"LAWYER?!" Screamed Hildey. "GET OUT!"

A white-haired lady, now beside her, yelled into her
ear. "HILDEY! GET YOUR HEARING AID! HE'S OUR
LAWYER!"

Hildey's fiery face drained to a gray-white, and Adam
suddenly worried if she was going to have a heart attack. The
woman in brown turned to her friend. "Margaret, could you
please take Hildey inside. Check her numbers, she may need
insulin."

An almost collapsing Hildey was led away. At the tall
woman's nod, the other ladies moved off, and Adam felt he

should apologize. "I never meant to upset her."

"Hildey gets excited easily. Margaret is a retired emergency room nurse and will take care of her. I'm Sister Josey, one of the directors here. Wynoma said she was sending someone."

"Adam Martin." He shook her hand and then looked down the wide lawn, past the cabins to a group of seniors sitting before easels on the edge of the Lake. Adam snapped another photo of a young woman, who was pointing to an elderly man's painting.

Sister Josey supplied. "That's Amiee's painting class for the Senior Men's Club in town. They love having a day out here by the lake." She looked at him nervously. "The Foundation pays for the bus and their lunch."

Adam had memorized the entire two folders. "Amiee? Is she the girl who drowned her baby?"

Sister Josey's face folded into pain. "When she threw the baby and herself into the river, Amiee was sure that a unicorn had promised them both a life of wonder in a golden kingdom under the water."

Adam shot another angle of the class. "She was off her meds?"

"But here her medication is monitored quite closely." Sister Josey seemed to be feeling him out. "There is so much unused land here. If the Foundation could build a few more cottages..."

With regret, he had to ground her in reality. "Sister, if you all had to leave?"

Sister Josey looked about her. "I and maybe three others could manage to get by, but life would be a lot less pleasant." She sounded just a trace bitter at that and then became sadder. "But the rest here, because of physical or mental disabilities, would hopelessly sink through any ragged safety net."

Sister Josey seemed to be looking to him for comfort,

but instead, he only said, "Perhaps you can show me around."

She nodded, and they started walking to the right line of cottages as he asked, "You weren't one of the original Foundation beneficiaries?'

"No. Only three are left. Hildey, Madame Terri, and Florence. I was taken on after I left the convent."

He wondered if it was an offensive question, but still asked, "You had a crisis of faith?"

She seemed faintly amused at the thought. "Oh, no. I joined the Sisters when I graduated high school, and I taught mathematics and physical education at St. Elizabeth's in the City. But over the years, our immigrant parishioners moved to the suburbs, and our new students tended to be Protestant. Fine children, but eventually the diocese did not have a large enough congregation to pay for the school. With St. Elizabeth's gone, it was decided that our order must disband." It seemed a painful memory for her. "Years ago, our order's younger nuns coming in would have cared for our retired sisters, but..."

Adam nodded, not saying what he thought of the Church that after decades of loyal service, dumped its aged sisters on their families and state's deficient charities.

Sister Josey was continuing brightly. "Several of St. Elizabeth's sisterhood were privileged to come here. The Foundation has been God sent for us."

An elder lady using a walker to struggle by glared at Adam's phone camera. Sister explained. "The Pancoffs and their lawyers have been here taking pictures."

"They've actually come on the property?" Adam asked sharply.

"The Pancoffs have been coming here for years, and they seem to know when something is going to go wrong."

"Such as?"

"The pony that bucked a child at the orphans' party. Then a few years ago a newspaper reporter discovered

Florence's cats."

"Cats–how many?"

"The Health Department found twenty-one. We didn't know she had so many, she was feeding them in the woods. When they took the cats away, Florence wouldn't stop crying." Sister sighed. "The newspapers dubbed her the 'Cat Woman,' and the Pancoffs went into court again. Your grandfather..."

"Great Uncle Quentin."

"A saint of a man. He straightened things out."

"Has Florence any cats now?"

"We watch her very carefully and officially restrict her to three adult cats, all neutered. We give her one month to find a home for any strays." Sister's face betrayed guilt, as she amended, "When kittens are involved, we give her a little more time."

Adam followed Sister Josey's firm strides, wondering just how much he could trust her version of things. She seemed to sense his Doubting Thomas attitude when she stopped at the fourth whiteboard cottage. "Come in and see for yourself." On the porch, a fat, white cat with a strange orange and black ringed tail stretched out on the wicker love seat. Sister seemed to apologize for the cat. "Florence spoils them so."

Sister Josey knocked, and then opened the door at the, "Come in, deary." The porch cat jumped down and ran inside ahead of her.

As Adam walked in, he found himself automatically smelling for cat urine, but there was no odor. He looked at Sister Josey.

"The Foundation budgets for special chlorophyl cat litter and Claire comes in to feed the cats and clean out the litter pans twice a day. It has to stay hygienic. Someone, we assume it's the Pancoffs, keeps calling the Health Department on Florence every six months, but since we've been checking, they haven't found anything wrong."

Adam nodded.

Sister Josey pointing to the neat room. "Most of these cabins are about the same," she explained. "A living room, small kitchen, bathroom and one or two bedrooms." To Sister's obvious embarrassment, a large one-eyed, gray tom cat arched his back and spit at Adam.

A tiny voice came from the corner. "Down, Plato! He's my 'attack cat,' or he was a 'he' until the Revenuers got him."

Sister turned to him. "This Adam Martin, Florence–he's our...our friend.

"Do you like cats?" The thin voice came from deep within the overstuffed corner chair that dwarfed the tiny, silver-haired lady, yet smiling, young eyes peered out of the age folded skin. She was stroking a young looking ginger cat, who purred and arched her back to receive every bit of Florence's attention. "This little pretty was born on the Fourth of July. We named her sisters Liberty and Independence, but they had to be adopted out. I think they were part royal Siamese, with blue eyes and such delicate eating habits. They pull their nibbles out of the dish with curved paws." She imitated a paw with her hand, then stroked the cat again. "I named this one Marie after my old friend because she had ginger-colored hair." Rubbing her head against the elderly lady, the cat purred deeper. Florence pointed to the cat who had come with them. "That white one with the striped orange tail is Tiger Rose. I think she was a spy in WWII."

"Would mind if I took some pictures?" Adam asked politely. Florence just smiled, and Marie seemed to preen as she arching her back to be petted again.

Leaving Florence, they passed several cottages, and Adam noted that Madame Terri's had a two foot by three foot, gaudy sign out front, *'Physic Consultations, Psychometry, Aura Readings.'* Sister Josey explained, "She isn't allowed to receive cash for her readings here so Terri mainly just comforts old clients." As they spoke, a woman, who could be

Betty White's younger twin, came out on the porch holding a golden Pomeranian in her arms. "Oh, yes, Houdini," she stage-whispered to the little dog. "He is more than a match for those nasty, greedy people!"

Adam just nodded politely.

Sister Josey pointed to one of the larger cabins. "We have three living there. It is so hard to turn others away, but we do."

Her tour ended in the two-story, main meeting and dining hall overlooking the lake. In a pleasant lounge room with a wall of windows, Adam stood before at a life-sized oil portrait of Marie Pancoff. The strawberry-haired woman was painted sitting, obviously in this room. She was dressed in a pink flowered, ruffled organza gown and held a small, nibbled cookie in her hand, with a fragile Limoges teacup beside her. She benignly looked down at him with calm, azure eyes, as if certain he was up to saving her legacy. Unfortunately, he didn't have any such confidence.

Yes, by his standards the Resurrection Sisters Foundation monies were well spent, and yes, these ladies shouldn't be turned out on the street for another shopping center. Never-the-less, if John O'Brien was half as good as his reputation, the court was probably going to invalidate Marie Pancoff's will. For a brief moment, Adam considered having Madame Terri try to spiritually contact his Great Uncle Quentin for some idea of how he was ever going to defend this case.

For the court date, Adam had originally planned to summon all of the Resurrection Ladies before the Judge, but Judge Kustanick had notified him that he wanted a preliminary meeting restricted to just lawyers in his chambers. Unfortunately, Adam arrived late to find, that while he had only his notes and photos, his honorable opponent John O'Brien had brought all his three clients. Smiling triumphantly, the Pancoff relatives sat in the judges' large modern-art decorated chambers, so before they were even starting, Adam pictured the scales of justice tipping ever so slightly in favor of the plaintiffs.

Not even bothering to look up at them, Judge Kustanick studied their file. "Actually, I have some complicated ligation come up–could this be finished today or postponed, for say a September date?"

Immediately grabbing at the chance, Adam said, "The defendants would agree to a postponement."

Before O'Brien could respond, one of his clients spoke up. "No–we can't. We have a closing date in August."

"Closing?" The judge looked up.

"For the property. It will be the Crystal Lake Mall, that will bring jobs and people and money to the community. We have a generous offer for the land." She actually got up and dropped a paper on the Judge's desk.

He studied it, seemingly impressed. "Yes. Very generous."

The woman continued. "We're selling now."

The second woman there objected. "Tatiana, we should hold an open auction for the land, because we'll get a better price!"

"This is no better price! We have to take this before they change their minds!"

The Judge looked annoyed. "Excuse me, are we discussing the disposition of a property that you do not, at this time, own?"

"It should've been ours! It will be ours." Tatiana sourly finished.

From the look on the judges' face, Adam mentally pictured the scales of justice shifting to tip ever so slightly in his favor.

"Mr. Martin," the judge studied the paper-work before him. "The Marie Pancoff Foundation for Perpetual Reincarnation Care, a.k.a. The Resurrection Sisters?"

Adam looked up. "Yes, your honor, it was the clear intention of Marie Pancoff, that her close friends, and later, other members joining the Foundation..."

"Objection!"

"To what Mr. O'Brien?" The judge asked in an annoyed tone.

"The Foundation should be limited to those who were on the property while the mentally incompetent Marie Pancoff was alive. And we believe several of those people have died."

Adam wished he could sound half so authoritative as he interrupted the Pancoff's lawyer. "Pardon me, your honor, but in page 3, paragraph 4, sub-unit 6, it clearly states that the Foundation is limited to the current members and, I quote, *'those whom the Board shall deem necessary and eligible for future membership.'* There is an attached list of current membership in your file and three of the ladies are original beneficiaries. The list may be added to in the future as it was Mrs. Pancoff's intent that the Foundation continue its good works into perpetuity."

Tatiana Pancoff was outraged. "Good works?! A scam artist telling fortunes?"

"Madame Terri doesn't charge, and it's more in terms of psychic counseling of her old friends."

"Worthless vagrants dining on steak and lemon mousse? Uneducated idiots that don't even realize the value of the land," the sister-in-law added.

O'Brien sought to cut his clients off. "The heirs are charging mismanagement of the Foundational assets."

Adam defended. "I have balance sheets to attest that the assets are being correctly utilized within the bounds of the original donor's intent and..."

Tatiana cut him off. "Aunt Marie was crazy! She should never have been allowed to make a will!"

The Judge looked at O'Brien. "At the time of Miss Pancoff's death, your clients challenged their aunt's competency and failed in court. Is that correct?"

Their lawyer nodded. "An unfortunate decision. Now, your honor, we are claiming that the Foundation is null and void because, after seven years, your court will be pronouncing Mrs. Pancoff missing and presumed dead."

Judge Kustanick looked confused. "Missing and presumed dead? She was dead. She is dead! I saw a death certificate in this file." He riffled through the papers. "I thought I saw it."

Adam had it ready, passing his copy to the Judge. "Yes sir, Marie Pancoff died in her own bed on May 1st, attended by her physician, the late Dr. Connor Morgan. Marie's body was buried in section 7, lot 26 of the Pinewood Cemetery in the plot with her parents."

"So she's dead." Determined the Judge. "Why would I pronounce her 'missing and presumed' dead, if we know she died and was certified buried?"

John O'Brien spoke for his clients with a firm finality that denied any other interpretation could possibly be made. "Marie Pancoff set up the Resurrection Sister's Foundation to take care of herself when she was reincarnated."

"Reincarnation and resurrection are absolutely ridiculous beliefs, however," the Judge interrupted, "obviously per the lady's wishes."

At the interruption, O'Brien's voice grew frostily. "That was over seven years ago. Seven years, eight months to be exact. In that time, Mr. Martin's clients have not found an infant that shows any physical marking or past life memories, or any other indication that Marie Pancoff has reincarnated. So, since Marie Pancoff cannot be shown to be reborn and alive and currently being cared for by the Foundation recipients, then her grieving family must bow to the inevitable and have her declared missing and presumed dead."

The Judge sat dumbfounded. "You're saying that if Marie Pancoff is declared dead a second time, then the court must determine that invalidates her previous instructions and declare the Resurrection Sisters Foundation ended, by reason that their founding purpose was never consummated?"

Tatiana cut in triumphantly. "In which case, the land reverts to her relatives. Myself, my brother Peter, and my sister-in-law, Ogla Pancoff."

With a sinking feeling, Adam knew that the Judge would have to find for the plaintiffs.

Clearly unhappy about that, Judge Kustanick turned to Adam. "Do you have anything more to say on your clients' behalf?"

"May I approach?"

Kustanick looked briefly at his clock, then nodded.

As O'Brien joined him, Adam started laying out eight-by-ten computer printed photos on the Judge's desk. "This is the Main Foundation building, and the sisters celebrating in the group dining hall. The Foundation's party for underprivileged children. The Sisters' pony classes for the handicapped..."

"Any pictures of them feeding the starving Nigerians? " Tatiana asked acidly.

The Judge looked at the pictures. "If I invalidate the Foundation these people will..."

Adam continued. "Due to mental and physical disabilities, most will be out of their only homes and probably wind up wards of the State of Missouri."

Judge Kustanick looked to the Pancoffs. "With such a large financial offer on the table, perhaps an out of court settlement could be reached that is mutually beneficial for all parties? A simple million or two could probably take care of these ladies for the rest of their lives?"

Her husband started to say something, but Olga cut him off. "Those scam artists stole our inheritance! We will not give them a penny!"

The Judge regretfully looked to Adam as he continued,

"Unfortunately, this court can not find the Resurrection Sisters Foundation's good works a valid reason for their existence if the original basis for the Foundation is invalid."

The Pancoff's were looking pleased, yet their Lawyer seemed to have a healthy respect for a Martin, even if he still needled Adam, "Do you have any pictures of the convicted confidence woman or the crazy cat lady?"

"Florence?" Suddenly it hit Adam, a way out. "Actually, I do." He pulled another photo from his file. "There is ninety-year-old Florence living in her comfortable cottage. The Foundation restricts her cats, so she's only allowed three now. That ginger one she is cuddling in her lap is her latest. That's Marie, named because she was a dainty eater and has the same hair and eye color as Marie Pancoff."

Tatiana cut in. "The old lady dyed her hair!"

"But it was strawberry blonde by her preference," Adam brightly continued. "That ginger-colored kitten was born July 4th last year in the woods at Crystal Lake. Cats have an average gestational period of 63 days, so in theory, that cat born on July 4th could have been conceived on May 1, the same month, maybe the same day, maybe even the same hour as Marie Pancoff died."

Judge Kustanick looked puzzled, saying nothing.

It was the Pancoff's lawyer, John O'Brien, who just stood there with a look of disbelief on his face. "So you are telling this Court that the Foundation premise is legally valid because?"

Finally seeing it, Judge Kustanick started to smile as Adam delivered the coup de grás. "When Marie Pancoff set up her eternal care Foundation, she never specified that she was coming back as a human..."

A not so legal fling, with a Succubus

"Your cousin George said that you had inherited an unorthodox law practice and that you understood about people who were...different." Clymene Cronin sat in his dark wood office, eyes modestly downcast. The twentyish woman sitting before Adam Martin was too strong featured to be termed Hollywood beautiful. A classic nose, thick, long, black hair tied back simply, and a trim figure mostly hidden by a shapeless business suit.

She pushed court papers across his desk. "Jason Warren has gotten an order of protection against me."

Adam studied them. "If he has this order against you, you can not step on his property, or get within five hundred feet of him."

"I know. I'm a court clerk, and he's a bailiff. I can't go to work. Now, he says I'm still in violation of the order. I'm due in court in two weeks, and he's told everyone I'm having sex with him."

"It shouldn't be too hard to prove otherwise. We just have to pin him down to several dates when he claims you had sex with him, and then prove that you were somewhere else under strict observation. Perhaps a monitored sleep clinic... "

"But I am with him—I mean I will be with him when he summons me again."

Adam stopped for a moment. "You have a key to his house?"

Sounding pained she said, "No–I don't need one. Mr. Martin, do you know what a succubus is?"

"Sort of..." Adam twisted in his chair. Some of Great Uncle Quentin's books were on the shelves behind him. Selecting a worn, leather-bound grimoire, Adam consulted the index, turned to page 526 and read out loud. "According to the Midrash, succubi and incubi are the gets of Father Adam and Lilith. Unclean spirits that have sex with mortals, after being summoned. They suck the blood, seed, and energy from mortals."

"I'm not a vampire, and I don't take some man's seed to Hades!" She seemed insulted at the mere suggestion.

Adam closed the book. "It's been my experience that these books only get about twenty percent of the facts right."

"I do get energy from men. You need that when you don't get much sleep."

Adam had the distinct feeling that she believed every word she said. "How will you go to Mr. Warren?"

"When he calls me, I am condemned to consort with him in spirit form."

"Uh huh." In the two months since he inherited Quentin's practice, Adam had discovered that there were a lot of people, creatures and things that he never would have believed were possible, but this was a little too much. "If you're only a spirit, what kind of sex can you have?"

"Very fulfilling, I'm told," she answered frankly.

"Have you ever charged money for this sex?"

"No." She didn't seem offended or surprised by the question. "It's not required."

Adam was having a very hard time believing the quiet woman before him. "You don't want to go to this Jason?"

"It's not up to me."

"You don't love him?"

"No." She was quite firm on that.

"Do you love anyone else?"

She lowered her eyes to study the floor and Adam just waited. Finally, Clymene said softly, "There is a man. I want to be like a human woman with him. I would like to live with him and maybe have his children. Succubuses can if we have sex in bodily form."

"Who is this man?"

"He's a guard in the courthouse, Bennie Adams. That's his second job while he's building up his own landscaping business. He takes me to the movies and picnics, and we rented a rowboat. Now he's talking about us buying a house together."

"That sounds nice." She seemed so happily innocent, but Adam had to ask, "Have you had sex with him?"

"Oh, no."

"But you have had sex with other men in the courthouse?"

"They usually don't tell on us or others never believe them. Some men think it was just a very intense, erotic dream."

Concerned for her Adam had to point out, "If your Bennie is working in the court, he'll hear about this order of protection."

She looked anguished. "He has heard! But he just thinks Jason is lying. He says I should get a lawyer and sue Jason for slander."

"How many men have you had sex with?"

She frowned. "Just in this country or way back in Greece?"

"Just a general idea," he encouraged.

She seemed to be mentally totting up figures, but finally, the numbers became too great for her. "A lot, I guess."

"Have you been tested for HIV or other communicable diseases?"

"Why?" Clymene seemed to find the question puzzling.

"When I'm having sex with these men, I'm in spirit form. I can't catch anything."

Adam had to think about that one. "Okay. Have you had real physical sex?"

"Bennie and I, we've kissed with our tongues." She shyly blushed.

Adam nodded. "That's a start, but we are going to have to do something about Jason."

"He's addicted."

"Men get addicted to succubi?"

"Oh, yes." She seemed deadly serious. "It's really quite common and very dangerous. Some men never get over it. Some I'll do just once, but others keep calling and thinking about me. Some refuse to stop having sex. They don't eat and don't go to work. Sometimes they die. Rough sex can be very hard on the heart." She sounded like she was pleading. "I don't want to do it anymore. Maybe with Bennie, I could stop..." She looked at Adam and sadly said, "You don't believe me."

"I believe that you believe what you are saying." He silently cursed his awkward phrasing.

She reached into her handbag. "The moon is filling, soon it will be full." She handed him a small parchment roll tied with a tiny, purple-silk ribbon. "If I am with you, then I can't be with Jason. Maybe if he's away from me long enough, he'll get over me! You will have to believe me, to help me, so when you go to bed tonight, slowly read this out loud. Then after the first time, all you will have to do is think of me, and I will be summoned."

That night, Adam went up to the apartment that was above his law offices. He read a Clive Cussler thriller until 10:30, and then he decided to turn off the light. As he reached across the bedstand, he saw Clymene's parchment roll where he had emptied out his pocket contents. Slowly, he slid the silk ribbon off and unrolled a five-inch by four-inch document. It was in ancient Greek. He couldn't understand much of it but stumbled over the words as best he could...

Suddenly, a woman pressed down on top of him. He felt her naked weight, her heat, her full breasts, and her long mare's tail hair falling over his chest. She smelled of sandalwood. Clymene was sliding her warm tongue into his open mouth, twisting her hips on his. Pulling his shorts. Sucking at his shoulder. She couldn't get enough of him! It was his every teenage wet dream!

In the morning, as Adam showered he would have thought it must have been a vivid dream if the soap didn't sting the fingernail claw-marks on his back. He made himself a cup of tea and oatmeal. Feeling great, he was taking two steps at a time on the wide, carved staircase as he heading down from his apartment to his law offices.

In the entryway, his tall, forbidding Cherokee secretary stood there staring at him. "Have a restless night?"

Adam had to remind himself that there was no possible way Wynoma could see the healing scratch marks on his back or smell that faint whiff of sandalwood, yet he still felt guilty. Having sex with a client was really unethical, but he was keeping Clymene from lying with Jason, and from being in violation of her restraining order while he could prepare a defense for her. Those were sufficient mitigating circumstances.

The next night before bed, Adam found himself showering, shaving and putting on a little aftershave lotion and even straightening up his bedroom a bit. But before he had fully stretched out on the bed, Clymene was on him. Thrusting her tongue into his mouth, reaching with urgent hands to guide him in. This time he was ready not just reacting as he got on top, and on the bottom, and sideways.

During the next week, he found himself less and less able to concentrate on dry legal papers as he forced himself to research Jason Warren's work and life. He didn't find much, but he thought it would be enough for the hearing next Friday.

And it was time to stop summoning Clymene. That night, Adam put on a sweat suit and ran for miles and miles. Finally, totally exhausted he fell into a sound asleep, but just before dawn, he woke with that pleasurable tightening of a morning erection and the faint scent of sandalwood. Suddenly Clymene was on him.

Later his secretary found him searching through volumes in the Game Room. "Wynoma, did my uncle have a book that gives...say counter charms against possession by an apparition?"

His secretary stared at him darkly. "The spirits cannot take you unless you open to them."

Adam smiled weakly. "Yhep. Just exercise the old will power. That's the Martin way. Right."

That night when Clymene zapped in, Adam held up his hand. "Wait! Just talk to me! That's a sex thing, too. Talking sex. For a moment, we just talk—okay?

She panted as she crouched doggie style naked on his bed.

"Can you talk in spirit form?" Adam asked her.

"Yes, but why..." Her voice was husky, sexier, more compelling, and the smell of sandalwood was deepening as it overwhelmed him. With great difficulty, Adam tried to marshal his thoughts as he noted what a voluptuous figure she had. "In the courthouse, have you had sex with any of the other men?"

She reeled off a list of names that included several judges and his staid cousin George Martin.

"Thank god, we've pulled Judge Claire Goldstein," murmured Adam.

"I don't think I've ever been with her." Clymene seemed to be trying to remember.

"Judge Goldstein is not a lesbian," Adam supplied.

"Oh." Clymene looked at him. "Didn't your book explain that a succubus can become an incubus if the summoner wishes a male?"

"I missed that." Adam thought about it. "How do you look as a man?"

"You have to summon me."

Curious Adam said, "I'd like a man."

Clymene instantly transformed into a dark-haired, muscular male with large hands and extra-large everything. Hungry eyes locked with Adam's as he moved in...

"**Bring back the female!** Please–I summon the female!" Begged Adam.

By next Thursday, Adam was finding it difficult to walk and was falling asleep at his desk. Wynoma just stared at him, her pale lavender eyes getting harder. "You are going to court for that Greek one?"

"No! We haven't done Greek. I mean–yes, I have...Clymene. Ms. Cronin. She comes from Greece. And I'm defending her. I'm her lawyer. Court, yes, that's where I am going."

"Friday?" She asked coldly.

"Yes, Friday." Trying to clear his mind, Adam looked about. "What day is today?"

Wynoma stared at him, and then from around her neck, she took off a leather cord. Hanging from it was a flat black stone, pierced and polished as a pendant. "You don't hear evil voices when you wear this."

She handed it to Adam. Looking at it, he realized it was incised with a stylized bear. He slipped it over his head and strangely felt better.

That Friday Clymene sat next to Adam at the defendant's table. He realized Judge Goldstein was seeing Clymene as he had, as a somewhat shy, modest court clerk overwhelmed by false accusations. It was a good impression.

Clymene had also told Adam her Bennie was in the court. Adam worried about that realizing he would have to be very careful questioning the complainant to keep Bennie's illusions intact.

Adam called Jason Warren to the witness stand. Jason was unshaven with trembling hands and red-rimmed eyes. The judge was sure to see he was in the late stages of withdrawal, but fortunately, she just wouldn't ever guess what kind of withdrawal it was.

"Mr. Warren, did you not place a protection order against my client, Miss Clymene Cronin?"

Sounding distracted Jason said, "She keeps forcing me to have sex with her."

Adam tried to appear surprised. "Forces you? She does? At your house or hers?"

"Mine. In my bedroom."

"Mr. Warren, I've done some checking. You live with your mother in her house, don't you?"

"Yeah." His eye twitching he looked to Clymene, then looked away.

"Is your mother at home when Miss Cronin is...visiting you?"

"Ma don't hear so well."

"But I've spoken to your mother, if I called her to the witness stand, she would say that she has never seen Ms. Cronin in her house. Isn't that true?"

"Clymene just comes to my room."

"And has sex with you?" Adam gave him a big smile. "Gee, why are you complaining?"

Everyone in the courtroom laughed, except the Judge and Bennie.

Ignoring them, Jason continued. "She's so wild–sometimes it hurts."

"Was she at your house last night?"

"No...she hasn't been around lately."

"Uh huh. Because you got the order of protection against her?"

"No. She was still coming to me with the order."

"Coming to you. How does she get past your mother?" Adam asked as if he couldn't figure it out.

"She appears in my room," Jason said defiantly.

"Appears?" Adam gave a questioning look to the Judge and then stared back at Jason. "Do you open a door for her? Or open a window?"

"It ain't like that."

"You don't want her coming to have sex with you.

Your mother doesn't let her in. You don't open a window. The doors must be locked in that neighborhood. Did you ever give her a key?"

"I just read the Greek stuff..." He looked to Judge Goldstein. "You gotta keep her away. She flies through walls."

"Flies?" The Judge sharply asked.

"She's a ghost or something. You gotta keep her away!" Jason looked terrified.

At that, Adam turned to the Judge. "May I approach the bench?"

Judge Goldstein nodded, and the D.A. joined them.

In an undertone, Adam hotly argued. "Your honor, on this unhinged man's ravings my client has been humiliated and embarrassed by an unfair order of protection that has barred her from her place of work!"

The D.A. just looked at Jason Warren and shrugged.

Judge Goldstein raised her voice for the courtroom. "Mr. Warren, I am dismissing your charges against Ms. Cronin. I will see that your order of protection is rescinded, and I am placing an order of restraint on you! You may not visit or disturb Ms. Cronin at her home or in her workplace. Any violation of this Court's order could lead to proceedings against you." The Judge continued, "And Mr. Warren, the court strongly suggests that you speak with your doctor about possible medicinal intervention." Then Judge Goldstein turned to Clymene. "For the record Ms. Cronin the court apologizes to you."

Bennie looked relieved and happy as Clymene joined him.

After Adam packed up his papers, he found them out in the hallway where Bennie was proposing. "Honey, instead of a diamond ring I've put a down payment on a house. It's a small one, but it has three bedrooms and a yard for kids. Anyone of the judges here will marry us?"

Clymene beamed at him with tears on her long lashes. "Yes. Yes!"

But when Bennie went back on duty, Clymene turned to Adam. "I must pay you for your legal work."

Adam said, "Do you still have anymore of those rolled parchments in your purse?"

"Yes. We always carry them."

"Who makes you carry them?"

"I don't know, maybe my mother did, or her mother..." She said vaguely.

"Your payment to me must be that you do not carry them anymore! Give them all to me, and you must wear this around your neck." He handed her Wynoma's spirit protection necklace. "When you wear this, you will not hear anyone calling to you at night, unless its Bennie."

She looked at him with tragically-aged eyes, that knew better than he. "You will still call to me–you must! And I must come to you." Clymene finished hopelessly.

"No, ma'am." Adam replied, and he had to add, "And take it easy on Bennie. He's human. Maybe just once a night only two or three times a week. You want him to last, okay?"

Clymene left with a bride's blushing smile.

That night Adam determined to go cold turkey with lots of long runs and cold showers. He got through without summoning Clymene by staying up most of the night, working out difficult numeric puzzles. Still, he could faintly smell sandalwood, and at dawn, he knew he had to try to sleep, but there was some fool ringing his front door bell. Still dressed in sweatpants, Adam padded down from his apartment to the main hall.

He opened the door to Jeremiah Martin. His tall uncle was dressed in camouflage, and he was smiling down at his tail wagging, black Labrador. Adam had actually caught Judge Jeremiah in a soft moment as he affectionately scratched the dog's ears. That unaccustomed smile faded from Jeremiah's angular face as he looked Adam over. Since his parents died, Adam was always a bit afraid of his formidable uncle.

Jeremiah eyed Adam closely. "That secretary of yours called. She said you were looking a bit run down."

To play for time, Adam bent down to pet the dog. "Hey, Lucifer." The black lab smelled him and then growled deeply, baring his teeth. The Judge was the only man Adam knew who could breed vicious Labradors.

Adam looked back up to his uncle. Those merciless, icy blue eyes that had sentenced thousands of guilty people bored through him. Adam just tried to relax and have faith in his ability to lie. "Yeah, might be coming down with the flu, but business is picking up. I was in court yesterday, and I saw Cousin George in the hallway."

"How's he doing?" Jeremiah usually sounded like he was doing an interrogation from the bench.

"Great. He showed me pictures of Debbie and the kids. Nice life he's got."

"If you were free, I was going to ask you to come out with me, but you look like something the dogs dug up and chewed. Did you ever get that medical insurance?"

"Still working on it."

"I'll be back at sunset. If you don't look better, we're going to find one of those walk-in clinics. They'll have to take a look at you."

"I'll be fine..."

"Get to bed!" The judge sentenced.

But getting to bed was the last thing Adam dared do. Smelling sandalwood in the car, he wildly drove down to St. Louis. At lunch, Adam managed to get his cousin George alone outside the court house complex.

"George, you were with her—Clymene?"

His cousin wouldn't meet his eyes. "When my mother-in-law had that heart bypass, Debbie took the twins to Philadelphia to help out for two months."

"You had Clymene?"

Normal, boring George whistled slightly. "Oh God, it was great! Toward the end, I was only getting two hours of sleep before I had to get up for court. Man, that whole last month I didn't win one case. I was so happy, I just couldn't prosecute anyone."

"But you beat it! You got away from Clymene, how?"

George thought back. "Debbie was coming home, and I just kept thinking of her. Maybe her divorcing me. I still carry pictures of Debbie and the kids, that I've got to stare at sometimes to banish thoughts of Clymene and that smell of sandalwood. It was hard, but I did it."

Adam looked away. He didn't have a Debbie and kids coming home to him. "Thanks."

Seeing his downcast look, George added. "There is a way out for you too, you know."

Adam looked at him desperately. "How?"

"When you get that relaxed, warm feeling at night even before you envision Clymene and call out her name..."

"Yes." A desperate Adam was starting to feel a bit of that warmth right now.

"Well, when you start thinking about her-- you have got to start picturing Uncle Jeremiah. Think of that stern face. Think if the judge ever finds out you've been screwing a client..."

In a sudden, frigid realization, Adam he knew was permanently cured of his succubus.

The Pied Piper of Sleeping Giant

"Judge Franklin J. Martin is raising Krugerrands for the ransom?" Adam Martin didn't dare laugh out loud, even at the thought of his perfect cousin, the Martin family's best hope for the next Supreme Court's Chief Justice, raising a ransom of gold coins for a Pied Piper?

Even on the phone, Adam could picture it all. He stood just under 5' 9" and the renowned, Connecticut Judge, Franklin J. Martin, was only 5'7", but HH Martin (Hang 'em High) Judge Jeremiah, stood an imposing 6' 4", magnified by his constant angry demeanor. Now his uncle growled at Adam. "Stop gloating you, cretin! Franklin doesn't deal with boogeymen and vampires. How is your practice going?"

"Slows down towards Halloween, everybody's busy."

"You will be consulting for your cousin. Since we can assume your credit cards are maxed out, he will be buying you a plane ticket for tomorrow."

"Actually, I have several court dates coming up," Adam blatantly lied.

"If necessary, I'll have Jereusila claim you're needed in her court."

Jereusila Martin Obermeyer. Aunt Jerusie was Jeremiah's twin sister and a judge in Missouri Federal District Court. She was only 6' tall. Resigning himself to the inevitable, Adam asked, "Who am I billing for this?"

"You want pay? For an opportunity to help your renowned Cousin Franklin? Maybe have some of his judicial excellence rub off on you?"

No chance of that Adam silently vowed. But Jeremiah had raised Adam's college money within the family, and the perfect Judge Franklin and his prominent lawyer wife were probably major donors. "I'll need a hotel and expenses."

"You'll stay with your cousins, and you'll have thirty dollars a day."

"Eating in Airports? Dining in Connecticut?"

"Thirty-five," came the Jeremiah's acerbic reply.

"What are the details of the case?"

"I'll have Franklin call you."

*   *   *

Actually, Adam found himself immensely enjoying that call. His perfect cousin started with, "Your help is not needed. The police are investigating, and my only connection is that the kidnappers specifically named me as the party who had to collect and deliver the ransom."

Adam was truly loving this. "Police grilling you as a confederate? You need a good criminal lawyer?"

"It wouldn't be you," came Frank's tart reply.

Okay, time to get serious. "You're raising Krugerrands for what?"

"An alleged talent agent booked twelve children, ages 7 to 11, for the filming of a soft drink commercial. The advertising campaign was based on the theme of the Pied Piper fairy tale and was being filmed in Sleeping Giant State Park."

"Any parents there?"

"They were instructed to drive the kids to the park, help them get into their filming costumes, and then leave."

"Costumes?"

"That's irrelevant." Uncharacteristically, his cool cousin Frank actually sounded annoyed. "The shoot was a fake! There is no Terrific Tots Talent Agency. There is no Pied Piper Soda! The commercial was just a ruse to get the parents to drop the kids off and go wait at the local donut shop until the talent people called."

"They didn't call."

"Near sunset some parents found a ransom note on the trail and some sort of pathway chopped out of the undergrowth to a solid granite cliff. There they found a sheer rock cliff that was painted."

"Painted?"

"With an eight-foot-high set of doors."

"Doors? For the Pied Piper to magically lure the kids into the mountain?" Adam mused. "Did they do any ground penetrating radar?"

Frank rarely exploded. When dealing with incompetent lawyers, his voice just grew more tightly precise. "Actually, they did, which was ludicrous. It's solid rock. There could be no children inside there."

"The note said what exactly?"

"You didn't pay. So now the kinder are gone. Mine magical flute drew them into the mountain. My magical notes will not open this wall until you deliver 10 Krugerrands for each child. You must not call the polizei.." Adam noted that Frank even gave the proper linguistic bark for the German word for 'police.' "If you ever wish to see your kinder again."

"Krugerrands, why not Goldmünzer coins?" Adam mused.

"By their illiterate, inaccurate syntax, I presume they were only trying to sound Germanic."

"10 Krugerrands per kid. With gold in four figures for an ounce, what does that add up to?"

"Irrelevant! The ransom was raised. Placed before the pathway closest to the cliff wall, and the police have covertly monitored the drop. Nobody has picked it up, except two curious tourists from Denver who had a whole swat team drop down on them."

"Didn't the kidnappers say something about not getting the police involved?" Adam pointed out. "Police check out the parents? Kids' relatives?"

"Only guilty of wanting to see their kids in show business." Frank sounded resigned, but said, "I don't see where your talents can be of any service."

Adam smiled into the phone. "I assume you have advised his honor, our eminent Uncle Jeremiah, of that fact?"

Tightly, Frank stated, "I've e-mailed your flight

information. Marti has offered for you to stay with us, but I understand you want me to arrange a motel room near the park?"

Connecticut in September? "With an indoor pool and work out room, and a mid-sized rental car. And yes." Adam was feeling expansive. "Make that two rooms. I'm bringing a lady friend, maybe, two." With that, Adam had the pleasure of disconnecting the conversation. He didn't have to be psychic to sense his distinguished cousin's seething, but Adam figured he would have the Foundation for the Resurrection Sisters pay for his lady friends' plane tickets and rooms out of their entertainment budget. They deserved a trip to the East Coast, and he had a strong feeling that the sisters might be very useful.

His honor, Judge Franklin J. Martin met him at the New Haven Airport, with keys for a rental car and two motel rooms, and although Frank probably was surprised, the perfect judge didn't show it when he was introduced to Adam's two girlfriends. Sister Josey, still dressed as if she were in the convent, gave him a shy smile as Frank took some of Madame Terri's multiple suitcases from her. Childlike Terri, a bubbly, doppelganger for Betty White at seventy, looked everywhere at everything and even the parking tarmac seemed to fascinate her. "Freshly paved!" With difficulty, she carried a bulky, beige animal carrier. In the parking lot, Terri immediately put the carrier down, and kneeling before it she released a sharply barking, golden Pomeranian, eight pounds of brillo fur who danced around her knees. "Poor Houdini, such a long trip behind bars."

Ever following closely, Sister Josey took a leash out of her handbag, bent down, and clipped it on Houdini's collar, then handed the end to Madame Terri.

Madame stood up and looked at Frank with great joy. "If I do good, the Foundation is going to buy me a Pomeranian puppy, another white one to replace Tooter. A pure-bred one.

Tooter was a rescue dog, but he had a purebred pedigree I'm sure. Purebred dogs are so expensive, you know."

Frank nodded gravely. "I think your motel accepts pets."

Adam looked at Sister Josey. "I'm told the path to Sleeping Giant Mountain is walkable but a little steep, maybe Madame Terri needs to rest until tomorrow?"

Still playing with her tiny, bouncing dog, Terri didn't look up. "We go to the mountain now." Her face darkened as suddenly she became serious. "The trail is getting fuzzier–all those little children lost..."

Frank drove ahead, and Adam followed in the rental car with the women. They arrived at a state park in the forested foothills. Adam noted purplish mountains in the distance, with closer foothills just beginning to yellow and flame for fall. Walking past two, blue-walled easy-up tents, Adam found himself drawn to a box truck parked close to the trail's starting point. The old truck was painted a scratched green, and Adam found himself touching it. It felt dirty. Wrong. It felt dead. He was aware Frank was frowning at him, but that only made Adam want to touch the truck more.

Madame Terri had joined Adam. "You feel something, don't you?"

"What?" The truck's emptiness was filling his mind.

"When you were a boy, I told your Uncle Quentin that you were quite psychic."

Adam shook his head. "No."

"That's why he picked you. So I could train you." But the clearness of her that had just been suddenly faded to fuzziness as she looked around, appearing to be lost. "But I've gotten so old. It's hard for me to concentrate now, everything skiddles so..." Then the other Terri was back as she smiled brightly. "Well, you'll grow into it, especially hanging around Quentin's secretary, Wynoma is such an old soul."

Sister Josey was gently hurrying Madame. "The sun

will be going behind the mountains."

Frank took them past the blue tents surrounded by yellow police tape as they headed up the dirt trail. Immediately, Houdini pulled at his leash, squatted, and started doing his business.

Sister Josey looked embarrassed. "We usually have plastic grocery bags with us, but not today."

Madame Terri smiling, shrugged. "Dogs gotta go." They continued on their odd odyssey until the path curved. Dropped at the left edge of the dirt path, was a leather bag, obviously stained from an earlier rainstorm. Madame Terri moved to it, looking down at the closed satchel. "Gold. So much gold." Madame Terri's face pinched in pain, and on a warm September evening, she drew her sweater around her arms and started to shiver.

A concerned Frank asked. "Do you need my jacket?"

Madame Terri shook her head. "No. The evilness is here. Can't you feel it? They want the money, that's all they are thinking of! Just the money."

"The gold?" Frank said.

"No. No." With an angry look on her face, Madame Terri turned slowly looking in each direction. "The gold was just a joke! They're laughing at you. No, they always knew they couldn't get the gold." She turned and faced the woods to the left. Beyond some weeds and trees, a sheer cliff of gray granite rose. It was only fifty feet off the trail, but it was fifty feet of brambles and tilted rocks slabs.

Sister Josey looked definitely concerned. "It's too rough for you, Terri."

Madame looked at her small dog. "Too dangerous for Houdini, you keep him here." Saying that she started into the brambles. Helpless, Sister Josey held the leash as the Pomeranian sharply barked and fought, wanting to go with his mistress.

Farther up the steep path, Frank also objected. "This is

out of the question for her."

But Madame Terri determinedly forged on into the undergrowth, and Adam had to hurry just to give her his arm. The senior citizen surprised him with her strength as she pulled him towards the rock wall. Millions of years ago, the mountain had split, leaving a sheer rock cliff that rose hundreds of feet. The base of raw rock and boulders had been roped with yellow police tape, but Madame Terri just climbed over it all and strode forward.

Then suddenly, she stopped and looked about her feet. "Clothing?"

Adam didn't understand because he just saw trampled milkweeds, cut blackberry canes, and tiny pine seedlings on the rocky ground.

Frank's voice came from behind them. "They found the children's Pied Piper costumes here. Heidi type dresses for the six girls and lederhosen, mock-leather shorts for the boys, that had been rented by a slender, twentyish woman. She was not identified as such, but was probably the talent coordinator who called herself 'Sher Sinclair,' With their parent's help, the children changed in the two tents down in the parking lot. Then the parents were told to leave until called. Afterward the parents found only the tents, a cooler with soda and melted ice cream. All items you can buy for cash at the local Walmart."

Adam looked. "The children's street clothes?"

Frank spoke with unease. "Still in the tents."

"Any descriptions of the film crew?"

"The parents saw two men in their twenties, olive-skinned complexions. The talent coordinator, Ms. Sinclair, was a slender, fair-skinned woman in her twenties, with a blonde pixie haircut. Possibly wearing a wig as the woman renting the costumes had short, black hair."

Madame Terri appeared confused. "Three lost boys?"

Frank shook his head, patiently correcting. "No. Six boys and six girls."

Madame Terri looked from the vines to the flat rock ahead. "They wanted you looking for a Pied Piper."

On the cliff, someone had taken spray paint and made two rough rectangles, each about eight foot tall using black and dark gray paint to give the sketch a little shadow and depth. Someone had taken time to add swirling curlicued hinges and massive, round, door-knockers to capture the essence of medieval cathedral doors. It was just a speedily drawn outline, but Adam had to admit the effect was eerily artistic.

Frank spoke behind them. "The note said the children were in the mountain, but..."

Adam moved forward to assist Terri, as she struggled to get closer to the doors. "I must feel the rock!" She announced firmly.

It took Adam on one side and Frank on the other to half lift her to the sheer granite wall so Madame Terri could spread both open palms on the rock. Then she bent her head down and squeezed her eyes tightly. There was a long silence, ended by the excited barking of Houdini as a worried Sister Josey drew closer.

Finally, looking old and tired, Madame Terri turned around. "We're done here. There is nothing in that mountain but solid rock. The children were never here. They never left the parking lot. The painted 'gate' and decoy clothes were just more of their clever little jokes like the resort clothing."

Frank looked at Adam. "Did you tell her about the that? But you didn't know." He seemed to be struggling, not able to believe this woman could psychometrize rocks, but still forcing himself to fairly weigh the evidence before him. "The parents reported the talent agent dressed theatrically in filmy blouses and capri pants, with long, colorful silk scarfs on her neck, kind of a cruise hostess look."

"Wicked. Wicked people." Showing her tiredness, Madame Terri seemed to need more help getting back to the main path. There she stopped and stared fixedly down at the leather sack. She bent and touched the leather briefly, and then, leaning on Adam's arm, she stiffly bends lower to touch the gravel around it. "You can take back your sack of gold, they won't come for it. They aren't returning the children."

Sister Josey asked softly, "Then they're dead?"

"No." With a pained face, Madame Terri looked down the pathway to their cars. "It would be better if they were dead... for what is going to happen to them." She stared back at the mountain and shook her head helplessly. "I can't tell you where they are. I'm just too, too old." She looked deeply into Adam's eyes. "Can you? But you aren't trained, and you are fighting it!" Looking about to cry, Madame Terri started down the path. "All blonde children with blue eyes. All for money. They're monsters! Monsters!"

When they reached the parking lot her face transformed, from a grim accuser to a happy, slightly childish old lady."Can we go somewhere for dinner?" She asked brightly, as she looked at Adam. "Will the Foundation pay for that? Someplace nice with linen tablecloths and old barn beams, maybe on a river. Can I have shrimp cocktail? They're so expensive now, I remember when they were free with the meal."

Adam nodded to Madame Terri, noting the sharp blue eyes of Frank following this. Yhep, Adam was probably going to have to explain, or at least try to explain, the Resurrection Sisters Foundation to his holier than thou cousin. Oh, hell.

Frank soon found them a wood-beamed restaurant overlooking a waterfall, with very expensive, delightful shrimp dishes. Leaving them there, Frank took the dog back to the motel after making an appointment to meet them for breakfast. When it came time for the dinner check, Adam was pleasantly surprised to find Frank let them run his credit card before he left.

As they got back in the car, Madame Terri looked up

at the dark sky. "We will go back to the mountain tomorrow when it's quiet."

Adam didn't want her climbing that trail. "To the cliff face?"

"No. Just the parking lot."

He didn't expect to see Frank again that night, but when Adam drove into the motel parking lot, he found his cousin waiting to help settle the ladies into a room that adjoined Adam's. When they were alone, Frank quietly asked, "Madame Terri specified blond-haired children. You didn't tell her that, did you?"

"No—were they?"

"Yes, all light hair with blue eyes," Frank spoke cautiously.

Definitely not wishing to try and explain Madame's powers, Adam just said, "Maybe she saw some television coverage back in Missouri."

"There has been no coverage."

"Twelve kids kidnapped? No coverage?" Adam stared at his judge cousin. "How in the hell did you manage that?!"

"Some vandalism in the park is the cover story for people seeing the police. Of course, some local newspaper people know, but so far, because of the danger to the children, we have been able to keep this off the front pages and newscasts."

Suddenly Adam felt sorry for his convention-bound cousin. "When this breaks, there will be a media circus—no, a media crucifixion—of you and anyone else involved in the coverup. All the talk shows are looking for bleeding meat, and you are denying them twelve fresh helpings of baby carrion."

Frank ignored that. "Madame knew there was gold in that bag, without opening it." Frank stared at him—this was Judge Franklin J. Martin questioning a hostile, recalcitrant, and possibly guilty witness.

This is what Adam got for trying to help? "You

seriously think that Madame Terri, Sister Josey, and I are in on this?"

Frank looked at him for a long time, before he spoke. "No." Again, there was a long hesitation. "The alternative..."

"Madame Terri is a genuine psychic." Frank started to object, but Adam held up his hand. "I don't even believe it myself sometimes. Even with what I have learned from Great Uncle Quentin' unorthodox law practice. There are people..." He looked at Frank's steady blue eyes. "We're not even going to get into that."

Frank raised an eyebrow. "But if she knows things?"

Adam nodded. "She can't control it too well. She can't pick lottery numbers–believe me, I've tried. Madame's wrong almost as much as she is right. She's seventy and lately in poor health, but they tell me when she has that really strong feeling she *knows*. Right now, she can't tell us where those kids are, but we have to give her some time."

Left unsaid was how much time did those children have?

The next morning, Adam rose early and dove in the motel pool. Cutting through warmish water, he could almost swim away from his problems, but as Adam surfaced, he looked up and saw Sister Josey poolside, primly dressed in her soft green sweater and suit pants. "Mr. Martin."

"Please, it's Adam."

"Adam, we were watching television, and the news has broken about the Pied Piper, the gold, and what they are calling 'Stonegate,' all the news media seems to be very angry about the cover-up and your cousin's involvement."

"They mention us?"

"No."

"Good!" Adam reluctantly swam to the pool's edge. Getting dressed in his room, he heard his cell phone ring again, picking it up he looked at the screen to see the number. Jeremiah was calling. That's the fifth message left since yesterday, Adam would have to answer sometime. And say what? What did he have to show for an airplane ticket to Connecticut, rental car, two motel rooms and three people eating meals? It really wasn't his fault, but from Jeremiah's view, Adam shows up in Connecticut, and Judge Franklin Martin's pristine reputation is immediately flushed down the toilet. Adam let the call go to voicemail.

Frank met them for breakfast at Pop's Diner, across from the motel. He downplayed the news leaks and then followed them back to the park. At Sleeping Giant, both Adam and Madame Terri seemed to be drawn to that truck.

She instructed Adam. "Touch the metal with your full hand. Close your eyes. Try to free your mind. You'll get impressions."

Adam tried. All he felt was painted steel, uncomfortably hot from the sun. He smelled the stink, something like Houdini had done another one. Adam squeezed his eyes shut tighter. Something he felt...like the truck was dead?

Adam opened his eyes, and Madame Terri was staring at him, saying, "They planned to take the children away in the truck, but it died!"

A dark blue Crown Victoria had pulled up alongside their cars. When Adam hurried over, he was introduced to a friend of Frank's, Detective Jerry Ramos, who was head of the task force on the kid's disappearance. Skipping the niceties, Adam babbled, "The truck. It's dead–probably mechanically broken. It might've been the kidnappers!"

Frank looked to Detective Ramos, who patiently explained, "The truck is an unregistered junker with stolen plates, that was bought for cash a week ago in Norwalk. The police garage guys hot wired the ignition and tried to start it. The starter is dead."

"Then the kidnappers would have needed another truck..." Adam excitedly said.

Ramos nodded. "Three miles from here is a cheap rental place. We think we've identified the truck. It was rented with an unreported, stolen credit card. The truck was returned to the place after it closed. The kidnappers probably figured if they returned it, we wouldn't connect with it with the Sleeping Giant children. Wiped really good but the forensic guys are still going over it, and they've gotten some hairs they think might be the kids, DNA testing will take time."

"Any G.P.S. recording?" Adam asked fast.

"On the truck? Nope, it's an old army surplus."

"Was the mileage checked?"

"Oh, yeah, that we know. 263.7 miles. Which round trip, would give us an arc of 130 or so miles, from here that could be all of Connecticut, parts of Rhode Island, Massachusetts, New York, or upper New Jersey. The owner described the renter as a young, muscular Italian or Spanish looking guy, unfortunately, no security camera in the desk area. We're checking the Connecticut driver's license. It's real–but address and name appear to be faked. When our guy drove the truck away, the rental owner said he was headed northwest. The truck was dropped off after the rental agency closed, and the owner never saw the renter's car. From the poor quality outdoor cameras we know it wasn't parked in his lot, he was a walk in.

Soon Madame Terri was off in the grass, throwing a stick for Houdini, nothing was happening, and a bit later, both Frank and Detective Ramos left. Feeling like a total ass, Adam hung around the parking lot until lunchtime, while Madame Terri alternately romped with Houdini or stared morosely at the unmoving truck.

They had lunch then returned to the park. Nothing. That night, back in the women's motel room, in near tears Madame Terri perched on the bed with Houdini curled in her lap. "I can't–can't see anything. I'm too old. You should have taken Inga with her Scandinavian runes or Helen with her crystal ball."

Sister Josey placed a comforting hand on her shoulders. "You're the best. The strongest."

"But it's been days! Those poor children are suffering..."

They sat silently for awhile and then Sister Josey reminded her. "In the past, you've used a map to dowse for well water?"

Adam saw Madame Terri perk up. "Yes. We need a map!"

From the rental car, Adam got a complimentary map of Connecticut which both women spread out on the bed and studied. "No." Madame pronounced. "We need a better map!"

Adam found a bookstore where Sister and Madame Terri could sip mocha café lattes while he searched through the selection of maps. As he shelled out $17.39 for three maps, Adam wondered if he could submit the receipt as an expense to Frank. Then Adam pictured Jeremiah's grim face. The lattes could go on the Foundation's Entertainment budget, but could he justify the maps? No, he'd just have to take their price out of his own pocket.

Back at the motel office, Adam borrowed scotch tape to join a map of New England with one of New York and one of the Mid-Atlantic States, giving him what he hoped was a radius of 130 miles from Sleeping Giant in all directions. While he taped, Sister Josey modified a crystal pendant necklace of Terri's fashioning it into a crude pendulum, which Madame Terri held out over the maps on the bed.

As Houdini whimpered, Madame Terri closed her eyes and tried. Opened them and tried. Then closed them again looking like she was asleep. Finally, showing great strain, Madame sat exhausted on the bed, staring down at the useless pendulum chain in her hands, suddenly she sharply looked up. "Adam, you try it!"

She hurried over to him, her thin arm around his waist, pulling him towards the maps. Madame Terri took his hand in surprisingly strong, warm fingers. "Here, put your index finger on this red circle we made for Sleeping Giant. Close your eyes. Do you feel anything?"

Regretfully, he shook his head. "No."

Madame Terri was rotating his hand in ever-widening circles. "The children. Think of the children. They're frightened, they can't understand why Mommy and Daddy haven't come back."

Adam really tried, but could only say, "I'm sorry. I'm not psychic, I can't think of where the kids can be." Miserably, he opened his eyes to stare into Madame Terri's focused face.

In a quiet, controlled voice she said, "You do not know where the children are so your conscious mind can never reason it out. The answer must come from outside of you. The spirits want to tell you, but you must stop blocking them! You must relax, thank them for their help, and then let them come through you."

Adam obediently closed his eyes and tried to block his mind of any thoughts. Madame Terri was slowly rotating his hand again in ever-widening circles. Suddenly, Adam pushed his index finger down. He opened his eyes, expecting to know the answer, but it wasn't land. His finger had stopped on the Atlantic Ocean. "That's water."

Sister Josey looked to Terri as Madame studied where is his finger still pushed into the map paper. "Visions are often not understood. It could be a boat." Madame brightened. "Yes. A boat the Spirits are showing you that's going to the children. Close your eyes! Try to let them tell you where the boat is headed for."

He did. Madame Terri was no longer touching his hand, but this time as he circled, Adam felt a definite pull on his index finger. Of course, it was just his subconscious, trying to make everybody happy, but almost without his control, his finger slid across the paper and stopped. Adam opened his eyes. His finger was still on the water, no, actually it was pressing down on a section of New Jersey coastline.

Hovering nearby, Sister Josey drew a red-penciled circle around where Adam's finger had stopped. Contented, Terri picked up Houdini as she lay down on the other bed. "That's it. It's too dark now, but tomorrow, after we meet Frank for breakfast, we'll drive to New Jersey. Should we bring him with us?"

In resounding unison, Adam and Sister chorused, "No!"

But that proved a little more difficult. While they waited in line for a table at Pop's, Madame airily informed Franklin that they were going to New Jersey to see the ocean.

Adam amended. "Since the ladies are here they should see some highlights. Maybe the Atlantic City Casinos and the Boardwalk."

His cousin quietly studied him, then said, "I have a counter offer. Today I'll arrange three package tours, with meal vouchers and hundred dollars worth of chips for each of you to the Indian casino up by Mystic, my treat."

Madame Terri dimpled so cutely at him. "Oh, no. Adam and Houdini think New Jersey is so much more scenic. Too bad you can't come with us, but Adam says you've rescheduled so many court cases lately." She wagged her finger at him. "You shouldn't do that."

Frank looked at the three of them, his judge's eyes immediately targeting Sister Josey for the poorest liar of the bunch. Under his gaze, she reddened and looked down at the floor. "Yes," Frank concurred. "I have got to get back to court." He looked up as the waitress approached. "They have our table. Adam, could you please order me a western and a black tea. I just have to step outside to make a phone call."

After they finished breakfast, when they left the diner, that unmarked, dark-blue Crown Victoria with its multi-radioed dashboard was pulling over to them. The driver's window lowered, and Franklin introduced them again. "You met Detective Ramos at the Park."

Sister politely nodded to him. "How do you do."

Frank continued. "Jerry will be your guide to New Jersey today."

"But he's so busy looking for the kids," Adam protested.

"Consider it my day off," returned the taciturn Ramos.

"Good," said Madame Terri smiling coquettishly, as she opening up his car back door and slid in. "But we have to stop back at the motel, because Houdini wants to see New Jersey, too."

While they waited for Sister Josey to walk the dog, Adam brought over the Frankenstein mess of a map and tried to spread it on Ramos' dashboard.

The detective looked at him in disbelief. "You've taped together three tourist maps, with three different scales..."

"I know." Feeling like an idiot, Adam just said, "We're looking for a warehouse, on the ocean where a large boat will be coming in."

Ramos stared from the map to Adam, saying a bit testily. "New Jersey has over a hundred miles of coastline on the Atlantic."

Adam pointed. "This area here–we thought we'd start there."

Ramos peered at it. "That circle covers South Amboy to Union Beach. Do you guys have any idea of how much ground that is?"

"Yes," said Madame Terri pertly. "So we had better get started."

The detective sat back in his seat, searching Adam's face. "If you have a lead on those twelve kids, I'll put in a few calls, and there will be five states worth of cops searching the entire coast of New Jersey."

"No! Christ! Don't." Adam shook his head. "Look, we just want to satisfy Madame Terri's hunch. It'll be better if I take my car, and it's just the three of us on this snipe hunt, okay?"

Ramos sighed. "Frank Martin says you need an escort and I'm to be it. I don't argue with the judge. Let's start with South Amboy." He began entering it into his G.P.S. as an excited yapping grew nearer. "Is that dog housebroken?"

"Yes." Adam lied, hoping Sister Josey had remembered to bring the cleanup wipes this time.

They crossed from the Merrit Parkway taking I-95 through to New York City, with a delighted Madame Terri trying to see everything. At each state line, Ramos picked up his radio mike and was soon talking to some old police friend. From the Garden State, he turned off on to local roads, headed towards the water. Wanting to be anywhere else, Adam looked out the windows at New Jersey's endless wetlands that regularly sprouting clusters of white, gas-tank farms.

Detective Ramos finally spoke. "I know you're looking for a warehouse, but today most of the stuff is shipped in cargo cubes, like that white, red, and green rubik's cube over there. They're stacked out in the open."

Madame Terri directed. "Then we'll have to find an old warehouse. It might be closed." Actually, there were quite a few. As they drove past, Adam nervously wondered if they should check them, but Terri just sat in the car, alternating between looking out the window and sweetly playing with Houdini in her lap. Adam figured they'd get lunch, drive some more, and then head back to Connecticut at sunset.

Suddenly Houdini barked sharply, Adam turned and saw Madame Terri sitting up and intently staring ahead at a section of old warehouses they were passing.

"Do you feel, Adam? The evil?" She demanded.

No, he didn't. "Can you turn back?" he asked Ramos. Madame Terri was twisting against her seat belt to stare back at one of them.

Ramos asked. "Here?"

Adam could see Madame Terri was lucid and hunting, but that wouldn't last long! "**Turn now**!"

Ramos barely braked as he twisted the wheel hard into a wide U-turn, throwing them all against the car. Sister Josey paled, and Terri yelled, "Wheeee!"

They parked the car across the street from a row of large, one story warehouses.

Sister Josey asked, "Could you please crack the windows for Houdini? We should leave him in the car."

But when they tried to, Houdini jumped back onto Terri's lap, barking and growling. "You want to come too?" Terri asked. "You want to protect me?"

The dog wagged his tail and whined as if begging.

"Okay." Terri nodded. Sister Josey helped them both out of the car. Ramos was finishing a radio call, asking his New Jersey buddy to check the license plate of the only other car parked in sight.

Adam stood there uncertainly looking around at what seemed to have been an abandoned neighborhood since WWII. Although he couldn't see past the warehouses, he knew they were right on the Atlantic as screeching seagulls swooped above them, and he smelled salty sewage and dumped diesel fuel.

Ahead was a row of gray-brown wood warehouses, each behind its gated chainlink fenced yard with 'No Trespassing' signs everywhere. He moved closer to where Madame stood blocked by a rusted padlock chain on the wide truck gate. Adam could get toe holes from the chain link fence, but he looked up to the top to curved coils of razor wire, no, he wasn't climbing that. He doubted if he had the chutzpah to ask a police detective if he carried bolt cutters in his trunk, but for some reason, Adam *knew* he must get into that yard!

It was Sister Josey, who apparently had the instincts of a burglar, who found it. Off to the side, she discovered a small, walk-in entrance gate. "The padlock's been sawed. See, if you just lift this latch here, we can just walk in." She looked a little doubtful about this, but Madame Terri and Houdini were already going in, hurrying ahead of them.

Bird droppings and rubbish littered the tarmac as Adam followed Madam Terri to the steep steps that lead to the loading dock. Balancing herself against the wall, Madame climbed right up, because the steps were too high for Houdini, he danced at the bottom and barked his frustration. Coming behind him, Adam scooped Houdini up and climbed to the loading dock.

The loading doors of the warehouse were not just closed, they were nailed shut with massive, weathered two-by-four boards. Adam put Houdini down as Madame Terri spread her palms wide on the small office door ahead as if listening to her inside voices. The door had a '**No Unauthorized Persons Allowed**' sign, and its glass window had three bullet-hole halos in it, but when Madame Terri turned the knob, the door opened. She just walked in with Adam and Houdini following.

Inside was a dark, rubbish-filled warehouse, with the only light coming from high, gray-paned windows. The urgent feeling that was driving him was gone, and when he looked beside him, Adam also saw Madame had gone. In her place was a confused, frightened Terri.

"Why are we here?" She asked.

Oh, shit, Adam looked around. They weren't alone. A tall woman in a very short skirt was hurrying up to them, with a male figure in overalls just behind her.

Looking angry the young woman shouted. "This is private property! I'm calling the police!"

Adam had a flash of male response to the yellow scarfed blonde with her long sexy legs, which cooled as he quickly tried to concoct a cover story. Then he remembered the description of Sher, the fake talent agent.

Madame Terri was ahead of him, smiling widely as she

hurried up to the woman. "You work here, dear? So dusty! You like scarves? I love them too, is that real silk?" With both hands, Terri quickly reached for the yellow scarf artistically knotted around the young woman's neck.

She tried to step back, but Madame Terri moved too fast, and with both hands, she yanked the scarf down. "That's a big Adam's apple for a lady! Where did you three bastards stash the kids?"

Ms. Long legs Sher shoved Madame Terri away, knocking the older woman to the floor. Houdini charged, biting at the blonde's ankle and woman tried to kick him away as Adam got between Sher and Terri. The kicked Pomeranian bounced off a wooden crate, but growling viciously with claws scrabbling on concrete, Houdini bounced back. Sher howled in pain, as the dog bit again and again. Giving Adam a chance to get a glancing punch off her jaw. That's when the other guy in overalls swung, hitting Adam in the shoulder with a two-by-four. Rims around his eyes were blackening out as Adam sank down, seeing another guy dressed in jeans joining the fray.

Laying on the hard concrete, Adam saw Houdini circle Sher, jumping up from behind to latch on to her calf. The screaming Sher's legs were bleeding badly as she kicked out. The kicks threw the tiny Pomeranian into the air, but the moment the dog's paws clawed floor, he was back attacking! Savagely biting Sher with those tiny but shark-sharp teeth. Then Overalls swung the two-by-four like a baseball bat and hit the dog. Houdini gave a yelp and rolled with his neck at an old angle.

Madame Terri moaned on the floor behind Adam. Wondering if that board had broken his arm, Adam forced himself up to hopelessly fight.

But now he had allies. As Overalls raised his two-by-four to hit Adam again, Sister Josey grabbed his arm from behind and was yanking him off balance, throwing him over her hip. Down, he screamed in pain, as Sister powerfully stomped his arm with the sound of bones cracking. Detective Ramos's punch flattening Mr. Jeans.

Adam screamed to Ramos. "Don't you have a gun?"

Pulling his arm back, as he ducked a punch from Sher, Ramos shouted, "Just to escort a couple ladies through New Jersey?"

Officers in riot gear were rushing in. Asking no questions, they just rounded up the three Detective Ramos pointed out, and Adam realized, outside of hiding an enlarged Adam's apple, they had no proof these guys were guilty of anything, so he and Madame Terri were the aggressors. Holding his throbbing shoulder, Adam mentally touted up the charges they'd have against him: trespassing, unwarranted search, assault on warehouse employees times three, falsely triggering a Police SWAT team, who must have been cued by Ramos buddy's license plate check–all on the word of a senile fortune teller and a crazy lawyer? Well, if Adam spent the rest of his life in a New Jersey correctional facility, at least Uncle Jeremiah couldn't get his hands on him.

Adam looked at the three warehouse guys under police guard. Maybe if he got their handcuffs taken off? Apologized profusely, and made some sort of financial arrangement? Two policemen bounded in with leashed German shepherds. From his car, Ramos had gotten a black, zip-locked evidence bag and the handlers soon were holding edelweiss braid trimmed lederhosen for the excited dogs to scent.

But at that moment Adam had realized that Terri was gone. Holding his arm tight and ignoring the pain, he hurried to find her. In the back of the dark warehouse, he found Madame Terri standing back straight and alert, looking thirty years younger. Flat palmed, she was running her hands up and down a solid wood wall, no, it was a huge door. From the massive hinges and handle it must have once been a meat locker. Everything on it was ancient and stained, except for a shiny new hasp that was locked with an even newer looking padlock. Helplessly, Terri yanked at that lock.

Barking wildly, the police dogs pushed them aside, and a cop from behind used his gun barrel to pry up the hasp. The door swung open, inside was a stinking hell. Two toilet buckets, a burning propane lamp, and twelve cringing, filthy children, all huddled in the corner, too afraid to even cry. Silent, but alive.

Adam helped carry out one of the kids, comforting the little guy, with thumb stuck in his mouth. "You'll be with Mommy soon." Out into the sunlight, more police cars and ambulances were arriving. Adam gently transferred the boy to a friendly looking EMS woman, and then he looked around. Where was Madame Terri? Sister Josey?

He found them inside the warehouse, heads bent, as they knelt on the concrete floor. Sister Josey's hands were folded downwards, as she softly recited. "Forgive our trespasses, as we forgive those who trespass against us..." Saying nothing, Madame Terri gently stroked the fur of the stiffening Houdini. That little yapping, midget of a dog with the heart of Rottweiler.

Finally, Madame Terri looked up at him, her black eyeliner running down her ruined makeup. "I want to take him home."

Adam nodded.

＊   ＊   ＊

After the hospital in New Jersey, Frank insisted they stay in the motel a few more days until Madame was stronger before traveling back home. Madame Terri was just bruised, and Adam's arm wasn't broken, but two of his ribs were cracked. It turned out Sister Josey was a fourth-degree black belt; the Resurrection Sisters were always surprising him. But all of them were worried about Madame Terri, she had stopped switching into her childlike, happy states, and she just sat on the motel bed, staring at the wall, barely talking or eating.

Adam tried again. "We'll get another dog."

"No." Madame Terri shook her head. "No, I don't want another dog. I couldn't save Houdini because I was too old."

"Houdini would want you to have another protector," Sister Josey soothed.

"No, I'm not going to live much longer. When I'm gone, I don't want another dog to be alone." She shook her head with finality.

When Adam dropped off the car at the airport, Frank met them at the rental desk. He was holding a pet carrier which he brought over to Madame Terri, but she only looked at him saying adamantly. "I don't want another dog, I told you that!"

Frank put the crate down, opened it, and lifted out a golden, fluffy fur ball which he set on the sidewalk. Immediately, the little Pomeranian puppy took a dominant stance and barked a challenge to the giants surrounding him.

Madame Terri looked longingly at him, but she made no move to pick him up. Shaking her head no. "It's better he goes to someone else, he needs a real family."

Letting the little barking puppy approach to smell her, Frank reached into the crate and took out a second ball of white fur. This one's big, round, dark eyes stared at Terri but stayed timidly quiet in Frank's hands.

"Oh, twins," Madame Terri whispered wistfully.

"Two males. Brothers," Frank explained.

Terri looked at the golden puppy, cautiously smelling her shoe. "You're Houdini the Second, and your brother is Thurston. Two great magicians." Madame Terri swooped down to lift the golden one in her hands. "Are they pedigreed? Not that it matters." She cooed to the puppy, who was licking her face. "You're so luvvy."

Knowing she really wasn't caring, Frank told her, "They are the pedigreed sons of two champions."

Madame Terri now had one puppy in each arm as she looked pleadingly to Adam and Sister Josey. "Will the

Foundation let me keep them?"

Resigned, Adam shrugged. "The more, the merrier..."

"We have a flight to catch." Sister Josey gently herded the two puppies back into the carrier and shepherded Madame Terri toward the airport entrance.

As Frank helped him load their luggage onto a cart, Adam asked, "How are the kids doing?"

"Dehydrated, bruised, undernourished and will have nightmares for the rest of their lives, but other than that, they're fine. The New Jersey Troopers notified the Coast Guard, and they intercepted a tramp steamer heading into the abandoned warehouse's waters. The search found a windowless, locked, and sound-proofed cabin with old, worn toys and blankets on the floor, which the Captain claimed was for his grandchildren. They're probably guilty, but Guard had to let them continue on their way to the Caribbean. Still, they will be under surveillance from now on. Your three warehouse guys, on the other hand, are in a bidding war for who will be allowed to go state's evidence."

"Part of a child sex ring?"

"Nope. Three college buddies pulling a one time scam. They'd been promised a small fortune for a dozen blond kids. Planned to live like royalty on the islands and get Sher her operation."

"Will we have any legal problems?"

"Doesn't look like it. Detective Ramos is covered under the 'in pursuit' doctrine, and now the papers are making me out to be some sort of hero." That figures, the perfect Franklin always came out admirable, but his cousin was continuing. "They don't know about you yet, but I'm being interviewed today, and you three certainly deserve all the credit."

Adam flinched. "No, thank you! Most of my practice consists of keeping my clients out of the news." He wanted to change the topic. "Those puppies..."

"Are my gift to a great lady," Frank said very firmly. "And I want you to bill me for **all** your hours and expenses." He was just about to leave, but Frank was continuing. "You know, Adam, Uncle Jeremiah was correct about you, not that he will ever admit it. He used to say someday you would amaze us all. He was right."

Firebug

"The little arsonist is facing jail time, and I hear his court-appointed lawyer bugged out." Silver-haired and angular faced, Judge Jeremiah Martin usually sounded like he was pronouncing a death sentence, and that he was enjoying doing it.

Why hadn't he inherited some of his family's tall genes Adam thought, as he suggested, "Anybody think the kid might be, say a pyrokinetic? A natural fire starter and he just might not be able to control it?"

"Pyrokinetic–you make that up yourself? Or you dug that out of Quentin's compost pit of files of his 'special clients'?" Jeremiah sat forward, indicating this meeting was about to end. "It's all hogwash, but you might able to get the kid off with that pyscho babble."

Adam was confused. "I'm your nephew, I can't appear in your court."

"Nathan Delling is appearing in juvenile, before Judge Hansen. He's eleven years old."

"An eleven-year-old doesn't understand about using fire as a weapon...he should get supervised probation."

"Unless they find out about the family history." Jeremiah pronounced sourly.

"What history?"

"I had the duty of sentencing the grandfather to prison for arson twenty-two years ago."

"He's out now?"

"No. Set fire to his cell."

Adam was definitely confused. "But you want me to defend his grandson?"

"The family has no money."

"How am I going to be paid?"

"Pay? Your Cousin Franklin's wife does twenty

percent of her practice pro bono."

"They can afford it."

"How much do you want?"

Why in hell would the notoriously parsimonious Jeremiah Martin want to pay for this kid? Why would the rhino-hided, prosecutor loving Jeremiah want this kid to walk free? "Is this related to that victim's warning letter on your desk?"

Jeremiah's glacial-blue eyes grew large. "You dared read the papers on a judge's desk?"

"Yhep. You learn a lot that way. That letter is not a judge's warning, it's some guy coming up for parole that victimized you. Who was it? What did he do?"

Ice radiated from Jeremiah's eyes. For a moment, Adam felt he was a child in trouble, standing before his uncle as the judge pronounced, "We're finished here–except what payment you want for representing the Delling boy?"

Adam always needed money, but he got one of those *strange-knowing* feelings that there was something he should do. "I'll defend the boy... for a favor from you to be named later."

"What?" Jeremiah stared at him. "You know I can't do anything for you in the courts."

"Yes, sir."

"Yet you expect me to be stupid enough to agree to an 'unnamed favor'—you could want anything!"

"The favor will be, by your standards, reasonable and doable, but it won't necessarily be one that you want to do."

"Games? You bill your clients with games? No wonder you're always broke!" His uncle raged. "You gave me two loopholes, doable and reasonable by my standards!"

"But not pleasant," Adam reminded him.

Jeremiah leaned back, in his chair, thinking it over. "Do you do this with all your clients? What if afterward, they just refuse to pay your cockamamie fee?"

"That offer only goes to the ones I know who will be honor bound to pay up."

Jeremiah waived a dismissing hand. "Your client will be in court shortly."

At juvenile court, Adam cornered a friendly guard. "Max, there's a Nathan Delling, an eleven-year-old coming up, do you know his parents?"

"Sad. A kid his age. The mother's over there. She's been here since we opened, and I think that's the grandmother joining her."

Adam walked over to two shortish women, both with long, brown hair pulled back with rubber bands. The mother looked like she rode motorcycles in her worn leather jacket and jeans, and the grandmother was an older, heavier version. Both had worried worn faces.

The mother was telling the grandmother. "I called Legal Aid again. They don't have anyone to send over today. She said maybe we could talk to Judge Hansen and get more time."

"Ms. Delling?" Adam asked.

They both looked at him, seeming afraid to admit to their names. Finally, the younger one nodded. "I'm Sara Delling, and this is my mother, May Delling."

Adam smiled at them. "Ladies, I understand you need a lawyer?"

The grandmother turned away, saying tiredly, "We don't have any money."

"I can work pro bono–free."

Relief and just a touch of 'what does this guy really want?' warred in Sara's face, but she said nothing.

"Who are you?" Demanded the grandmother.

"Adam Martin, Attorney at Law."

"Martin? Any relation to Judge Jeremiah Martin, that second-rate bastard?"

Adam quickly corrected her. "Madam, please!

Jeremiah Martin is a **first-rate** bastard, anyone in the Martin family would be happy to testify to that under oath."

"He killed my husband."

Adam firmly returned back. "The jury convicted your husband, and my uncle just sentenced him."

"And we should let you 'help' my grandson?"

"You got anybody better?"

May looked hopelessly to her daughter, and Sara firmly replied, "Ma, he's all we've got." Unhappy, the old lady nodded. Sara to turned to Adam. "They put Nate in jail for two weeks."

"Not jail," Adam gently corrected. "Probably a youth holding facility. It's usually not that bad as he'll have his own room, games, desert, and television..."

Sara ignored that. "Can you get him out?"

"Is there someone at home who can supervise him twenty-four/seven?" Adam asked.

"We all work–me, mom, my boyfriend, but we could all rotate our jobs, so there was someone at home."

"Do you live in an apartment?'

"A house." The grandmother added. "But it's already mortgaged."

"Single-family?"

"Yes."

"Is the house separated from others by a lawn?"

"Small one. Why does that matter?" Asked the confused grandmother.

"Okay, let's go into court."

After about an hour, Adam saw the police lead in a dark haired boy. They'd actually handcuffed his hands with a chain like a leash to the officer. The boy was small for his age with hair shaved close, probably by the grandmother. He looked about dully then saw his mother and grandmother, and his face lit up. He pulled at the chain to reach them. The officer looked down and let the kid walk to the low visitor's galley gate. His mother ran her hand through his hair, and his grandmother murmured something encouraging to him.

"Nathan Delling. Arson. Three counts." The court bailiff called out.

The judge was looking at her file. "Do we have counsel?"

"Yes, your honor, Adam Martin." Adam stepped up to the defendant's table.

The judge looked up but didn't smile. "We don't get many of your family in juvenile court, Mr. Martin?"

Adam looked at the child saying carefully, "Your honor, Nathan is eleven years old, and I don't think he is that much of a danger to the court."

The judge looked from Adam to the child and focused on the chains. "Oh, my...was anyone killed or injured in these fires?" The judge looked at Adam.

He had to admit, "Mam, I just got the case five minutes ago."

The judge looked to the prosecuting attorney. "Was anyone injured in these fires?"

The young woman was busy adding dates into her cell phone. She looked up, seeming to be startled to be asked a question. She had to pick up her briefcase and start digging for the kid's file.

From the audience came the grandmother's timid voice. "No injuries. No big damage. A fire in school bathroom's waste can. A fire in the library, in a pile of papers, and the librarian stamped it out fast. The one at the holding facility, but the cameras showed Nate didn't do anything to start it."

The judge looked to the cop. "Officer, why is that child in chains?"

"He runs fast," replied the cop sounding tired.

The judge looked back at her case papers. "Take those chains off him. If required, they can be used in transit only, but not in my courtroom or in the holding facility."

The officer nodded and got out his keys, as Judge Hansen continued to Adam. "So if you've just taken over the case, you'll want time to research it?"

"Yes, mam, but the boy's been away from his family for two weeks."

The judge looked at the mother and grandmother. "That might be safer for them."

Working at sounding firm and confident Adam said, "There are three adults living in a private, single-family residence, with a lawn between theirs and the other houses. They are willing to provide supervision at all times."

The judge looked to the other table, where the prosecuting attorney was still searching through her papers for the charges. "Ms. Tenna, are you raising an objection?"

"To what, your honor?"

"To my releasing the boy into his families' custody?"

"Yes," she said definitely. "I am objecting."

"What is the objection?" The judge asked sharply.

"He's dangerous, isn't he?" The DA seemed to be asking the court.

The judge looked over at the little guy, twisting in his seat to see his mother, then she spoke in a low tone to the lawyers. "Approach, please."

Adam and the D.A. walked to the judge's desk bench. In an undertone, she spoke to Adam. "The child is innocent until proven guilty, but a child, who repeatedly sets fires, cannot be allowed to return to our schools and movie theaters."

Adam raised his hand. "Your honor, I still have not presented our case yet."

The judge looked to the D.A., who hadn't even bothered to look at Nathan, while the prosecutor said, "He's dangerous and must be maintained under lock and key. We are talking permanent removal from the family and institutionalization until he turns twenty-one. He started a fight and fire in the school library, it's just pure luck he hasn't killed anyone yet."

The judge looked at Adam. "Mr. Martin, chances are we will have to institutionalize the boy. Wouldn't it be just cruelty to let him return home for only a week?"

The D. A. Interrupted. "And there's the danger to his family! And the community!"

Adam looked back from the grandmother's pleading eyes. "Your honor, his closest family members are willing to trust their lives with him. The community is protected from fire by the lawn. He's only eleven, I think the court can let him have a little comfort."

The judge looked at her clerk. "The boy will be released into the custody of his mother. This case will resume next Monday."

As they left the court, Adam wondered if the District Attorney would dig enough to find out about the arsonist grandfather? He'd bet against it unless the answer was in her cell phone. Outside in the hallway, Adam wrote down the address and phone numbers of his new clients.

During that week, Adam interviewed Nathan's school teachers. Ms. Gleasen said Nathan was a bright kid with a bit of attention deficit, who had to be constantly directed. The librarian added that "Nobody saw him start the fire. Nobody found any matches or a lighter on him." As Adam suspected, in the library, the other kids picked on Nathan because he was small, and he just got mad, and fires happened.

His next visit was to the Foundation of the Resurrection Sisters. The sisters were running some sort of bar-be-que for the Senior Citizens Club down by the lake. Adam found Sister Josey struggling with a huge tray of buttered corn.

"Let me carry that for you." He lifted the very heavy tray from her.

"Can you stay for the chicken roast?" she asked.

"Yes, but I have some questions. Have you ever heard of a person who can wish it and have a fire start?"

"Fire-bugs. We have one here, Nora. She started the bar-be-ques grills today," Sister Josey said matter-of-factly.

"She can control it?"

"In a very limited fashion. When she concentrates, she can sometimes start fires. Briquets dripping with lighter fluid aren't that hard to ignite."

He looked at the ladies and guests. "Is she here?"

"No, Nora is very shy. She doesn't like being around people, so she helped with the setup and then hurried back to her cottage."

"Could I speak with her?"

They tried. Nora wouldn't open the door to Adam, and Sister Josey kept apologizing. "I'm sorry. You and your Uncle Quentin have been so good to us."

"Sister, there's an eleven-year-old boy on trial. When he gets excited, fires just start around him, and his grandfather may have had the same problem."

"Oh, no." It was a story she'd heard before.

"Could there be an opening for him and his mother here?"

She stopped and looked up and down the two lines of twenty-four neat little, gingerbread-trimmed cottages. "There's one we keep open for visiting families."

"If I brought him here, could Nora train him to control himself?"

"I think several of us could work with him, Nora, myself and Madame Terri."

"There is a danger to you..."

She smiled that off. "We are all put here for a reason."

A delighted voice called. "Adam!" Terri, dressed in a purple tie-dyed robe befitting a fortune teller was walking over. "Look at my babies!" She happily carried two fluff balls of Pomeranian puppies, one white and one gold colored. The golden one growled at Adam. "Look how they've grown!"

Then there was an almost imperceptible shift then Madame Terri now looked up into his eyes, and her face radiated pain. "There is a man close to you. He's made a mistake, but it wasn't his fault, and he suffers so. He can't move on, you have to help him, Adam."

Her golden puppy barked for her attention causing Terri to look down at him.

"Who is he? How do I help him?" Adam asked.

But in that brief moment, the all-knowing Madame was gone and in her place was the slightly childish, puppy loving Terri. "They're so sweet." Terri looked up at Adam. "I don't know how you will help him," she started vaguely, but ended brightly, "but I know you will."

Guessing that would be all he'd get out of Madame for today, he had another problem to solve. After the bar-be-que, he headed for Federal court for an appointment with the Honorable Jereusila Martin Obermeyer, Jeremiah's twin sister. She made him tea in her chambers.

"Aunt Jerusie, did you know that Jere was getting a victim's notification of a parole hearing for one August Camdon?"

"August Cameron." As she sat down, Jereusila's face became very tight and judge like.

"Why the notice?"

"Your uncle gets a lot of death threats as he can be a very harsh sentencing judge. They give him the most dangerous cases because they know he won't back down. Won't be intimidated."

She was evading his questions, so he pressed. "This was a victim's notification? He was injured?"

Jereusila met his eyes but still wouldn't answer. "Why is this any concern of yours?"

"At his request, I'm defending a Nathan Delling who

is accused of arson."

Jereusila leaned back in her chair. "Nathan Delling?" She thought for a bit. "He's an arsonist who Jeremiah put in prison. He died in jail, how can you be defending him?"

"I'm defending his eleven-year-old grandson," Adam said firmly.

"Eleven years old and an arsonist, already?" Jereusila shook her head. "Delling was sentenced after the Cameron trial. I've always wondered if Jeremiah would have been less harsh if it wasn't just after what they did."

"Who did what?"

"It's not important."

"Yes, mam, it is important! I can't tell you how I know, but it is **very** important." He set the teacup down.

She sighed. "You knew Jeremiah was married? To Sara?"

He had to think hard about that. "She died when I was about seven."

"They had a little six-year-old, red-haired daughter, Sandi." It seemed to pain Jereusila to remember.

"They were killed in some sort of an accident...a car?"

"No, we didn't want you kids to know. The Klu Klux Klan was causing trouble in those days, and Jeremiah had sentenced one of their own. They wanted to get back at him, and they knew Jere had a cabin on Thomson's lake. They found his wife and daughter there. Killed them, and then burned the bodies. They had just been sentenced when the Delling case came up before Jeremiah. Delling had burned down his ex-boss's lumberyard."

"Was anybody killed?"

"No."

"Yet Delling died in prison?"

"In a fire that he set himself! That fire also killed his cellmate."

Adam thought back. "Jere's never spoken about it."

"He never remarried, always afraid it could happen again. He could never stand to see Franklin's daughter, Samantha because she looked so like Sandi. Your generation doesn't know much about the story, and it's better forgotten.

"No, mam. Some things shouldn't be forgotten."

Contacting Laura Cameron was a bit harder. Adam decided to fudge his name a bit, and soon, Adam sat before a sweet, round-faced woman. "You visit your husband in prison every weekend?"

"Yes. Augie never was a bad man really." She looked so pained. "He has never even seen his grandchildren."

"You can bring them into the prison."

"Augie has never let me."

This he felt would be tricky. "I want to talk with him, but he's refused to see me."

"Why Mr. Adam?"

"Actually, it's not Mr. Adam. It is Adam Martin."

Her face hardened. "Did your uncle send you?"

"No. He doesn't know I'm here, and I'd rather he didn't know."

She stopped at that, then said, "Will your visiting help my Augie at his parole hearing?"

Adam figured it wasn't a lie if he just evaded the issue. "I need to understand what happened years ago. If the parole officers know he cooperated, it might help him. Could you call your husband, and ask him to see me?"

At the prison sitting across the visitor's table, Adam stared at a square-faced man, white-haired, with scarred hands, and face harshly lined, but still looking strong. He'd been in prison since he was twenty-two.

"What do you want to know?" asked August.

"What happened? You were in the Klan, and my uncle sentenced your friend..."

August cut him off. "Your uncle was a bastard!"

"Still is." Adam dropped his smile. "But you were three men, I could see you going after him, but a woman and a six-year-old child?"

There was genuine agony in August's eyes. "We were drinking, and the whiskey was thinking. We weren't going after them, or even him. We went up to his cabin to burn it. Martin's car wasn't there, and we didn't think to knock. Joe started pouring gasoline, and Billy lit some branches. We started a fire all around the cabin. We didn't know there was a basement and didn't know there was anyone hidden there until the woman and her kid started screaming." August stopped, almost unable to control the pain flooding back.

Adam reached out and took August's hands between his. That's when, in a flash, Adam knew about the scars. "You tried to fight your way in."

The old man looked at something in the distance. "That was a different man. Joe and Billy are dead, and I'm gonna die here. Only going to go before the Parole Board to please Laura. She won't divorce me, and she keeps visiting," August said, "Look, me saying I'm sorry won't help your uncle, but you might want to tell him I still get those dreams. Where I hear that woman and baby screaming in agony, where I feel my hands burning. That might make Jeremiah Martin happy!"

Sunday, Adam visited the Resurrection Sisters again. Sister had talked Nora into seeing him, but Nora wouldn't even meet his eyes as they talked. She was a mousy woman with gray-brown hair, small, fragile hands, and she kept trembling with him in the room. Not much of a witness if she would agree to testify, which she wouldn't.

After they left the cottage, Adam told Sister Josey. "I need her to testify."

Sister was painfully apologetic. "It not like she doesn't want to. She just can't."

"Sister, I don't have anyone else! Please, this is the

court's address, be there at nine yourself, but I really need her. The boy needs you both!"

In court, Sara and May had brought in Nathan, dressed up in a blue suit and little red tie, but Adam was desperately wondering where was Nora and Sister Josey? He started his presentation on the history of pyrokinetics, most of the material from the field of Science Fiction.

Judge Hansen asked to see the books he had brought, and then she said, "These are fiction or histories bordering on the lurid. Do you have any court decisions that substantiate the phenomenon of unconsciously causing fires?"

All Adam had been able to find were court cases with arson precedences that he did not want to show. "Your honor, after each incident my client was searched, and there were no lighters or matches found."

There was noise from the back as the door opened, and a strained looking Sister Josey walked in holding Nora's arm, almost pushing her. Nora looked terrified, and Adam knew a terrified witness wasn't going to make much of an impression as an authority in the judge's eyes. Preparing for court Adam had thought about buying magicians' flash paper to hype a demonstration, but then discarded the idea. Now he desperately wished he hadn't. "Your honor, my expert witness, has arrived, Miss Nora Brenner."

Finally, Nora came up and nervously took the witness chair, but she just sat with downcast eyes. Adam tried to relax her by talking about her childhood. What fire starting history her family had, and what fire starting felt like. Nora's soft voice could barely be heard, and the judge looked impatient. The District Attorney was completely absorbed in keying texts into her cell phone.

The judge put an end to it. "Thank you, Miss Brenner, for your interesting history, but I do not think you can be referenced as an expert witness. Mr. Martin, do you have anything else?"

They'd lost unless Adam did something. Anything.

"One moment your honor. We would like to do a little demonstration. Nora will set fire to the papers in my hand."

A stricken Nora looked to Sister Josey. Adam looked over at nun sitting in the visitor's gallery too, she was shaking her head '*no.*'

Yet Adam scooped up Nate's commitment papers and held them out before Nora. "Burn them."

"I can't," she said in a tiny voice, probably only he could hear.

"Set them afire!" he commanded.

Nora looked at Sister Josey and back to Adam, saying miserably. "There's too many people here, I can't."

"You can't?? YOU LIED TO ME!" He moved closer to the witness stand, keeping the papers out of her reach, but pressing closer and closer into her personal space. "The nun told me you lighted huge bar-be-ques! **THE NUN LIED TO ME?!**"

"Sis–sister doesn't lie!" Bawled out the now crying Nora. "Please, I want to go!"

She started to get up, but Adam blocked her with the hated papers.

On the edge of his vision, he could see the court guard moving over to intervene, but Adam looked to the judge. Ever so slightly Judge Hansen raised a staying hand to the guard, and he stopped but hovered close.

Adam turned his full anger on Nora. "**You're running away**? The Judge is going to put you in jail for lying!" A terrified Nora shook her head as Adam pressed harder. "See these papers! The judge is putting Sister Josey in jail—for the rest of YOUR LIVES!!"

Nora looked desperately at Sister Josey, and then looked back at Adam, her eyes finally focused in anger. He said nothing. Breathing hard, Nora now glared at the taunting papers he pushed towards her, her mouth set, but she seemed to stop herself and looked back to Sister Josey.

Sister Josey commanded and pleaded at the same time. "Nora, do it!"

Before Nora's head had turned back, Adam actually felt the first heat, then in small waves, the temperature increased. Would it be enough? Were the papers too far away from her? The judge had to see Nora wasn't touching them, but Adam moved them a bit closer.

He found himself looking down as the heat was actually becoming uncomfortable. The papers in Adam's hands were starting to smoke at the edges, ever so slightly, Adam gently exhaled, blowing the air down to help things just a small bit.

More smoke–then tiny yellow flames broke out. Pivoting carefully so as not to extinguish them with his movements, Adam turned towards the judge. "Your honor, she did not touch these papers–you saw it!" Flames were catching, growing and he could feel increasing heat near his fingers. "It was all ignited by emotion, by getting angry. Nora is a born pyrokinetic, but she has learned to control it. Nathan was picked on in school, and being a naturally born fire-bug, he got angry, and fires happened. He did not know what his subconscious was doing, but like Nora has trained herself to control it, he can be trained too!"

Like being mesmerized by a swaying cobra, the judge stared at the growing flames in his hands. "Put them out! Now!"

Adam dropped the papers to the floor and stamped on them as the bailiff had rushed over, dousing them with a fire extinguisher. "Your honor, I have arranged a slot for my client at The Resurrection Sisters Foundation. They will allow the mother and boy to live on their property, while he is being trained at no expense to the State."

Finally, the District Attorney became alive. "No! Delling Nathan must be removed permanently from the custody of his family and placed in an institution!"

The judge looked at her and drily asked, "Do you know of any totally fireproofed juvenile correctional facilities that the State of Missouri has?"

The D.A. didn't answer.

"Mr. Martin," the judge continued, "Does this facility..."

"The Foundation for the Resurrection Sisters."

"Are they aware of the boy's special history and the possible danger?"

Sister Josey stood up in the visitor's gallery. "Yes, Ma'am. I'm Sister Josephine, retired from the faculty of St. Elizabeth's and now a Director of the Foundation. The Board has made a full review of his case, and we feel we can help him. Nathan will be boarded, schooled, and protected, and his special fire control training will begin immediately."

His grandmother looked crushed. "He won't live with me anymore?"

The judge shook her head. "No, I can't allow that at least at this time." She looked at Sister Josey. "Will the family be allowed to visit?"

"Of course, the Foundation is not a prison."

The judge looked troubled. "What is to stop him from running away?"

Sister Josey looked lovingly at Nathan. "We have fishing, puppies, and strawberry shortcake."

Nathan and his mother both smiled. "He'll stay," Sara said.

The judge nodded. "Mr. Martin, for the beginning, the court will expect weekly reports of his progress. If it seems to be going satisfactory, we will revisit this matter in four months...?" She looked up.

Sister Josey looked concerned. "He's only eleven, getting control will be hard at first. Perhaps six months time?"

The judge nodded. "Mr. Martin, the boy will be given

probation and is remanded to the custody of his mother, as long as he remains on the premises and under the supervision of The Foundation for the...

"Resurrection Sisters," Adam supplied.

"In six months the Court will re-visit the matter, examine his progress, and discuss if Nathan can be returned to his grandmother's and school. If his probationary period is satisfactorily completed, his court record will be expunged."

The D. A. looked up. "Your honor for the arson charge, the state recommends a term of no less than..."

Impatiently the judge interrupted her, "Ms. Tenna, I''ve already disposed of the case."

"Oh." The District Attorney said as she sat down, getting back to her smartphone.

The guard opened the bar gate, and Nathan ran into the arms of his mother as his grandmother stroked his hair. Also smiling, Sister Josey, with Nora, walked to them.

Three days later, Adam had made an appointment with his Uncle Jeremiah in his chambers. The judge started off with, "Don't want to know how you finagled it, but you got the Delling kid a get-out-of-jail card. So I now I owe you an unspecified favor. I assume you plan to just hold this over my head and enjoy yourself a bit before you tell me what it is to be?"

"No, sir," said Adam quietly.

"What do you want? Money? One of my prize labradors?" The judge stared at him as if trying to puzzle it all out. "It can't be court related, and it has to be doable and reasonable by my decision."

"Reasonable, but not pleasant or something you want to do." Adam reminded him. "At three o'clock this afternoon, August Cameron is coming up for his parole hearing."

Jeremiah went dead white. "He'll be denied!"

"No, sir, not if you go before the Board, and in the names of your wife and your baby daughter, you ask for clemency for him." Adam kept talking fast. "He never meant to kill your Sara or Sandi, he was only there to burn what he thought was an empty cabin. August's has served almost a lifetime with a clean prison record, and he has a loving family to go home to. If you will just testify for him, he'll walk free."

White skinned and so angry he barely could get the words out, Jeremiah spat, "How can you care for that piece of..."

"I don't!" Adam found it awfully hard to explain. "It's even more ludicrous than that! Jere, I care for you, you over-sentenced Delling for that arson charge, and you've worried about that for years. Delling's dead so there is nothing you can do for him, but you can help August Cameron and his family. And it's time you let the spirits of your wife and daughter finally rest."

Jeremiah said nothing and just sat there, so Adam continued. "We had better get going, unless you want go back on your word for the first time in your life, and I don't have to be psychic to know you won't."

To Be Like Others

"My niece chooses to disfigure herself. She is much too young to make that decision!" said the woman sitting before him, speaking with a heavy Greek accent.

Adam Martin looked over at the imposing woman. "If your niece is under the age of consent, there might be something we could do."

"She was born only two hundred and fifty-seven years ago."

Okay. This was going to be one of his late, Great Uncle Quentin's special cases. Adam's tall secretary entered, carrying a silver tray with a squat bottle and two cut-crystal glasses. Setting it before Adam, she wordlessly poured the clear liquor.

Madame Alexis Ceto looked delighted. "Ah, Ouzo. Wynoma, you always remember!" Madame reached for her glass, then waited for him to get his. "A toast...to old friends and family, it is like being on my island in Greece."

Although Madame head was swathed in a green silk al-amira hijab, the fact she was drinking alcohol meant she wasn't a devout Muslim. That her "young" niece was two hundred fifty-seven years old meant that those war land claims his Great Uncle Quentin negotiated for her could have been in World War II or even World War I. As Adam lifted his glass, Wynoma silently retreated, closing the door behind her.

Madame continued. "Dear Quentin had such strange clients. I believe Count Throlman was one of them, is he still drinking blood?"

Adam covered by sipping the burning liquor, better not have too much of this, if he wanted to keep a clear head. "As a friend of Quentin's, you know he couldn't discuss his clients' cases or appetites."

"Your uncle and I... were very intimate, is that the right

word?"

Looking at her bold, beckoning eyes, Adam was sure it was. And whatever Madame's age, she didn't look a day over forty, and a voluptuous, earthy forty at that. "You're here about your niece?" He reminded.

"I need you to travel to Tucson with me."

"Arizona? I'm sorry, I'm only licensed by the courts in Missouri."

That did stop her for a moment, but then, "Never-the-less, you are simpatico. In dealing with Dia, this is what is required."

"What is her problem?"

"My very foolish niece is allowing herself to be operated on by a lying charlatan!"

"Who is this doctor?"

"Dr. Christian Olsen." She spoke the words with bitter contempt. "Of the '*Miraculous Beginnings Clinic.*'"

Adam turned to his laptop and keyed in a search, and soon he was pulling up the sophisticated website of a plastic surgery clinic that billed itself as the '*ultimate in undoing Nature's missteps*'. Their motto was '*Be like others*', and Adam did a 'ctr copy' on the doctor's certifications, checking them out on the Internet. Finally, he reported. "A man named Christian Olsen has earned the plastic surgeon credentials he claims. Those of his nurse-practitioner wife, Inger Olsen, check out." To dig further, Adam typed in 'Dr. Olsen sucks' as he asked, "What is the exact procedure being done?"

Here the bold woman hesitated for a moment. "Have you ever heard of Gorgons? Of Medusa?"

What Adam knew of Greek mythology, he recited. "Because Poseidon had raped the beautiful Medusa in Athena's temple, the Goddess cursed Medusa and her sisters who were," he left off the word 'hideously,' "transformed by turning the Gorgons' hair on their heads into stinging snakes. A mortal who even looked at the sisters was turned instantly to stone."

Madame Alexis laughed. "Foolish myths! There were no Gods involved! My people are descended from the star visitors. We, like humans, are made in their image, but perhaps we Gorgons are a bit closer to the Life Bringers." She gave him a tantalizing smile. "We can interbreed with humans, so we must be relatively close." Alexis started pulling the tightly wrapped green fabric from around her neck and head. "It will be good to be out of this smothering scarf."

As the silk fell away, Adam stared almost hypnotically as the thickly entwined brown, black, and yellow braid-like ropings on her head started to uncoil. When they twisted free, Adam saw various-sized snakes emerge. Ten, twenty--too many to count, all with black diamond patterned scales and two dazzling yellow eyes with black reptilian slits. Some of their diamond-shaped heads were tasting the air with black-forked tongues while others swung widely backward, seeming to look at his office from all angles.

Adam stood up and started toward the door. "My secretary might come in..."

Madame Alexis just laughed deeply. "Wynoma has seen my children and much, much more, I expect."

Almost hypnotically drawn, Adam walked closer to her. "Well, I'm not turned to stone, so that part of the Gorgon myth is false."

From behind her, the largest, dominant Snake was rising. It swayed behind her head in a king cobra-like strike pose while Alexis watched Adam, apparently approving of his curious reaction, but she gently warned. "They all can bite."

He stopped. "With venom?"

"If they were excited, it would be fatal to you."

"Must be a rough mating."

She smiled with wide, white, square teeth. "There are those that are strong enough, like Quentin."

Adam wanted to change the direction of the

conversation. "Can't you control them?"

"Do you ever have an erection, when you would not wish it?"

Not even realizing it, Adam was raising his hand towards her head, and her snakes instantly drew back. Some hissed and opened white-fanged mouths, with the huge one rising from behind her head just swayed closer to mirror his movements.

"They're afraid of you," Alexis cautioned. "Put your hand up in the air and hold it about a foot from my face."

Adam did as instructed. The larger snakes stayed still, but smaller, thin ones from behind her ears stretched out towards him. They flicked forked tongues at his hand, tasting the air near him. Adam had never been a fan of snakes—especially venomous ones--but he found himself filled with curiosity. "Can I touch one?"

"Let her come to you."

Adam kept his arm out, as a medium sized one swayed to it, finally twisting around his hand. It's scaled skin wasn't slimy, rather it felt smooth and dry. Slowly he withdrew his hand, studying how each of the heads reacted. Some withdrew, some stayed in position, and one close to him turned its head to the side as if to see him from a different angle. "They seem to have separate intelligence. Can you see through their eyes, like the ones behind you? Can you see 360 degrees?"

"When you step into a pond, can't you feel the cold water with your toes and warm air with your fingers—it all becomes one sensation in your mind."

As they stood there, Wynoma entered, not seeming to look at Madame Alexis as she walked to the four large windows of Adam's study. With her dark, Cherokee face inscrutable, as usual, Wynoma lowered the green window shades. "I hear the trucks coming to spray the apple orchard."

Madame nodded approvingly. "I didn't even smell them. Thank you." She turned back to Adam. "Dr. Olsen will cut the snakes from Dia's head! My niece desires to be normal, but she can't. It's been tried before...my own foolish sister was a client of Quentin's after her horrible mutilation."

Adam looked at his empty calendar. With business down lately, he certainly had time for the Cetos, and he needed to pay for that apple spraying, but, "You're talking me traveling with you, that would be travel expenses and eight billable hours per day. I don't see this arrangement as being in your best interests. A lawyer based in Tucson might be a better way to go, I can get a referral?"

While he had looked away, Madame Alexis had taken out her checkbook and was writing. She reached over and handed him a check. "In advance. Now, you fly with me this evening?"

The check was in American dollars, on a Massachusetts bank. For six figures, yhep, the lady could afford the billing, but he put the check down on the desk. "Before I commit to this, I have to do some research, and then I would like to meet your niece. When is the operation?"

"This Sunday. She won't put it off."

"Six days. That's cutting it short. You fly down tonight, and I'll follow later." As she started to leave, Adam wondered out loud. "When you have to go through airport security?"

Alexis smiled. "The boarding terminals for private jets are much more civilized. And a friend has graciously arranged Greek diplomatic passports, so we are never subjected to those demeaning searches."

When she left, Adam did some more Googling. Dr. Christian had several very popular videos on the Internet. He seemed to broadcast his practice that way, two giggling babies joined at the head, a boy afflicted with 'alligator skin,' a hoofed man, and then his miraculous surgery. Would Dia Ceto's snakes wind up as a billboard flash on the net? That Adam might be able to legally prevent.

He studied more of Dr. Oslen's cases, on the unauthorized sites the results were not always so '*Miraculous.*' One of the twins was left permanently brain damaged, and the former alligator man committed suicide. It may have been posted by someone jealous of Dr. Olsen's publicity successes, but Adam got the distinct feeling the rest of the plastic surgery community was not that impressed with Olsen's self-proclaimed '*miracle scalpel.*'

Next Adam researched the Internet for "Gorgons," "Medusas," and "Snakeheads." There must be Gorgon communities somewhere on the Internet, but he couldn't find them. When Adam looked up, Wynoma was looming above him. "You've been sitting there for hours." She carried a tray with a bowl of very delicious smelling stew, probably made from those chickens she raised.

"Getting nowhere." He looked at her impassive face. "You've seen Madame's snakes before?"

"Years ago."

"Did Quentin have any other Gorgon clients?"

Her impassive face was impossible to read as she answered, "Perhaps, before I found him."

"This file you put here on Madame Alexis. It's coded red, and there's that mark there 'ᛉ.'" He pointed to a pen-written symbol on the top. "Is that my uncle's handwriting?"

"Yes."

"Can you look through my uncle's special cases file drawers, and see if you can find me any other folders with that marking?"

She nodded and left as he started devouring the soupy stew which came with a hunk of her homemade cornbread. Obviously, Dia Ceto was of legal age, and her aunt couldn't dissuade her from an operation that might be damaging. What would change her mind? By the time he finished eating, Wynoma had found four more files.

The first was on Madame's sister, Katarina Ceto.

Katarina's case file was a horror story. When Quentin was called in during the 1940's, she had already had the operation, and her head was a mass of regrowing two-inch stubs. From the operation, Katarina was blind and had lost her ability to smell. She couldn't seem to maintain her balance as she tried to walk across the floor, and despite Quentin's efforts at getting her massive doses of painkillers, an agonized Katarina suicided.

The death certificate referenced "an unfortunate house fire" with an unidentifiable body. Quentin had scribbled a side note '*Si puteat sepeliant illud altius,*' and Adam tried to remember Aunt Jerusie's Latin lessons as he roughly translated "If it stinks, bury it deeper." In other words, the best his great-uncle could do for the Cetos was start a fire that covered everything up.

That left three more files: Rufus O'Donnell, Ravi Bendu, and Jepson Clark. Not stated outright but from the services performed, they were probably for long-lived Gorgons. For all three, Quentin had 'found' birth certificates. For Rufus, he arranged passage aboard the liner Queen Mary for a nurse and a surgical patient wrapped in head bandages. For Jepson, there was a balance sheet, and series of notations that looked like Quentin had been paying off a blackmailer.

Adam got back on the Internet. His search for Rufus O'Donnell turned up nothing likely, from the dates, if Rufus were still alive, he was presumably living under a different identity. There was a death certificate for Jepson, but a being that lived several hundred years might find it practical to have Quentin arrange a 'death' legally, so he could go elsewhere and be young again.

The most recent contact had been with Ravi Bendu in 1992. On the Internet, Adam hit the jackpot with a clinic website for a medical doctor in Wyoming, who also seemed to be an internationally known expert on herpetology. Yhep, he could see a Gorgon specializing in the study of snakes and their venom. The website had a photo of Dr. Ravi Bendu, a rather swarthy-skinned man, appearing to be in his mid-thirties with rather handsome features wearing a white turban.

On a hunch, Adam got on the phone, called the doctor's office, and requested an emergency consultation tomorrow. Then he phoned Madame Alexis and said he would meet her on Wednesday evening in Tucson. Just before going upstairs to his apartment, Adam started to put Madame's check on Wynoma's desk for her to cash tomorrow, but he had one of those '*knowing feelings*' again. Instead, he just folded the check up and stuck it in his wallet.

Paying for the airfare with his credit card, Adam flew to Wyoming and rented a car. Like his own office, Bendu's clinic was located way out of town, off by itself on a great deal of land that allowed for privacy.

When he sat down in the doctor's office, Bendu was blunt. "You have inherited your uncle's files, and if I pay sufficiently, you will remain silent."

Adam could answer that without hesitation. "The Martin family has had many generations of maintaining client confidentially, and that is not going to change. Actually, I'm here to hire you as a consultant for a client of mine. Doctor, I'm going to ask you a hypothetical question: A female of Gorgon blood has been told that she can be successfully operated on..."

"Removal of her appendages?" He looked pained.

"Yes."

"It can not be done, not without causing untold damage." He face radiated his horror at the thought. "These are not snakes just sitting upon our heads. Each appendage grows through a hole in the skull from the brain, and its sensory input is intrinsic to the being's total functioning. The attachment of each appendage's network of muscles leaves its mark on that skull, and that is why Gorgons are always cremated to destroy the evidence of those multi-orificed skulls."

Adam interrupted, "There was a case in the 1940's, where a female Gorgon underwent the removal..."

Bendu finished for him. "She was plagued with chronic, agonizing pain, loss of balance, loss of the sense of smell, taste, and a resulting blindness. Yes, there is one in every generation who is foolish enough to try this. Sadly, I lost a first cousin."

"I don't understand, if her eyes, nose, and tongue were intact, shouldn't she have maintained the senses of smell, taste, and sight?"

"The sense of taste is dependent on the sense of smell. When her appendages were removed, she lost the equivalent of thirty or more noses. Her sense of smell would have been reduced to that of a homo sapiens, and for a Gorgon, that is truly being deprived."

"And the blindness?"

"That's a bit more complicated. Yes, in theory, her two front-facing eyes should have remained functioning for a limited field of forward vision..." He stopped as if searching for the English words. "Humans have a condition called 'sympathetic ophthalmia.' When an eye is injured or destroyed, a swelling of the uvea in the uninjured eye can cause bilateral blindness. It is a condition sometimes possibly treatable in a homo sapiens, but with Gorgons, removal of the tentacles generally causes permanent systems destruction."

"The case notes from the 1940's indicate a regrowth of the appendages?"

"A stunted regrowth. It has been heard of, but the sensory heads will not regenerate. If your client is a true Gorgon, she must know this?"

Adam looked at him, wanted to ask, but did not.

Understanding, Bendu gently smiled and removed his turban. His appendages were short, black, flat faced and sea snake-like, but waved quite strongly at Adam. "The females of the species are much more showy. This young girl–have you seen her?"

"Not yet. I've only met her aunt, who was magnificent. I'll be flying out this evening to talk with them both."

Bendu smiled sadly. "It is a pity as I would like to have met the niece. With travel for us being more restricted, our families grow smaller. I am one hundred and twenty-five years old, and I have never found a mate."

"I'll mention you, but..." Adam didn't want to raise unjustified hopes.

"But the Gorgons are a stubborn race. If this young female has decided..." Bendu shook his head sadly. "She will need care afterward. As a doctor, I can find diagnoses to cover the large amounts of painkillers she will need. We could try to preserve her forward eyes, the medical options available to me are better than the ones in the 1940's, perhaps something can be salvaged." He finished, as he pushed one of his business cards to Adam. "There will be no charge for this consultation, and if you have any questions, do not hesitate to call me again."

Adam studied him. "You have an Internet web site for your practice. Have you ever tried to use the worldwide web as a way to contact more of your kind? Maybe find a female?"

The doctor shook his head. "Too risky."

Adam thought about it. "I could set up a site for you, password protected. Of course, it would be visible to Systems Administrators, but if you were all careful to maintain the conceit that you guys were just using Gorgon personas, we could create a contact database. If each you added relatives and Gorgon friends, we might develop quite an online network."

Bendu didn't answer for a time. He seemed to be wary, but interested. "I would like to talk more about this."

Adam nodded. "When I get back. Hey, endangered species got to hustle a bit more."

As he passed the airport bank, again Adam thought about cashing Madame Alexis' check but didn't. Instead, he just put the flight to Tucson on his credit card.

Madame Alexis' travel agents had arranged for three suites at the Whitestone, an older but gracious establishment. Adam found his rooms had a king sized bed, sitting room, and a balcony with a decent pool below, if only he had the time to swim. Adam unpacked and then called Madame Alexis' suite.

They went together to her niece's rooms down the hall. With her head covered in a black striped scarf, Dia opened the door, but then she walked away from them, sitting dramatically so she could look out at the window at the purple hills in the distance.

Her aunt cajoled a bit. "This is Adam Martin. He is the nephew of my great friend Quentin, and he is a lawyer, too."

Adam walked to sit opposite Dia, allowing her space, yet catching her eye. "I just spoke with a doctor, who is also a Gorgon."

He saw a flicker of interest in Dia's eyes.

"Pureblood?" Her aunt asked.

"I don't know. He's a medical doctor and an expert herpetologist. Handsome looking guy, he seems to think that the operation is going to..."

"I've heard it all!" Dia got up, restlessly pacing the room. "You're all wrong! Dr. Olsen assures me that with his advanced surgical techniques he can cure me."

Her aunt's voice radiated anger. "Being Gorgon is not a disease!"

"It is for me!" She looked at Adam. "Please leave!"

To her aunt's obvious distress, Adam did just that.

Thursday, using Dia's name, he made an appointment with Dr. Christian Olsen's office, gambling his supposed client might not find out about it.

The Miraculous Beginnings Clinic was in a two-story, Art Deco building. White stucco inside and out, the building had large circular rooms scattered with chrome-trimmed furnishings. The waiting area was huge and two stories high. It should have been rather attractive, but Dr. Olsen had decorated the place with painted-canvas, bed-sheet sized panels. They were yellowing, antique freak show adverts that had once embellished the tents of traveling carnivals. While the receptionist logged him in, a sick stomached Adam studied tawdry versions of Mermaid Girl, Alligator Boy, the Pin Headed Twins, and the Human Headed Chicken.

A lavender uniformed nurse escorted Adam past reception into the clinic. As he was ushered in the door, Adam walked under an elegantly lettered motto '*To Be Like Others'*, and then in the doctor's office Adam got an even more disturbing view. Dr. Olsen's office continued with the leather seated, chrome piped furniture and glass-topped desks, but the entire right-hand wall was decorated with recessed glass tanks.

Adam expected tropical fish, but when he walked over to the thirty-gallon tanks, he realized they were built in terrariums. They must have been accessible only from a room behind the wall. As Adam studied one, he saw some artfully arranged rocks, sagebrush, and a slithering inhabitant, a sand-colored sidewinder. There were two banks of four tanks, each holding a venomous snake, more deadly than the one before: an Eastern rattler, a banded coral, a bog tank with a dark scaled cotton mouth curled on a floating log, and finally, a black mamba.

Adam heard a noise from the room beyond the wall, and the coral snake desperately slithered to the side as a heavily gloved hand reached in with a snake hook.

In a moment, the nurse opened the door, staying as far away as she could as Doctor Olsen entered carrying an open tray, with the brightly colored red, yellow, and black coral snake curled within. Christian Olsen playfully prodded it with the snake hook. "Like to touch a killer?"

Adam smiled back. "Not unless you give me those gloves first."

The doctor only laughed and sat down. Adam got the feeling that playing with his poisonous snake was apparently the doctor's subtle form of intimation. The low sided tray stayed on the desktop between him and Adam as the doctor began. "You said you're a lawyer for the Cetos?"

"Yes."

"Dia didn't mention you." The doctor seemed to be keeping one eye on the snake.

"Actually I was hired by her aunt."

The doctor looked interested. "Have you seen Madame Alexis, without her cowl?"

Adam ignored that. "Doctor, I've researched the operation you plan to do. It has been tried before, but in every case, it was a crippling failure."

"Those surgeries weren't done by me," said Olsen radiating confidence.

"Several of your patients and operations have wound up on the Internet as entertaining videos. There is some talk in the medical community of pulling your license for disregarding patient privacy."

"But I am still licensed." The doctor smiled smugly.

Adam's attempt at intimidation wasn't working. "The Cetos do not wish publicity. How many of your staff know of Dia's appendages?"

"We have carefully protected her privacy, only myself and my wife, Inger, who is a nurse practitioner, has seen Dia without her scarf. Her file is kept here locked in my office, and her need for secrecy is why the surgery is being done on a Sunday when the clinic is normally closed."

"How many will be doing the surgery?"

"Just my wife and myself."

There was a brief knock on the door, and Dr. Olsen called out. "Enter."

A tall, blonde woman in lavender scrubs with a stethoscope hung from around her neck entered. "Chris..."

"Mr. Martin, this is my wife, Inger." Olsen seemed to say that more to alert her of Adam's presence then introduce her.

But she didn't see Adam as all she focused on was the coral snake coiled on his desk. "Why is that thing out?! Put it back! I've warned you..."

Dr. Olsen angrily interrupted her. "Inger! This is Adam Martin, a lawyer for the Cetos. Not Dia, her aunt."

Still keeping an eye on the snake, Inger turned to Adam. "Lawyer?"

"We believe this operation is a mistake and will only injure Dia, possibly opening you and your husband to a malpractice liability suit."

An obviously concerned Inger looked to her husband. "Chris?"

Her husband ignored her. "When my Dia tells me she doesn't wish my services, then she'll no longer be my patient. Until then, I think, Mr. Martin, I'd rather you leave my clinic!"

It went just as poorly when Adam got back to the hotel. He tried to get Dia to postpone the operation, so they could study it more and maybe talk with Dr. Bendu. She looked like she might be thinking it over, but then Madame Alexis just imperiously ordered her niece to obey! Both women's snakes writhed and rose above their heads, lashing about in their fury. It finally ended with Madame Alexis throwing on her scarf and furious glaring at her niece. "If you do this–this sacrilege, I will have nothing to do with you again! You will have no money! No family!" Flushed with anger, Alexis turned to him. "Adam! We leave this fool! "

When he didn't get up, Madame Ceto glared at him, and then turned and went to unlock the deadbolt. Automatically, Dia pulled up the red silk shawl from about her shoulders and her aunt waited, until her niece was fully covered before Alexis dramatically swept out of the room.

Dia sat there, her shoulders tight, and not looking at

him so finally Adam commented. "She sounds a lot like my Uncle Jeremiah. When I inherited my Uncle Quentin's law practice, Jeremiah ordered me to sell it or else. I don't think your aunt is about to abandon you, and you know that."

He waited, and when Dia didn't speak, Adam continued, "Why don't you postpone the operation, say, just a week. We both could meet with Dr. Bendu. He's a Gorgon, and he'd like to meet you. Actually, he was very interested in meeting a possible mate."

The girl sat righteously wrapped in her own tragic misery. "I want to be away from them. All them. Dr. Olsen says I'm going to be normal."

"If he's wrong? Removal of her appendages caused your Aunt Katarina blindness and agonizing pain."

"You are my Aunt Alexis' servant, and she has said you must leave."

Adam still sat there. "I'm not your aunt's or anybody's servant! I want to be your lawyer, maybe your friend. Will you let me come with you to the doctor's office Sunday?"

"To try to stop me?" She asked defiantly.

"No, I can't do that. Only you have to make the choices for your life, just as you have to live with those choices."

She bit her lip. "My Aunt Alexis would not allow you to come."

"I don't think I'll be working for your aunt Sunday." He said with a touch of regret, Madame's check would have come in handy.

Looking towards the door where Madame Alexis had exited, Dia said, "If you come, you must promise not to try to halt the operation?"

Reluctantly, he nodded.

She actually looked a bit relieved, but only said stiffly, "They will send a limo for me at 8:00 A.M."

The next two days, Adam didn't see much of Alexis or Dia. He mostly just sat in his room, researching on his laptop, and the more he learned about Dr. Christian Olsen, the more he despised the man. Dr. Olsen's site showed a patient covered totally in hair in front of the 'wolf boy' freak show poster, the vampire toothed woman was forced to smile for the camera for his clinic's Halloween card. On Sunday morning, Adam got up early and dressed, but before he knocked on Dia's door, he went to see Madame Alexis.

Dressed in a white hotel robe with a towel twisted on her head, she let him in, and then turned her back on him, walking out on to the hotel balcony. Outside it was hot and smelled of dust and traffic, but seemed less confining than the room as Alexis just stared out at the hills.

Adam tried. "It is her decision."

"She's a baby." Alexis sounded so pained.

"Dia shouldn't go alone, and I think you should go with her."

"To watch her deliberately disfigure herself? To reject our heritage? No, and you will not go either!"

Figuring this was coming, Adam reached into his wallet and pulled out her folded check. It hurt, God he needed that money but, "I can only handle one client's interests at a time. Right now, Dia needs me more than you do, so I'm returning your retainer. Thanks." Not taking it, she continued to stare out at the mountains, so he went inside and placed the check on her table as he left.

He knocked on Dia's door. She opened it, looking a bit frightened but excited. "Oh, I thought you were the limo driver."

"Nope. It's not eight yet."

"Did you talk with my aunt?"

"Yes."

"I'm not changing my mind, and I don't want to talk about it!"

There was a lot he wanted to say, but she wasn't going to listen to it. Frustrated he just sat down on the couch and waited with her.

She seemed to be tearing up but just sat on the chair facing him, until the limo came.

At the clinic, the outside doors were locked, and Inger had to open them. Adam noted the doors were locked again after they entered. Dr. Olsen came into the waiting room, reaching up and removed Dia's pink butterfly scarf as he smiled confidently. "When you leave here today, all will be different." Both he and his wife were now dressed in worn, green scrubs.

Were two enough for an operation of this magnitude? "Who is doing the anesthesiology?" Adam asked.

"My wife," Olsen answered carelessly.

Adam went after that. "On your website, neither of you were listed as a qualified anesthesiologist?"

Dia warned, "Adam, you promised!"

He stopped. "Can I come in with her?" Adam asked.

"No," said Dr. Olsen.

As his wife led her away, Dia looked back at him, frightened but still determined.

Adam forced a smile for her. "It'll be okay."

Dr. Olsen followed them, locking the reception door behind him, and when they left Adam started working out a plan. If Dia was in pain, Dr. Olsen could give her enough pills to get her back to Greece. Would the aunt help them? Unlike Judge Jeremiah, Adam figured that Alexis would relent, but should Adam take Dia directly to Dr. Ravi instead? Alexis had a private plane, could they use that?

As Adam sat there, he tried to look at the magazines but found himself staring up at more of those sideshow canvas sheets of dog boy, the half man-half woman, and the pinheaded sisters. Well, at least they had jobs and a carnival community that accepted them for what they were.

He felt so helpless. Could he have arranged a restraining order against the clinic to play for time? On what grounds? Could he call the cops and report the wife as unqualified to do anesthesiology, therefore performing an illegal operation? His cousin Franklin would have come up with some obscure, nineteenth-century statute that would have ended this operation. Some stinking lawyer Adam was, sitting there while his client was being permanently maimed! Miserably, he kept looking at his watch. Only three minutes later than the last time he looked. Adam picked up a travel magazine, turning pages to tourists skiing.

That's when the woman started screaming.

Adam ran to the door. Dr. Olsen had locked the office door behind him, but it was a weak, standard, inside door. Adam only had to give two strong kicks before the lock gave way. Limping from the door, he headed in following the hysterical screams, passing the doctor's office, before turning on to a long hallway with four or five closed doors. Following the loud sobbing, Adam opened a door to a brightly lit white tiled surgery.

Dia lay on the table, with her shoulders, waist, and legs tied down with surgical strapping. She had a mask over her nose and mouth–oxygen? Her eyes were closed, her face a greenish white, but Adam could see her chest rising slightly, and the various, free-standing monitors she was plugged into were registering vital signs in shooting shining lines. Even to Adam's untrained eye, they looked abnormally low. And although Dia was unconscious, her green, yellowed bellied snakes were awake, writhing wildly, hissing at him and the screaming woman in the corner.

With her surgical mask still covering her shrieking mouth, Inger was pressed against the wall, as she stared down at her husband. He was slumped on the floor, next to the operating table.

Adam looked at Inger harshly ordering, "Stop it!"

The nurse stopped screaming, but when she spoke her words were edged with hysteria. "She murdered Chris! Those snakes of hers bit him again and again!"

Adam moved to the doctor, trying to get a pulse from his ankle as Dia's snakes bent over the table above him, spitting with opened long-fanged mouths. No pulse. Christian Olsen was nothing but a stiffening body. Adam stood up and moved to Inger. "You murdered your husband!" He shifted to protectively stand between Inger and the hospital bed. "You're not a licensed anesthesiologist! Neither of you should have been operating!"

"I gave her a huge amount of pentobarbital..."

"You didn't knock out her snakes!"

"I warned Chris!" She furiously ripped the surgical mask from her face.

Dia choked and seemed to be fighting the oxygen mask. As one of the light lines dropped, the first monitor started a steady warning beeping.

"Something is going wrong!" Adam looked at her. "You've got to help her!"

"I won't touch that freak!"

"That mask on her face?"

"Chris' body weight is cutting off the oxygen line. The mask has got to come off, but I'm not touching her!"

"Where is Dia's clothing?"

"In the examining room through that door. I've got to call the police. Chris is dead!"

Adam had to get control. "Don't call the police until I get Dia out of here! They can't know about her!"

Inger reacted in fear. She looked up at the ceiling near her, and Adam could see a camera. "My husband has filmed all stages of her treatment. This is being filmed now."

Shit! Adam firmly told her, "You have to get me all of the DVDs concerning my client, all pictures, and records you have on Dia, or, mam, when we start suing for malpractice and violation of privacy we will own this clinic!" He was bluffing, but Inger started out, pressing herself against the wall to keep as far away from Dia's wildly hissing snakes as she could.

Now two of the monitors had alarms sounding. Adam moved forward. He had to get that mask off of her, but his foot stubbed against the mass of dead doctor that lay alongside the table.

Adam moved around the bed to the other side. Taking a chance, he extended his arm and pulled an IV needle out of Dia's arm as red blood puddled on her pale skin. Her raised snakes followed his every move, hissing as he got closer. Adam grabbed up several towels, wrapping them around his arm to use as a snake-bite shield, and he moved in slowly, but firmly. "Guys, I'm trying to save momma. You understand me?"

Like angry bees, the green heads with black beaded eyes swarmed protectively above her skull. Adam looked up at the monitoring equipment. The beeping was getting louder–Dia's heart rate was failing. She was dying.

Adam slowly reached forward and pulled at the mask's hose, but it was firmly strapped on. If he was going to release the velcro straps holding it, he would have to reach into the snakes' striking zone. Dia's facial skin was turning purplish. The snakes hissed, but as he moved his hand close to her head, they allowed him to rip away the velcro strapping.

With the mask gone, the unconscious Dia took loud rasping breaths.

She moaned weakly, but the lines on her monitoring equipment started to rise again, so Adam hurried into the next room. Grabbed up her belongings, including the butterfly printed head scarf, he hurried back.

When he reentered the surgery, Inger stood in the other doorway. She was holding two filing folders in her hand, and one uncased DVD that must have just come out of the recording equipment. He reached out, but she pulled them back. "Chris said this documentary was going to pay for our kids' college educations. Pictures of the snake-headed woman..."

Was she as uncaring and cruel as her husband? Adam doubted it, but it was time to present the new widow with a winning argument. "Your husband's cutting-edge recording equipment is digital. Do you know why courts demand the original photographic negatives? To see if images have been manipulated. A court can't do that with digital photography. Change a few of the numbers in a computer, and you can have a picture of me embracing Martha Washington on board a UFO. So your 'documentary' will be nothing but a freak flash on the Internet!"

She straightened her shoulders. "I'm calling the police."

"And saying what? Admitting that you were acting as an unlicensed anesthesiologist? You'll lose your Nurse Practitioners' license. Your husband died by your acts–you may wind up in jail. Who will support your kids?"

The children argument got her. "What'll I do?"

"You'll do what I tell you! Now go sit in the waiting room!"

Adam ripped off the face mask and scrub hat from Olsen. He'd have to leave the operating gown on. Stiffening his resolve by counting up his felonious acts so far, Adam reached down and grabbed the doctor under his shoulders. He pulled and felt the full meaning of 'dead weight.' Dia moaned again as she was coming out of sedation. Her snakes were becoming more active, so desperation gave Adam a bit more strength. This had to be done before the widow changed her mind!

He dragged Dr. Olsen from the surgery to his office. There Adam tried to heave the body up onto his chair but wound up just letting him slide to the floor. Picking up the snake tray and hook, Adam went out into the hallway. There was a closet like door right next to the doctor's office, it had a lock, but it was open. Here in a narrow, dark space, there were the backs of the terrarium tanks on one side and Olsen's recording equipment on the other. Adam found the CPU and hit the eject, the disk drive came out empty. Maybe he could trust the wife. It'd help if he could make her an accessory to the cover-up.

Then he turned to the two banks of venomous snake tanks. It made his skin crawl to look at them, rattler, slithering striped coral, and cottonmouth. The black mamba would have the most dangerous venom and looked like it had fangs closest to Dia's beauties.

Where was Olsen's protective gloves? Adam didn't see any, and he hadn't time to look as he opened the steel screen on top of the mamba's tank. With the hook, he reached in and started pulling the snake up. It coiled around the hook, rapidly twisting upwards, reaching for his bare hand. Skin crawling, he dumped the snake into a tray and with the hook, held its head down as he ran back into Dr. Olsen's office.

Using the hook, he threw the snake on Dr. Olsen and tossed the tray on to his desk. Wiping it fast with his jacket sleeve, Adam threw the hook down by the doctor's hand. The deadly black mamba dropped off Olsen's body, and on the carpet, it slid towards Adam. Scared sick, he ran backward, slamming the door shut on that slithering death whip. Could it get under the door?

Adam could hear Inger sobbing in the waiting room, but he was more worried about Dia. When he reentered the surgery, her snakes had stopped hissing. They seemed to actually recognize him, obediently pulling back to curl against her head. Adam undid the strapping at her feet and then decided to chance moving to her waist strap. As he was loosening it, Dia opened her eyes. Seeing him, she pleaded. "Am I?"

Adam stopped and looked deeply into her eyes. "You are beautiful. Just as beautiful as you were before."

"Dr. Olsen?"

"Suddenly decided to give up surgery." Adam started released the straps holding her shoulders. "Pull those monitoring-tapes off your chest, we have to get you out of here."

She looked up towards her snake-like appendages, her face full of guilt. "I killed him, didn't I."

Adam stopped and stared directly at her. "No! He stupidly killed himself! He and his incompetent anesthesiologist wife! Look, Dia, death isn't that nice. Police questioning isn't fun. Jails aren't that comfortable. Being a treated like a freak on the five o'clock news sucks! I think sunning yourself on a beach in Greece would be a lot more fun."

Dia just sat there. All her green snakes writhing wildly in no particular pattern or direction.

Adam picked up her head scarf. If her snakes were going to attack, they would probably stiffen and raise to strike first. As he moved closer, Dia looked at him, and then her snakes seemed to relax and weave back into a tight nest encircling her head. She took the scarf from him and finished putting it on herself, Adam left her getting dressed.

Picking up Olsen's 'Dia C.' files, he headed for the waiting room, finding himself sweating as he passed the doctor's office with that killer slithering loose inside. In the waiting room, Inger had gotten control of herself and had stripped off her operating gown. She was now wearing a blue blouse and pants, and by her defiant body language, Adam knew he had big trouble, even before she pronounced. "I'm not going to be part of your coverup!"

He needed a winning argument. Losing her license? Tying up the sale of her husband's practice? Naked Notoriety? He'd tried those, and their effects had worn off. Adam needed something more. In a brotherly fashion, Adam leaned over her and lowered his voice. "You saw what Dia did to your husband? As a Gorgon, she's relatively immature. But she has family, and they are all capable of a lot more venomous stings then what killed your Chris. Yes, I can't stop you from talking to the police, but don't be surprised if they don't believe you. And when you are done talking, you are going to walk out of that police station by yourself. Just think of spending the rest of your life grabbing your children and running every time you see a woman wearing a scarf or a man in a turban."

She blanched.

Adam continued. "Your husband's gone. You have yourself and his kids to take care of. Without scandal, you can sell this practice for good money, and he must have life insurance? Do you want to try and explain to them how your husband was killed by a mythical creature?" Adam was watching her face, trying to see if his arguments were taking hold. "After we leave, you call the cops. Say you and your husband were using Sunday to catch up on office work. You heard a noise–probably him falling. You've warned him in the past about playing with his pets. You opened his office door, saw him slumped dead on the floor with the mamba sliding off him. Knowing by his skin color he was beyond help, and afraid of the snake, you closed the door and called the police. Do it exactly like I tell you and everything will be all right!"

Inger just sat there.

He had to get Dia out of there. "Give me the keys for the outer door!"

Inger did.

Getting Dia back to the hotel in a taxi was a nightmare with Adam afraid she was going to throw herself out of the speeding cab. When she reached the hotel, Dia seemed drained, walking like a robot as Adam steered her toward Madame's suite.

But once they entered, Alexis was all over her niece, hugging Dia as they both cried. Finally, with Dia resting on her bed, Alexis turned to Adam. "Will there be any embarrassment?"

"I don't know, but if you both are on your way to Greece any possible extradition for questioning would be a lot more complicated."

Madame Alexis nodded. "My pilot is on standby." As Adam was about to leave, she turned to him. "You mentioned a young man–a doctor?"

"Ravi Bendu. Medical doctor. Herpetologist. Unmarried. He'd love to meet your niece. Of course, he's only one hundred and twenty-five years old."

Alexis smiled widely. "For us, age is of little matter. On my island, there are some very interesting snakes he might wish to study, I will invite him."

Adam took Ravi's business card out of his wallet and gave it to her. "I'll ride with you to the airport." If the police stopped Dia, he wanted to be there.

At the airport, before Madame Alexis got out of the limo, she reached out and brushed his cheek with her warm lips. "My invitation for you to visit is open, any time you wish it. I think Quentin found his stays with me quite pleasurable."

It was tempting, but, "I've learned it's not good policy to have romantic relationships with clients."

"A pity." She slid away, then looked over at him. "But it would be just as pleasant for me to entertain an intelligent man on my island to just discuss world affairs. Keep it in mind." She kissed his cheek again, and then hurried her niece into the gate of the private jet terminal.

When he got back the hotel, Adam ruefully realized he had dropped one client and never asked Dia to pay him. Providing she even had any money of her own? Not only had he lost his billable hours, but he'd run up rent-a-car bills and airline tickets that would now be coming out of his own pocket. If he ever found out, Uncle Jeremiah wouldn't be surprised. Adam went back to the hotel and at least got a swim in for his money.

The next morning when he checked out, he was

pleasantly surprised to discover the bill had been paid by Madame Alexis, and the desk had a sealed envelope for him. He ripped it open to find a first-class airline ticket and a folded piece of paper. It was a check from Madame, double the original amount and Adam grinned widely to see all those lovely, lovely zeroes.

While waiting at the airport, Adam bought a local paper. Big headlines, famous surgeon accidentally killed while playing with pet viper. Adam quickly read down to the last paragraph, with its memorial arrangements.

Inger Olsen was having her husband's body cremated and the memorial service to scatter his ashes was scheduled for Thursday, so the police weren't holding the body. To Adam that sounded very good. Threatening a widow with death by multiple snake bites was not exactly what Uncle Jeremiah sent him to law school for, but somewhere Adam knew Great Uncle Quentin would be smiling.

Adam's Dryad

"They're going to cut her down–kill her!"

These were friends of his secretary, Wynoma. The man, Wolf, with shoulder length white hair stood even taller than his 6'2' secretary. But where she was silent and Cherokee, Wolf was a four hundred pound white man whose baritone voice resonated throughout the whole mansion.

"Who is cutting her down?" Adam asked.

"The stinking State!" Boomed Wolf.

"They're stealing our land–just taking it," supplied Rowena. She rambled on as Adam nodded and studied her. He saw a fortyish, dark braided Viking like maiden, dressed in a homemade, purple tie-dyed gown, and Adam soon learned that if he allowed her, Rowena would talk all day.

After giving up waiting for her to stop and take a breath, he finally broke in. "The woman being killed is?"

"Kasha."

"Her last name?"

"It's just Kasha," Rowena rolled on, "at the Commune, we feel that last names are an ownership thing. Why should a woman lose herself because she marries? Why should a slave have to take the name of his master? Why..."

Wynoma's quiet firm voice overruled Rowena's. "Perhaps if you went and met Kasha, it would be easier to understand."

Rowena quickly objected, "Will Kasha speak to him? I mean, she will speak to him, but will he hear her?" Without stopping the stream of her words, she looked at all of them in turn. "Wouldn't it be something if when the Cossacks from the State came to kill her, she just yelled at them, and they went away? Wouldn't that be great...."

Wolf talked over her. "You can follow us."

As they started out, Adam turned to Wynoma. "Will I

hear Kasha?"

"You are your Uncle Quentin's heir, if you listen very carefully in the stillness, you may hear her." She looked down at him. "Take off your shoes and socks, it will help."

"Take off my shoes–why?"

"We are all rooted to the Earth. You connect better with bare feet."

He looked, she was in worn moccasins.

Wolf drove a bronze colored van that alternated rust holes with painted yellow leopard-spots. Leaving his shoes on, Adam followed Wolf with Wynoma in his old pick up. Heading into a rural area, they turned off the highway at a hand-carved sign, '*Love Haven Commune, Founded 1969*", which stood beside another hand-painted sign, '*Fresh Herbs, Eggs, Cheese and Goat's Milk-Raw.*' From the entrance, a rutted dirt road led through the trees.

Finally, at a clearing, Adam parked the truck. He saw several homemade, one story buildings of weather-grayed wood, including a long, low central house with multiple doors for multiple families? There were two or three free-standing cabins, and on the other side a long bank of hen houses with some chicken-wire enclosures, but those must be only for night protection because all about several flocks of chickens were ranging free. Walking around Adam could smell baking bread and chicken manure.

While Wolf spread the word, Adam walked farther and saw a few black and white goats that were fenced out of a good sized garden—veggie? No. He saw lavender and lemon verbena, and he smelled basil and oregano. This must be the commune's herb garden.

Adam counted ten adults coming out to see him, and he was introduced to people with names like Storm, Iris, and Freya. Nobody under forty and most a lot older. No, from one of the small, free-standing cabins, he saw a twentyish couple with four-year-old twins.

While Rowena was talking at him, Adam looked to see if Wynoma was mixing with her friends. If so, these would be the first people she seemed to socialize with, but no, the tall Cherokee woman just stood by herself, waiting until they all walked to a twisted wicker-vine arch that was spray-painted gold, and interwoven with pink and blue silk flowers. It leads to another path into the birch woods.

As ever, Rowena rambled on, "With their superhighway running through here, everything will be gone. Kasha. All the trees breathing in the global warming carbon, trees that protect us..."

In the next clearing, Adam passed a serious garden that spread over a couple of acres, with tall rows of ripening corn, wide-leafed squash, staked tomatoes, and several varieties of green beans. Alongside it was two long rows of sunflowers stretching their heavy, yellow heads to the sky. If he couldn't get anything else for the commune, he had to get them the right of the last harvest!

Rowena flowed on. "Canning gets us through the winter, but they're going to bulldoze this garden. All gone! We won't have any food. Of course, we won't have a house or a root cellar. There won't be a commune, so I guess the State figures we don't need to eat..."

They walked to another edging of trees, this predominantly made up of old firs with wildflowers at their feet. Adam noted that even with the weeks of drought they'd been having, everything here seemed to have stayed very green. Another golden wicker gate grandly arched before a red-pine needled path through the forest that finally led to a large, high grass clearing. In the center of that clearing stood the biggest, widest tree Adam had ever seen. He had to bend his neck to study the shading canopy above him. An oak. An ancient one.

All around that oak, someone had set roughly-cut knee high granite blocks, making a ring rather like a tiny

Stonehenge, overshadowed by some great, gray-trunked tree god.

While he stood there looking, others walked to the tree, touched its bark lovingly with their hands, and then they went back and sat down on one of the granite seating cubes.

Rowena stood alongside side Adam. "Do you hear her? Kasha? I don't, but Wolfie does. They sing duets together. She's there, and others hear her." Rowena turned to look at Adam, maybe to read his reaction. "She's a Dryad."

Dryad? Greek Nymph? Adam mentally pulled up more data. "A female spirit living in a tree?"

She nodded and started talking again.

Adam found himself tuning Rowena out, trying to listen to the stillness, but he wasn't hearing anything. He should take his shoes off, but he felt stupid doing that. Wynoma had walked across the clearing barefoot now, as a red cardinal flew to the lowest branch of the oak above her. Then two yellow something or others fluttered by, and Adam watched them alight on the lower branches.

A tall, dark chocolate skinned woman he had been introduced to as Iris came to him. She was dressed in a brilliant cobalt silk kaftan with concentric rings of gold, and she carried a six foot tall, carved wooden staff with an almost round, clear crystal on the top. He gathered that the others treated her as some sort of priestess. As he watched a bright red robin flew close to her head, then flashed up to the branches above her.

While Rowena talked in the background, the priestess asked him in a low voice, "What is your favorite?"

Adam started. "Favorite?"

"Bird?"

God, it's going to be question and answers? He said the first thing that came into his mind, "Bluejays."

The priestess nodded, turned to the mighty oak and whispered something.

Adam asked her. "You're talking to the tree?"

"To Kasha in the tree."

"Is she talking back?"

"Can't you hear her?"

No, he couldn't. Adam had a brief, mad vision of getting some judge to move his court out into this clearing while Adam had Iris translating for Kasha. Well, then all of them would have someplace to live—the looney bin.

A bluejay flew to the branch above him. Adam pulled out his cell phone and started taking snapshots: Iris near the tree; the oak's towering branches, and the others of the commune sitting on their individual rocks. Maybe he could come up with some sort of a religious exemption from the Highway Authority? Would the court accept an outdoor Wiccan Cathedral?

The heavyset, gray-haired woman, Alice, passed out meat pastries from her basket and eight-ounce paper cups. Adam nearly refused, but then had a feeling that it was some sort of ritual for the tree. He put his pastry down on the granite block, as Wolf followed Alice, with a jug. "My home brewed Heroka." He gave Adam a generous pour.

Adam sipped honeyed vodka, smooth, and strong. He looked about. Nobody else was drinking–he should have waited until they all were served, Adam realized they must be doing some sort of communion rite with the tree. Two more bluejays were squawking after the first one.

When all had been served, the priestess nodded, turned to the tree, stretching her arms to the sky, and sang out a benediction, thanking the Mother for the beauty given them. Five more bluejays flew into the Oak's branches.

As one, the commune sat, ate their pastries, and drank their brew in silence. With the Martin family's rigid adherence to court discipline, Adam had learned early to accept quiet waiting, but finally, he looked around and asked, "If this land is taken, what is going to happen to you guys? Where are you going to live?"

They looked from him to the tree.

The fact that they didn't seem to have any other plan than relying on him and a tree concerned Adam. "You have to be making contingency plans."

Everyone looked sort of blank, then Rowena started babbling again, "We're going to chain ourselves to the tree. Get network coverage..."

Adam shook his head. "Network news doesn't count for much these days. Have they offered you a buyout?"

Storm looked to his boots. "They talked about it, but we can't prove it's our land."

Another complication, Adam groaned inwardly. "Are you guys squatting?"

"No, no!" Rowena supplied. "This land belonged to MaryAnne Ramsey's family for generations. She started Love Haven Commune, and she left it to all of us when she died."

Uh huh, Adam probed. "That is registered at the County Seat?"

Wolf looked embarrassed. "To register, you had to pay a fee. We never got around to it."

Great. Adam asked, "Do you still have the papers?"

"Somewhere." Wolf looked to Storm who looked to Freya who looked to Iris.

Without much hope, Adam ordered, "Make finding those papers for me a top priority, okay?"

Rowena just brushed it aside. "Everyone around here knows we own the property."

Wolf interrupted. "We've pay the taxes!"

"That's good," Adam nodded. "Could you get me paperwork on that?"

Glancing from one to the other, Wolf and Storm didn't look so confident.

Finishing their brew, most the commune members left. Adam was ready to leave, but Wynoma still lingered. She stood away from the tree, looking at it, but not talking. It was hard to hear with the tremendous squawking racket anyway, Adam looked up and realized there must be twenty–no, thirty–bluejays decorating lower branches of the Oak tree. He took some cell photos, and then just waited for Wynoma to start walking back with him.

When they finally reached the main clearing, Adam started to walk towards his pickup, startling a small brown hen who squawked as she darted out of his path. She quickly blended into the tall grass before him, but as Adam started to put his foot down, from just behind him he heard a melodious voice of a woman, saying firmly, "Don't!"

He looked down and nestled in the grass before him was a speckled brown egg. The hen, still watching him, must have been sitting on it. Adam changed his direction and looked about, nobody near him, but he had heard that woman's voice so close, so clearly. Not a shout, but still loud, as if someone had been right next to his ear.

Wynoma stood by the car, looking at him, and he asked her, "Was that you who said 'Don't'?"

She shook her head. "You heard Kasha, she was protecting the chick, he's ready to emerge."

Now, Adam didn't even know if it had been an actual voice, or had it just been something he heard in his mind? As he drove back to his law office and farm, he wondered what exactly he had heard? And more importantly, how was he going to save Kasha and the Love Haven Commune?

The next day, Adam drove to the Department of Transportation. Sitting across from a drawing board, Adam listened, as a very, weary engineer patiently pointed out. "My responsibility is to make the roads of Missouri safe for you to drive. When we build a new road, it always means taking somebody's property. Somebody is losing the family barn, generations of memories, momma's house, auntie's restaurant, dad's school, or great-grandpa's outhouse. They get a lawyer.

He/she comes here, and we argue, then we go to court, but my road gets built!"

"If your road could just be moved a mile or so?" Adam started.

The engineer cut him off. "Then somebody else would be in here giving me heartburn."

Adam looked at the figures on the sheet Wolf had given him. "There are twelve adults in that commune and two minors, who will be homeless and without their farm income if you condemn that property."

"It is condemned. Technically they're already homeless, and they've now reached the point where they must vacate so demolition can be completed."

"You're taking their homes and livelihoods and only offering enough compensation to let them stay for three months at a Super 8 Motel?"

The engineer went back to marking his blueprints. "Compensation is not this department."

Adam went to Compensation. And Relocation. Citizen's Advocates. And Historical resources. And the EPA, between Federal, State, County, and Town, it was actually fifteen departments, before Adam ran out of authorities to appeal to.

End results: Adam felt sure he could get the Love Haven Commune's land claim refiled in their names. He might get an order allowing them the right of the last harvest, and he could get all the Commune members recognized as owners to be compensated. He might even get that compensation increased, but in the end, without a court order to the contrary, the highway was going through. The Commune's buildings and Kasha's Oak would be bulldozed down.

So unless Adam could come up with an overriding, significant historical, religious, or geographic status that took priority over drivers' safety, they had lost. Time was running out, and it was all on his shoulders. From the Resurrection

Sisters, he picked up Sister Josey and Madame Terri. Maybe the retired nun or the bubbly fortune teller could speak more clearly with this tree and translate for him. Moreover, he wanted a disinterested second and third opinion on this wood nymph's existence.

They walked to the clearing without an escort of commune members. If either of Madam Terri's Pomeranian puppies ran over and peed on that Oak, Adam knew he had a problem, but the golden colored Houdini II, the aggressive one, stopped stiff-legged in the middle of the clearing. For a change he didn't dare bark his usual challenge, while his brother, the quiet, white fluffed Thurston, also stopped, studying that tall tree with big black eyes as he growled softly.

Not told why they were here, both Sister Josey and Madame Terri softly walked to the tree with great respect. Sister Josey looked as if she was entering some contemplative state that left out the world around her as she stood before the Oak and laid her palm on the tree's rough bark. Later, Adam saw Sister Joesy's lips moving, as if in silent prayer or soft conversation.

With perfectly coifed golden-hair, Madame Terri looked high into the leaves and smiled contentedly, and then she laid her hand on the rough bark as she walked around the full circumference of the tree's trunk. She stopped several times and seemed to be searching for something about two or three feet from the ground.

Adam joined her. "What are you looking for?"

"The hole."

"What hole?"

She started walking around again, looking higher up this time–at about three and a half feet off the ground. There was a hole in the tree, where there must have once been a branch that later rotted away. Madame Terri pursed her lips. "Of course, it would be higher, that was a few hundred years ago." She looked at him, shaking her head disapprovingly.

"You men."

Adam asked, "What?"

"A lonely, Greek man lived here. Very lonely and at dark nights he deposited his seed..." Madame Terri stopped, looking from him to the hole in the tree's trunk.

As he got it, Adam found himself flushing. "That created the Dryad?"

"It helped her bind herself to this tree. She used to come out and dance naked with him." Madame Terri grew terribly serious. "Kasha, that's her name, isn't it? But Kasha is not a Dryad, Dryads are wood nymphs. They live in a tree, but they can come out and dance or run away. Kasha is older by hundreds of years, and she chose to become a Hamadryad."

"Hamadryad?" questioned Adam.

"She has become one with the tree," confirmed Madame Terri.

"How do we get her out of there?"

"You can't. Kasha will live as long as her tree, but when it falls, she must also die."

"You feel her there?"

"Yes."

Adam didn't want to ask, but he had to know. "What is she feeling?"

Madame Terri listened to the quietness. "She's very afraid now." But the Madame shifted to her happy Terri stage. "But she knows you will take care of things."

Adam needed more. "Do you feel anything else?"

Madame Terri looked around. "The commune people have good karma, and there are Native American spirits still here. There must have been an ancient graveyard nearby, or they come here because of Kasha."

Before she left, Sister Josey pulled a chain from her neck and hung an oval St. Elizabeth's medal on a piece of rough bark that stuck out from the tree. Adam felt it should be a medal for St. Jude–patron of lost causes. As they were leaving, the Pomeranians followed Madame Terri, but both dogs constantly looked over their shoulders at that looming tree.

Adam took a few more cell pictures, dropped the Resurrection Sisters off, and then headed back to his office. He got an emergency court hearing scheduled and not much else. He dialed his district attorney cousin. "You know anything about Judge Suzanne Harris?"

"She's pretty fair," George Martin said.

"Favor the State's case?"

"The State usually has a better case," replied the St. Louis prosecutor.

"Do you know if she believes in, say, spirits or...."

George cut him off, "I doubt that very much. Judge Harris is very conservative. You can meet her as she's being honored for her work with the Audubon Society next Friday, and will be there giving a speech. Only cost you a hundred and twenty-five bucks for a ticket."

After he rang off, Adam looked up to see his silent secretary had entered. "Wynoma, besides yourself, did Uncle Quentin have any dealings with, say, Native American tribal leaders? "

She nodded.

The next morning, Adam stood before a sign that read. *'The Hopewell Tribal Reservation, Home of the Sacred Mound Builders.'* It stood in front of a rather beat up R.V. with flat tires, and behind that was a 1950's split level house. The muddy yard was cluttered with kid's toys, and as Adam walked up, he saw *'Chief Big Eagle Flies'* scrawled on the mailbox. Adam knocked on the door to the house. It looked like the lock, as well as the bug screen, was broken on that door. Finally, a big man opened it, shorter than Wolf but with a bigger, solid beer belly. He had deeply tanned skin, high cheeks, a wide African nose and introduced himself as *'Chief Big Eagle Flies.'*

Adam started off with a question. "Did you get the name Eagle Flies from your parents or the tribe?"

"Actually, my mother named me 'Robin' because it was the first animal she saw after I was born. I got christened "Eagle Flies" when I was a paymaster in the Navy. 'Big Eagle Flies' is the cleaned up version."

As a three-year-old screamed in the kitchen, Chief Big Eagle led Adam inside to a Rec room on the lower level. "Used to know your Uncle Quentin. He did some work for us because the blasted State and Feds keep claiming my tribe is extinct."

"Quentin worked on that for you?"

"Got this land registered as a State Reservation, which was the first step to Federal recognition, but then your uncle died," said Big Eagle like Quentin did it just to screw him.

Adam looked out the window at a wheelless pickup in the junk strew backyard. "How big is the Reservation?"

"An acre and half, but when we get our Federal recognition, we can claim one-eighth of the State. But we really need that Federal kissoff for our own casino–can you fix that?" asked Big Eagle hungrily.

"Casinos cost money," said Adam.

"Got a guy from Singapore who'll pay for the structures, if I get recognition!"

"You got money to pay for legal fees?"

"You work pro bono, to make up to my people for what the whites did by taking our lands?" The Chief asked hopefully.

"No."

Big Eagle actually seemed to approve of that attitude in a lawyer. "Could you work on consignment? We get the casino, you get paid?"

Adam looked around. "Let me get this current case finished, and then we can talk about it. As my secretary told you on the phone, the State has condemned my client's land for a new highway. They live in the *Love Haven Commune*."

The Chief looked at him, and then shifted his eyes to the '*Tribal donation*' can sitting by the open beer on his end table.

Adam fished out a twenty and fed it to the can. "My clients are hoping you might know of any Native American graveyards or sacred sites that might be on their land?"

"Wynoma said you'd be bringing beer?" asked Big Eagle.

"Four cases, out in my pickup."

Satisfied Big Eagle settled back on his recliner. "Yhep, that land was sacred to my tribe. My grandfather told me this as we sat around the fire of our sweat lodge, after my first bow and arrow hunt."

That sounded good. "Really?"

"My great-great-grandmother is buried there in an unmarked grave. The tribe pulled the tents and horses across it to hide her resting from the evil spirits."

"Can you testify that under oath?" Adam quickly asked.

"Sure can."

"Okay, as our expert witness, we can probably get expenses for you and more beer."

"Only got to know one thing," the chief asked. "Where the hell is Love Haven Commune?"

Adam took him out there. When they got to Kasha's clearing, the Oak was decorated with about a hundred squawking bluejays. Chief Big Eagle actually stopped, looked long up at that tree, and then abruptly turned around and pushed back on to the pine trail.

While Big Chief Eagle Flies wouldn't go near the Oaktree clearing again, he spent the whole day walking the rest of the land. At first he was sure his ancestors had placed those granite blocks around the tree, and Adam had to get him off of that one, but as they walked around, Chief Eagle Flies found a spring sacred to his tribe, a cremation site (no bones left naturally), and ritual, tribal dance grounds. The Chief told him, "If I get an extra hundred and fifty bucks, I can get the real deer hide, beaded, Injun suit out of hock—feathered headdress and all. Look great in court."

Adam ponyed up the money.

That week in court, Adam found himself getting nervous as Big Chief Eagle flies was a no-show. He managed a continuance, and then furious, he drove to the reservation. Out front by the R.V., a twentyish male was in a screaming match with an Indian looking female, and three toddlers had taken that opportunity to start sitting splashing themselves in a mud puddle. No one answered the door, but Adam could hear someone in the back hammering on a car, so walking around he found Chief Big Eagle working under his truck hood.

"We had court today." Adam started evenly.

The Chief looked up calmly. "Yeah, 'bout that. Can't give you your hundred and fifty back–you want the beaded Injun suit?"

Adam couldn't believe him. "I need your testimony!"

Big Eagle looked back to his truck. "Can't-do. We're in negotiations, seems the State thinks they might be able to help us with my tribe's recognition with the Feds. They contacted me!" The Chief was wiping his hands, and now finally he met Adam's eyes. "Look, man, forget that trash pit of a commune! We could have millions from a casino, and you can be the Tribe's lawyer. We'll be getting a real reservation, maybe a couple thousand acres of State land, and we could adopt the commune guys into the tribe. They can grow their beans and corn on tribal land. Or just sit back and count the money rolling in from the slot machines. I've waited my whole life for this!"

Despising his stupidity, Adam just stared. "All that State re-consideration coming through, just when you showed up on my witness list? What a coincidence," he finished bitterly.

The Chief had the grace to look ashamed. "Look, it's me—my wife, five grandchildren, my daughter, and her friend's just moved back into the R.V. My son, and his wife's have been living in the basement for three years. And the daughter-in-law is pregnant again. White man was real clear, if I testify for you, no reservation and no casino."

"Chief, hope you got your deal in writing and triple notarized, cause I think come next week you're going be in the same condition as I am now. And, buddy, it hurts!" Adam slammed his truck door, and burned rubber getting out of there. '*Alley et proditor, et moietur solus*' Ally with a traitor, die alone.

He headed to the Commune and found himself drawn back to the Oak tree. In the clearing, he took off his shoes and socks, walking barefoot on the grass. Rowena and the priestess, Iris, were covering a woman with a blanket as she lay beneath the tree's encompassing branches.

When the priestess came back, Adam softly asked her, "What is that?"

"Usually we bring infertile women just to stand and hug the tree, but Lily and her husband have been trying to have a baby for eighteen years. She wants to sleep here tonight, so that Kasha may decide to help her."

Adam took a picture of the woman lying there, but he needed a stronger case to save this Commune and its Oak tree's inhabitant. "Iris, I said I liked bluejays and the tree...Kasha..."

"Called the bluejays to her branches," she finished serenely.

"I can hear her a little, but I can't speak with Kasha, can you do it for me?"

"I'll try. What do you want me to say to her?"

"Could she bring, say something unusual for Missouri,

a bird like a flamingo?"

Iris frowned. "From Africa? That's too hard."

"Okay. Judge Harris is an Audubon Society enthusiast, and she likes birds. If we could get a rare, endangered bird living in the Oak tree's branches, and I could photograph it..."

"What bird do you want?" asked Iris, her face serene.

Adam didn't know. "Do you think Kasha could figure out which is the rarest?"

Iris walked from him, and facing the Oak tree, she raised her arms and closed her eyes. He didn't hear anything, and Adam didn't see her lips move, but he just knew to wait.

It was a long wait, most of the afternoon. A single wren flew through the branches, some pretty yellow birds with black wings came to alight, but then Iris looked up and nodded her head to him. Adam followed her eyes, as a big bird, then another landed in the tree. They had wide wingspans, maybe more than twenty inches across their wings tips and he thought they looked like woodpeckers with black bodies, half black wings with white tips. The first one had a sharply pointed red crest, and its mate had a black crest. Endangered species? Was it an endangered Ivory-billed woodpecker? Those had been in the news, so Adam rapidly took as many cell photos as he could, until the birds flew away.

In court, the state engineer sat with his maps, along with the Department of Transportation's attorney. Judge Suzanne Harris seemed to accept the need for another highway, bad sign. The judge allowed Adam to set up a projection screen and they all sat patiently through his slide presentation on the Commune, its history, its importance as a nurturing community, and its fresh food relationship with its neighbors. They were letting him run out, until he got to the Oak tree. He pointed out that the Amerind tribes considered it sacred and it was the oldest tree in the County, maybe the State. That it supported a unique interrelationship of flora and fauna. Adam showed pictures, saving the Ivory-billed woodpecker to the last, cagily letting the judge identify it.

"That bird? You saw it land in that tree? Are these recent photos?" Judge Harris excited asked.

"Yes, ma'am, two, maybe a breeding pair, your honor. I was wondering if they are Ivory-billed woodpeckers? They're on the edge of extinction."

Judge Harris looked at the photo of the large male, flying just above Iris. "How big was the wingspan?"

Adam took a guess. "Twenty, thirty inches."

"It looks like it may be twenty-three," the judge supplied, not taking her eyes off the photograph.

"Then it is an Ivory-billed woodpecker?" Adam asked again hopefully.

"I don't think so," said Judge Harris. "No, indeed, these pictures are terrible, but from the red crest, the wingspan, the black and white tips, I think you have found two Campophilus Imperialis."

"Is that almost as endangered as the Ivory-billed?" Adam asked.

"It's extinct!" The judge pronounced. "At least it is in its ranges in Mexico, to have it here is a miracle!" Judge Harris finished in a reverent voice.

Adam turned to two the State's table. "Maybe if the highway map could be redrawn? Just miss the Oak and the Commune?"

The engineer didn't even look at him. Instead he just started to pack up his drawings. The State's lawyer looked tired, asking the judge, "Is this bird on the protection listing?"

Judge Harris happily bubbled. "Yes! This is fabulous! I am temporarily staying the State's condemnation. We'll send out Audubon Society members, and if they find this bird, I will be ordering a permanent stay of eminent domain on this property!"

The State's lawyer pointed out in a patient fashion. "Your honor, the road is already under construction."

"You will just have to go back to the drawing board and find another way!" With that, the judge adjourned court and started asking for directions to Love Haven Commune.

When Judge Harris ordered a temporary stay of demolition, the whole Commune behind Adam went wild. Wolf's deep baritone shook the walls, leading "Vee vott!" cheers for Adam and the judge, but Adam had been watching his opponents' table, knowing with a gut feeling that something had gone horribly wrong.

The State's attorney took a single page of a pre-written form from his file, handed it to the clerk and very, carefully, for the record, drily announced. "The State wishes to appeal." He presented no supporting paperwork showing the road's necessity; no appeal to passenger and vehicular safety; no mention of loss of time and money to the State with stopping present construction.

Adam moved to him. "Sir, if the road could just be moved a bit. Just half an acre, we could come to an understanding that would please everybody." The lawyer just smiled politely at Adam as he picked up his briefcase and left.

Rowena danced over to Adam, a letter in her hands. "Yesterday, we got an order to vacate immediately–guess we can tear that up! We're not moving!"

Adam took it from her frowning. "I wouldn't ignore this. There may be some confusion whether the judge's stay covers your buildings as well as Kasha's Oak. Remove everything from the Commune that you value, dishes, pots, toys, books. Just keep what you need to sleep there, but keep living there. Somebody must be on the site at all times!"

Adam left the court, with a deeply disturbed feeling. It felt wrong like he had lost, but since he'd won, there was nothing he could do.

Yet something was being done, he could sense it.

It came on Saturday morning, at dawn with a desperate phone call from Rowena. "The Police are here! They're rounding us up! They've got bulldozers! They're going to kill Kasha!"

Adam started calling. The Federal Court had overridden Judge Harris's stay, and other courts wouldn't open for hours yet. In desperation, Adam dialed every Martin he knew, starting with Judge Jeremiah and getting no answer. Finally, Adam got his cousin at home. George's sleepy voice answered. "District Attorney's office. No–this my home. What time is it."

Adam started. "I'm e-mailing you a stay of demolition. I need it now!"

"What?" George sounded like he was yawning.

Adam gave a fast explanation of the legal side, leaving the hamadryad bit out, but soon Cousin George was finishing for him. "Uncle Jeremiah's off fishing, and he'll be back late Sunday evening. The Federal courts are in recess, so Aunt Jereusila's on her way to the Caribbean. None of the State Night Court judges would dare overturn a Federal Appeals court. Saturday's court won't officially open until nine, not that it will matter because anyone you or I can get to now will not overturn the State's appeal of Judge Harris's decision."

Adam was desperate. "If you could get to a Federal Judge? Endangered species?"

George must have been reading the e-mail Adam had shot him. "You're desperately trying to stop the demolition of a farm, that has seven buildings that have an aggregate value of only six thousand dollars? Are you kidding me? Adam, is this one of your jokes?"

"George, I must stop this demolition!"

George was silent, then said, "Is this for one of Great Uncle Quentin's special clients?"

"Yes." Adam didn't feel an explanation about dryads and hamadryads would help.

George relented. "Okay. I will get dressed, go down to the court, and I will do my best for you—but Adam, these guys at the state have been doing eminent domain seizures forever. As soon as they got the appeal, that tear down probably started."

"The property is still in contention!" Adam protested.

"If there is no property, there will be no contention." George recited drily. "Adam, it will be all over before I can get to a judge."

"The Oak tree on the property is a protected, endangered bird habitat! That's what's important, try to save the oak tree! I'm going to the site, call me!"

"Yhep."

Adam swang by the cottage on his property where Wynoma lived, but she wasn't there. Then he raced like the devil to the Commune, bouncing his truck on their rutted dirt road. As George predicted, the state hadn't wasted any time. The long, multiple family house, the freestanding cabins, and hen houses had been bulldozed. Now everything was a massive pile of gray wood, tar paper, ripped leather-bound books, and balled chicken wire. He stepped on cracked china plate and saw a single, terrified Rhode Island Red hen running into woods.

He walked down past the truck gardens. He'd gotten a special court order to specify that the Commune be allowed to get their last harvest in before any demolition, but when he reached the main garden, the construction gangs had set up their Porta-johns in the center of the cornfield, and it looked the workers had been deliberately taking shortcuts, flattening rows of beans, and sunflower seeded heads, trampling the tomatoes and squash. The workers had also driven their trucks through the pumpkins and cucumbers.

Adam walked alone to the trees encircling the scared clearing of Kasha's Oak.

Two parked bulldozers were already there and about ten yellow helmeted construction workers, and at least twelve, riot-gear armored State Troopers with shotguns. The over armed troopers surrounded the nightgowned dressed Commune members, who huddled together like sheep, looking at the Oak tree and rock seats that were inside yellow caution taping. Rowena cried on Wolf's big shoulder, and the big man was openly crying too.

Trying for a bluff, Adam moved to the worker who was giving orders, announcing that he had a stay of demolition! The foreman just signaled for a trooper, who told Adam he could shut up and stay quiet, or be arrested, his choice. Adam drifted to the side.

Sister Josey and Madame Terri were also there, how did they know? Had someone from the Commune called them? Or had they heard Kasha, herself, calling out for help? He could feel Kasha now, not her words, just her terror.

Sister Josey had her head bend in silent prayer as her hands worked her rosary beads, and Madame Terri held her two puppies close and stared in helpless misery, as several workers surrounded the tree. Their biggest chainsaw was only thirty-six inches long, and the tree was over four foot in diameter.

Standing by himself, Adam heard a low sobbing, a hopeless crying as he looked about clearing. Just within the trees, across the way stood the tall dark figure of Wynoma, but the sobbing he heard wasn't hers, it was in his head.

Adam stood helplessly as the buzz saw screamed, and the workers cut into the dried bark of the ancient oak. A cloud of sawdust and ripped wood fragments pelted them.

The woman in his brain screamed—high, agonizing cries of pain as Adam clenched his eyes shut.

When he opened them, the workers had cut two huge wedges on either side of the mighty Oak.

The tree still stood.

It took a bulldozer three slamming hits before the tree finally cracked and crashed to the earth, taking out the woods and planted fields beyond with its mighty branches.

When the huge oak finally smashed to the trembling ground, the screaming in Adam's mind stopped.

Then all he heard was silence.

Rowena was yelling to him, demanding that he have the troopers arrested! That he sue the State! Adam knew he should go to Wynoma to console her on the death of her friend, but feeling numb and sick, he just walked back past the devastation. As he drove his truck home, George called on his cell phone with the 'stay of demolition' order he had gotten. Numbly, Adam thanked him.

Sick, Adam just sat there in his office. All day. As sunset darkened the room, he didn't have the strength to turn on his lights. He just sat there, letting his failure bury him.

He really heard nothing, until the grandfather clock in the hall boomed long. Then Adam looked at his watch. Eleven o'clock. He should go to bed, but he didn't think he would sleep, not ever again, not with that woman's death screams echoing constantly in his mind.

Almost without realizing it, he was dialing a number. Uncle Jeremiah's line. Why would anyone call the ultimate in lack of sympathy, Judge Jeremiah? Maybe Adam needed to be brutally yelled out of his funk.

Jeremiah's voice boomed over the phone. "Do you know what time it is?"

"Eleven," Adam answered in a dead voice.

"Adam? What do you want?" The voice on the line had switched to professionally neutral.

"To talk."

The line was dead for a moment, then the judge's voice sounded quieter. "What do you need to talk about?"

"You practiced law before you were a judge?"

"That's before you were born."

"My father had a criminal law practice before he died?"

"Never much good at it, Justin wanted to help people,

but my brother had no patience with the law's endless constraints."

"He didn't?" That would mean Adam wasn't the only Martin to fail as a lawyer.

"My brother never wanted to be a lawyer actually, Justin wanted to raise quarter horses."

"I never knew that."

"Shame you were so young when your parents died."

"Uncle Jere, did you ever defend any capital cases?"

"Yes."

"Win them all?"

"No, most of my clients were guilty as hell to start with."

"Did you...ever have one, that was convicted...but might have been innocent?"

"Ivan Jacob Japlonsky."

"Was he innocent?"

"I thought so. Couldn't prove it."

"He went to prison?"

"Until they hauled him the fifteen miles to the gas chamber."

"Did you...?"

"Witness it? I was his lawyer, and I failed him. I had to watch him die."

"What did it feel like?"

"Sounds like you already know," answered Jeremiah.

"Yeah." Adam let the words fade off, then, "How do you get over it?"

He was silent for a moment, then said, "You don't. But in this life, you just have to keep walking."

"Yeah."

"Can you drive?" asked his uncle.

"Drive?"

"Have you started serious drinking?"

"No."

"Then C'mon over to my house. It's been awhile since I hoisted one to Japlonsky. You'll stay the night. Getting real stinking drunk with a friend helps, believe me."

The 'judge' a friend? Maybe he was. Maybe he was Adam's best friend. At least tonight he was.

Only the World's Second Best Alchemist

"Western Bank called. Checks are bouncing--again!" pronounced Adam's severe-lipped secretary, as she loomed over him.

"I meant to put in that deposit yesterday. I'll do it right now." Adam dropped the Sudoku puzzle book.

With her long black hair piled up in a top knot, Wynoma seemed even taller as she cut him off. "Not your account. Professor Paracelsus'!"

Adam was totally lost at that one. "Who is Professor Paracelsus?"

"A long time client of your Uncle Quentin's. His first client, I think."

"One of those in the 'special files'?"

"Of course, the man's a few centuries old."

"And he's not too good with his finances?"

"Your uncle set him up with sound investments with the exception of those Confederate bonds, but Paracelsus is always going behind our backs and pulling out principal for some transmuting rabbit dung into gold scheme."

"Rabbit dung? He's an alchemist?"

"He fancies himself that. You will go to him, find out what he is doing, and then tell him how he will no longer do it! Then you will get some money into his checking account."

"If he's bouncing checks, how is he going to pay me–us."

She narrowed her eyes. "He will pay us out of the assets you find! After you straighten out his finances, tell him you will be dropping by every month to supervise. "

That was a change. "Wynoma, you usually supervise the clients' finances?"

"I want you to go there--personally!"

As Adam put on his coat, he asked, "Did Uncle Quentin always straighten things out when you sent him?"

Her eyes softening she almost showed emotion. "That one time, Paracelsus talked your uncle into investing in the Mars colonization scheme. You will not do anything that foolish!"

"Yes, mam." As she started to leave his office, Adam stopped her. "Wynoma, we haven't talked about... since Kasha's death. I'm sorry I failed your friend."

As Wynoma looked down at him her face was as impassive as ever. "There is a time for all things to end, and Kasha's season had come. You tried all you could do to save her oak, and for that, Kasha's spirit and I thank you." She turned and left.

It was a forty-five-minute drive to Aureolus, Missouri. There at a crossroad, Adam found a massive three-story, gray-wood board building that ran one hundred eighty maybe two hundred feet back. It was seventy feet across in the front, with two big flat glass display windows, and was probably built in the early 1800's as a general store. A rusted, visible gas pump stood beside it, and now the lower floor was occupied by an old-style drug store. On the rolling land behind it, Adam could see a yellowed vineyard which might be good growth coming in the spring? An asset?

Inside the building to his right, Adam saw a red-veined marble fountain counter. A young blond kid was shwooshing soda water into a chocolate milkshake can for two teenage girls. To Adam's left was a long, polished wood counter, with bottles of medications behind it. In the further back, straight ahead, were shelves for heat wraps, hot water bottles, walkers, and aspirin.

Adam walked about, this room must only encompass a third of the building's depth. He looked at the cough medicine bottles and dusty Yu-gi-oh cards, it didn't look like this place got much traffic.

Behind the drug counter, a middle-aged man of medium height faced away from Adam as he poured the red liquid into a medicine bottle. Adam walked over behind him and patiently waited. The man kept filling and capping his bottles, then he carefully packed them into a shipping box.

From behind him, Adam heard the soda jerk call out, "Professor, ya got a customer."

Instantly the professor turned around: square, full face; reddish-brown hair, with streaks of gray; van dyke beard; half lense reading glasses, perched on his nose in front of lively, piercing black eyes. "I didn't hear you, sir. What can I do for you?"

Adam smiled. "Actually, I think I'm here to help you. Wynoma sent me."

That seemed to disconcert him. "Ah, yes, poor Quentin passed away. You're....?"

"Adam Martin, his great nephew."

"And you're here for?"

"Maybe we could speak privately?"

The professor looked regretfully to his bottles. "Fed Ex will be here for this box shortly, and I've only have a few more to fill...?"

"I can wait." As the professor went back to his pouring, Adam walked about a bit, noticing the stamped tin ceilings, worn wood flooring, and some really nice, framed medical prints. Could those prints be sold? Finally, he headed over to the marble soda fountain and sat down on one of the red-topped, round chrome stools.

The clerk had been flirting with the girls but immediately came over. "Sir?"

"Do you know how to make a brown cow?" Adam asked.

The clerk thought about it for a second and then started squirting chocolate syrup into a tall soda glass. He mixed in some milk and soda water, then two scoops of vanilla ice cream, finally squirting in more soda water. As Adam was reaching for his wallet, the professor called over. "Steve, he's my lawyer, it's on the house."

The tall soda came with a spiral of whipped cream and a deep red cherry perched on top. The chocolatey brown cow tasted even better than it looked, and Adam found himself slurping the last rich dregs, when the professor called out, "Steve, take this box to the truck and then mind the store. Buzz upstairs if you need me."

Professor Paracelsus wiped his hands as he nodded for Adam. Leaving a tip for the teenager, Adam followed Paracelsus to a door in the back of the drugstore, that lead to an even larger storage room, filled completely from bottom to nine-foot ceiling with crates, boxes, and barrels. Shower stools and neck collars were piled upon buggy wheels and a small cannon? This place was an antique pickers dream!

They went through another door, into what looked like a small winery with a wooden grape press, and then up steep wooden stairs. Here the door was substantially locked, and the professor stumbled for a key. Inside was a large apartment living room, with an Empire sofa set next to a Swedish modern dining room. High backed Shaker chairs stood around a Victorian poker table, and every wall shelf, tabletop, and empty floor space was filled with stacks of ancient books.

The Professor indicated the sofa for Adam to sit down, as he sat across in a carved, medieval-like throne chair. "That what-is-it secretary of Quentin's sent you?"

"Wynoma's Cherokee."

Paracelsus looked at him over his glasses. "Wynoma just passes as Cherokee. Hers are a much older people, but then women are so vain about their ages." The Professor took off his glasses and laid them on a stack of leather-bound books, that covered his end table. "You are here for?"

"You seemed to have forgotten to put money in your

checking account."

"Ah." He looked irritated. "*Quid imperia amittatur pro inopia turpem aurum?*"

Adam thought for a moment, then translated. "What empires lost for want of filthy gold?"

"You speak Latin?" The professor seemed surprised but then said, "But, of course, you are a Martin. About the money," Paracelsus smiled a trifle bitterly. "It's not that I forgot, I'm just a bit short this last decade or so..."

Adam smiled back. "Well, that's what I am here for, to work out your finances. Do you have a spreadsheet?"

"Pardon?"

"On your computer, do you have a financial sheet, say, listing credits? Debits?"

The professor raised a quizzical eyebrow. "Computer?"

"Handwritten ledger books?" Adam tried.

Still a bit of a baffled look on the Professor's face.

So Adam tried again. "Cigar boxes stuffed with your bills?"

Paracelsus immediately rose up. "Of course, and while we are at it, do you like homebrew?"

"Always." Adam was realizing this was going to take a lot longer than he had planned.

The professor walked towards the front of the building through another door that he opened and locked behind him. Hearing his footsteps fade off, Adam decided to take a snoop about. First, he picked up Paracelsus's glasses and looked through them, and as Adam expected, they were plain glass, just part of the illusion.

He started to walk about the room noting a nice collection of books, heavily weighted to chemistry, biology, astronomy, and what is now called 'new age.' Okay, they needed room to work. Picking the poker table, Adam was moving books off to the floor stacks, and soon Paracelsus returned with three over-stuffed cigar boxes and a dusty, unlabeled green bottle, sloshing with a dark colored liquid. Every client of Great Uncle Quentin's seems to have begun their consultation with a shot. Okay, his uncle Judge Jeremiah wouldn't approve, but it relaxed everybody.

While Paracelsus left again to fetch glasses, Adam started putting the unpaid bills in piles, first monthly, then he realized he'd have to set them up in yearly categories. Paracelsus came back with two bulbous brandy snifters and started to pour something chestnut colored that gave a pungent, smokey aroma to the room. Adam looked up. "That's all—I'm driving."

Stopping, they both sat back in their seats, using their fingers to warm the bowled glass. Finally, the Professor lifted his in a toast to the Martins, past, and present, and Adam reciprocated, then found himself swallowing the very best brandy he had ever tasted. "You brewed that? It's a masterpiece!"

"Napoleon thought so," said Paracelsus looking satisfied.

"You have a vineyard out back—maybe instead of peddling medicine, you ought to be bottling wine?"

"Did until 1920."

"Stopped in the 1920s? Prohibition has been over since the 1930's?"

"But they look at your paperwork so much more closely now. I'll probably need a new birth certificate, the last one your uncle got me shows me at ninety-four. I think I look maybe forty-five?"

"At least." Faking I.D. wasn't exactly a course he had taken in law school, Adam wondered if Wynoma knew the procedures? "Where are the receipts from the drugstore?"

The alchemist sighed. "Since those HMO's came in, you have to be a chain to be recognized and get the medical insurance business. I still do some special compounding, a lot for fertility specialists, and progesterone suppositories. So few people make up anything from scratch anymore."

After about an hour, Adam canceled his dinner at Aunt Jerusie's and got his laptop from the car to begin a spreadsheet for Paracelsus' finances. The finances looked worse on Adam's computer screen then they had appeared in the cigar boxes, which meant this was going to be another pro bono job.

Paracelsus was doing a third pour of brandy, but what Adam needed was something to sop it up like dinner. "Professor, you don't have any property taxes here?"

Paracelsus looked guilty. "Yes. Those. Taxes, yes." He looked about vaguely, moved a few books here and there, and finally came up with several envelopes, mostly unopened.

Adam soon found the foreclosure date of next week. "This we have to get straightened out immediately!"

"They do send some nasty letters. Can we sue them for threatening?"

"Not when you are this far behind."

"Well, with all my collections here, they can't just throw me out," said Parcelsus righteously.

Adam painfully recalled the recent wreckage from the State's bulldozers at the Love Haven Commune. "Actually they can and they will."

Paracelsus poured himself an even larger brandy.

When Adam got back to his office late that night, he found Wynoma had waited for him as she sternly asked, "Did he give you anything to drink?"

"Brandy. Great stuff."

Her face never changes. "No, I mean a potion that he compounded?"

"No." And Adam finished righteously, "I will never drink any potion he whips up!"

She glared at him. "You will drink it!" After that command, she looked less severe as she asked, "Have you straightened his finances out?"

"Mam, I don't even think I've gotten to the worst yet!

And when I'm done, there isn't going to be anything to pay us."

As she put on her coat to leave, Wynoma said firmly, "You will settle his affairs, and you will drink what he offers."

The next three days had Adam sitting up in Paracelsus' apartment, trying to reconcile a molehill of pharmacy receipts and with a mountain of bills. The brandies helped.

Paracelsus also could whip up a great chicken crepe and asparagus lunch. As they ate, Adam mused, "Your name Paracelsus–I seem to remember a medieval alchemist of that name..."

"Actually Renaissance. I was a natural healer, but they considered me a magician. I use the name once every century." He looked at the mound of bills. "I used to get royalties from a lot of my books...I don't remember any coming in, in a long while."

That might be an income source. "When was your last book published?

"*Studies of North American Indian Herbs,* in 1912. Got a lot of information from Wynoma for that book."

Adam regretfully shook his head. "I'll check, but I think if it were published in 1912, your copyright would probably have been twenty-eight years, and then could only be extended for another twenty-eight, so fifty-six at the max. Have anything after 1978? That's when it became 'life of the author' plus seventy years?"

Paracelsus sadly shook his head. "No."

"What is your actual birth date?"

"11th, November 1493."

That interested Adam. "Then you're a contemporary of Nostradamus? He's another alchemist who is big now."

Professor Paracelsus spoke disdainfully. "For those prophecies of his? Nostradamus couldn't distill vodka! I did his medical compounding, and then he made up all that prophesy stuff. '*Keep it vague,*' he'd tell me. '*Let them figure it all out. It'll all fit somewhere down the line'."*

"So Nostradamus was a big phony?"

"Still is, he's doing a lot with corporate forecasting now."

"He's a alive today?"

"He's only alive because of my longevity elixirs."

Adam brightened up. "You have an elixir that grants immortality that we could market?"

"No." Paracelsus looked down sadly. "One of the herbs I used is now extinct. Industrial Revolution pollution was terrible, you know, even wiped out the white moths–they showed up on the black, sooty tree barks and got eaten by English sparrows."

His endless narratives were interesting but getting them nowhere. "Okay, if you want to keep this property, we have to come up with a dependable income stream for you. But first, you have got to raise the money for the property taxes! Now, you've got lots of antiques that I could sell for you..." As Paracelsus face dissolved into tragic pain, Adam tried to soften the blow. "Maybe, we could just hock them. I'm sure you want everything up here, so let's go down to the storeroom. Looks like a lot of stuff you don't really need."

Down in the storeroom, Adam pulled out a sword in an ornate metal scabbard. It was covered with the grime of ages, but when he pulled out the saber the wickedly sharp blade still looked well oiled. "How about this–a Civil War piece?"

"Actually that's Eighteenth century. Given to me by Gilbert du Motier, Marquis de Lafayette."

That captured Adam's attention. "Lafayette? As in General Washington and the American Revolution?"

"Oh, yes. I was living in Buck's County, Pennsylvania when I first met him. I was a student of Machiavelli, so we talked of him. Lafayette appreciated someone who could converse in French. Somewhere, I think in that trunk, there are some letters of his when he was back in France as a leader of the Garde National. Nice, eager boy but not much of tactician. Certainly not a great political mind."

Adam put the sword back. "With a story like that, you should keep it. How about this spinning wheel?"

Paracelsus beamed. "That belonged to Betsy Ross. Now, they claim she didn't sew that flag, but she did!"

Two hours and three hundred and thirty-six riveting anecdotes later, a beaten Adam accepted the fact that his client was an unreconstructed, unstoppable hoarder, and the plan of 'pawning a few of the antiques' was a no go. Wearily they climbed back upstairs.

Ignoring Adam's pessimism, Paracelsus was positively bubbling. "Did you want to meet Nostradamus? He'll be in Missouri this weekend for the annual rock and mineral show. Every year we get together and exchange homebrews. Quentin used to join us."

A warning bell went off. "Rock and mineral show?"

"We always have to replenish our supplies, an alchemist needs a standard stock of rubies or emeralds to grind up. Some sulfur mineral..."

Adam cut him off. "But you're not spending anything on credit until we get your finances fixed up, right? Maybe you should skip the show this year."

Paracelsus looked unhappy but mumbled acerbically, "Well, Nostradamus is a pompous ass anyhow."

Adam thought about. "Maybe it's time you wrote another book. The story of the first and second best alchemists. You can set the story right, tell it how it really was– claim the first Paracelsus was an ancestor of yours, and you have insider, family information. Do you have any of your journals from that time period?"

"Always saved what I could," but he sounded doubtful.

Adam sat there. "With two chapters and a proposal, we might be able to get an advance. Can you put some sex into it? Maybe you should read some of the current *'panting breaths, bodice rippers'* stuff."

That seemed to insult him. "Not necessary! Your sexual revolution has gotten us almost to the freedom of the Renaissance period." Paracelsus smiled contentedly. "Currently, I have two lady friends, twin sisters. They give acrobatics classes at their gym, so after the kids go home, we have the mats and trampoline pits to ourselves. They think I'm forty-four and can't believe I can keep going with both of them until dawn. Want to join us?"

Great, a six-century-year-old man was getting a lot more ass than him. Desperately Adam wanted to change the subject. "How about throwing in some doomsday prophecies in your book? The 16th century 'Paracelsus' could have predicted World War I, Princess Di, and stagflation?"

"It's always a matter of time and priorities," the professor said sadly. "With the spring warm up, the vineyard will need tending. I've got my medicine compounding, and writing takes so long, even with your magnificent fountain pens. When Samuel Clemens was here..."

"Mark Twain? You knew him?" Adam was talking to a man who spoke with one of his heroes. "Is he still alive?"

"No," said Paracelsus sadly. "Do you want Sam in the book, too?"

Adam thought about it. "No, that can come in a sequel. One of many sequels."

"He left me a letter machine that's buried under the books on that desk." With difficulty, Adam and Paracelsus dug out a spidery, black, Hammond.

"Mark Twain gave you a typewriter?" said Adam looking at 1880's writing machine with awe.

"Never could do much with it," grumbled Paracelsus. "It's faster for me to use a quill."

"You don't have to write the book, you could just dictate it."

"Hire an outsider to come up here?" The professor

really looked unhappy about that.

"No, sir, you already have a genie upstairs." Paracelsus followed him up to Adam's open laptop. "Now I'm pulling up a writing program with a new document." Adam clicked on an Icon and started speaking into the computer's microphone. "This is how you will write your book." Paracelsus's jaw dropped as that exact sentence appeared on the screen before them.

"You just talk to it?"

"We'll have to train the software to recognize how you pronounce words, then you'll just talk your fabulous stories right into the computer!"

Soon Adam had Paracelsus dictating to his laptop. As the alchemist's words appeared in courier type across the glowing screen, the centuries-old man shook his head and marveled. "Truly magical!"

Adam nodded. "Well, the bookselling will take awhile, so we have to get some cash now, or you won't have a parlor to parlay in."

Paracelsus went back into his private rooms again and came out with a small vial and an antique, leather fire bucket. "Your uncle used to drop by every year for an ounce or two of this."

"More brandy?" God, that evil looking brown stuff Paracelsus was now holding stank worse than a baby's diaper. " No sir, I'm over my limit as it is today."

"This is medicinal. Take the whole ounce at once-- chuck it down fast."

Still worrying about the negative money situation, Adam absently mindedly took the vial and swallowed it. The horrible, disgusting oil torn at this throat. His guts–his whole body started to wretch. Desperately, Adam looked about at the priceless books and handsome Persian rug on the floor. He was trying to hold it back but couldn't...

Paracelsus passed him the bucket. Adam started

heaving and couldn't stop until he thought his guts were twisting inside out. Eyes streaming, he looked up. "I help you-you poison me?!"

"No! My dear boy, you are just more sensitive than your uncle. I'll have to adjust the formula. At the beginning, you'll have to come maybe semi-monthly, maybe weekly to build up your tolerance to the doses..."

"No, sir! No thank you!" Black phlegm coated his tongue and throat, and Adam's empty stomach still painfully contracted.

"Your uncle's life was extended quite a bit."

Physically and mentally sick, Adam still looked with horror at the dropped vial on the floor. "Immortality?"

"No, maybe only an extra two hundred or maybe two hundred and fifty years. Since we are started with you at a younger age than Quentin, it could be longer. In your nineties, you'll really be a hit with the ladies," finished Paracelsus confidently.

Adam let Paracelsus take some of his hair and fingernail clippings to analyze, all the while swearing that 'the ladies' and Wynoma to the contrary, he was never going to drink that stinking shit again! But if Paracelsus was staying in business, the alchemist-would-be author needed cash right now. "Sir, if we don't come up with the tax money this week..."

"You know, for years I have been so close to turning rabbit dung into fourteen karat gold," mused the alchemist.

"On the Periodic Table lead is very close, so don't they generally use that as the base metal to transmute into gold?"

The Professor flipped his hand, dismissively. "Lead to gold? Anyone can do that."

Adam suddenly saw a light dawning. "Anyone? Have you ever done that?"

The Professor looked at him as if he was crazed. "It's simple. It'll just take over night, if I have any Unicorn Blood left." He vaguely looked at the walls of bottles as he muttered to himself. "I might have enough for just five or six."

Five or six troy ounces of gold? Adam was elated. "This unicorn blood is it blood from a white, one horned, horse bodied creature that can only be captured by a virgin?"

Again Paracelus looked at him like he was demented. "Good lord, no! No animal's blood is used at all! There were times when alchemists could be burned at the stake for owning a 'stone from heaven.' Those ridiculous Inquisition fools! So we labeled everything for safety. Actually, the vial labeled '*Unicorn's Blood*' is smelted from a meteor that I found in Siberia that glows blue in the dark. Wish I had more of it."

From the potion he drank, Adam was still sweating and nauseous when Paracelsus finally came back wearing heavy gloves and carrying a tiny, glowing vial. "Not much left. Might make only four. Do you still want me to try?"

"Yes. Try, right now. Gold would be nice." Adam pushed.

They had to go downstairs and dig through the mess to find Paracelsus' hoard of lead ingots. Following the Alchemist back into his apartment rooms, Adam helped him set up the gold making apparatus in a laboratory surprisingly devoid of clutter.

The next day, when he returned, Adam stared at five, softly-shining gold ingots. Not just the expected five troy ounces, but actually five pounds of gold bars! "Uh, will this test properly?"

"As twenty four karat gold, yes. Of course, it'll only be as pure as the lead bar it came from."

"This isn't fairy gold, is it?" Adam pursued.

"You believe in fairies?" Paracelsus seemed surprised.

"I'm learning a lot about...different things. Will this stuff just vanish on the full moon?"

"No, it's real gold. Your scientists now can make gold from lead, it's just too expensive to make it practical."

Paracelsus gave him a beat up, old carpet bag to lug it all downstairs.

Could Adam pay the County clerk with gold? No, he would have to sell it. He could claim his client was a jeweler, who was retiring or died. Maybe he should only sell one bar at a time, a pound of gold would be worth what? He had to get Paracelsus' taxes and penalties up this week, but one bar might do it. He took out his smartphone and Googled the price of gold.

If this stuff tested as pure as Paracelsus claimed, there would be more than enough for the taxes, the checking account problems, and all of Adam's billable hours! With the ingots loaded on the passenger seat, Adam started thinking about just where he would cash this stuff in? Wonder if Cousin George has a listing of reliable St. Louis pawn shops?

Haunts of the Goryo

In his bedroom, Adam adjusted his suit jacket and tie again before he went downstairs to meet his new client. This was apparently his first normal client, not part of his uncle's practice of supernatural beings with their unorthodox problems. Wynoma had said this client was a 'Mr. Herman' from an engineering firm.

Going downstairs from his apartment, Adam sat at his office desk. He was early, so he just tidied up the desk, stuffing all the papers in drawers, and closed his laptop. The polished cherry desk looked substantial, even with its trim of arcane symbols carved into the edges. The handsome Italian, green-leather, and gold embossed desk set was a graduation gift from the Franklin Martins, and it too looked impressive.

But thinking more, he decided it might be better to give the impression of being a busy lawyer. Adam reopened the laptop and took some papers out again, spreading them out in neat piles. Still, with time to wait, he looked around the room, wondering if he should remove some of Uncle Quentin's more exotic touches to make the law office more his own? At least the basalt Rain God should go.

Wynoma ushered in a briefcase-carrying man who was even shorter than Adam. A small, thin-mustached man he instantly recognized. "Uncle Herman?"

His usually inscrutable Cherokee secretary blinked. "I'm sorry, I didn't realize you were a Martin?"

"It's Obermeyer," Herman corrected. "And this is purely a business visit as my company wishes to hire Adam's services."

Adam asked, "Wynoma, could please get us...two beers?" He looked to Herman. "Dark, German bock, if we have any?" Herman gave a small, quiet, conspiratorial smile, as Adam led him over to the less formal drum table and chairs by the windows.

As his secretary discretely left, Adam sat wondering just why in hell would a staid, no-nonsense engineer consult with a lawyer, whose practice ran to psychometriests and vampires? Especially when that quiet, unimaginative man was married to Adam's aunt, the honorable, Federal Judge Jereusila Martin Obermeyer.

Jereusila, like her twin brother, Judge Jeremiah, was over six foot tall. When Jere's blond hair turned silver, Jerusie maintained hers as a honey blonde, but with their glacial blue eyes, habitual authority, and tart tongues, both easily overawed those around them. Still, over the years Adam had noticed that Herman was capable of standing up to the frightening Jeremiah, and Herman actually seemed to rule the household in the face of the formidable Jereusila. In fact, Adam couldn't conceive of a problem the mild Herman Obermeyer wasn't capable of taking care of.

But until Wynoma returned with a tray of tall, foaming glasses of dark brown beer, they chatted in generalities, which was unusual from the normally quiet Herman. He just figured his uncle had something to say but couldn't, so Adam talked along, occasionally prompting. "And your kids?"

"Your cousin Alician is expecting--again. Morgan has switched his major--again. The rest are about the same." Herman stopped and then started more formally. "But I'm here for business reasons..."

"You know I can't charge you," stated Adam.

"Of course you can, and you will!"

"When my parents were killed, I lived with Grandma Martin, but you, Aunt Jerusie, and Uncle Jere helped raise me."

Remembering those times seemed to make Herman look regretful. "Most of that time, I was traveling for business, Jereusila was struggling with our five children, and Jeremiah isn't known for his nurturing nature."

Adam wryly smiled. "Jere has his moments."

"Never-the-less, your aunt and I are very pleased that this inheritance seems to be working out for you. A working farm with planted corn fields, orchard..."

"Those fields are actually leased by a tenant."

"Huge flock of chickens."

"That's Wynoma's. My secretary also has a life interest in that cottage on my property."

"But you have your Uncle Quentin's law practice..." finished Herman obviously sharing in the family pride.

Now, after all that uncharacteristic conversation, Herman seemed to be ready to get down to business, so Adam just sipped his beer and waited. They drank for awhile, then finally, Herman continued, "I've been overseas recently, months in Japan. My engineering firm has been dismantling an eighth-century Samurai's house."

"Japanese warrior?"

"It has been moved and is being reconstructed pretty much log-for-log, on a private mountaintop in New York on the New Jersey border. The plans were for a premiere Hibachi restaurant overlooking the Ramapo Valley."

"Sounds good."

Herman hesitated. "There have been problems." Adam waited, and his uncle seemed to be having difficulty figuring out how to phrase it. Finally, obviously comfortable with the dry facts, he continued. "This project was to have been completed November last year."

"It's March."

"Yes, they've missed the holiday trade, and financially it's a total mess." Herman stopped again. "Years ago, I had come to Quentin with a strange problem. He worked it out." That seemed to amaze Herman. Still, he let that trail off. "But we shouldn't be going into that now..."

"Why is your project behind schedule?" Adam asked gently.

Herman seemed very uncomfortable with this as he

said, "A number of problems. There's a group that opposes moving Japanese heritage to the United States. They've been fighting us in court and they, or someone else, have been sending anonymous threatening letters. Then there has been vandalism at the site."

"That's a concern for the police."

"Yes, they're working on it, and we've hired a New Jersey private security firm. Actually, this is the third security firm working on the project."

"How far are you on the house?"

"It's nearly completed. Should have been done and open months ago. Quite an interesting engineering job, but..." Again Herman seemed to stop and force himself back on track. He opened his briefcase and took out a disc. "Can you play a DVD on your laptop?"

Adam got the computer and set it up on the table between them. Soon he was watching dark security camera footage of a cavernous room at night. The site was only lit by moonlight streaming in the wide windows, but the screen showed a dark ceiling held up by massive, painted, peeled log posts, amidst construction work, with wood posts and beams stacked about on the flooring.

That was it. No movement. No sound. Then suddenly crashing as a window exploded with shards of glass, raining down to the floor. Adam moved forward stopping the DVD. Reversing it, he then replaying it three times. Now that he knew what to look for, he saw that the shadow smashing the window was a ten-foot post that rose and flew across the room from the right side. Adam did another replay-stopping it just as the beam rose. It seemed to rise by itself, fly across the room, and smash out the window.

Adam's eyes were on the computer screen. "I assume this is a digital image. It could have been manipulated?"

Herman sighed. "The window was smashed, and the beam showed evidence of the damage. There were two experienced, bonded, security guards on the property--knowing their company is about to get fired--yet they swear under oath that they saw no one."

"That's the only camera?"

"There were four more in the building and several outside. On the other interior cameras, there is a recurring problem of the footage blurring or whiting out, so we've replaced all of them several times, upgraded them to sound. That DVD you are watching is the only clear recording of the vandalism we have."

"Who else was up there that night?"

"And outside camera shows some blurring, the post falling out of the broken window, and hours of the guards patrolling. And a few browsing deer."

Adam sat back trying to come up with a reasonable explanation. "Have you checked for, say, magnetic anomalies on the site?"

"We set meters and had some unexplained rises, but nothing that could have lifted a hundred pound wooden post ten feet long and throw it across the room." Herman shook his head in frustration.

"So you're looking into a paranormal explanation?"

"Yes." Herman looked embarrassed. "Yes, Quentin had operatives..."

"Sensitives." Adam nodded. "I'll need to travel to New York with two of them. We'll need money for the ladies, three hotel rooms, and one rental car. Is your client willing to pay for this?"

"Yes. You will be hired by my company, I will give you a retainer today. As soon as you give me flight arrangements, I'll rent rooms for you at the motel my company has contracted with on the New Jersey side."

Adam visited the Resurrection Sisters that afternoon. It was decided Madame Terri, and Inger would be the best for ghost hunting, so a day later Adam was landing in Newark airport, with a dog carrier case under his seat. In his carrier was the white Pomeranian puppy, Thurston. The bubbling, always excited, Madame Terri had the second carrier with Thurston's golden brother, Houdini II. Tall, reserved Inger, with her blonde hair showing just a hint of silver, made up the menagerie.

The motel in New Jersey was like Herman Obermeyer practical, with no frivolity; clean, with a decent free, hot breakfast, and no pool or exercise room. Adam should have been more specific.

In the rental, Adam drove Herman and the two ladies up to the construction site at sunset. They turned off the interstate on to a two-lane paved road, then off onto a private asphalt drive under a massive, steel Torii gate painted scarlet. As he drove under that gate and the road climbed up steeply, an impressed Adam asked, "How high is that gate?"

"Four stories, it was imported from Japan. Took two cranes to set up," Herman said proudly.

That road twisted its way up and around the low mountain, well, more of a very high, steep hill, soon they came out on top, to a little bit of Japan. Adam saw a landscaping of bonsai trees, little red, arching bridges over koi ponds, and an open work tea house, obviously for the wedding party photographs.

The Samurai's house was magnificent. White walled with dark timbering, the one-story building of rambling construction featured layered eaves, hand carved doors, and yellow painted carved window trims. Herman said three guards were constantly patrolling, but Adam noted, "No crews working?"

"We're rehiring," said Herman wearily.

The massive front door did have a lock, and two of the guards joined them. It opened, but Thurston balked, barking and backing away, pulling at his leash, until finally, Madame Terri looked about and then handed the guard the two

Pomeranians' leashes. "Yes, Thurston, you two should guard the outside," Thurston whined as his mistress walked away, but as Madame Terri entered, Houdini lunged, pulling his leash free and running after her.

Hesitating outside, Inger looked pale, and when she finally forced herself forward, she raised her hands in front of her chest as if to defend herself.

Concerned Adam asked, "What do you feel?"

"Deadly cold. Death. Injustice." Without looking at him, she walked into the darkened door. Adam was followed by Uncle Herman and the second guard.

Only the weak ceiling security lights were on. The entrance lobby was full of heavy, oriental furniture for the waiting guests to come. The openwork ceiling was a marvel of slanted, polished beams, forming multiple, eight-pointed star designs. Quite beautiful, but by the reception desk, a huge glass display case had been shattered. The floor was still covered in the shards, and Adam could see a leather shield, with a black falcon device painted on it. It was viciously slashed, with long, deep ruts.

Herman came up behind Adam. "That was the first of the serious vandalism."

"Did you have security then?"

"Just one man. Only two cameras."

"Those angry Japanese history lovers?"

"May have authored the threatening letters, but they seem to have given up when we moved the house from Kagawa."

"Nothing stolen?"

"No," said a mystified Herman.

"This looks expensive." Adam reached down and picked up the shield. He felt a brief flash of fury take over his body.

But totally unaware, Herman was continuing, "It wasn't cheap– it is an authentic, hand crafted reproduction of an eighth-century noble's shield."

Adam smelled something as he took a deep, unpleasant breath. "That stink?"

Herman shrugged. "I don't smell anything myself, but we brought a chef in to look at the kitchen, and he threw up. He said it smelled like a slaughterhouse. Some of the workmen quit for the same reason."

"Dead animal in the walls?"

"We called in a pest control service. He smelled it at first, but then he said the smell went away. He couldn't pin it down, and the exterminator said that dead animal smells don't come and go like that."

Madame Terri was leading them as they walked into what Adam figured must be the main dining room. There was some light from the fading sunset, but again the weak ceiling security lights were the only real illumination. This galley was a story and half high. A huge ancient post and beam room with windows along the sides, giving mountaintop views. Even under construction, with its intricate wooden details, the hall looked impressive.

Madame Terri slowly moved to the center of the room as Inger reluctantly followed, leading the rest. At Terri's feet, Houdini stiffened as he looked across the room and Adam could see the hair rising on the Pomeranian's back, as the little puppy growled deeply.

Adam advanced to Madame Terri and Inger, and as he looked in the same direction they were staring, the room became kind of hazy. Like there was a swirling grayish vapor that distorted the view behind it.

Covering her nose, Inger cried out, "The stench! It's horrible!" She was making choking sounds. Alarmed, Adam looked at Madame Terri. She had protectively reached down and picked up Houdini, holding the dog close to her. The little puppy was barking his head off, trembling uncontrollably.

Inger screeched, "I see them–kimonos–blood!" Inger

didn't know which way to run. Adam grabbed her arm and dragged her to the security man. **"Take her outside! Stay with her!"**

Helpless, Herman just stood there watching, as Adam ran back to Madame Terri. With her one arm, Terri tucked Houdini tightly against her hip and then she then reached out and took Adam's hand, giving him a reassuring squeeze. Madame forced them both to walk forward towards the bloody tableau forming.

In his mind, Adam could hear screams of rage, screams of death pain! Harshly accented words. Japanese?

Now, holding Madame Terri's hand, he saw figures forming before him. Terrifying, bleeding males, one disemboweled, his stomach contents pouring to the floor, another headless figure, his body kneeling with his head rolling toward Adam. A central figure wore leather armor and raised a katana sword above his head, aiming for them. Red, purple, and black kimonos and slashing spears, all the more horrible, because the creatures before them were sometimes solid, sometimes translucent.

If he hadn't been holding Madame's hand, Adam would have run himself. "Can they hurt us?"

"I don't know." Madame Terri lowered her voice. "They haven't so far." The horrible apparitions didn't retreat, but they didn't move closer either. "If only we knew what they were saying..."

"Can't you tell?" Adam asked. "They're spirits–don't you hear them in your mind?"

"Well, I know they are angry," she sounded exasperated. "But I don't know why. They're obviously cursing us! But I can't understand Japanese."

Finally, the horrific visions faded, but the sickening fecal and decomposition stench still hung over the dining room. "Nobody is going to eat in this place," Madame Terri said covering her nose.

Herman walked over to them. "You saw something?"

"You didn't?" Adam said.

Looking baffled Herman shook his head. "No."

"Do you smell the stink?" Adam asked.

Again Herman shook his head. "No."

"Okay," Adam ordered his thoughts. "We need a psychic familiar with the Japanese language. The Japanese guys who bought this place originally, have they ever seen the hauntings or smelled something bad?"

"No, but they might not have told me..." said Herman helplessly.

"They're not sensitives," Madame Terri said as she kissed the top of Houdini's head, and then put him down on the floor. The dog whined pitifully, staying close to her ankle as Madame Terri looked to Herman. "These visitations–they've been getting worse, haven't they?"

"Yes."

Adam realized his responsibility was to protect Madame Terri. "Could they hurt you?"

She shrugged her thin shoulders. "Beings that can throw a heavy beam across the room and that can slash leather can kill a human, but they haven't yet." Madame Terri frowned with concentration. "I feel they are trying to communicate. That they are frustrated and getting angrier because they feel they're being ignored." Then as suddenly as ever, the wise Madame slipped into happy Terri. "This has made me so hungry. Are we going out to dinner? A nice place, maybe Japanese? Is there one around here?"

Herman shook head. "How about a really good Italian?"

Smiling brightly, Madame Terri led Houdini out.

His uncle turned to Adam looking pained. "Have I got to send to Japan for a psychic?"

"There should be an easier way," said Adam. "Let's have dinner first."

Inger refused dinner, with her hands still shaking she only wanted to return to the motel, so they left her off with the dogs. Herman, Adam, and a bubbly Terri sat down for some really good antipasto. Herman was passing the bread basket to her when Madame Terri touched his fingers. A concerned look suddenly crossed her face, as she took his hand within hers. "You're afraid. You're facing bankruptcy."

Adam could see that Herman paled.

Still holding his uncle's hand, Madame Terri continued, "You're afraid of telling your wife. Oh, that is so foolish, she loves you so much. She'd never care about money." He seemed to try to pull his hand away, but Madame held it. "You have had some very bad thoughts. That was wrong. Call Jereusila tonight and set things straight."

Herman's face flushed a deep red, and he couldn't meet Adam's eyes.

Back at the motel, after they helped Terri carry take-out dishes to Inger and the dogs, Adam followed Herman to his room.

"What she said..." His uncle started.

"Why didn't you tell me how bad it was?" Adam asked.

"There's nothing you could do."

"I could have saved you some money, Inger and Madame Terri could have shared a room, instead of business class we could have flown cheaper."

Herman looked away from him. "I don't want your aunt to know."

"Know what? That you could be bankrupt? That you're thinking of suicide?"

"That was just...late at night," Herman said ashamed.

Adam couldn't understand. "This is just one project. Your engineering firm is worldwide!"

At first, Adam thought he wasn't going to answer, but then Herman said in a low voice, "Business has been dropping off. This Samurai house project was God sent. When the problems started happening, the legal suits from the historic nuts, and the accidents, well work slowed, costs went up. The Japanese partnership owning the restaurant couldn't meet payrolls, so I talked my partners into investing, but things got worse, and we had to keep shoveling money into an endless pit. And now, with ghosts, I can't see..."

"We will get this straightened out," Adam stated, with calm conviction.

Herman gave him a cold eye. "I've lived with Martins all my adult life. I know that false 'curtain of confidence' you guys try to project."

Adam gave his uncle a lopsided grin. "Okay, tonight I want you to give Aunt Jerusie a call. Tell her what is happening financially, and let her reassure you that no matter what, everything is going to be fine between the two of you. Hey, remember, what the family always says: *'she's a judge, she can get bribes,'*"

Herman actually laughed. Then he turned serious again. "What are you going to do? Look up a Japanese medium in the yellow pages?"

Adam nodded. "Pretty much that." Back in his room, Adam got on his laptop, Googling New Jersey, Psychics, Ramapo. Then not happy with what he was getting, he tried mediums and fortune tellers. Finally, he got a lead just over the state border, a mall in New York was having a 'Psychic Fair' with twenty-three sensitives. He only needed one who could translate Japanese.

That next morning Inger was still too upset to go out, so Adam took just Madame Terri to a large, three-story mall. The 'fair' was booths and stalls scattered throughout the open spaces in front of the stores. Going to the signing in desk Adam paid the twenty dollars each 'registration' fee, for himself and Madame Terri for their membership pins and a map.

He also got receipts for his expense account, presuming that if the restaurant ever opened he would be getting reimbursed. The registration came with a map of the fortune tellers were apparently spread over three floors. Adam decided to start on the lowest level, questioning prospects with Madame Terri.

But when he turned around, Madame had mentally slipped away, and in her place was the slightly childish Terri, who was looking eagerly at a store window. "Would you mind if I just went in and tried on that darling, yellow blouse. I think it's silk."

Adam said regretfully, "We're short on time..."

"Oh, but that blouse is so perfect." She looked at it again. "You said I was going to be paid for this trip–we will be paid, right? Then I can afford the blouse?"

Adam found himself pleading, "Can't we find a Japanese psychic first?"

"You will find her, dear." She started walking towards the beckoning blouse. "Now, why don't you just go and ask them if they understand Japanese."

"Without you, how will I know if they are genuine psychics?"

Madame Terri thought about that a minute. "Well, if they are faking, they're going to try to make up something that you would want to hear. So go to each of them and ask about your love life. If they say you are going to have a number of beautiful women deeply in love with you, Adam, you'll know they're phonies."

"Yhep." Adam nodded as she went off to Lord and Taylor's. Okay. The registration had gotten him an annotated map of the psychics' booth locations. Studying it, he noted that each reader charged their own fees, ranging from ten to fifty dollars. Ruefully, Adam realized if he couldn't rid Herman's site of those horrifying apparitions, any psychic fees were probably coming out of his own pocket.

Adam looked down the list of names, 'Donna the Great,' 'Iris of the Lotus,' 'Barbara, Seer to the Presidents,' 'Madame Chang Kai,' and 'Kobara' sounded oriental. They were on the bottom level so he'd approach them first.

Madame Chang Kai had a pop-up tent hung with origami butterflies. She looked Oriental, so Adam shelled out twenty dollars to sit in her chair and shake an oatmeal sized box until bamboo strips fell out and madame 'read the fortune numbers.' "I see a brunette and a blonde lady, who likes you so much. Have you met them yet?"

"No."

"And there's a redhead here. You are so lucky in love!"

Walking a bit farther, Adam found an I-Ching coin reader, who was Korean-American but didn't have a clue of how to speak Japanese.

Adam smiled and moved on. He greeted the very Caucasian looking, henna-haired Kobara, who said she was raised in the Orient. She said twenty-five dollars for a gemstone reading.

As Adam sat down, she handed him a cup. "Just shake it and think of your greatest desire."

He thought of exorcising bleeding eyed monsters, and then at her direction, Adam spilled a colorful sprinkling of semi-precious stones out on to her black velvet mat.

She smiled with cigarette-stained teeth. "Oh, so many young ladies are after you!"

Before starting with either the Astrologer or the Gypsy, Adam took stock of the situation. Two memberships at twenty dollars a piece, two readers, one at twenty and one at twenty-five. He was already down eighty-five dollars, and he had nothing to show for it. He got out his cell phone and goggled the translation program. 'Hello' in Japanese was *koa'nichiwa*. Maybe 'Good morning' would be more polite, that was '*Asa yoi.*' What else did he know? '*Soyŏnara*?'

Adam started methodically going stall by stall, greeting

each psychic or clairvoyant in Japanese. Friendly smiles, some hopeful faces, some disappointed looks when he didn't sign up for a reading, but no Japanese response. Then Miriam, an aura reader, got highly incensed with his Japanese greeting of '*Asa yoi*', thinking he made some sort of an "Ass you!" comment, so at the next walled stall, with it's massage table, he went back to '*Koa'nichiwa*' for Princess Iris and her 'New Age Regeneration'.

With her bright purple contacts, Iris stared deeply into his eyes. "We could have a private session in the hotel next door. They have special rooms with hot tubs. I could give you a sensual, spiritual message, that will totally open up your sexual Chakras. For only a hundred and fifty dollars," she murmured seductively.

Adam caught the escalator to the next level and tried his '*koa'nichiwa*' on a woman who did something mathematical and predictive with your birth date to find out how many reincarnations you had lived.

Finally reaching the third and last level, a discouraged Adam noted he only had three more psychics on his mall map. He moved to a booth walled with strings of translucent, rainbow-colored beads. The face sitting inside wasn't Oriental, it was a light cream-skinned Afro-American, with delicate features and decidedly green eyes. She sat behind a card table with a sign that read 'Tarots by Zelda.'

He bowed slightly to her. "*Kon'nichiwa.*"

She immediately smiled and responded, "*Anata wa higongo o hanasemasu ka?*"

"I beg your pardon?" Adam asked.

"I said, do you speak Japanese?" She replied.

"No, but you do?" Excited, Adam sat down on the folding chair before her table.

"When I was a kid, my father was a Marine stationed in Kobe. I returned to Japan to do my dissertation."

"How much for a fortune?"

"Twenty-five for a tarot reading."

"Great." He paid.

She spread a mixed deck of Playing, Tarots, and Gypsy Witch cards face down. "Think of your greatest problem and then select twenty cards and give them to me. Try to select the ones that you feel call to you."

He started picking, praying this psychic wouldn't focus on his love life and as he handed her the cards, he noted she carefully kept them in the same order. When he had selected twenty, she removed the rest of the deck, and then laid down a sort of square, starting with crossed cards at the center and working her way out, ending in a long, four card tail.

She started slowly, "You're very afraid of failure. The people that you care for have such high expectations. You constantly feel the need to prove yourself. Especially now." She looked at him.

He prodded. "The project I'm working on..."

Zelda seemed to ignore that. "Your family loves you, but they just worry about you. You are a lot more competent than they realize." She looked back down at the cards again. "There is a man. He has just hired you. He's always thought well of you, an uncle? Not by blood. I see an 'H.'"

"How will his project turn out?"

She pursed her lips in effort. "Give me nine more cards from the deck, thinking of him."

When Adam did, she laid a small, flat pyramid of Tarots on top of the first one. He saw the Emperor, nine of spades, a mountain with lightning, nine of diamonds... "You are part way to solving his problem, but it will be on you to come up with the solution."

"Is there one?"

She seemed to be trying to concentrate, then shaking her head Zelda said, "I don't see it now...but I do see you as part of a solution."

Collecting all her cards back into her deck, she looked

up at him. "Would you like another question answered? Just think another thought, and phrase your wish or question in a yes or no sentence. Don't tell me what it is–just think of it."

"Yes." What the heck, he might has well get his money's worth, so he thought about his love life.

She nodded. "Select twelve more cards."

Adam did. He saw the Hanged man, the Queen of hearts, Something with a wolf before a mountain, the Queen of clubs...

Zelda studied them carefully. "You've had some terrible luck with love. In the coming year, I see two women. One connected with the water. You may meet her at a beach or lake."

"Nice looking?"

"Beautiful...on the outside...but she's really quite ugly inside."

That figures. Well, Adam should be concentrating on his client's business.

But Zelda was continuing. "There is another woman. Worthy to be your mate. Intelligent...a very fast runner, she loves to run. She has amber eyes and long, reddish fur..." Zelda looked up, shocked. "I meant reddish hair." Then she looked back down at her cards. "But they say fur?" Zelda seemed alarmed when she looked back at Adam. "What are you in to?"

Leaning forward Adam lowered his voice and said, "Actually, I'm not so much interested in a reading as I am in hiring your services for a client of mine."

Zelda's face turned stony, as she protectively gathered up her cards. "No, sir. You seem to have misunderstood my services. Why don't you go down to the second level. I think Princess Iris and her massage table are just what you're looking for!"

Oh, shit. Adam fumbled for his wallet, pulling out his business card, but when she wouldn't take it, he placed the card on the table before her. "Ma'am, I did not mean what you are thinking! I am a lawyer with a client who needs a sensitive who speaks Japanese."

She glanced at the card. "A lawyer from Missouri, with problems in New York? Get away from my booth, or I'll going to start screaming for mall security!" Zelda sounded like she meant it.

Oh, great, Adam was rising to leave, when he heard a delighted voice behind his shoulder. "Oh, you've found a nice one." Madame Terri moved in and handed Adam three shopping bags. "I do hope Herman will pay for this. Otherwise, I'll have to return them all." She turned her dazzling Betty White smile on Zelda. "She speaks Japanese?" Madame Terri reached out, and Zelda hesitated, but then politely shook Madame's hand.

Not letting Zelda's hand go, Madame Terri took her other hand and enfolded it. "Yes. Yes. You are strong! Totally untrained, but this psychic fair business is the very best way for you to practice. Adam frightened you? Oh, he's really quite harmless and very sweet. Now, my real name is Rose Kear, but I work under Madame Terri. Zelda is only your reader's name. What is your real name, dear?"

'Zelda' looked from Adam to Madame and then decided it must be alright. "Megan Jefferson."

Madame Terri continued. "Megan, that's lovely. Adam's client has a haunting problem, several ghosts. Very, very nasty spirits that we want to get rid of."

Megan looked confused. "I'm not an exorcist. I'm sorry..."

Adam interrupted. "You're a sensitive, and you can understand Japanese. These ghosts yell things that only a medium can hear. They haven't hurt anyone yet, but they've done considerable physical damage."

"Goryo," said Megan.

"What?" Adam asked.

"Goryo were Japanese nobles who were killed in clan warfare or were unjustly executed for their politics. Because the proper Shinto burial rituals were never performed, these men feel they died disrespected. They hate all the living. The Japanese people believed that goryoes have caused epidemics, flooding, even warfare...but why in hell would a goryo be in New York?"

"We'll explain that. What do you charge by the hour?" Adam asked.

"Twenty-five dollars for a reading."

"That lasts ten minutes?"

"Usually, fifteen," Megan corrected.

"Okay. It's Sunday, so the mall closes at six, I am prepared to offer you eighty dollars an hour if you will join us at the construction site tonight. We will stand inside the building and hope something materializes, so maybe you can translate what they are saying."

Megan quickly looked from Adam to Madame Terri, who said, "Oh, take the job, dear! You don't have a date tonight." Terri looked at Adam. "She's almost as bad with men as you are with women."

Insisting on driving her own car, Megan followed Adam's up the mountain to the work site. Getting out, she was entranced with the stone lanterns, bonsai trees, and the Samurai's house.

There were several men working outside, but the security guard had to open the building. Madame had called and had Herman bring up the white-furred Thurston. She explained, "He's so embarrassed he didn't go in the last time, Thurston's going to protect me now." When she saw the dog, Megan gave Adam a really hard look, but she followed Madame Terri inside. Coming from the late afternoon sun, it was quite an adjustment, with only upper-security lights casting long shadows across the ancient dwelling.

Megan seemed fascinated by the starred ceiling design,

and the wood blocked prints, but that starry-eyed wonderment vanished when she stopped at the smashed display case with its broken spear and slashed shield. "Goryoes can kill," she said softly.

He could feel her fear and thought she was going to leave, but squaring her shoulders, Megan started walking forward again. In the shadowed main hall that ran lengthwise across the building, Megan touched the polished woodwork murmuring, "Your engineers brought everything over."

"Including the ghosts," Adam finished.

But it seemed nothing was there. So they stood. And waited silently. For three hours.

Thurston's doggy nose smelled it first, and he barked hysterically to warn of the coming apparitions. As the stench of dead human flesh seemed to clog Adam's nostrils, he looked to Megan and Madame. Scooping up Thurston in one arm, Madame Terri moved to the girl's left side, ordering Adam, "Take her right hand. Give her your energy!"

A wide-eyed Megan stared into the thickening darkness ahead. "Goryo! It's Goryo! That one there was beheaded by the Emperor because of lies! He curses. *Anata o fakku*! You must go away! They have no peace—they will give you no peace!"

Now even Adam could see the swirling white, purple and black robes–sometime transparent, sometime solid. The scarlet bleeding bowels! The swinging raised swords!

"You don't listen!" Megan translated in a yell, then she cried out softly. "I can't take much more of this!"

Adam tightened his hold on her hand. "Can you translate. Tell them we are here to honor them!"

Megan barked out, "*Anata wa, kono ie o sonchō shimasen!*"

"Ask them why are they angry? Why did they destroy the shield?"

Megan seemed to be translating for the most menacing

warrior. "The shield placed in the cabinet was of his hated enemies. Those who took his castle killed his wives and children!"

Adam was feeling a bit more confident, as negotiation was Martin territory. "Tell them we wish to honor them and their deaths. Ask them what ceremonies they want done, what clan badges, what armor, and what kimonos they want displayed in their house?"

The Goryo still swirled in bloody, headless and disemboweled messes, but Adam realized the stench was receding.

The next evening, Adam had Megan showing the Goryo catalogs of reproductions of noble garb and weapons that Herman had agreed to pay for. Inger had been very upset about running away, so Adam tried to make her feel better. "You're more sensitive than us, of course, you would have run." She insisted on helping Madame Terri build a temporary shrine to the Goryo in the lobby, with flowers, incense, food and drink as offerings.

Seeing it, Megan concurred, "The Goryo spirits are feeling respected. This will be one restaurant that will never require human security guards."

By the end of the week, there were new crews working inside and out, and a delighted Herman expected them to be finished before the revised opening date. Adam, Inger, and Madame Terri flew back home that next week, with bonuses, new silk blouses, and two boxes of dog biscuits for the Pomeranians.

To complete this matter, Adam flew back to Newark for the 'Samurai House' restaurant's grand opening. They did it up in style, with the New Jersey Governor and the New York City Mayor in attendance. Adam escorted Megan there for an excellent hibachi dinner, and as they enjoyed shrimp and steak, Adam devotedly hoped they wouldn't need any of Megan's translations.

Sitting in that ancient hall, he did have a feeling of being surrounded by the spirits, but it was a good feeling. The Goryo were satisfied, and the diners were delighted.

That night after everyone left, Adam had management hold off locking up the restaurant until Megan could convey his personal thanks by pouring sake offerings to the spirits of the house at their newly constructed miniature shrine.

Flying back home, the only thing Adam hadn't figured out yet was what exactly had been the problem that his staid Uncle Herman had that required the special services of Uncle Quentin? Adam figured he might get that out of Wynoma or maybe the special client files?

Still Fighting the Not So Civil War

Wynoma was there with yet another of Paracelsus's life-extending potions that were just about killing Adam.

He grabbed his briefcase. "I'm late to meet George after court."

At six -foot two, his secretary out reached and out weighted him as she blocked his exit. "You have time to drink this."

"As an alchemist, Paracelsus stinks. I'm his lawyer, and I'm sure he's only two centuries old."

"His potions extended your great Uncle Quentin's life. They will extend yours, but only if you drink them!"

"It'll make me sick!"

"It is medicine."

Someday he was going to have to explain that he was the boss and she was the secretary but in the meantime. "Let me take it into the bathroom, so I can vomit in there." She actually followed him into the bathroom, making him look back at her and say, "May I have some privacy? " He started unbuttoned his pants, hoping to scare her away. "I'm gotta pee first."

Wynoma just stood in the doorway, staring at him.

"What do you think? I'm gonna behave like a little kid and dump this eternal life right down the toilet because it tastes like hell?" Which was exactly what he planned to do.

Unimpressed she stood like a redwood, unmoveable as Wynoma counseled, "Try to keep it down this time."

Adam took the green glass vial and pulled out the cork plug. Shit, it stank like a flattened skunk. Adam poured himself a paper cup of water, and then a second cup in preparation to washing the stuff down, but he had to admit since he'd been taking Paracelsus' potions, his love life performance had increased; if he only he had a girlfriend to impress with his new endurance.

His ruddy skinned, Cherokee secretary just stared, her strangely pale orchid eyes never leaving him.

"Heads up." He lifted the vial to salute her and then poured it down his throat. Or tried to, as it seemed his whole body was wrenching.

"It needs to stay down to work," she reminded him sternly.

He felt too sick to even try to wash the vile taste down. "This stuff is supposed to get better?"

"When Paracelsus gets the formula right, but with that sweat breaking out... and your body still smells wrong, I will tell him to adjust it." She walked out of the bathroom.

Adam put the wooden toilet seat down and just sat, not thinking he should even try walking until the unstableness of his body stopped. He noted that the hallucinations were starting early as the small black and white square tiles of the bathroom floor had risen and were swirling like tiny ballet dancers.

After the first of those potions Adam had started to drive home, but when the road lifted to the sky, he pulled off. Cops found him there, and he failed the field sobriety test but passed the Breathalyzer. And even though the cops hauled him to a hospital, blood tests hadn't shown any known drugs. Thank god, Judge Jeremiah hadn't heard about that one.

Today, he had planned to drive into St. Louis and have dinner with his Cousin George's family, but now he could only crawl on the floor back to his office. From the floor, he pulled himself up into his chair, where he could reach his phone to cancel George. When he could safely talk again.

Then, as usual with no law clients begging for his time, he opened up his laptop. He started scrolling through hundred and forty messages: cheap remortgaging and land sales in Alaska, fundraisers for the Bar Association, Boy Scouts, and local occult society. From his mail, apparently, Quentin had made the mistake of donating to everything.

As Adam worked online, his fingers began to dissolve and run over the keys, and the molded plaster ceiling seemed to be dripping down. Yhep, if Paracelsus ever gave up his pharmacy, he had a great future developing synthetic peyote.

The phone rang. Was it really ringing? Or was this another hallucination? Where was Wynoma?

After four rings, Adam reached out, but with his vision off, he had to reposition his hand twice. Should he answer? This might be a client, and he needed paying clients. He slurred, "Adam Martin's law firm."

"Hello, dear." The bright, cheery voice on the phone chirped to him. It was Madame Terri of the Resurrection Sisters. "Can you envision me as a six-foot-four Confederate Calvary officer?"

Actually, even on Paracelsus' drugs, Adam could only picture Madame Terri as a perky seventy year old with blonde, bubble coiffed hair, a lavender pants suit, and pink-trimmed running shoes. "What's your brigade?"

"I don't know. But my horse's name is Brownie," she proudly responded. "Since I'm stuck in bed, I've..."

Instantly concerned, he asked, "Why are you bed bound?"

"Stop being such a mother hen! My new gentleman friend and I were dancing, and I twisted my ankle." Great, even a seventy-year-old got more dates then he did, but she was babbling on. "So Sister Joesy set me up with a computer. I've always been interested in the Civil War, did you know they fought around here?"

"Yhep. Uncle Herman used to do some reenacting. We'd dress up in blue uniforms and go out and shoot cloth wadding out of our muzzleloading rifles." He suddenly got a horrific vision of erratic Terri with a gun. "You aren't doing that, are you?"

"This is all on the computer screen. You just talk and argue about which general got it wrong and talk about living in the camps. I'm Trooper Kear, and I've made some new friends." She slowed down. "And there is this one friend..."

Here it comes, another client who couldn't pay.

She was continuing. "He really needs a lawyer, but I don't think he has any money. Still, what he wants fixed is not for himself."

Judge Jeremiah had endlessly lectured Adam about lawyers who ended destitute, because they didn't charge for their only asset: legal advice, but he just smiled wryly. "Tell him to call me."

"I don't know his real name, or if he has a phone. A lot of the people on this site are shut-ins. I only know him as 'Big Rob.' I was telling him about some museum being sold for a strip mall, and he is so upset about it, saying they can't do it! Adam, can you go online?"

"Sure."

"The site is 'fight_it_again.' Some reenact the Napoleonic Wars, some refight Vietnam, and we do the Missouri Civil War battles on weeknights, at eight p.m.. You should study up and pretend that you are an actual soldier. It's fun!"

That Tuesday night, Adam found himself signing up for free as he chooses a persona. The program suggested some actual soldier's names he could assume, but, remembering his re-enacting with Uncle Herman, he choose Cpr. Martin, attache to Brig. General Thomas Ewing of the Union forces. The site was sort of a blog, with soldiers randomly typing in and it seemed to be equally divided between academic types wanting to show off their knowledge and wanna-be-soldiers rehashing 'their' war stories. Adam found he could type in a neutral comment then just sit back and read the scrolling answers.

He waited until Big Rob signed on and started typing again:

Cpr. Martin: **Big Rob. Trooper Kear told me you needed a lawyer?**

Big Rob:	**Cpr. Martin? You a college educated esquire? Why ain't you all higher than a corporal?"**

What was a proper Civil War response?

Cpr. Matin:	**Got demoted. Drank a little too much.**
Bulldog:	**Martin–you're Union! Finally, I got an extra boy on my side!**
Drummer Boy:	**Won't help you!**
Big Rob:	**Hold! I need to talk to Cpr. Kear. Now, I got a legal hassle for you to settle. What would this cost me?**
Cpr. Martin:	**What rank are you?**
Big Rob:	**Buck Sergeant.**

Adam seemed to recall a Confederate soldier got eleven dollars a month, while a sergeant got nearly twenty.

Cpr. Martin:	**What can you pay?**
Big Rob:	**I guess...I got five dollars, I could give you. Hard money.**

Now, if Big Rob was keeping in the 1860's persona, five dollars would have been over a week's pay. Or was he really a shut-in, on a wounded veteran's meager pension, so maybe five bucks cash was all he could pay? Adam had one of those *'knowing feelings'* that Madame Terri encouraged. Big Rob was a good guy, and five bucks was all he could pay.

Cpr. Martin	**Five dollars would suit me. What's the problem?**

There was a hesitation, then the typing on the screen began.

Big Rob:	**Stone River is selling a museum they got no right to sell!**
Cpr. Martin:	**Townships are short of money now. They're selling what they can't maintain.**
Big Rob:	**The land, buildings, and a maintenance fund was donated by**

	Martha MacIntyre's will in 1848. Part of the deed said that if Stone River township ever stopped using the School House Museum for educational purposes, they had ta return all of it to the family.
Cpr. Martin:	The family? You a MacIntyre?
Big Rob:	Yeah, but I don't want any money. Martha meant that museum to carry our name down! The MacIntyre name.
Bulldog:	What's this got to do with fighting? We're gonna redo Fort Davidson!
Cpr. Martin:	Big Rob, give me your e-mail.
Big Rob:	My what?
Cpr. Martin:	Big Rob, your computer mail address?
Big Rob:	I ain't no good with this newfangled stuff! You kin meet me here, swimming in the river.

Adam nodded, he's not planning to pay me, so he doesn't want to give me his real name and address. He also had that flash of lawyer's instinct which told him, that although Big Rob was basically honest, his new client was holding something back.

The next morning, Wynoma announced there were no paying clients, so Adam started researching the Martha MacIntyre School House Museum deed. Stone River Township was in St. Francois County and its online stuff only went back to 1999, so Adam found himself driving to the Stone River courthouse. As he stopped to refill his pickup's gas tank, he doubted Big Rob's 'five dollars' would include expenses.

In Stone River, Adam talked with the town clerk. "Yhep, we're selling the Museum property. Nice acreage and it's got a small pond that they give nature walks by, but the town's got a construction company to purchase it for a new mall. Of course, that's not the real reason why they're selling it," said the clerk sourly.

"No?" Adam asked.

"One of the well-connected guys down the road cain't stand the shooting sounds."

"Bullets?"

"Part of that property backs to a hillside that's an outdoor rifle range, and the Boy Scouts, local cops, and re-enactors use it on weekends."

"That insurance must cost the town a lot?"

"Don't cost nothing–there's a trust that came with the property that pays for upkeep, everything. 'Course when they sell, that trust gonna go into General Funds and wipe out the whole town debt. Councilmen like that."

Maybe Adam's new client did expect the property and the trust to revert to him? That might give Adam a hefty contingency fee. "Could I see that deed?"

"Nope."

Adam looked up to argue, but the clerk patiently explained. "Lost all the records in the Town Hall fire back in 1897. All we got is reconstructions from taxes paid. No deeds from before 1897. You might try the Schoolhouse itself, maybe they still got a copy?"

The Schoolhouse was one story, built solidly of fieldstone, with two entrances: one for boys, one for girls. It once had four large classrooms and two outhouses.

"One is set up as a display classroom, and the rest are lent free as meeting rooms for local organizations," Miss Rawlings, the volunteer curator explained. "In 1822, the MacIntyres built the school for their boys and the children from nearby farms. When the new school was built, their daughter-in-law, Martha, donated the land for the town's educational use. Its focus has grown over the years, from history to nature studies. We get the second and third graders bused here for their field trips, and we show them real slate blackboards and McGuffy readers." Her face lapsed into sad lines. "Well, we did. We're packing now." She indicated the open cardboard boxes that lined up along the wall.

Adam studied the children's desks, each wooden seat and back providing the frame for the next student's desk, with holes in the desktop for the kid's ink bottles. He looked at the yellowed pull-down maps and dark gray chalk-board. "Where will you be taking the antiques?"

She hesitated, obviously not wanting to think about what was coming. "The town board wants it all dumped. We can probably store some of it in Mr. Banerk's garage, for a time..." Her face looked even sadder. "Maybe money for a smaller museum can be raised."

Adam nodded. "I've been told that the property came with an entailed deed. That if the town stopped using it, it would revert back to the family." Adam watched her face.

She looked hopeful. "Would that still hold up today?"

"It might."

"I've never seen the original deed...but there are boxes of papers..."

"Could you look around?" Adam handed her his business card. "And call me if you find anything related to the donation."

Her face had brightened considerably. "Oh, if you could save the museum, it would make so many people happy. We get the children, the Reenactors, the Wild Flower Club..."

Adam decided to try the town library next. The reference librarian was sympathetic,"My daughter takes drawing classes there," but she couldn't help.

The next night, Adam signed online.

Cpr. Martin:	**Big Rob.**
Big Rob:	**Soldier! We're going into battle.**
Cpr. Martin:	**First the School House. How did you know there was an entailed deed?**

Big Rob:	**Heard it from... heard it from my grandfather. He heard it from his. All you got to do is find that deed in the Town Hall.**
Cpr. Martin:	**The Stone Creek Town Hall burnt down in 1897.**

There was a pause before:

Big Rob:	**So then we lost that one too, right?**
Cpr. Martin:	**Not yet. I need you to come into court and testify to hearing that...**

Other voices scrolled across the screen:

Bulldog:	**Maybe this time we Union guys got repeating rifles!**
Drummer Boy:	**And we captured a wagon load of them from you! Yeah. Let's play it that way!**
Cpr. Martin:	**I want to speak to Big Rob.**
Big Rob:	**Sorry, Cpr. Can't go to court with ya.**
Cpr. Martin:	**If you are homebound, we could do a bedside deposition? I can get a judge to do that.**
Big Rob:	**This School House battle's over, boy. Sorry, I wasted your time. Now, Bulldog, how many bullets do these new rifles fire for you Yankees?**

Adam watched the scrolling screen with its battle details: The Johnnie Rebs were Sgt. Big Rob, twelve-year-old Drummer Boy, Cousin Samuel, and Capt. John. The Yankees were Union Joe and Bull Dog. They didn't use the jargon of academics, yet each seemed to have the depth of a PhD. in the War Between the States, as for hours they rehashing every detail of the Missouri Campaign.

Adam couldn't understand it. Virtual reenacting took tremendous discipline, yet rather than let himself be deposed by Adam, Big Rob would give up his goal of stopping the Stone

Town School House sale. Logically it made no sense, but Adam started to get one of those strange-knowing feelings again.

The next day he called the Resurrection Sisters and got Madame Terri. Ever her flirtatious self she began, "Adam! You've got to come over and see what my Houdini has learned..."

Adam wasn't in the mood for Pomeranian cleverness. "That Sgt. you told me about, Big Rob, with the School House..."

"You saved his museum?" She asked happily.

"I'm trying, but I need him to appear court."

She sounded confused. "He can't do that."

"I can do a bedside deposition at his home."

Madame Terri's voice got very serious. "Adam, you are supposed to be practicing."

Talking with Madame could be very difficult. "Practicing law? I am."

"No, dear, your psychic abilities." Madame Terri's voice took on a tone of recrimination. "Your Uncle Quentin chose you to carry on his practice because I told him--of the Martins--you had the strongest innate metaphysical abilities. You're not working on those! Adam, you have to just let your mind free itself of preconditions, relax, and allow voices from the other side to guide you."

"Big Rob is dead?"

"Well, he never told me, but I think so. Haven't you felt it?"

Adam couldn't believe this. "You've been talking to a dead person?"

"Dear, I'm a psychic medium, I do that all the time. Crystal ball, glass computer screen, what's the difference?"

He couldn't accept what she found perfectly normal. "A deceased Civil War soldier is speaking over the Internet?"

"Why not?"

Some days Adam would trade his Great Uncle Quentin's law practice for a bagel and a cup of tea. "Madame Terri, how do the dead get on the Internet?"

"Ask him, not me. Although, I don't think he'll know. Adam, in this life somethings just are, and you have to accept them."

Yeah, lately he'd been accepted more and more, or was it all just Paracelsus's potions melting his brain? No, he couldn't get a Civil War Ghost accepted as a witness in court. His next move was the Jefferson City Library, but when he drove to the State Capitol, he found no records of the Schoolhouse transaction. But there were Civil War military records with the Army of Missouri, under Maj. Gen. Sterling Price. He found there were over 2,000 Confederate causalities at the Battle of Fort Davidson and the surrounding areas. Davidson was near Stone Creek. Adam searched the microfilmed lists, stopping at Sgt. Robert MacIntyre.

Big Rob fell in a brief skirmish following retreating Union troops. As the afternoon wore on, Adam went out, got two rolls of quarters for the copy machines and a bag of burgers that he snuck back into the Genealogical section. By seven p.m, Adam finally located a Stone Creek church, with the burial sites for Captain Robert MacIntyre in 1864, and his mother, Martha Banister MacIntyre, in 1858.

The next day, Adam drove to Stone Creek and the Christ Redeemer Church. An elderly man in jeans was digging a post hole to replace a rotted corner in the graveyard fencing and seeing Adam approach he looked up with a friendly smile. "Not too many people drop by here."

"I'm Adam Martin, a lawyer. Are you the sexton?"

"Sexton, preacher, gardener, retired history professor, Jonathan Fuller." The churchman slipped off his work gloves and shook Adam's hand with his thin, dry fingers.

Adam explained. "I've been doing some historical research on the MacIntyre family, in regards to Martha

MacIntyre's original deeding of the School House Museum. "

Jonathan shook his head. "So little respect for history today, and they really don't teach much to the kids, preferring a propagandized 'social studies.' Then our leaders dump what concrete history the kids could get interested in."

"Would this church have any deeds or papers related to the MacIntyres?"

"I'll show you what we have, but I've read and refiled it all, and I don't remember seeing anything regarding that transaction. Got a lot of the MacIntyres in those books I'm always writing."

"You write?" asked a surprised Adam.

"Local history of the Civil War in Missouri. Nothing ever printed, the university publisher said you have to have a different angle, something fresh, old family sources that nobody else has got. But I keep gathering stuff, here and there." He looked about. "The MacIntyres built this church in 1815, and most of them are buried here."

"What about Sgt. Robert MacIntyre?"

"Reburied here when his family found his grave, dug him up and brought him back in an ox pulled wagon. Luckily Robert wasn't in the trench grave. Missouri stayed a border state, but the MacIntyres were state's rights believers. Robert and his cousins mustered out to General Price's troops."

Jonathan was walking to the thin, metal gate. "Cemetery's big by county standards. Many of those blue and grey soldiers that died hereabouts were buried alongside the locals." Jonathan surveyed the land. "Ain't changed a lick since 1860's. They shot a Civil War documentary here without having to fix much up."

Adam looked about, seeing cattle grazing in the distant fields enclosed with neat stone fences, a dry gulch, the old church on its quiet lane. "There are those phone lines following the road." He pointed out.

"Old time poles that looks a bit like telegraph lines." As

they turned the corner of the church, he finished. "What really spoils it is those fug-ugly high tension wire supports, cutting across the land along the dry creek bed. Looks like giant Martian robot warriors tramping across the farms. Shame they scarred the land with them in 1980. Monstrosities.

"Bringing power up from New Madrid. Course St. Louis needs the juice, but the farmers say the cows miscarry near those lines because the power kinda spills over. Saw a guy on TV stand near one of them once, holding a fluoresce light tube in his hands, and the dang thing lit up from just the spill over electricity in the air." Jonathan was walking Adam to the back of the cemetery, just before the dry creek. "Sgt. MacIntyre was re-buried with several other local soldiers, even a few Yankees back here. In the 1870's, the town paid to put up tombstones for the war dead when the wooden head markers started rotting out."

Adam found himself in among neat squares of pitted, white marble reading 'Sgt. Johnson', 'Cpl. Timis', 'Pvt. Kastanik', and 'Col. John Grahame.' Jonathan had stopped before one lettered

'Sgt. Robert MacIntyre'. It came as a shock when Adam looked down and saw next to Big Rob, a plain white marble marker for 'Drummer Boy Samuel Scofield, born July 3, 1852 – Shot September 28, 1864'. Drummer Boy was just twelve.

Jonathan pointed to the left. "Robert's mother, Martha, is buried over there. Shame if she did protect that Museum, and nobody can find the deed." He pointed to the right. "Over there are the Pearsel graves."

"Pearsels?"

"Lawyers around here for generations. They probably did her will, and it would have been a tight one. Very precise men the Pearsels. You'll have to excuse me, I've got to set up for Church service, but you can stay or come back again, and we can talk."

"Yes, sir. Do you mind if I look around a bit?"

"Glad to have ya."

Adam tried to remember what the re-enactors had said, Drummer Boy Samuel talked of the excitement of war and of swimming in the rushing river. So did Stg. Rob and Bull Dog, but they were buried here, besides a dry creek bed that looked like it had dried up decades ago. Adam didn't see any other river nearby.

He walked closer to Stg. Robert MacIntyre's white marble stone. His was larger than the town stones, so it must have been raised by his family. Adam closed his eyes, and he really tried. Madame Terri said to empty his mind, but his mind kept swirling with problems. He'd look at some of the church papers before he left, but he figured Jonathan was right. There was no deed and nothing in the State Archives. Could he locate a secondary source? Maybe a town paper article about the donation? A diary written at the time? Maybe something from writings of the town officials? But there wasn't enough time, as the schoolhouse was slated for demolition right after the sale finalized at the council meeting next Thursday.

Then Adam heard it or more likely felt it. A faint voice in his head that broke up. "Cpr. Martin, esquire? You there?"

Adam opened his eyes and looked down at the grass in front of Robert's stone. "Yhep."

"Kin barely hears you, yet you feel closer? You know now why I can't testify?"

"Yhep," Adam said to himself.

"Then it's over, I guess."

That Martin stubbornness rose up. "Soldier, we've been losing skirmishes, but the war isn't over yet."

"Cain't hear you much..."

Adam spoke out louder, wondering if that would help. "I'll be with you Monday before the battle!"

He walked over and stood by Martha's grave. Did she know where a copy of her will was? Did Rob have time to give her grandchildren before his last battle, so she would have descendants? Adam tried to reach Martha's mind with his but couldn't. He walked over to the Pearsels: Abraham, esquire, Philip, and George. Last burial of a Pearsel was ninety years old Margaret, in 1922. Adam really tried to mentally contact them, but nothing.

The field tone church was small, with room on wooden benches for maybe fifty parishioners. Most of the windows were clear glass, but when Adam went in, he noted it boasted one really fine stain-glass window high over the altar with soldiers flying Union and Confederate flags. He checked it was from Tiffany & Company. In the side addition with the minister's office, Jonathan showed him some of the history manuscripts he had written, and as the church, they were clean and solid. After they both looked through more of the church records, a discouraged Adam returned home. He was like a young hound fidgeting on the trail, so eager to go, but he had no scent to follow.

Still, there was one person he hadn't tried. Adam dialed Judge Jeremiah Martin.

"Hello, Adam. Are they disbarring you yet?" Came the cold, impassive voice.

"Not yet, Uncle Jere." Adam continued brightly. "I'm trying to locate a lost deed. The lawyer of record was a Pearsel from Stone Creek."

Jeremiah gave it some thought, before replying. "Don't recall ever hearing of him."

"The Bar Association doesn't keep records of deceased lawyers?"

"No."

"No other place the information could be found fast?"

"If you want to dig into history, go speak to the oldest lawyer in the district."

"Stone River Township?"

Jeremiah Martin gave it more thought. "Winthrop. Will or Warren something Winthrop. He'd be in his eighties now."

"Retired?"

"Last time I heard, he was still in general practice."

"Thanks." But before Adam hung up there was something he had to ask, "Jere, about August Cameron being paroled, you okay with it?"

There a silence for a time, then his uncle said quietly, "Surprisingly yes. Seems like even you can get one right once in awhile."

Lawyer Willard Winthrop was a heavy-set man, with a huge stomach and bigger laugh. He was delighted to see Adam in his office, and he wandered on and on. "Shame about the School Museum sale. Big mistake, the town's getting a bunch of money but losing something so much more valuable for its citizens. My great-granddaughter tells me they hold butterfly picnics out there."

Adam tried to get him back on track. "I believe that Martha MacIntyre donated the School House Museum, with the stipulation that if the town ever allowed its educational functions to cease the entire bequest would revert to the family. "

Willard's eyes opened wide. "You got a deed to prove this?"

"That's the problem..." Adam had to admit.

"The fire of 1897?" His new friend finished. "That kinda washes things away."

"The family should have had a copy."

Sitting back deep in thought Willard finally said, "The MacIntyre name died out hereabouts in the 1950's. There were a few daughters who married into other families. Be a lot of work, but the Stone River Genealogy Society could probably trace down an heir for you. The Society meets every Thursday at the School House Museum. But chances are the daughters or nieces wouldn't have kept the old folks' papers."

"The lawyer writing it up would also have kept a copy for his files."

Willard nodded. "They always did that in those days."

"I think the lawyer's name may have been Pearsel?"

"Abraham Pearsel? No. When was that property deeded?

"1858."

Willard seemed to be running decades of lawyering through his mental computer. "Lordy, that goes back to his father, Philip Pearsel. The Pearsels have been lawyers with offices on Main Street for generations."

"There's no Pearsels registered with the County Bar?"

"That's because the last three generations have been daughters. The current one would have to be the great-granddaughter, Mary Anne Mckenna."

The name stuck a tiny bell. "She has an office on Bank Street?"

"Second floor, mention I sent you. Son, hope you can save that museum!"

Mary Anne looked at him strangely, but Adam was thankful for the respectability of the Martin name as he explained about the School House Museum.

She nodded. "My girl scout troop used to meet there. There are records from our law firm in storage in the basement. My mother's, my father's and maybe my grandfather's, but I can't take the time to go through them. I'm sorry."

"Could you let me search?" Adam held his breath, private client files, the answer should be no, but he was a Martin, and it was for a good cause.

She was considering it. "I'll let you see the storage area–but it's an impossible task."

MaryAnne took him down to the basement and unlocked a wooden door that leads to a storage room with boxes in stacks eight foot tall. Some were properly labeled with their contents, others weren't.

"I'll let you search, but this will take forever, and as I understand it the museum sale will be finalized at the next council meeting Thursday?"

"You have a ladder I could borrow?" Adam brightly asked.

She nodded, but asked, "I don't mean to be impolite, but what are you going to be paid for all this work?"

"Might get a whole five dollars in hard cash out it," Adam cheerfully explained.

That night he called the president of the Stone River Genealogy Society, she was willing to help but time was running against them. On Tuesday, he recruited Wynoma, Madame Terri, and Sister Josey to help open boxes as he glanced through the files. On the third day, MaryAnne and the volunteer curator from the museum had joined them. They got back to 1903 when Abraham had taken over the practice, but that's where the boxes stopped.

MaryAnne had come down with cups and a pitcher of ice water and found the searchers were all covered with sweat, coal dust, and discouragement. Sadly Adam announced, "Well, it was a long shot," as he climbed the ladder to finish piling the last boxes back up.

"You know," MaryAnne was thoughtful. "I have an elderly cousin, Belle. She never throws anything out.

"Yes!" Madame Terri exclaimed delightedly. "We need more boxes!"

But getting up in Belle's storage required climbing a steep wooden ladder through a hole in the rafters over Belle's garage, a former livery barn. Adam forbid the Resurrection Sisters and anyone else over sixty from going up, but of course, the ageless Wynoma never listened to him, so it was the two of them, sweating in a hot loft as they started on another seemingly endless mound of boxes. The cellar had been damp and moldy, while the loft was sticky and dirty. These paperboard boxes were fortunately accurately labeled year by year in an elegant, looping script, so after much dust raising and box moving, Adam finally got to Philip Pearsel's records.

In them were generations of MacIntyre files, yellowed paper bundles in manilla envelops tied with white string cords. Martha was supposed to have dictated her will on her deathbed, so they looked for a box that covered1858. Wynoma found it first, and with trembling hands, Adam rapidly sorted through. One labeled bundle held a complete, handwritten copy of the School House Museum transaction, including Martha's will, and a letter with Stone River's sign off acceptance of the terms.

Wynoma held the battery light above him, even she seemed to be smiling as Adam read out loud the iron clad codicil that stated "if the Stone Creek School House Museum shall ever cease its educational functions, the entire land, building(s), and trust funds will revert to the MacIntyre family or descendants of same."

At the Town Council meeting that evening, Adam passed out photostated copies of the registered deed and agreement. From the genealogy society, he had already located two MacIntyre descendants who would be absolutely delighted if the property and maintenance trust reverted to them. Hearing that, Stone River's Council unanimously decided to cancel the property sale and retain the MacIntyre School House Museum and its substantial trust intact.

Feeling very satisfied and proud, Adam logged on to the re-enactor site. He had news to tell, but first, he had some questions of his own that needed answering.

Cpr. Martin: **Big Rob. You remember dying?**
Big Rob: **Last I remember of Stone Creek was choking on blue smoke, then a mighty pain on the side of my head.**
Cpr. Martin: **Then you're a ghost?**
Big Rob: **I don't think I'm up to scaring children and cart horses. Even my wife didn't believe in haunts.**
Cpr. Martin: **But you can talk to me?**
Big Rob: **Swimming in the rushing river with**

	you.
Cpr. Martin:	You're on the Internet.
Big Rob:	Inner what?

How do you explain computer chips and electricity to a man who only ever knew woodstoves and candles?

Cpr. Martin:	Sort of a telegraph, with written words and pictures.
Big Rob:	Don't see pictures–jes hear your words.
Cpr. Martin:	How long have you been able to contact us?
Big Rob:	Time don't mean much anymore.
Cpr. Martin:	After your...after the battle, you could talk to others in the churchyard?
Big Rob:	Yhep. And heard some of those that walked near, but they didn't seem to hear me.
Cpr. Matin:	Could you contact your mother, Martha?
Big Rob:	No.
Bull Dog:	We gonna fight a battle or talk all night?
Drummer Boy:	You were closer to us Cpr. Martin, now you're away?
Cpr. Martin:	Big Rob, something happened, so that you heard other people?
Big Rob:	We started hearing water, rushing. Getting louder. The river started calling to us. I kinda swam in it, and it's sort of warm and fast running.
Cpr. Martin:	Do you know when you first started swimming in the river?
Big Rob:	You want a year? Cain't count them anymore.

Cpr. Martin:	What were others in the river talking about when you first went in?
Big Rob:	When I started swimming in the river, there was a hullabaloo over a U.S. Hockey team that beat the Canadians in the Olemics?
Cpr. Martin:	The Olympics? That was 1980, when the high tension power lines were constructed over your...area.
Big Rob:	Power Lines?
Cpr. Martin:	Kinda lightning harnessed. It must be amplifying your thoughts. Can you hear others in the churchyard?
Big Rob:	Lord, yes. One time there were over two hundred of us. But most have grown silent.
Cpr. Martin:	Maybe they have moved on.
Big Rob:	My wife, Henni was always talking about loving Lord Jesus Christ and playing harps in heaven throughout eternity. Sounded kinda boring to me.
Cpr. Martin:	Near death, people say they experience a bright, white light, and a tunnel they have to go through to meet with friends on the other side.
Big Rob:	I jest got wacking on the head, real hard.
Cpr. Martin:	In the rushing river, have you gone out and met any others that are...like you?
Big Rob:	You mean dead? Hard to tell, but I think so. Years ago there was guy. Claimed he was in Napoleon's army. He wasn't faking it. Ya jest get feelings about some folks who are

	lying and some who are the real thing. Corporal, I had two sons and a daughter. Wondered how they made out?
Cpr. Martin:	I'll look into that for you.

There was a pause, then:

Cpr. Martin:	This is upsetting you?
Big Rob:	Don't mean spit now. Can't rightly even picture my wife much anymore. Only remember that painting of Henni, in the yellow silk dress, with her chestnut hair tumbling down. Glad it's over for her.
Cpr. Martin:	Will it ever be over for you?
Big Rob:	Others here talked of that pulling feeling I get some time. Like you're being called. Those others are gone. Must've answered that call.
Cpr. Martin:	They say gh–spirits stay earthbound because they can't accept that their life has ended.
Big Rob:	Like that blue belly, Bulldog, always fighting the war again. And poor boy, Samuel, shot in battle while drumming commands. The boy can't seem to understand that his life was over afore it began.
Cpr. Martin:	Maybe there is something else.
Big Rob:	Wings and harps?
Cpr. Martin:	Maybe you could reincarnate. Be born again. Samuel might be up for another life. One that he could fully live if he would just let go?
Big Rob:	Maybe. But I guess we all hate to charge over a hill when we cain't see

what's on the other side.

Cpr. Martin: **Then you plan to stay?**

For a time no answer scrolled across Adam's screen. He found himself holding his breath. Then:

Big Rob: **Won't leave. At least until Drummer Boy and Bull Dog are ready. Don't want them to be alone.**

Cpr. Martin: **I have a friend, Prof. Jonathan Fuller, who takes care of your graveyard. He's writing books on the Civil War. If I get him online, will you answer questions? Maybe tell him that at holidays your family made it an obligation to pass on stories from your great-great-grandfather? That you can give him facts of 1860's warfare and camp life no one else knows?**

Adam waited. Again, no answer, and then letters typed across the screen:

Big Rob: **Sure. What the hell. I ain't going nowhere.**

Cpr. Martin: **I've got good news. We found the deed. The MacIntyre School House will continue as a community museum.**

Big Rob: **You did that, Corporal? Well, then I owe you your five big ones!**

Adam shook his head as he typed back:

Cpr. Martin: **What, is in your back pocket? I'd don't have my shovel with me.**

Big Rob: **No shovel. Hand trowel'll do it. It's buried a foot deep in a jelly jar. That's how we used to pay off our cottonmouths.**

Cpr. Martin:	**Cottonmouths?**
Big Rob:	**Supposed Yankees who spied for me. They'd leave the information in a hollow stump. If'n it seemed good, I'd pass on directions to the jelly jar.**
Cpr. Martin:	**The money's still there since 1864?**
Big Rob:	**Unless some bastard got to it first. That mini ball kinda intervened before I passed it on. You start at the center of town, by the Congregational church, then take Millers Road....**

Big Rob's directions were simple, so simple, that Adam found himself afraid. How many non-ghosts were reading that site's scrolls? They could beat him to the jelly jar! At dawn, Adam headed down Highway D, but quickly he ruefully realized that all of Big Rob's markers were gone.

Well, not all of them, so he started at the old Congregational church on Main Street. He followed Main Street for about a mile, coming to the crossroads, with a big, two-story, gray wooden store. Now it sold English riding gear and rhinestone poodle collars, but he figured that in 1864 this could have been 'Avery's Feed and Grain.' That gave him what looked like a modern road called Robertson that might have once been Miller's Way?

There were several old churches, with graveyards along the Miller's Way/Robertson, but none looked like the one-story, board one that Big Rob had described. Of course, Rob couldn't remember the church's name.

If Avery's Feed was wrong, Adam could be way off target, but he had the feeling that he wasn't. Big Rob had said that in an ornamental iron fenced the graveyard, Adam would find a statue of the Archangel Gabriel and at its base would be the inscription, '*Peaceful Be Ye Rest,*' in the center of a family plot. Big Rob couldn't remember the family's name either, but Adam was to dig twelve inches or so down directly under the

'B.'

Reaching the next town, he turned his pickup around and rode up and down Robertson multiple times. There were several churches with graveyards, and one graveyard all by itself, that may have lost its church. All the cemeteries seemed bigger than what Rob described, but it had been nearly a hundred and fifty years since the sergeant last saw it. They could plant a lot of people in all that time!

At the closest church to Rob's description, Adam parked and walked past white painted aluminum siding that could hide boards. Big Rob had described the marble angel as being bigger than life size and in a straight line between the tallest pine and a huge weeping willow.

There were no big trees in this graveyard, but of course, they could've been cut down. A lot of 1800's graves and family plots, but no big angel. He found several cherubs. Had Big Rob's memory enlarged the marble angel? Made it a strong-faced man, instead of baby-faced cherub? There was no inscription like '*Peaceful be*' on any of the cherubs.

Next, Adam tried a boarded-shut brick and wood church. He was walking its graveyard at lunchtime, and although Adam felt hungry, he couldn't stop hunting. Bordering this churchyard he found several large pines that could easily be two hundred years old, but no weeping willows or marsh beyond. Could that have dried up?
Damn. He should have brought a metal detector, but of course, then he'd probably find coffin nails all over the place.

After two more churches, he stopped at St. John's and put a trowel back in his pocket. The graveyard had tall pine trees with no weeping willows, but this church was a two-story brick instead of the one-story wood-board Big Rob had recalled. Still, out front, Adam found a bronze plaque saying the church was rebuilt in 1925, replacing one lost in a fire. Okay, this might be it, he started walking.

If he was arrested for grave robbing, how could he ever

explain this to Judge Jeremiah? Adam kept walking. Some recent burials in family plots, one with fresh flowers and some granite headstones going back to the 1900's. No, over there were older stones, like the area Rob described, but without the fence.

Beyond the granite headstones, Adam could see aged, white marble markers, some with iron star veterans' flag holders. He walked over, there seemed to be a large rectangle of older graves that once might have had the fence around them. Yes! He could see an isolated section of decorative iron railings in the back. By walking around, Adam found a granite post that once marked one of the corners. This was the original burial ground in the 1800's.

He walked to the rear of the oldest section. There wasn't Rob's marsh, but now, although overgrown, he could see a small rock-lined ornamental pond obviously from groundwater. Still, among all the tall obelisks, sculptured urns, and pitted, marble mausoleums, Adam couldn't see a bigger than life archangel, but back near the small pond area, Adam did find a huge, time grayed, weather checked tree stump. The big willow?

Adam lined it up with the biggest pine and started to pace down the tomb lined paths. Up front, a car was pulling into the cemetery. He had a reflex reaction to run and hide, but Adam just kept walking. This was ridiculous, a wasted day's work all for a jelly jar stuffed with five rotting dollars? Hell, it was left by a Confederate soldier so it would be stuffed with five worthless Confederate bills. Course, if the glass hadn't broken, and it was authentic Confederate paper, he could sell them at the antique market. For five of Rob's dollars, he might get a hundred or so? Or maybe twenty dollars? Where was that marble, angel?

He glanced over to the parked car where a fortyish woman was helping an elderly lady get a pot of white daisies out of their car, then Adam looked back at the narrow pathway between graves. That's when he saw a solid, white arm and trunk on the ground with sculpted robes and one broken tipped wing. In the shade of the pine tree, the archangel had fallen, and now Gabriel was covered with vines of ivy. Following the sculptured robes, Adam found its marble base also hidden by heart-shaped leaves. Kneeling down he ripped the strong vines away to reveal '*Peaceful Be Ye Rest.*'

He could hear distant digging. The daughter and mother planting their pot of daisies? Should he wait until they left? Well, maybe they would just think he was planting flowers on some grave. Adam took the trowel out of his pocket, lined it up with the "*B,*" and started to carefully dig into the black, damp earth as he smelled the earthy, pottery smell of graves. Soon he was down twelve inches. Nothing. The women's car doors were opening and shutting as Adam kept digging, making the hole bigger. Deeper.

The trowel kept hitting small rocks, then he hit something hard. Bigger rock. He angrily pried it out and threw it away, feeling like a fool. Was this a joke? Big Rob's ghostly idea of fun? Send him on a snipe hunt? The ghosts would be laughing their asses off at him at the next re-enactment. The hole widened and deepened as Adam frantically kept digging.

Suddenly the trowel tip hit something that clinked like glass. Adam threw the trowel down and started gouging at the dirt with his fingers, clawing at the mud and sharp rocks. There was something there! A tin can? It was a smooth cylinder covered with clay like mud. He grabbed the trowel again to pry around it.

Finally, he could pull it free, wiping muddy clay off with his hands, he saw smooth glass, a Mason jar intact, with the zinc lid corroded in place. He shook it. Heard loose somethings clattering inside. This was a Civil War artifact, used by a Confederate spymaster for the Missouri campaign. He should take it to some university archaeological laboratory, have the screw cap removed with an acid bath or electrolytically....oh, hell. He smashed the jar on the Angel's marble robes, and in the pine trees' shade, several objects fell to the earth among the glass shards. Five small coins.

He held one up to catch the light, and it gleamed. An Eagle design and he could make out a date of 1858. He had five, one-ounce coins of pure gold. Yeah! He'd accept Big Rob's five solid gold pieces as fair payment any day!

Oh, Such a Luscious Lady of the Lake

"She says she's a mermaid. She's lying!"

"Unless she's under oath, misleading the police, or trying to defraud someone, lying is not illegal," Adam explained.

"You're a prosecutor?" asked the black-haired woman angrily.

"Actually, I'm not–I'm Adam Martin. I think you have me confused with my cousin, George Martin."

"Oh, the guard called you Mr. Martin." She sounded really frustrated. "Then you're not a lawyer?"

"I am a lawyer with a private practice. George's office is—let me write down his address on my card."

"You don't think he'll help me, do you?" The woman looked so defeated.

Adam looked at his watch. "Court seems to be running over, so I have some time. Want to sit on that bench over there and tell me about this mermaid of yours?"

The woman before Adam was big boned, and she spoke with a slight Spanish accent. She could have been late forty to fifty. Her hands were red and rough, and she wore a blue work-shirt and jeans. She sat down, a bit away from Adam, telling her story in tired fashion like she had repeated it many times. "My name is Gina Mountalvo, and I do house cleaning. My Thursday for fourteen years is Joe Thomas. A very nice man, a bit slow, since he had the stroke, but he's doing better. Least he was doing better, now he's sick all the time. Because of her!"

"Why does he think she's a mermaid?"

"Mr. Thomas writes books. He does them on Cryzootal...fake animals," she finished.

"Cryptozoology? Study of animals or creatures, that's existence has not yet been proven?"

She spoke contemptuously. "Bigfoot! Mothboy!

Mermaids! One day, she knocks on the door. This woman, Merissa, and her brother, Neal. They claim Mr. Thomas has a photo in his book of their 'grandmother.' A naked woman with a fish's tail, sitting on a rock in the ocean."

"This Merissa, she has a tail too?"

"No. She says she's only one-quarter mermaid."

"So, one grandparent?"

"She says they were stopping to see Joe, but their car needs fixing. He gets excited and wants to interview them. They say they are traveling on, but they could stay with him until the part for their car comes in."

A mental alarm bell went off for Adam. "He let two strangers move in?"

"Men are such fools over a pretty face!" Gina said with contempt.

"For how long are they staying?"

"That was March, now it's June. She and her brother are living there, rent-free. Since Merissa started feeding Joe 'health foods', he starts getting sick. Now, he wants me to find a lawyer. He wants to redo his will and leave it all to his mermaid. Do you do wills?"

That afternoon, Adam found himself following Gina's car into farm country outside St. Louis. She stopped at a two-story white board house set on overgrown pasture land. Gina knocked, and the door was answered by a thin, friendly looking man in his thirties. "Hi, Guys." He looked quickly at Adam's briefcase and then said, "I'm Neal Grogan. Merissa's out cutting flowers, and Joe's in the living room." Neal had a goatee beard and dark blond hair. He ushered them inside.

In a dead voice, Gina informed him, "He's the lawyer Joe asked for."

Neal's face brightened considerably, as he shook Adam's hand. "That'll make Joe feel a **lot** better! He's been so low lately, Merissa's going out of her mind."

The front door behind them opened, and Adam turned

to see the most beautiful woman in the world. Taller than Adam by a good two inches, Merissa was wearing a tight, blue tie-dyed t-shirt and jean shorts. Her long, blonde hair was tied up in a twist, and her blue-green eyes were dancing, as she carried a basket full of wildflowers. "I've got to do an article on these perennial blooms," she explained to Adam. "I'm a freelancer for the magazines, mostly travel. Merissa Grogan." She put out a hand.

Adam shook her slender hand. "I'm Adam Martin. A lawyer."

She held his eyes for a moment, and then still holding his hand, Merissa led him into a white board-walled sitting room with comfortable overstuffed chairs. A man dressed in a green plaid shirt and slacks was sitting there reading his paper. He brightened to see Merissa, but Adam guessed any breathing male would cheer up seeing her.

"Joe, Gina brought you that lawyer you wanted, Adam Martin, not that you should be thinking about making wills." She smiled warmly at him like he was the only one in the room. "I've found some wild mint that will have you feeling much better!"

"Thank you, honey." The older man started to rise but seemed to be weaker than he expected. He sank back a bit and then had to use both his arms to push himself upwards. "Adam and I are going to talk business." Leaving the other three in the sitting room, Joe led Adam into a tight office, overflowing with six filing cabinets, shelves of books, mounds of pictures, papers, and several scanners. Even with his computer and printer, Joe still had a beat up, green Hermes typewriter. Adam noted Joe's own thick books filled several shelves over his desk.

Joe had to clear a pile of newspaper clippings for Adam to sit, and then Joe sank down into his wooden, swivel chair. In his comfortable surroundings, Joe sat up straighter and looked better. "Martin. Are you any relation to a lawyer named

Quentin Martin?'

"He was my great uncle, and I inherited his law practice."

Joe's eyes lit up. "There were rumors in the exotics community that Quentin handled a number of, well, not so ordinary clients. I wrote him several times, trying to get him to meet and talk with me..."

"And?"

"He regretfully cited client confidentiality."

Adam nodded. "That would be a problem."

"You know of my books?"

"I've seen them."

"If any of your clients are anxious to come out of the closet?"

"I'll be happy to pass along your name," said Adam, politely but not holding out much hope.

Joe swiveled his chair, looked up into the shelves and took down a book, scribbling his name on the front piece. "I'd like you to have this."

Adam took it from him. Joe had signed his *Exotic But Real Creatures* to him. "Is the picture of Merissa's grandmother in here?"

The happiness kind of fading a bit from Joe's face as he said, "In the back on page 173. I'd like to have your opinion."

Adam turned to a foggy, black and white photo of a woman, with her upper half that of a human and lower half that of a fish. She sat on a distance rock in the ocean. The woman was naked from the waist up, her long dark hair artfully covered her pendulous breasts, with her tail harder to see as it was partially obscured by foreground rocks.

He studied the picture. "The woman's torso muscle mass isn't as prominent as you expect for a constant swimmer, and the tail's proportion to her chest, it would seem to me, it should be bigger to support that upper body." Adam looked back at Joe. "But then a mermaid spends most of her life supported by water."

"Anything else?" His face remained unreadable, but Adam had the feeling that Joe was looking for an honest appraisal.

Adam looked down at the page-sized photo again. On the desk next to him, Joe had a rectangular magnifying glass, so Adam picked it up and studied the mermaid's face closer. "Her hair is long and streaming, but it looks like she has spit-curl bangs?"

Joe appeared uneasy about that, but said, "It would have been a style in the 1950's. Of course, Merissa says that her grandmother had contact with humans, and sex with them. " Joe looked back at the open book. "But I've always had my suspicions about that photo. The cameraman was a local fisherman that I could verify. Seemed honest. He said he'd seen her sunning two or three times before, and that's why he had the camera. But..."

"Did he ask for money?"

"For the picture? Oh, yeah, a lot! But I've used that photo several times. It's been in my publicity and was the cover for one of my later books."

"Merissa says she's a descendant of this mermaid?"

Joe nodded. "She thinks it might be her grandmother, but she isn't sure." He seemed to have dropped the skeptical scientist as he adopted true believer enthusiasm, speaking excitedly, "She knew the time period and where the picture was taken."

"That's right here in the book." Adam pointed out to him.

But Joe was waxing poetically. "Mermaid myths appear in almost every area of the world. There were the Greek Sirens, the Inuit Ikalu Nappa, Havfine in Norway, even the Maori's had Ngarara. It's either a very, very ancient myth that's spread, or there's something to it." Joe leaned forward to emphasize the importance of this. "Merissa's never asked me for money, and she has refused to let me photograph her. I have seen her swim underwater. One night, she was under a full twenty minutes! No human could do that."

"Did you ever see her swim in daylight?"

"Nope. Like a lot of unusuals, she doesn't want to be seen. Doesn't want to capitalize on her 'difference,' but you know, the time I have had with her has been the culmination of my life's work."

"I understand you want to make a new will?"

"Yes, I'm leaving it to all to Merissa," said Joe with resolve.

Adam hated doing this, but, "A woman you just met?"

The scientist was back. "I'm no fool. She's not in love with me, God, I wish she were! But, she is a creature that I've waited my whole life to see! I sat for three years staring out at Loch Ness. I've climbed the Himalayas to photograph melting snow prints, the closest I've gotten to a Yeti. I've marched through Amazon jungle, lugging camera boxes and sound equipment, and didn't find that sixty-foot anaconda. Then I'm sitting in my own house, and a beautiful mermaid just walks in and gives me the greatest thrill of my entire life."

Adam wanted to get back to the will. "What about your family?"

"Distant cousins that have nothing to do with me. I'd always planned to leave it that way."

"Your current heir?"

Here Joe hesitated. "Gina, my house cleaner. It's a business relationship, but she's treated me like a friend for years, and helped me quite a bit when I had my stroke."

To disinherit Gina didn't seem totally fair to Adam, maybe he could nudge Joe a bit. "Perhaps you can have both of them as your heirs? Split it?"

He smiled lopsidedly. "Sounds like you don't have much of a realistic idea of a writer's finances. I still get some small royalties, but most of my stuff is out of print. Any money

I got from the books went back into research and travel. All my 'estate' consists of this house, its contents, and the land. I'm leaving that to Merissa." Joe seemed to think a bit, then said. "Maybe, if anything happened to Merissa, you could make Gina a secondary beneficiary?"

"That could be worked out." Adam took a legal pad out of his briefcase and started making notes. The will outline was simple, finished in a few minutes, but the wild tales of exotic creatures that Joe had hunted filled the rest of Adam's day. They only stopped when Merissa came in, bringing a tray with chamomile smelling tea and a sandwich, gently scolding, "Joe really needs his rest." It was dark when Adam packed his briefcase and walked outside as Merissa with Neal followed him to his car.

She asked him, "Did Joe tell you about me?"

"Tell me what?" Adam loved playing dumb.

"About Neal and I being descended from a mermaid?"

"That is fascinating." Actually, she could have been reading addresses from the phone book, and Adam would have found that just as engaging, as he studied her finely chiseled face washed in full moonlight.

"You think I'm a fake taking advantage of Joe, don't you?" She asked.

Adam managed a neutral tone. "Being a mermaid is a bit out of the ordinary."

Merissa looked directly into his eyes. "Got a little time? I'd like to show you something."

Her brother looked back at the house. "Merissa, Joe?"

She looked up at the lights on the second floor. "Joe's going to bed, and he'll be asleep in a few minutes. I gave him some herbs in his tea to help him get rest." Merissa looked back at Adam. "Now, would you like to take a walk with me?" She took his hand to guide him. "The Mer people have much better night vision."

She led him behind the house, through a field, and

towards some shadowed saplings.

"You are a Mer?" Adam asked.

"Merrow. It's an Irish name. Of course, the Mer have no country citizenship and are all over the oceans."

"Both you and your brother are Mer?"

"Neither of us have tails, as you can see. Neal and I were both born with my mother's webbed fingers and toes, but unfortunately, the doctors removed the skin folds shortly after birth. Actually, Neal doesn't seem to have gotten as much of the genetic inheritance as I did. My brother hates to swim, he can only do it for an hour or so. His lungs aren't capable of breathing underwater."

Taking the subject seriously Adam asked, "There are no Mer men?"

She looked at him quizzically. "Where would the Mer babies have come from? Mers can interbreed with humans, but my mother, Neal and I were born without fish tails, although my mother had a brother born with the full tail, who stayed in the sea with my grandmother."

They walked on a worn dirt path, winding through a grove of dark trees while Adam just enjoyed holding this slender, but strong, woman's hand. Walking alongside her, he kept wishing her brother wasn't following so closely.

Adam came out to a marshy clearing on the edge of a good-sized lake. To his left, there was an old fishing pier, but Merissa just headed to the ledge of rocks overhanging the dark water. She stood in the moonlight, looking hungrily out over the lake, then without even seeming to think, she started stripping off her blouse and shorts, bra and panties, dropping them down on the rock.

Adam tried to control a very primitive reaction.

Merissa turned back to him, as she said, "Do you have a watch?"

"Watch?"

"Yes."

Not taking his eyes off her curvaceous body, he pulled back his sleeve. "Yes, and when push this, it lights up. I can do a stopwatch too."

"Time me." Saying that she swung around and dove into the black water and disappeared in a splash. Dark ripples were ringing out to the rocks sticking up from the water offshore.

Adam checked his watch, 10:36. He waited. 10:38. Normally holding your breath was one, maybe two minutes. Japanese Ama pearl divers, bred for generations, can do just eight minutes. The longest record he heard of was seventeen minutes. 10:40. Where the hell was she? Had she hit her head against a rock on the bottom? There were rocks sticking out of the water. Had she gotten tangled in some tree roots?

Adam started taking off his shoes. "She's down too long!"

"No!" Neal grabbed his arm. "Be patient. The lady's a mermaid. A true Mer!"

10:51. If Merissa was under there still, she was dead. He's have to use his cell phone to call 911 to get rescue to recover the body, and then explain why he stood there like a dummy while a woman drowned.

Suddenly, arching like a graceful dolphin, Merissa shot out of the water and dove back under, disappearing, and then shortly surfacing to roll on her back. With her breasts glistening in the moonlight, she expertly back-stroked in a long, lazy circle.

Neal was behind Adam. "Check your watch."

"10:59." Yhep. The lady was a fish, but a very, very warm blooded one.

Laughing with delight, Merissa swam back to the rock ledge, still staying in the water. "The water's fine," she whispered seductively to Adam.

He just stood there in amazement.

She pulled herself up and on to the rocks and Neal

moved beside her, primly handing his sister her blouse. Merissa slipped it on but ignored her brother's obvious disapproval.

Looking back into Adam's eyes, she said, "Neal, Joe shouldn't be alone so long. He's been coughing in his sleep a lot. Can you go back and listen for him? I want to talk with Adam for awhile."

Not looking happy, her brother left.

Adam sat down on the ledge beside Merissa, getting some of the water puddling off her on to his pants. She inclined her head and watched him. "You didn't seem to be shocked or surprised. Most people don't even believe mermaids exist."

"Since I've inherited my great uncle's law practice, I've seen some amazing sights."

"Can you tell me about them?"

"Privileged communication," he had to reply regretfully.

She smiled at him prettily. "What –say– if I was your wife?"

A jolt went through his body. "Well, if you were my wife you'd meet them when they came to my office in our house."

She looked out over the smooth lake reflecting the opal moon and dark willow trees. "Do you swim?"

"Yes."

"The water's really fine." She reached out, touching his face with a wet hand that was still warm, then leaning forward she kissed him on the mouth. "The Merrow think differently about a lot of things humans seem to have trouble with. We're a bit bolder." Now, with both hands, she urgently pulled at his shirt.

"Didn't you have enough?"

"Of swimming? Never."

Adam looked around fast seeing no house in sight. He stripped off his tie, shirt–all his clothes, dumping them on a rock.

Merissa was already in the water up to her breasts, and

her long hair floating around her. A sparkling path of fragmented moon reflections left a trail behind her.

Damn, that water was cold! The bottom under Adam's feet was an unpleasant, squishy muck, then they were in deeper water, Merissa put her arm around his neck, kissing him, pressing her full breasts against his naked chest. They rolled in the water, with Merissa playfully pulling him under and kissing him in a shower of bubbles. He had to kick them both up. "Honey!" he gasped. "I'm a human. I've got to breathe!"

She just laughed and started kissing him again.

When they climbed back on to the bank, Adam had enough of a workout, but Merissa was pulling him down on the moss. She wanted more than kisses, but Adam held back regretfully saying, "Hey, I don't have anything."

Merissa didn't understand. "Anything?"

"Protection. We don't want a baby the first time."

She giggled. "The Mer people are only fertile once a year. We pup in the Summer and mate in the Fall. June is not my time."

But it certainly was Adam's. Afterward, they helped to awkwardly dress each other and then headed back to the house. Adam insisted on seeing Merissa to the door with its yellow porch light still on. As she was concentrating on opening the sticking door, Adam snuck a cell phone photo of her, and before going in, she gave him a fast, goodbye kiss.

He had a long drive back to that strange Queen Anne house and law practice he had inherited from his Uncle Quentin. He'd grown to love its endless rooms filled with lightning gods and stuffed monkeys, but a woman like Merissa, what would she think of it? Maybe they could sell it and get something conventional? But Adam really didn't want to do that. Maybe he didn't have to sell. Merissa was a travel writer that had been around the world many times—maybe she would appreciate Adam's spook house?

His secretary, Wynoma, and the farming tenant lived in

the first two guest houses, but there was one house left, that log cabin on the lake that could be cleaned up for Merissa's brother. Of course, there was plenty of room in the main house, but Adam didn't want Neal living with them. The way Neal looked at his sister was possessive and positively creepy.

At his desk, Adam loaded his cell phone pictures on to his laptop. He only had that one precious photo of Merissa with her light hair still wet, streaming in twisting coils. He studied her profile, those thick lashes and her finely cut nose, so beautiful. Adam made her his desktop wallpaper and then hurried upstairs.

Searching in the back bedrooms, he found a box of stuff he cleaned out of his uncle's bureau. Adam sifted through engraved gold pocket watches, an oversized ruby pinkie ring, diamond cufflinks, there–he found it! A gold stick pin, with a large, ocean-blue stone. He held it up to the light examining a shining star sapphire which, when reset, would make a wondrous engagement ring for a true daughter of the sea.

Looking in another unused bedroom, he found a small, filigreed, gold frame picture of an elderly woman, dressed in the fashion of the 1900's. He took this downstairs. Enlarging and cropping Merissa's photo to her smooth, curving shoulders, he printed it and put her headshot in the frame for his bedroom bureau.

Now, if he was going to see Merissa, he'd have to become a regular at Joe Thomas' house so he would need something more than just a will rewrite. Talking to Joe about his client's abnormalities was out of the question, so Adam started searching the downstairs bookcases. It seemed Uncle Quentin had every one of Joseph Mitchell Thomas' cryptozoology works, in fact, Quentin seemed to have acquired every volume available on alleged mythical beings, from *Journey Around Pathia* in the first century to the current *Encyclopedia of Magical Creatures*. Adam selected several illuminated volumes of medieval bestiaries to share which would entitle Adam to at least two visits, and probably more.

Adam returned to Joe's house on Thursday with the draft will. When Gina opened the door for him, he asked, "Is Merissa here?"

Gina glared at him. "No. The pretty one is out shopping with her brother. Joe gives her money for clothes, and Joe says you bring the will that gives her everything. So she can kill him." Gina added bitterly.

"Do you know who the previous beneficiary was?"

"Probably me." Gina looked at him, with a sour face.

"So maybe that's why you dislike Merissa?"

"I tell Joe to leave it all to the church!"

That Adam had trouble believing. "You don't want money?"

"I want money, and I work hard for money, but I also know what happens. My mother takes care of an elderly lady, my mother diapered and fed her and shopped and scrubbed that house until it shined! When the old lady died, she left my mother her house."

"That was fair," said Adam.

"The old lady's relatives didn't think so. Relatives who never visited her, and never returned her letters, never called her, they were going to sue my mother in court. Claimed unfair...unwrong...."

"Undue influence," Adam supplied.

"They were going to put my mother in jail!"

"No judge would have."

"No judge, no trial, my mother just signs the papers their lawyer hands her. Money is nice but not what comes with it!" She stopped and then smiled saying harshly, "Joe's has cousins. They don't even thank him for the checks he sends at Christmas. When he had pneumonia, I called them, but they were too 'busy' to visit. When Joe goes, if your pretty lady inherits, those cousins will be after her!"

"Then she gets a good lawyer to fight them, which is

what your mother should have done!"

Mouth shut, Gina led him into the office where Joe was sitting, looking out the window. Adam sat down, noticing Joe's coloring seemed to have gotten worse.

"You have the will?" Joe asked sounding tired.

"Only a draft." Adam was hoping he could stretch it out to two or maybe more visits just so he could see Merissa. "You okay?"

"Feeling like shit this last month. I just keep getting weaker and weaker."

"See a doctor?"

"Can't go for every little thing! I've got a cold, and Merissa giving me herbs. Feel better right after I take 'em, but I'm getting old."

Adam started unpacking his briefcase. "My uncle had a lot of books, some that I thought you might be interested in seeing. He had all of yours."

"You bring them to be signed?"

"If you don't mind, maybe next time. These are different ones I could lend you. Medieval bestiaries. Some on werewolves. Vampires..."

Joe's eyes lit up, as he eagerly reached for the books. While he glanced through illustrated pages, Adam looked around the room. There were several framed, out-of-focused pictures of Bigfoot, a drawing of the Fuji mermaid, and an interesting press clipping photo of a cemetery, inset with the head of a tattooed man. Joe looked up and saw him studying that. "Since you are going to be my executor, that is where I want to be buried. In the family plot over in Doylestown with the rest of them."

"Who is the tattooed man?"

"Was my grandfather. He did P.T. Barum's circus, the freak show. He met and married my grandmother there when she was billed as 'the incredible rubber lady.' I told Merissa I was going to take her to see that cemetery someday...she'll go at my funeral, I guess." After the brief uplift of seeing Quentin's books, Joe was slumping back into his seat.

They went over the will draft, then got to talking about the probability of a Big Foot surviving in Florida's swamps.

When he heard Merissa's melodious voice in the hallway, Adam made his excuses to leave with Joe buried in one of Quentin's velum pages. As usual, brother Neal was hanging around, so Merissa handed her grocery bag to her brother to carry in and walked out to the car with Adam.

Adam commented slowly. "You know Joe really should see a doctor."

She sighed. "I've been trying to push him, but men are so stubborn!"

They had reached his car. He turned, trying not to look like an overeager high school student as he asked, "There's a Bar Association dinner Saturday, and I've got tickets for it. It's kinda boring..."

She turned those incredible green eyes on him and him alone. "Adam, nothing about your life is boring to me."

"I could pick you up. We have to be in St. Louis at 7:30."

She briefly looked back at the house, and then said, "No, I'll come by your place. I'd like to see your house. When should I be there?"

"How about five, and I can give you the tour?"

On Saturday, Merissa showed up, draped in a flowing white gown reminiscent of the Grecian goddess she resembled. She wore her blonde hair down with just a touch of beige lipstick for makeup. Proudly, he gave her a tour of his downstairs offices and the apartment upstairs. He was hoping her 'Mer' nature would bubble over into a quickie, but she just looked about, and then said, "We'll be late."

Seeing his old beat up pick-up truck, Merissa said, "Let's take my car." As they started walking back to her red Prius, Merissa stopped and reached down to a string of white and pink, bell-like flowers, climbing a tall stem. "Adam, when we get back, can I dig up some of these? I'm making a wildflower garden for Joe."

"No!" A resolute voice came from behind them.

Adam turned to see Wynoma staring at them. Merissa certainly didn't appear overawed by his tall six foot two secretary as she just walked right up to Wynoma saying, "This is Adam's property, isn't it?"

Adam intervened. "Yes, but Wynoma has one of the guest houses here, and we have a division of labor. I do the law, and she's in charge of the flowers."

Merissa looked about. "Foxglove is a perennial that grows wild. You have a lot of them here."

Wynoma stared at her. "And they will stay here."

Adam took Merissa's arm to steer her to the car. "Honey, we're running late."

As he guided her, Merissa asked him, in a raised voice, "Who is the owner of this property?"

While she drove to St. Louis, Adam leaned back, proudly anticipating the buzz when he walked in with the most striking woman there. A discordant thought intruded. "We'll be sitting with Judge Jeremiah tonight so it might be wise not to mention that your family descends from the Merrow. In their worldview, most of the Martin family tends to be very unimaginative."

Turning on the main road, Merissa just gave a musical laugh.

When they walked into the Bar Association Banquet, a gratified Adam felt everyone's eyes had turned to the woman on his arm. There were eight chairs at each table, and Adam steered Merissa over to a front one. She sat down gracefully beside his tall Uncle Jeremiah.

Sitting across from Merissa was Adam's aunt, Jererusila, almost as tall as her twin brother. Sitting next to Jerusie was her dapper, shorter husband, Herman, who couldn't take his eyes off of Merissa. Jereusila introduced the others at the table, and Adam watched Merissa greet them as if she were sojourning royalty. Adam never felt prouder, as Merissa turned her luminous smile on Jeremiah. "Which one of you is the judge?"

"We both are," Jereusila answered. "I'm Federal, and my brother is State court."

"Oh, that's fascinating," Merissa purred.

But as the evening wore on, Adam realized that the legendary Martin total recall could be very hard on the uninitiated. With smiles and pleasantry, Jere and Jerusie questioned Merissa as thoroughly as if she were on the witness stand. "Oh, you write for travel magazines? How many pieces have you done? Can a writer earn a living on that?"

Jere would establish where Merissa traveled and lived while--as if on a tag team--Jerusie would follow up, gently pointing out when Merissa contradicted herself over a minor point on her mother's early death, or the dates when she lived on Butler street. It was no surprise when before dessert Merissa said she was getting a bit of a headache. Adam was relieved to make their excuses and leave.

All in all, for a Martin family gathering, Adam didn't think it had gone badly, but out in the parking lot, Merissa seemed upset. "Your family didn't seem too impressed with me."

"Aunt Jerusie's jealous. Uncle Herman couldn't get his eyes off of you, and every other man in the room kept envying me."

"But to your family, I'm not a lawyer," she said sounding resentful. "I'm a freelance travel writer, and that doesn't seem to be much of a job in their eyes."

Adam tried to get her to laugh. "I'm a lawyer, and I don't seem to have much of a job in Uncle Jere's eyes either."

Merissa didn't crack a smile, as she sat down beside him in the car, suddenly realizing. "I left my handbag on the table and, Adam, I don't want to go in there again. Could you get it?"

"Sure."

Inside the band was still playing. Uncle Herman had gone up to the bar, and with the exception of Jeremiah and Jereusila, everyone else at their table had left.

Proudly, Adam walked over to his aunt. "What do you think of her? Isn't she great?"

A strained looking Jereusila didn't answer him, but instead, she turned to her equally glacial-blue eyed brother.

Jere looked at Adam. "I think Merissa is a walking lie. I don't know what she is lying about, but I know she is. Your aunt also thought there is something wrong with her."

Adam felt like he'd been doused with ice water. "She makes one mistake on what year she lived in Washington, and you two are ready to sentence her to prison? For what crime?"

Jereusila shook her head. "Adam, we can't tell you what's wrong, but we're both telling you our alarms are going off."

An angry Adam stared at them. "Maybe it's just because you don't think your shlep of a nephew is good enough to attract a woman like Merissa? If it were George or the eminent Franklin, you'd feel it was a fine match!"

Jeremiah commented acidly, "Can't you speak louder? The waiters in the kitchen can't hear you."

Wearily, Jereusila looked at Adam. "Both of us would love to see you with a beautiful, intelligent woman who truly adores you, but Jere and I have been on the bench a combined total of over thirty years. We know when someone is trying to pull the wool over. Adam, all we want is for you to go more slowly, think before you get yourself into anything lasting."

Furious, Adam picked up Merissa's evening bag. "Thanks for your support."

*   *   *

The next day, when Wynoma brought the newspapers into his

office, Adam looked up annoyed. "Why were you fighting with Merissa over a bunch of stupid weeds?"

"You like her."

"I love her."

"Love? You've known her how long?"

"I only had to take one look."

His dark secretary stared at him. Finally, Wynoma said, "Someday you will find even the most beautifully ripe apple with smooth, unblemished skin can be full of worms."

The phone rang, and Adam picked it up, glad Wynoma was leaving the room. It was Merissa's voice on the line, and she sounded stressed and afraid. "Adam, Joe's sicker. I'm so worried. He wants you to bring the new will so he can sign it. Please come... I just want to see you."

Adam printed out the will and copies. At Joe's, he met the doctor in the hallway. "I'm Joe's lawyer. How is he?"

The doctor shook his head. "I don't understand, all of a sudden his heart's racing."

"Shouldn't he be in the hospital?"

"Won't listen to me." The doctor again shook his head. "It comes and goes, but he seems to be stable right now."

Actually, his color looked a little better when Adam went into his bedroom. Still Joe's thin hands appeared so frail resting on the white linen sheet. Adam noted someone had put a bouquet of wildflowers in a vase by the bed, probably Merissa.

"Hey, maybe you should be in the hospital?" Adam suggested.

"Yeah, like I can afford that." Joe shook his head. "I want you to take your uncle's books back today."

Was he feeling that sick? Or did Joe realize what was going on between Adam and Merissa? "You've finished them?"

Joe ignored that. "Where's my will? I need to sign it."

"You should read it first. Maybe think over the

changes?"

Joe was fumbling as he reached for his reading glasses, so Adam got them for him and a pen. As Joe started to sign, he said, "You know the mermaid legends always speak of the songs of sirens? Compelling, unearthly voices that call out to sailors? Merissa told me that since Mer people don't have a written language, that they keep their history in songs taught to each generation. At night, Merissa sings her family genealogies to me...to help me sleep."

When Adam came downstairs, he packed up his uncle's books as Merissa watched him. "Do you want to stay for supper. I've made a stew in the crockpot?"

He wanted to, she seemed to be inviting him for more than just supper, but it just didn't feel right. "No, thank you. I've got some legal work that must be finished tonight." As he started to walk past, she kissed him briefly on the cheek. Why hadn't he thought to bring the tie clip stone to show her? But now was not the time.

He was still working on contracts when the phone rang late that night. It was Merissa saying brokenly, "Oh, Adam. He's gone."

"Joe?" Adam found himself not believing it.

"He started vomiting. I called his doctor. The doctor was with him, but couldn't do anything." Merissa was just reciting as if she couldn't believe it either. " The doctor said his heart just gave out."

Adam wanted to take her pain away. "It happens. What are you doing now?"

Merissa sighed, then said resolutely, "Neal and I are packing. We have to move on."

She was leaving? He couldn't let her do that! "No. No, you don't. I'm the executor of Joe's will. He left the house and his property to you."

Merissa sounded surprised. "Me? I mean he talked about that...but I thought that was just to get me and Neal to stay on so he could learn more about the Mer people. He's only known me a few months."

"In those months you've meant a lot to him." But more important to Adam now was what Merissa meant to him. "You mean a lot to me. I don't want you leaving–in fact, I want you to stay the rest of my life."

There was silence on the other end of the line, then from Merissa's sweet voice, he could picture her gentle smile. "Oh, Adam...a proposal over the phone during funeral arrangements? Your timing stinks!" She laughed softly. "Let's get Joe settled first. Can you call a funeral home? Joe wanted to be cremated. Maybe we could have a service afterward and scatter his ashes to the wind on Friday?"

Adam thought of the cemetery with Joe's circus grandparents and family. "Isn't there a family plot?"

"No, Joe was most definite on cremation, to recycle his body with the earth, and I agree with him. We Mer also go back to the sea–our bones are in the white foam that laces the beach sand. We'll have Joe cremated, and then have an urn service for his friends. Can you make the arrangements?"

"Yes," said Adam, but her voice sounded so bereft it pained him. "Honey, I'll come over."

"No." She hesitated then. "Not tonight. I just want to be alone."

After his call to the funeral home, Adam opened his desk drawer and took out the small velvet box that held Quentin's star sapphire stick pin. Should he show it to Merissa, or just have a ring made first? He'd already proposed. But tonight she sounded so down, no matter what she had said, he should go over there right now and comfort her.

But something stopped him, he kept thinking about that newspaper clipping on Joe's wall with his family plot.

*   *   *

The next morning, he got out that sapphire again. Merissa was all he'd ever wished for, his doubts about her were ridiculous. Adam even had jealous pangs when she was teasing with her brother. What the hell was a matter with him? Yet he found himself dialing the St. Louis prosecutors' office, asking for his cousin.

"So what's the early call for, Adam?" George's cheery voice boomed over the line.

"Just a procedural question. All deaths aren't autopsied, right?"

"Yhep. Way too expensive, so if there are some minor questions, we might only order a partial study, say a drug scan run or a brain check. Want to come over sometime and look at my book of forensic pictures? Got some neat ones."

Adam hesitated. "This is purely hypothetical..."

"Oh boy, it's gonna be one of those," George sighed theatrically. "How old was this non-existing person?"

"Eighty-three. He had been recovering from a stroke but was doing well."

"Usually at that age, there won't be an autopsy unless there was some kind of complication. Did he die in a hospital–possible malpractice? You chasing ambulances now, cousin?"

Adam didn't respond to George's attempt at humor. "He died at home."

"Was he under a doctor's care?"

"Yes."

"Did that doctor sign off on natural causes?"

"Yes...but the doctor commented that he had failed so suddenly the death was unexpected."

"You haven't given me many details, but I'd say if it were my call, eighty-three, with his doctor's sign off, there would be no autopsy."

It was an eighty-three-year-old man, a natural death, if Adam just shuts up now, he and Merissa could be together forever. Adam looked across the dark wood of his desk to the laptop screen-shot of his alluring mermaid siren. "A man, Joseph Mitchell Thomas died last night in Jefferson County. He's going to Braden's funeral home, and I'm the executor of the will. At his main heir's request, he is to be cremated for a memorial service this Friday. The heir stated that it was Joe's wishes, but that wasn't what he'd told me. I know Jefferson is out of your jurisdiction..."

George finished for him. "I have friends."

"There might be nothing—there's got to be nothing! But, George, I just have to know!"

"If this autopsy is done, what will they be looking for?"

Adam could hardly get it out. "Possible poisoning over a several month period. May have been some local plant, like foxglove—they also call it digitalis. It used to be compounded by herbalists as a heart stimulus."

"Okay. Let me get a paper to write these names down. You're executor so you can send me permission for the autopsy, that'll save some paperwork. You should notify the funeral home we're coming." When Adam didn't respond, his cousin said, "It's always better to know."

To add to the depressive aura of the Friday funeral, they had a storm for the southeast with whipping winds and pouring rain. Adam arrived at Braden's funeral home early to complete the death certificate and make payments arrangements for the estate. The rather embarrassed funeral director was wringing his hands. "This is highly unusual. The police came, and they removed the body for autopsy. They haven't returned it! Do you wish to cancel today's service?"

"No, if people come out in this weather, we might as well just get it over with. There wasn't going to be an open casket anyway since Joe was supposed to be cremated by now. There's a blonde lady, Ms. Merissa Grogan. She'll be expecting an urn with ashes. Could you make one up? Fill it with sand or something?" said Adam in an emotionless voice. "I'll tell her we'll wait for a sunny day to scatter Joe's ashes."

"This is highly unusual," the director repeated.

"The estate will pay for your extra duties." Adam thought about it. "About the autopsy, I don't want anything said about that, okay? It would depress the funeral atmosphere."

"If you wish."

The wind and driving rain seemed to be getting worse, but surprisingly about twelve of Joe's friends and neighbors showed up. Gina and her husband were sitting up front, ignoring Merissa and her brother. Even in black lace, Merissa looked so beautiful, Adam found himself relaxing, knowing his captivating mermaid would never have done anything to hurt Joe or anyone else.

After the service with the rain pounding steadily, Adam escorted Merissa to the car, holding his umbrella over her. He hoped they could go for lunch, but Merissa said she was tired, and needed to be alone. Of course, her brother sat in the passenger's seat giving Adam a small smile.

Feeling down, Adam headed home listening to the radio warning of continued rain and flooding. Shit, just what he needed. When he pulled past her house, he saw several of Wynoma's chickens fluttering in the fenced yard and getting beat up in the wind. Where was she? With the rain pelting him, Adam headed over to chase the stragglers into their coops. Most had sought shelter, but he wound up soaking his good suit and shoes, chasing a few bird-brains until he could latch their coop doors shut.

Cursing softly and wet to the skin, Adam started sprinting back to his house. He could see a silver car–a minivan parked in front? He didn't recognize it. Automatically he looked up to the porch. She was there, Merissa, knocking on his door. At the sight of her, joy spread through his body. "Hey." He called out, running up the wide porch steps.

Those beautiful sea green eyes turned on him. She was still dressed in that black lace and now reached out, hugging him as if her life depended on it. "Adam, why are you outside in this rain?"

"Why are you out driving in this storm without a coat?" He asked as he started opening the door. He had to detach himself from her, in order to pull the door against the wind.

Inside Merissa murmured, "We're dripping on your floor."

He moved closer to her, saying softly. "Maybe you should get out of your wet clothing and slip into my nice dry bed?"

She slipped from his hold. "No." Her face hardened with determination. "I have to leave and head up to Minnesota."

"North? No way! With the flooding, the old bridge may be out."

"Adam, my mother is ill. I need to leave immediately."

"I thought your mother passed away?"

She stopped for a beat, and then worriedly said, "Well, I call Cousin Florence my mom. Like your Grandmother, she's raised me when my mom passed away."

"You can't go tonight. Not in this weather!"

Through the cut glass sidelights by the front door, Adam could see someone was getting out of the minivan. It was Neal, her brother, he was running through the rain and up on to the porch.

Merissa just kept talking to Adam. "I need money to put her into the hospital. Can I get an advance on Joe's estate? Just a few hundred thousand?"

"Honey, we're not even in probate yet."

She looked at him with the pleading eyes. "I'll sign my share over to you. Can you advance me the money?"

The wind and rain swept in the foyer again as Neal opened the door and blew in.

"I don't have that kind of money," Adam said to Merissa.

"Could you get it from a bank? Maybe put your farm up

for collateral? It would just be temporary until we settle Joe's estate," she urged.

Surely she could see he couldn't do this. "No."

Merissa pressed herself against him, and he could see her hard nipples through her thin black blouse. "Do you have any cash in the house?" she asked.

"Maybe a few hundred bucks," Adam answered slowly.

"Oh, honey. Get it for me, please." She was so close. He could smell her oriental perfume and feel her warm hands through his wet shirt.

But Adam felt something else, that *knowing* feeling. "Where did you get that van?"

Neal was speaking in a mocking tone. "We stole it, honey. Now get the money for us, please!" Merissa's brother had a gun in his hand.

Adam looked at Merissa. Her polished perfection now looked more like chromed steel as he asked, "You stole the car?"

She smiled, saying lightly, "Had to. Somebody at the funeral home called, they wanted to tell me the police haven't finished their autopsy on Joe's body yet. Adam, there was an autopsy?"

He played dumb. "Was there? Why?"

Merissa still spoke melodiously. "The police were coming to Joe's front door when we ran out the back. I didn't even have time to grab a coat, but you'll lend me yours, won't you, Adam?" She ran her hand down his arms in mocking affection.

"Stop touching him, sweetheart!" Her brother was saying. "The game's over."

While Neal held the gun on Adam, Merissa got money from his desk, travel food, and left to get his coat. Would they leave Adam tied up or just kill him? Adam had no chance against a gun pointed at him by Neal, but he might have with Merissa. But when she came back, Merissa's transformation was into total stone coldness.

Neal said, "Go out to the car. I'll finish up here."

Merissa looked from Neal to Adam. "No, we may still need him. We don't know how close the police are."

After transferring the gun to Merissa, Neal tied Adam's hands in front of him with one of his own neckties, then they set him in the front seat, besides her, with Neal in the back pointing his gun at Adam's head. Into that black curtain of rain, Merissa started driving.

Adam could feel the car pulling with the wind, and he could see a kid's stuffed tiger on the floor. Well, maybe he could keep them talking. "Neal isn't your brother?"

"You figure that out all by yourself?" Came a mocking laugh from the back. "We were in the foster home together."

Adam started again. "You aren't a mermaid."

Now Merissa just laughed, but this time it wasn't musical.

Adam really wanted to know. "How did you do the mermaid bit? Staying underwater for twenty minutes?"

Merissa's voice sounded lower. "Liked that? Almost as good as the sex?" His mermaid turned her head a bit towards him, slowly running her pointed tongue over her lips as she laughed at him. "There was a breathing tank near the rocks, tied underwater. All I had to do was swim twenty feet and around the rock. The darkness hid the bubbles."

He had to keep her talking. "That's a long swim in totally black water."

"With my swimming, I should have made the Olympics," she bragged.

Neal laughed. "She washed out for interfering with a competitor."

There was a tree down ahead, and Merissa had to concentrate, driving a little off the road to get past it. The wind howled so much now, Adam had to raise his voice. "You don't have to run. Joe died naturally."

Neal just laughed again.

Adam still pushed. "We go back and pick up my car. Drive this van somewhere and dump it. I'm a lawyer, and I was raised knowing every judge on the bench. Honey, you probably aren't gonna be charged, but if you are, I can get you off. Think about it, if you stick around, we'll end up with Joe's entire estate! There are assets you don't know about!" Would she believe that?

Merissa's face looked like she was considering it, but she just said, "That jealous bitch housekeeper must have turned us in. She kept screaming that I was poisoning Joe."

"They can't get you on undue influence, and I'll testify he was in his right mind." Adam left out car theft and armed kidnaping. "But if you leave now, it'll look suspicious. Honey, don't do this!"

Merissa looked at him, the calculation on her face. Would she believe he was still so besotted with her that she could trust him? She thought about it, and then said, "If it is going bad, if it feels bad, it's time to get out, that's kept us ahead of the cops since we were teenagers."

Neal didn't sound happy. "We've got no money. This car is hot, and we've got to get rid of him. We should have taken his truck."

Merissa seemed to have other concerns. "What's behind us?"

Adam and Neal both craned their necks to see behind. The rain had actually stopped, but when the lightning flashed, Adam could see a white and black car with what might be a light bar on top.

She slowed a bit, trying to see in the mirror and Adam could just about smell her fear. Then ahead, she had to slam on the brakes. Reflective orange striped barriers were blocking the road. The old bridge had washed out.

"Get out!" Neal yelled to Adam. Since the rain had stopped, the clouds parted for a three-quarter moon, and they saw gray trees, gray grass, and a stygian black river, swollen way over its banks.

With his hands tied, it was hard to walk on the wet grass and slippery mud underfoot. Should Adam shout out to the cop? That would probably get them both shot. The cop was getting out, but he hadn't been running lights, and he seemed more interested in examining the bridge wash out.

Merissa led down to the rushing river, and Neal had Adam's arm, hiding the gun by painfully jamming the barrel into Adam's back as they marched down the river bank.

"What the hell are we going to do?" Neal growled.

Insanely, a part of Adam still wanted to protect her. "Merissa, the cop's probably running the stolen car's plates. Tell your boyfriend to throw his gun into the river and give yourselves up now. I won't say you kidnapped me. Don't talk to the cops, unless I'm with you!"

She looked at him, smiling sexily. "And what–screw a judge and twelve jurors? A true mermaid can get out of this situation." Merissa was kicking off her shoes, and shedding his jacket and her tight pencil skirt.

Her boyfriend yelled, "Are you crazy? We can't swim that!"

She looked at him, leaving her black lace blouse on, and walked into the overflow that now covered her ankles. "You can't. Goodbye, boys," she said sweetly.

At his plaintive, "You're leaving me?" Merissa just blew them both a kiss and dove into the inky, swirling water.

Neal aimed his gun at the woman in the water just as the cop yelled out. "Hey, you!"

The cop was coming down the bank, as Neal swung the gun towards him, but Adam used his tied hands to chop at Neal's gun arm.

"**He's got a gun!**" Adam yelled to the cop, kicking out at Neal and knocking him down. The gun was lost in the mud as the cop ran toward them, leaping on Neal.

Adam turned. Even in grayness, he could make out Merissa's blonde hair and strongly stroking arms. She was an incredibly powerful swimmer, now swimming diagonally with the current, trying to work herself across to the other side, and she was making it.

But Adam saw a light-colored chunk sticking out of the river–wreckage from the bridge? Adam saw it, but Merissa didn't until it was too late, and the powerful wash slammed her head against it.

She went under.

Adam looked for her to surface.

He stared for a long time, but he didn't see her head rise again.

André Had a Life Interest...

Mr. Quentin Martin is dead, and the property he stole from me must be returned," pronounced the blue-brocade vested and silk-suited Monsieur Barre.

"My uncle illegally took possession of your property?" asked Adam, as he studied the thin, nutmeg skinned man sitting in his law office. "I find that hard to believe."

"It is true."

"Sir, what property are we talking about?"

"André Duclair."

Adam was confused. "André's house? His money?"

"André Duclair himself. Now he farms your land. He must work on my plantation."

"André, the man? You want him returned? Sir, you are in Missouri. Are you aware of the Fourteenth Amendment to the United States Constitution?"

"It does not apply."

"In 1868, human slavery was outlawed. André is not my property, nor was he my uncle's, nor is he yours."

"Your Fourteenth Amendment only covers the living. André is not alive because he is a zombie."

Well, that certainly cleared up a lot of things for Adam. "Alive or dead, I am not returning anyone to you, understand?"

Barre stared at him, with large black, death eyes. "I have been denied too long! You will return him to me. Do it now, and you will suffer less!"

At a loss for words, Adam just sat there and stared back at him. Finally, Barre stood up, bowed mockingly to Adam, and walked out.

Adam followed to the porch, mainly to see the loathsome man out of his house, and he stood there watching as Barre's rented white Lincoln Towncar drove away. Then Adam stepped down from the porch and walked the dirt driveway past his house. Beyond the orchard the pasture rose up, so André's one story, board house couldn't really be seen from Adam's rambling Queen Anne unless someone looked out the attic windows.

Per Quentin's will, André had inherited a life interest in the cottage and a percentage share of the farm profits. As he walked, idly Adam pondered the point of the law: if a man is already dead, can he inherit a life interest? What did Adam know about zombies? They were raised from the dead to work, and they can't tolerate salt. Could they ever die again?

He looked over the farm stead's well-tended fields, a few cows, pigs, and goats, all set before the forest. Finally, he saw straight-backed André Duclair carrying two buckets of feed toward the pig pens. Adam knew he would have trouble hoisting one of those huge, overfilled buckets, but André carried them easily. He appeared to be a normal, wiry muscled man, creamed-coffee colored skinned, with short, frost-white hair.

Adam knew he could call out his name and that André would not respond. He had always found the man sort of mechanical, if you tried to say hello, André would just keep on doing whatever chore he did the day before and would do the next day. Somehow, as the seasons changed, Wynoma seemed to re-program him for the different tasks, but other than that André ignored the world around him.

Yhep, the only way to 'talk' to André Duclair was to get in front of him, block his path, and force him to listen to you. Jogging, Adam caught up with André and ran around, stopping just in front of him. Blocked, André just halted and stood there, his black eyes staring towards the horizon. He had a two day, gray stubble on his cheeks–he must shave sometimes, but André always looked to have two days' worth of stubble.

"André," Adam started. "A Monsieur Jacques Barre was here, and he wants you returned to him. Do you want that?"

No response.

Adam put more firmness into his voice. "André, speak to me, please!"

"No," André replied.

Did 'no' mean he didn't want to go back? Or 'no' he wouldn't speak? This attempt at a conversation was going to take up most of Adam's day. "You do not to want to return to work for Monsieur Barre?"

"No."

Adam gave up trying to figure out what 'no' meant. "Okay. He says you are a zombie?"

No response from André.

"How did you become a zombie?" Adam was really curious.

André's eyes did not change their unfocused stare, but for a moment, Adam thought he saw a flicker of emotion on the man's face, as in a softly French-accented voice, André recited, "Many years ago, I was a rich man. A bad man. I cheated my brothers of land. Got many girls with babies, but did nothing to pay for them. Many in the town hate me. One day, I go to Barre's house. While he talks with his overseer, I see a gold coin on his desk. I pick it up, to slip it into my pocket, and I fall down. They carry me home. My sisters cry, but I can not move.

"They put me in a coffin in the front parlor of my house. The next day, they carry me to the cemetery. Shut out the light with a wooden lid. I see all this, but I can not move or speak. I hear the earth clumping on the lid as they bury me.

"Long time later, Barre's men dig me up. Then I slave in his fields many years. Mr. Quentin sees me work, and he asks me to tell him how to grow the little herbs. One day, Barre tells me to go with Mr. Quentin on a ship. I come here."

"Do you like it here?" No answer. "Okay. Just keep working." Adam stepped out of his way, and André moved forward toward the pig pens.

When Adam got back to his office, Wynoma had just returned from the bank. He felt he should explain to his secretary. "While you were gone, a Monsieur Jacques Barre was here. He wants André Duclair returned to him."

Her dark face rarely showed emotion–well, judging by André scale–Wynoma was a roaring bonfire of response as she now spoke in measured terms. "Quentin took André in lieu of payment of a debt. Has Mr. Barre offered to reimburse you for that?"

"Didn't mention it."

"André does not wish to be returned to Barre."

"But Barre seems confident that I will return him?"

She hesitated. "Men like Barre are used to getting their way. You will just ignore him." She was gathering paperwork from inside her desk before she went out again.

"Wynoma, there should be a file on André in my Uncle's special cases. Could you pull it for me."

His secretary hesitated but didn't unlock her desk drawer with the file keys. "I'm late for the Resurrection Sisters, and they are expecting me to supervise the monthly financial accounting."

"Then just leave me the keys, and I'll pull it myself."

Wynoma looked at the back of the hallway as if she was weighing his case. Finally, she shook her head. "That is not a good idea."

A flash of resentment hit him. "I can't be trusted to open up my own file cabinet?"

"There are things in it that could be dangerous, things that I must check first before you search, when I return, I will get the file for you. Now, you should go pick up your life extension potion from Paracelsus." Saying that she prepared to head out.

Adam nodded and made a show of going to pick up his truck keys, then stood by his pickup until she was gone. Hurrying back to his office, he headed over to her desk. It was probably crafted by the same master cabinet maker who had created Adam's. Polished, dark wood with lots of drawers and arcane symbols carved deeply into the trim. Taller than standard, Quentin must have had it custom made for Wynoma's six foot two frame, Adam thought as he focused on the locks.

When he was a kid he had been fascinated by magicians, and his uncles had encouraged that interest saying, 'Being a good lawyer is like being a magician presenting theater. You stage a scene for the jury and judge, focusing their attention on what you want them to see, and distracting them from what you want hidden.' Uncle Jere and Uncle Herman bought him endless tricks at the magic store, including several versions of 'Houdini's handcuffs.'

To make his many escapes, Houdini always carried a lockpick, sometimes in his nose, sometimes he had to regurgitate it. Adam hadn't had a lockpick in years, so he finally had to cut some number ten wires, then bend the heavy metal. In the past, Adam had tried using those bent wires on the 'special cases' cabinet itself, but it seemed to have a more intricate lock than one would expect on just a file cabinet. In fact, the locks on Wynoma's desk must also be custom, as they seemed to be resisting all his best efforts.

With his Martin stubbornness kicking in, Adam tried double pick combinations. It gave him time to feel a tinge of guilt over picking his secretary's desk, but hell, this house, and her desk were all his property!

Finally, the last tumbler clicked, and Adam got the top drawer open. Inside were several sets of keys, and he looked for a flash of yellow, a bright canary feathered fetish that Wynoma had attached to the special files keys. Yes!

Feeling like Willie Sutton, Adam hurried down the back corridor to the tall, steel cabinet and this time he got it open. Now, the first time he'd seen Wynoma pull out the 'Resurrection Sisters' folders, Adam had seen a file labeled 'Poxcow, Wynoma.' Maybe reading it, he could find out a little more about his mysterious, pale-eyed, 'Cherokee' secretary.

The Poxcow file was no longer there. Shit.

He went back to the top drawer. Nothing on Barre, Jacques, but there was a file on Duclair, André. Adam lifted it out noting there was not much inside. He found a promissory note, from one Jacques Barre, regarding a gambling debt. Apparently, in Haiti, Quentin had won a skilled agricultural worker in a poker game. Which would be a perfectly legal transaction, if you ignored the fact that the winnings were a human slave.

Adam checked the document's date, June 22, 1860–hell, slaveholding was legally protected in Missouri in those days! There was a ship's passage ticket from Port-de-Paix for André Duclair. And something manila colored at the bottom which Adam fished out. A small, sealed envelope, with a notation in fade ink that Adam had to take it over to the light to read. In Quentin Martin's elegant copperplate script it read 'gift from J. Barre.'.

Adam pressed his fingers on the envelope. What was inside felt small, flat, round and heavy. He felt something else too, felt it in his mind: cold, sickening, and repelling. Like touching the inside of a crusted, rotting-out sewer pipe. Adam let the unopened envelope fall back into the file. Barre's gifts were like his presence, something that afterward made Adam feel like he needed a really long shower.

After closing up the files and returning the keys to Wynoma's desk, Adam drove to Paracelsus' chemist shop. He walked past the soda fountain and headed to the pharmacist's counter where the jovial Paracelsus was handing a plastic prescription vial to his customer. "And, Bill, tell your wife I said to take this at night mixed with one ounce..." Paracelsus looked at his client's face. "Make that **eight** ounces of red wine."

The man's face brightened considerably. "Thanks, doc."

The alchemist turned to Adam. "You're a bit early, that potion I'm brewing for you has not yet matured enough."

Great! Vastly relieved, Adam relaxed. "Can we talk

privately?"

Up in Paracelsus's apartment, the alchemist poured him a tawny-colored brandy as Adam explained. "Have you ever heard of a Jacques Barre? Probably some sort of Haitian witch doctor?"

"Bokor. A sorcerer," Paracelsus corrected, as he poured another brandy for himself. "Barre? Something from the past...a man your uncle disliked passionately. What is this in reference to?"

Adam wondered how to phrase this. "I know this person who may be a zombie..."

"André Duclair?" Paracelsus asked without surprise.

"Yes. Barre claims to be his owner, and he says returning André to him is simply a matter of property law."

Paracelsus frowned. "You can't do that."

"André doesn't seem to care much either way."

"Zombies really aren't capable of making choices, but returning André to the conditions he came from would be wrong. Your uncle always felt he should have done something more for André's brothers in Barre's serfdom."

"First this zombie business. How does it work?"

"In its purest form, a man or woman commits sins against the community. They are judged by a secret, high Vodou court, and if found guilty, they are condemned to a life of physical and mental slavery. But of course, those courts aren't supervised, and power corrupts. The head bokor's personal feuds and the estate of a prospective zombie all have relevance to the outcome."

"Is there a possibility of appeal or parole?"

"No." He shrugged. "Unless you count the total destruction of the zombie's body, by say fire."

"How do they create a zombie?"

"Each bokor seems to have had their own formula, but a couple of ingredients are crucial, a powerful neurotoxin derived from the pufferfish, and a dissociative drug, such as datura."

"They eat or drink it?"

"They could, but in the breeding season, the toxin of the pufferfish is incredibly powerful. The unfortunate victim just has to touch a tiny bit of zombie powder, and it will be absorbed by the skin on his fingers. Immediately it paralyzes the body, giving the appearance of death, without the stiffening of rigor mortis, so the family buries the victim alive."

Adam didn't understand. "But when you embalm a body..."

"Oh, my dear boy, when you drain the body of blood for embalming you kill the body. You can't make a zombie with the Missouri funeral industry. You need a more primitive area, backcountry Haiti, some areas of Africa, South America–places where a body is buried without embalming. Someplace where the high priest isn't questioned about who is working his fields because although not very bright, zombies are known to be excellent workers."

"This victim, he's still alive in the casket?"

"Yes. Often the lack of oxygen in the coffin will kill the higher functions of the brain. And just going through the horror of the process, of being conscious as you are being buried alive, must twist something in the mind."

Adam wondered how Paracelsus could recite that horror so indifferently. "How does the bokor know how much oxygen is in the casket? I mean they could dig him up and find he's smothered?"

Paracelsus shrugged his shoulders. "So? They bury him again and zombie powder someone else."

Adam was still looking for a loophole. "Is this a mental state that André could be awakened from?"

"Unfortunately, no. Zombism is more than just the deprivation of oxygen. With zombie powder, the Bokor steals his victim's soul, so André is now truly the walking dead."

"Do you know where I could learn more about how to

fight Barre?"

Paracelsus was sipping his brandy slowly to savor it. "You need a Sangoma. Actually, there is a good one in St. Louis, Princess Yaya. I buy supplies from her." Paracelsus grabbed an envelope and started scribbling. "I'll write you directions to her shop and, if you would be so kind, I'll also make a list of ingredients I need to be replenished."

Before he left, Adam studied Paracelsus' list and asked, "What do you do with eye of newt?"

The Princess' dock was outside of St. Louis, along the muddy Mississippi. At first, Adam stepped on to the old bleached wood planking, wondering if it would hold his weight, but despite its rotted appearance, the docking was surprisingly firm. He walked across to a faded, hand-painted sign, '*Princess Yaya–Herbalist,*' and behind it, there was a tall post mounted with a small, swinging, school type bell with a pull cord.

Looking over the edge, he could see moored alongside the dock was a long, enclosed river barge, decked with grayed planks. It had a narrow walkway along port and starboard sides, and a kind of truncated pyramid shaped cabin that ran its length. In the front, he saw a higher, windowed pilot house that looked empty, but he didn't see a name or registration number on the flattened bow. Adam pulled the rope, sending the bell ringing with a loud clanging. From the shore, frogs jumped into the water with a few plunks, but nothing else happened. So stepping high, he climbed over the bulwark onto the boat's decking experiencing that slightly uncomfortable bobbing under his feet.

He walked to stern and a large hatchway. There Adam knocked and heard something stir inside.

The hatch was opened by a dark figure, who retreated inwards. Uninvited Adam descended into the cargo area. Going from sunlight to hazy darkness temporarily blinded him, until his eyes adjusted, and he saw the only dusty light came from a row of diamond-shaped, glass cones set in the cabin's roof. He was in some sort of herbalist's shop, with cords hung down from the ceiling, tied around dried herbs and snake skins. The bulkheads were shelved and crammed with jars of pickled frogs, pigs feet, and a lot of things he couldn't recognize. And a few things he could and wished he hadn't.

The cabin had a low ceiling causing Adam to raise his hand to push back a wide bundle of upside down tobacco leaves, just to see the little woman before him, who he assumed was Princess Yaya. She had bright red hennaed hair and long, yellow skinny fingers, and the princess was dressed in a flowing caftan, that had wide bands of yellow and green with stylized elephants marching across them.

"Who be you, boy?"

"Adam Martin."

She spread her skinny fingers and reached out towards Adam, then stopped, as if she had hit an invisible barrier. Princess Yaya drew back. "Who sends you here?"

"Paracelsus."

"No!" She shook her head, stepped a bit back from him. "Someone else watches over you." The princess looked around and reached to a shelf beside her. Taking out a repurposed glass jam jar, she extracted something yellowish--a dried scorpion. She held it by its head, and this she reached out towards Adam, stinging tail first as if in some sort of test.

He stood still, as Princess Yaya moved closer, and then as he watched, the scorpion legs moved in her fingers. That dead thing was now alive. Feeling sweat break out on him, Adam forced himself to remain standing still.

"Why do you come to me?" The princess asked.

"A man, Jacques Barre..." Her confident look seemed to crumble when Adam said that name, but he continued, "Barre wants something from me that I can't give him."

Firming her mouth, she moved towards him again. Then stopped before she reached him, and the princess looked down at her hand. That 'live' scorpion seemed to have curled up like a dead spider. She pulled back her arm. "There is one near you–she protects you. Your mother?"

"My mother died when I was five."

"No. This woman is very alive. Strong. Tall."

"Aunt Jereusila?"

"Yes. Your auntie, in the moonlight she walks barefoot in the woods as she sings to the owls."

"That's not my Aunt Jereusila." Adam grinned lopsidedly.

Princess Yaya put her hand down looking sad. "This one is powerful, she can stop me because there are things I must not do. She is strong enough to kill one like Barre, but she will not because she will not act in time. You both are too civilized for an evil one like Jacques Barre, give him what he demands."

"I can't."

"Then he will kill your auntie first and then you."

"If he is such a bad man, why do not the other bokors run a court and turn him into a zombie?"

"Why do the mice not bell the cat?" She looked at him with bright eyes. "I will sell you zombie powder. You get him first!"

Adam pictured himself trying a 'preemptive self-defense from living-death-by-zombie- powder argument' on some court. Didn't work for him. "No. Is there something else that you have that might help?"

She peered about her shelves. "His weapon is putting the zombie powder where you will touch." The princess took out a squat baby food jar that barely held three ounces of a thick amber oil. "Rub this on your fingers and palms every day. If you touch it, the oil will block the death powder from reaching your blood. Clean your hands at night with tree alcohol before you sleep, your skin must be allowed to breathe again. I give it to you--for fifty dollars."

"What if I eat or smell the zombie powder?"

"Then Barra has another field hand," she said without concern.

"Uh, I'll buy the oil." He reached for his wallet. "Any tax?"

The princess smiled tightly. "Tax man don't come here no more."

Adam could guess why. "Paracelsus sent me with a list."

"I know Paracelsus long time." Her stone face did not change. "For him, cash only!"

It was dark when he got home, and Wynoma didn't answer the knocks on the door of her house. He walked to André's. Again, no answer, but through the window, Adam could see André sitting in a straight-backed chair, just staring forward, waiting for the sun to rise and work to begin.

A little discouraged, Adam headed back into his own house, no note from Wynoma, and nothing much on the answering machine, only two calls: Uncle Jeremiah was coming by Sunday to pick up him for fishing, and some nutcase wanted to sue the President of the United States on contingency. Feeling tired, he closed the office and walked upstairs to his apartment.

Sometime during the night, he awoke again. Restless, he just couldn't go back to sleep, and Adam found himself getting up and walking to the windows. A waxing moon lit the outside so he could see Wynoma's dark house in the distance. Should he have left her a note saying Barre would kill her first? Somehow Adam didn't think Wynoma would need to be told. With the moon so bright, was she out barefoot in the woods singing to the owls? He couldn't see André's house from his bedroom, but everything was quiet.

Yet one of those strong urges, that Madame Terri was always telling him to pay attention to was making him feel unsettled, antsy. He pulled on pants and shoes, starting to head downstairs, then stopped and went to the closet, picking out a 30-06 rifle. Adam checked to see that it was loaded. He didn't bring a flashlight.

It was bright enough to walk down the dirt road to André's house. As he walked, Adam smelled manure, heard cows lowing and something big moving about in the straw. André's house was dark as usual, and his barns were dark, and everything seemed normal. Hell, now Adam wanted to go back and get some sleep, but he just couldn't.

Adam didn't know how long he was standing in that moonlight until he heard it. Tires on gravel. Adam stepped deeper into the tree shadows. Coming down his farm's driveway was a car, a big car, going slowly in the moonlight with its head lights off, heading for Duclair's house. The car pulled up alongside him, and he could see two men in the front seats.

Lifting the rifle, Adam stepped out, boldly yelling. **"You're on private property!"**

The driver must have hit the head lights. Now, in the dashboard light, Adam could make out two dark men, looking at him surprised.

Before they could fully respond, a bright light flashed close, from the discharge of a shotgun. A warning shot! The driver swung his car around wide in the farmyard, hit a milk can, then gunned the engine as he shot back out of the driveway, taking some bushes with him.

Adam raised the rifle, but, hell, he couldn't shoot two men. Couldn't shoot them for taking a wrong turn, which they could claim, but he briefly considered shooting out the back tires, while noticing there was no back license plate light. But they were gone before he could make up his mind.

As he stood there, a silent walking Wynoma joined him, smelling of gunpowder.

"They were coming for André," Adam stated.

"I will take him to my house," she said in a flat voice.

"Then they will come for you. I've been to a sangoma in St. Louis who says if we don't give up André, Barre plans to kill you first and then me."

Looking up in the dark, he couldn't see much in that shadowed face, but when she spoke there was no fear. "You opened the special cases file cabinet when I told you not to."

Adam had no shame. "Yes, mam, it's my cabinet."

"You are a fool!" Saying that Wynoma turned abruptly and walked towards André's cottage.

The next morning Adam reviewed his strategy. Well, if he had one, he would have reviewed it. Paracelsus was coming today to pick up Princess Yaya's herbal order, and Adam might get him to temporarily hide André in his chemist shop, but he felt that the problem with Barre was coming to an end. Either way, Adam must prepare.

Taking Princess Yaya's sycamore smelling oily salve, Adam rubbed it thoroughly over his hands, then he slipped the small, flat jar into his suit jacket pocket. With some digging in still packed moving boxes in a back bedroom, Adam came up with his childhood coin collections. Books of silver dimes, buffalo nickels, a silver cartwheel from 1873, even some loose coins. He carried some of them down to his office, laying them out carefully on his desk as if he were working on his collection. He added a few files from his desk drawer as a good magician sets the scene and directs his audiences' attention.

André Duclair's thin file was already on his desk, where Wynoma must have placed it. Adam opened it up, the boat ticket was there, the gambling chit, but no sealed envelope with Barre's 'gift.'

Again he took out the Princess' small jelly jar of salve, and Adam methodically rubbed it over both his hands. Rubbing deep into the skin and along the knuckles folds–as if he life depended on it–and it did!

Finally, he walked into the parlor Wynoma used as her office and reception area. Placing André's file down on his secretary's desk, he asked, "Where is the envelope?"

She sat there, not looking at him, but Wynoma didn't try to lie. "I do not wish you to touch it."

"Paracelsus sent me to a Princess Yaya. She gave me a protective salve to cover my fingers."

Wynoma looked up at him, obviously conflicted. "If the zombie powder touches any of your skin and enters your blood, I may not be able to save you."

"Maybe after all these years, the stuff is harmless?"

She looked down at her desk. "No. I feel evil still lurks there."

"Where is the envelope?" he asked firmly.

"Your plan is to have Barre pick it up—why would he be so foolish?"

Having spent years at family dinners, listening to judges laugh over their dumbest defendants, Adam acidly commented, "*Nunquam MINORIS AESTIMO stoliditate unius incitato by auaricie.*"

"That is Latin for?"

"Never underestimate the stupidity of one spurred by greed." Adam's eyes had followed her eyes to the center of her desk. He moved beside Wynoma, and reaching around her, he slid open the central drawer and extracted the small envelope. "When Barre comes in, warn me first, and then show him into my office."

She sounded surprised. "You made an appointment with him?"

"No, but his men failed last night, and we still have what he wants, Jacques Barre will come to us." That Adam could be confident about.

Sitting back at his desk, Adam re-oiled his hands a third time with the protective gunk, and then he picked up the coin envelope between his fingers. What if Princess Yaya was just a charlatan? What if the ointment she sold him was a worthless placebo? He would be the next blank-eyed robot marching after

André.

Taking a deep breath, Adam gingerly opened the envelope and dropped its contents on to the blotting paper before him. It was beautiful. A coin, soft, butter gold, with a tinge of green age residue, that looked like an 1870s double eagle? He didn't dare pick it up to check the date. Using a disposable tissue, he pushed it across the desk blotter paper to be closer to the edge away from him. He'd have to get Paracelsus' help in cleaning up this office afterward.

Then Adam waited.

At ten a.m., Wynoma announced the arrival of Monsieur Barre.

Adam was ready when she ushered him in. Staying seated behind his desk, he didn't feel the need to go forward and shake Barre's hand which also would reveal his oiled fingers.

Jacques just sat down in the chair before Adam's desk. "I have come for my property."

In his best lawyer voice, Adam said, "There is some question concerning your ownership."

"There is no question. I made André a zombie, therefore, he is mine."

"Actually," while he looked at Barre, Adam began gathering up his silver dimes, stacking them in an unthinking fashion. "Mr. Barre, you owed my Uncle Quentin a considerable gambling wager." Absentmindedly, Adam stacked some other coins as he talked. "He took André Duclair as payment of such." As he looked about his desk, Adam careless picked up the gold coin in his right hand. "If you wish André returned, then you must be prepared to make good on that wager." He carelessly laid the gold coin aside, "with appropriate interest added due to inflation."

Jacques Barre bared his teeth in a predator's smile. "I pay you nothing."

"Actually, I have the original script of your gambling

debt." Looking down again, Adam reached out and again brushed the gold coin aside with his fingers, as he looked through several files on his desk. "André's file was here..." Then he remembered. "No, I left that file on my secretary's desk. Excuse me."

Adam got up, walked to his door, carefully opened it with his left hand, and shut it behind him as he walked to Wynoma's desk. She just sat there, looking back towards his office door.

They both waited.

Until they heard a heavy thump. Adam headed for his office, followed by Wynoma, being careful to use a handkerchief to open the door even if he was using his left hand.

Inside, Barre lay stretched out on the blue flowered, oriental carpet. His body must have fallen, just after Jacques reached over to pocket the gold coin from Adam's desk.

Wynoma moved to Barre, looking down. "There. It's in his fingers! It is still poisonous!"

Adam nodded. "Yhep. Well, that's kind of justice since it was his coin to start with...he tried to get my uncle with it?"

"Yes. But I intercepted it, and I told Quentin to destroy that coin! He didn't. Paracelsus must melt it down."

Adam really didn't want that. "That is a rare antique gold coin, couldn't we just wash off the zombie powder and keep it?"

"No!"

"Yeah, well, what do I do with Barre? Maybe I should call 911?"

"You must not call a doctor–they can not help him, and they might get some of the zombie powder on themselves."

"We've got to do something with him."

"He is a murderer, many times over. André will bury him back in the swamp."

Adam looked down. "Ethically, I'm a lot looser than

most lawyers, but even I'd have a bit of a problem allowing a man to be buried when I know that technically he is still alive."

Wynoma raised a cold eyebrow. It didn't look like it would bother her one bit.

"Okay. Watch him," Adam continued. "I'm going to call Paracelsus. Maybe he can come up with something when we clean up this office. And I've got to get Barre's car out of here."

*   *   *

That Sunday as promised, Uncle Jeremiah dropped by. They were loading Adam's fishing gear into the back of Jere's pickup when his uncle looked over toward the orchard to see two men carrying shovels, one slowly walking behind the other.

Oh, shit, Adam silently cursed. Three more minutes and they would have been out of there.

Jeremiah looked up. "That's André Duclair, your tenant farmer?

"Yes, sir."

"Planting in the orchard on a Sunday?"

"Great work ethic. Works sunrise to sunset, seven days a week."

"Who is that shuffling behind him?" demanded his uncle.

"The new guy–he's learning the fields."

"Learning from a dummy like André? Where did you dig this one up?"

Adam smiled. "You might say, he's kind of André's long lost brother."

Shotgun Wedding

"They were betrothed at birth?" asked Adam.

"Tasha was four years old then, and she still is the only child of Carroll Jadwiga. He was in a business war with the rival Silver Van lines that was turning into a bloody feud, so when Slavek Wenceslas's only son, Misha, was born, your Uncle Quentin convinced them to do a business merger based on the strength of a marriage when the two heirs came of age," explained his secretary.

Adam couldn't believe it as he looked through the thirty-page betrothal contract. "All this was a business merger?"

"Both van lines were claiming the same territory, but after your uncle persuaded them to set up the betrothal, Carroll's Wolf Moving merged with Slavek's Silver Line to form Silver Wolf Moving."

"Tasha's twenty-four, and Misha's nineteen, no he'll be twenty this month. How do the kids feel about this? "

"I doubt if anyone has ever asked them." His tall secretary leaned over with a pile of parchment scrolls. "You will base the new business and wedding contract you are writing on these."

"Are they U.S. citizens?"

"Yes, but they think of themselves as international–citizens of the world."

Adam picked up the first of many long pages, some dated from the eighteen hundreds. "These contracts are written in Latin."

"The Jadwigas are Romanian Gypsy, and Slavek Wenceslases are Bohemian if Gypsies are to have a country affiliation, but Latin is a language they both can read."

"Pretty educated gypsies."

Wynoma raised a disapproving eyebrow. "Just because

you are living a different lifestyle does not mean you are uneducated."

When they were kids, Aunt Jerusie had been a stickler for teaching all of them Latin, but if Adam was going to have to translate pages of legalese boilerplate, he'd have to buy a good Latin-English dictionary. Maybe a computer translation program? "If this ever has to go into court, the judge isn't going to be too happy."

"The Jadwigas and the Wencelases–they don't go to court, they handle serious disputes in their own sort of ritualistic manner."

Adam looked up at his looming secretary. "So my job is to write up a marriage contract that cements their business interests?"

"Adding the international component, so that the families can be satisfied with all the terms. They pay well, and both factions will be here to go over the draft document next Thursday. The signing and the wedding are set for the following full moon."

That Thursday, the Jadwigas were in his office first. Tall, white-haired Carroll, with rock-cliff like features, and bushy black eyebrows. Adam tried to guess his age, if he was one of Quentin's special clients he could be, like Paracelsus, several centuries old, but Adam just guessed late fifties. His wife Tasha's stepmother, Jessie-Mae, was an easy forty with a still voluptuous build and expensive tastes in clothing. That was pretty much all he saw after amber eyed Tasha walked into the room. Full breasts, slender hips, long, dark reddish hair, and a quiet, sad smile...

Jessie-Mae was badgering her husband in a voice going shrill as he ignored her. "Oh, honey, this is positively medieval! Using your daughter to bind up a business merger!"

Tasha lowered her eyes under Adam's open gaze.

Adam wasn't getting paid to probe this, but, "Miss Jadwiga, you understand that a betrothal contract signed by your parents when you were four is not executable in any court in the United States?"

Her smile looked a little sadder. "I have accepted the terms."

With her father glaring at him, Adam continued to press. "Have you even met Misha Wenceslas?"

"Three or four times," she admitted.

"Have you dated him?" Adam continued.

Her father interrupted. "She had agreed to the union. It is best for all!"

Wynoma was ushering in the Wenceslases, bushy, black-and-gray haired Slavek looked even more formidable than the glaring Carroll. Slavek's veiled wife, Versperah, said nothing and stood in the back of the room, even after Adam got up and brought her a chair.

The unhappiest looking person there was Misha Wenceslas, who was dressed in the passé black leather fad with steel chain trims. Slackly lounging in a chair, he didn't even as much as look at his gorgeous bride-to-be, and Adam unhappily noted, that although Tasha eyed Misha with evident distaste, that didn't seem to be stopping the proceedings.

Adam handed each family a copy of the marriage contract. "It's in Latin. Will you need an English translation?"

Slavek shook his head. "No."

Carroll looked back at Adam. "The marriage will take place on the full moon. The Wenceslases are from the West coast, and my family is from the East. My marriage to my first wife was completed in Quentin's woods. Would you object to Tasha's marriage being consecrated on your property?"

"No." No more than Adam objected entirely to this mockery of a marriage. "You're welcome to marry here, but my house is better than the woods, it'll be more comfortable. How many people are you expecting?" He asked Carroll.

"Just my wife and daughter. Slavek?"

"My brother, Salveg, so it is the four of us and maybe

Oleg and some of the younger cousins. Misha wants his supporters."

"Ten-fifteen people. Would you like to have the wedding here in my parlor? You could bring a buffet for the dining room?" Adam offered.

Carroll didn't even seem to think about it. "No, under the moon. Wynoma knows where. Now, we must read this, if you do not mind."

"Misha, take the women outside," ordered Slavek firmly.

Jessie-Mae followed the Wenceslases, loudly complaining. "You want a wedding in the woods at midnight? That seems kind of creepy..."

Slavek and Carroll just ignored her, as both fathers and business partners settled in Adam's leather chairs to read their contract copies. Not seeming to be involved with the biggest commitment of her life, Tasha just walked out on to the porch, taking the opposite direction from her stepmother, mother-in-law-to-be and her depressed intended.

Adam should have remained available for questions, but he found himself following Tasha. She had walked along his wrap around porch to stand, gloomily staring out at the blossoming apple orchard. Adam studied her face with its neat, chiseled slightly slanted eyebrows, and attractively slanting amber eyes, with their thick, dark-red lashes. It didn't look like she was wearing any makeup, she didn't need to. In spite of being only as tall as Adam, this woman could have been a supermodel. Disturbed by the obvious mismatch he had to ask, "Why are you allowing this?"

She seemed to be shocked to see him there. "It is... tradition."

"Traditions can be changed. This is Missouri, not Transylvania!"

She smiled. "We come from Romania, or at least my grandparents did."

"But marrying a man–he didn't even meet your eyes in there! Surely you've dated some other guys that were much better than him?"

"I do not date. I work in the business, and I like the moving business. I am very good at it! When my father and Slavek are gone, I will run Silver Wolf Van lines. We are going international."

"What about Misha?"

She shrugged delicate shoulders. "He will spend the profits playing with his friends."

"Maybe by the time your fathers are gone, he may not feel that way. His mother obviously doesn't have any say in anything. And if you've never been with other men..."

"I am betrothed to Misha."

"Is your father holding you against your will?" That was a matter of the law Adam could do something about.

She turned those light, amber eyes to deeply look in his blue ones. "Oh, no, he wishes me to be happy. But I must marry one of my own kind. There are not too many of us around, and Misha isn't so bad. It's just he's become Americanized, so he's having more trouble with the arranged marriage than I am, but it'll all work out."

She reached out and put a warm, slender hand on his. Adam felt a thrill going through his entire body.

Her father found them on the porch, with a suspicious look on his face when he saw them standing together. "We want a section concerning each party's responsibilities concerning EU safety requirements. You add this, but the rest is acceptable." Carroll glared at Adam, but Tasha only moved between them and took her father's arm. Even as she tried to lead him away, her father still glared at Adam. "You fix the papers like my notes, before the wedding! We must leave now."

The Jadwiga parents had arrived in a shiny, black, monstrous sized F450 pick-up truck, while the Wenceslas parents drove a silver, equally as big Dodge Ram 3500. First, the Wencelases left, and then they were followed by Misha gunning his wide-white striped hooded maroon cobra.

Tasha seemed to linger, getting something out of her trunk and making a phone call. Her father had been driving out, but he stopped, turning off his engine, pointedly waiting for her to precede him. Finally, after looking shyly up at Adam on the porch, Tasha determinedly got into her low slung, silver Jaguar, and she pulled out with her grim father following.

His dark secretary joined Adam on the porch. "This is their way. You must accept it."

"It seems so unfair." Adam looked back at Wynoma. "If they don't want to marry in the house, maybe she could marry in front of the orchard? It'll look pretty, with the snowy apple blossoms, and I could make a vine wedding bower for her."

"No." Wynoma shook her head. "Your uncle had some Druid clients, who built a rough granite temple up in the pines before the cliff drop off."

Adam couldn't believe it. "Druids in Missouri?"

"He used to let them worship here until there were problems."

"What kind of problems?"

"They were having difficulties in getting virgins willing to volunteer for sacrifice. Finally, they kidnapped some barmaid, and Quentin could not allow that."

Adam nodded. "Yeah, being a party to kidnaping sacrificial victims, that could get messy. Where is this Druid temple?"

Following Wynoma's directions, Adam climbed up what was apparently a well-used game trail to the highest point on the property, and he came out of the white pines to a semi-circular, open-air temple made of rough, granite columns. Just before the cliff drops off lay a ten-foot horizontal slab, with a drain carved round it, Adam didn't want to think what that was for. Here, the enchanting Tasha would be joined in wedlock to that imbecilic Misha.

Adam kicked a rock in frustration. When he was a kid, Uncle Jeremiah had patiently explained the law and its relationship to society: lawyers and judges didn't make the laws, their duty was to make it all work. Although the law miscarries sometimes and some poor slobs get screwed, on the whole society is better for laws and contracts and codified traditions.

Not wanting to go back and work on the marriage contract again, Adam found himself pulling up some of the bigger weeds. Maybe he could haul two big pots of flowers up here to decorate that altar thingy, Tasha deserved something that at least looked as beautiful and perfect as she was.

On the Tuesday before the full moon, Adam opened a cream colored, heavy paper envelope finding it to be a gold embossed invitation requesting the presence of *Adam Martin, Esquire's* attendance at the Jadwiga-Wenceslas wedding. He didn't want to go, but there was a handwritten note scripted in purple ink. '*Adam, please come as my friend, Tasha.*' Even her handwriting was airy and elegant.

What wedding present do you get for people who can buy and sell the world? He'd like to give Tasha something nice, something that would make her remember him. Adam picked out two of his uncle's heavy, silver candlesticks, nice antiques, but if the Jadwigas were from the special client files, perhaps silver wasn't the greatest of ideas. Maybe he could find something in glass–did his uncle have any antique Tiffany vases?

On the Friday before the wedding, Adam was sleeping upstairs when the doorbell down at the front entrance rang. When Adam poked his head out of the window above he saw Slavek Wenceslas' monster truck parked in his front of his house, and beyond the porch, he could see Slavek and another man, who could be his double, waiting impatiently below. Adam pulled on a shirt and some jeans and headed down.

Out on the porch, Slavek introduced Adam to his brother, Salveg, as he explained why they were there. "My son, Misha, he wants a bachelor's party. He wants to go out and run with his cousins one last time before he marries, but he gets caught. My brother, he thinks you can get Misha out?"

"Maybe." Adam nodded. He'd need real suit pants if he were appearing in court. "Did they get him on DWI?"

"What? No. No Car. No driving. Yes, he drinks, then he runs, and does a little wild stuff. The Jadwigas, they must not hear of this foolishness, they do not like publicity!"

"Wild stuff–rape, robbery?" Adam asked.

"He gets hungry. Maybe takes some birds and kills them to eat."

It sickened Adam. Misha was marrying the most beautiful woman in the world, and he was nothing more than an animal torturer! But Adam was a Martin. He was this stinking kid's lawyer, and he had to get him bailed out. "What precinct is he at?"

"Precinct?" Salveg looked puzzled.

"Police station. Where are they holding him?" Adam asked.

Salveg sighed. "He's not under arrest. His cousins tells us they were out running, and Misha he gets hungry. He wiggles under a fence, so Oleg goes with him. They break into a cage. Lots excitement as the fowls fly about. The owners, they come. Oleg runs, but Misha, he's been drinking too much. They catch him with a net and lock him in a storage room."

Adam was shocked. "That's illegal! We can get them on unlawful restraint! You can't hold someone–well temporarily maybe--but then they've got to call the cops. But maybe we can get this cleared up before the cops show."

In his own car, Adam followed the Wenceslases down 64, into St. Louis, across town to Lindell Boulevard, then they parked in the St. Louis Zoo's lot. With a sinking feeling, Adam followed the Wenceslas brothers to a ticket booth. Adam should have questioned Wynoma more on why the Wenceslases was in Quentin's special client files. Salvek paid the entrance fee for the three of them.

Inside Slavek and Salveg raised their noses high and smelled the wind. All Adam could smell was popcorn and animal urine, but finally, the Wenceslases seemed to scent something familiar, leading Adam on a pathway to the left. Adam followed them to a chain link cage. Inside a sick looking, black furred wolf listlessly drank water from a metal pan. By the pained way he moved, that wolf looked like he had one hell of a hangover.

Slavek glared through the bars at his son. "You got caught–**before** your marriage!"

Misha, the werewolf, put his tail between his legs and kind of huddled against the back of the cage, as Slavek yelled at him in some nasty sounding language.

With the father shaking a clenching his fist and berating his errant son, Adam got a flashback to sessions with his Uncle Jeremiah. This wasn't getting them anywhere! Adam put a restraining hand on Slavek's arm. "Why don't you and your brother go over there on that bench and let me talk to Misha."

From the side, Salveg took his brother's other arm. "That's a good idea."

Talk to a wolf? Adam asked Salveg, "Will he be able to understand me?"

Misha's uncle answered thoughtfully. "By smell, he will know if you lie, or you are hostile, but I do not think he will understand commands or words like we talk now."

Adam looked at the wolf. "Can't he turn himself back?"

Father and uncle looked at each other, and then at Misha. "It should have happened already."

Adam had a horrible thought. "Sunrise–shouldn't he have had to turn back human or turn to dust?"

Salveg looked at Adam as if he was a fool. "Don't listen to that movie crap!" His uncle looked back to Misha. "But it is really hard to maintain the consciousness state needed to prolong a transformation, I don't know how he's doing it..."

A grim Slavek stated, "He cannot change in front of these humans!"

"Right. We've got to get him out of here." Adam moved to the gate looking at the heavy chain and shiny, new padlock. Could he pick it? Did the Wenceslas have bolt cutters in their truck? But then they would have to walk a wolf past the guarded entrance gates, and from the way Misha was cowering in that cage, Adam had a distinct feeling Tasha's betrothed didn't want to be rescued. Adam found a zoo guard who took him to Dr. MacClusky, Director of Mammals. As they walked back to Misha's cage Adam said professionally, "Dr. MacClusky, I'm Adam Martin, an attorney at law. My client's pet wolf seems to be locked up in your cage."

"Wild animals should not be restrained as domesticated pets," said the doctor with a superior tone.

"You have him locked in your cage," Adam pointed out.

"Our holding that wolf is an entirely different situation. This zoo is pioneering methods of induced estrous and the artificial insemination breeding of wolves, in an effort to save rare specimens on the verge of extinction. That wolf is a Canis Lycaon, a rare variation of Grey Wolf. Perhaps a survival of the thought-to-be-extinct Black Red Wolf, a species that must be bred to be preserved."

Slavek and Salveg were wisely just standing by, listening but not saying anything, letting Adam take point. "That's great, but not with this wolf. He's the property of my clients--actually of their client. The animal was being transported on the Silver Wolf Van lines and seemed to have escaped."

The director did not look happy at the thought of losing his prize. "Can you prove that?"

"Yes, sir." Adam turned to Slavek and Salveg. "Slavek, you have the van transportation papers for the wolf with you, right?"

Slavek looked blank, but his brother, Salveg, jumped right in. "I leave 'em in the van." He looked to Slavek. "Sorry, boss."

Slavek caught on, bellowing, "You losa the wolf. Now you losa the shipping bill! What'ya lose next–your head?'

Adam cut this off. "But Salveg, you can get them–the papers." He looked directly at Salveg. "The transportation order for one black wolf being transported from Oregon to Louisiana."

"Yeah," said Salveg. "Silver Wolf Van line has an office a couple of blocks away. I'll getta the papers." He hurried off, pulling out his cell phone.

Dr. MacClusky was very, very unhappy seeing his new prize exhibition trotting away. "Black wolves are endangered, and it would be illegal for a private party to possess one."

"It's perfectly legal." Adam pointed to Misha. "Ruff Ruff there has been raised by a rescue group since he was orphaned as a pup. Unfortunately, he's totally acclaimed to humans and could never go back in the wild."

The zoo official was getting red in the face. "This wolf belongs in a structured setting where he and his species can be studied and protected! In fact, we plan to breed him. That Texas gray wolf in the corner cage seems interested."

Adam looked at the brown, yellow, and black she-wolf with her ears perked up, and thought his wife-to-be, Tasha, might not be too happy about that, but he just said to Dr. MacClusky, "Breed him. That's a great idea. I'll pass it along to the owner, but right now this wolf is private property and in shipment with my clients."

MacClusky seemed to be weighing his options. "There were two wolves. The other one got away, the police are looking for him now."

"Two?" The second wolf must have been Oleg. "My client doesn't have two wolves, I don't think." Adam looked to

Slavek, and then back to MacClusky. "Did you get the second wolf on your security cameras?"

"It was too dark," said frustrated MacClusky.

That's good thought Adam, as Slavek boomed. "Just one wolf inna the truck."

Adam clarified, "Tell the police they can stop looking for a second wolf."

But the zoo official wasn't finished. "Your wolf killed and ate our rare yellow-crested, spoon-billed heron!"

"He ate it--raw?" Adam looked to the Misha, who lowered his head in shame.

MacClusky sounded aggrieved. "What do you think? Wolves microwave their dinners?"

The heron eating thing made Adam's empty stomach sickly contract, but he just said, "Since the Silver Wolf Van Line was responsible for accidentally losing our wolf, my client will reimburse the zoo for all reasonable expenses. If we just discuss this now, I'm sure we can reach an equitable settlement and send Ruff Ruff back on his journey."

The 'paperwork' Salveg brought back really looked good. A ripped off, pink copy of a multiple bill of lading, a receipt of the Louisiana client's payment, and even a photostat of the wolf's vaccination papers with a coffee cup ring staining it. Adam would have to remember Salveg the next time he had to fake some official legal documents fast.

MacClusky was definitely unhappy, but at five p.m., a really dejected Misha was being pole prodded into a traveling cage and then loaded in the back of one of his father's vans while Slavek wrote a hefty check to the St. Louis zoo.

The next morning, Adam hauled two huge buckets of white apple blossom sprays up to the stone altar, trying to make it look not so bad. When he came back, he decided to take another cold shower, the second today. He wanted to call Tasha just talk to her, but he only had her father's number. Instead, he decided to go out running. He was coming back, sweaty and tired, when he passed Wynoma's cottage, and saw her outside, using a big chisel with a steel hammer to slam away at something metallic.

Adam went over. His secretary was chopping up what looked like an antique, black tarnished, ornamental plate with a Tutor shipping scene.

Wynoma gave him a sharp look. "You keep thinking of that girl!"

"She deserves better."

"Tasha has made her choice." Wynoma slammed down the hammer, chipping off another small piece.

Adam didn't understand. "That plate looks neat. With all that black tarnish, it might be solid silver."

Wynoma just gave him a sour expression. "You run—I break up plates."

He took another shower and looked through his closet for something to wear to Tasha's wedding.

That night at ten p.m., the Judwigas truck came, followed by Tasha's Jaguar. Jessie-Mae was in a cream-colored suit, carrying two garment bags, and she hurried over to Adam on his lighted porch. "Can we change in your house?"

"Of course." Realizing he hadn't straightened up his apartment, he showed them to a large bathroom off the downstairs hall.

Tasha looked as if she was going to say something to him, but Jessie-Mae was hustling her away. "Hurry, honey."

Carroll Jadwiga looked very uncomfortable in a midnight-blue tuxedo custom fit to his massive shoulders and barrel chest. He glared at Adam. "My daughter has asked you to her wedding, but I know what you are thinking! You don't cause trouble for our deal!"

Even looking up at the formidable man, Adam still answered sarcastically, "No, I wouldn't do anything that would interrupt dumping your daughter to facilitate Silver Wolf's international expansion."

Fury crossed Carroll's face, and Adam realized that if Carroll was a werewolf like Misha, he was going to get killed. From behind him, Tasha called out. "Pappa! We have to climb the hill and be there before the Wenceslases get there. It is the tradition!"

As she and her stepmother stood in the lights of his foyer, Adam could see Jessie-Mae dressed in a filmy pink mother-of-the-bride formal. She was fussing over Tasha' long hair, not that anything needed to be done to the lustrous, loose curls of red.

Adam's Tasha wore a close fitted red leather bodice, over a red peasant blouse and long red satin skirt. There were elaborate black-bead and silver-thread embroidery all over the wedding outfit, and Adam realized the embroidery designs repeated the phases of the moon.

For a moment, Adam let himself fantasize that the white orchid bouquet Tasha carried was for their wedding, and he found himself just smiling at her. "You look beautiful."

Seeing that, her father roughly barked. "We are late!"

After getting a flashlight for Jessie-Mae, Adam followed them as they started up the hill under the full moon, with everyone ignoring Jessie-Mae's prattling. "This is all wrong! The bride is supposed to come last, with the groom waiting for her at the altar! She is the final person so all the guests can concentrate on her! Not that we have anybody watching this travesty of a wedding..."

Adam realized that a tall figure followed them. Was Wynoma invited or did she just come? And where the hell was the official who would perform this miserable, mockery of a bridal ceremony?

They need not have hurried. When they reached the temple drenched in white moonlight, Tasha walked to Adam's flower pots, touched the fragrant apple blossoms with her fingertips, and looked back at him with a shy, sweet smile. "Thank you."

Her father moved menacingly closer to Adam, and Tasha walked off to stand by herself, looking down at the ravine, as she held her small wedding bouquet of white orchids. They were all there before ten thirty. The 'midnight' wedding was to be at eleven, but Adam checked his watch at eleven twelve, eleven twenty, and eleven forty-one, no official showed, no in-laws, and no groom. From Adam's standpoint, it was looking pretty good.

He walked over to a glowering Carroll, who was getting a continual earful from Jessie-Mae. "Your daughter should have had a wedding at the Hyatt! With hundreds of guests! What about all your business friends–we've gone to all their weddings! They're not invited to your daughter's? It'll look like we're ashamed of Tasha!"

Adam gently interrupted. "Excuse, me, Mrs. Jadwiga, I'd just like to talk over some business to your husband." It was obvious that Carroll was furious, but even he could see that his wife walking away was a good thing.

When she reached to Tasha, Adam spoke quietly to Carroll, "My uncle arranged the betrothal to stop you guys feuding, but you know, I don't think Quentin ever planned for Tasha and Misha to actually marry. You and Slavek have been working together successfully for two decades. So the kids don't join in blood, but you guys can still make a binding contract for Silver Wolf Van lines to go international."

Carroll glared down at him. "There are things you do not understand."

"Maybe I do. I'm Quentin's nephew, and I have his records, so I know why you think a marriage partner might be difficult to find, but..."

With a look bordering on cold hatred, Carroll stared down at Adam. "My daughter wishes this joining!"

"Tasha wishes to please you, and she wishes to advance Silver Wolf Van Lines internationally. You are letting Tasha sacrifice herself for your company when that isn't necessary! If she marries Misha, is your daughter going to wear a veil and be silent like her mother-in-law? Is she going to stand back like an obedient wife, while Misha parties and runs the company into the ground?"

Carroll actually looked like he might be thinking it over. Unfortunately there were sounds of boots on the pathway below them.

Veiled Versperah came first on the arm of her brother-in-law, Salveg. Then four young males followed, looking a little embarrassed, they must be Oleg and the other cousins Adam guessed. Finally came Salvek, leading Misha-the-wolf on a rope.

Adam hurried to Salveg. "He can't turn back?"

Misha's uncle shrugged. "Like a guy with a shy bladder, he can't. After he's married, he should be okay."

Adam looked at Tasha. In the moonlight, she was biting her lip and looking at Jessie-Mae who was loudly asking. "Where is Misha?"

Slavek hurried over to Carroll and Jessie-Mae. "Misha's sick, but according to our customs, the wolf here," he pointed to Misha, "can stand in for him."

Jessie-Mae looked from Slavek to Carroll. **"What?"**

Carroll looked at his daughter, and Tasha sadly nodded her assent. Carroll turned to his wife. "This is a Romanian custom. Good luck for the wedding couple. Salveg, he marries Tasha to the wolf."

"She's marrying a big dog? This is your custom?!" Screamed Jessie-Mae as she ripped off her corsage.

"Jessie!" Carroll started strong, but his little wife cut him off.

"Tasha's been my daughter since she was four years old! I'm **not** letting her marriage be turned into a circus with wild animal acts!"

With everyone's attention on the fighting Jadwigas, Misha saw his chance and pulled the rope free from his father, bounding off into the woods.

Slavek was loudly cursing, Salveg hurried to his side, reminding his brother. "There are *others* watching!"

Before her father could reach out to her, Tasha threw her bouquet over into the ravine and ran in the opposite direction from what Misha had taken.

Adam hurried over to both fathers. "This wedding is off! At least for tonight! I want you both to come into my office tomorrow. We have to make a separate, binding contract for Silver Wolf's international business after that is settled, then we can talk with your kids and find out what's going to happen going forward. Okay?"

Slavek started to object, but his brother interrupted. "Yes! Take the business out of the wedding! This we do, Slavek, you talk to the lawyer tomorrow!"

A shamed Slavek turned to a glowering Carroll. "The Wenceslases mean no offense to your fine daughter, my son, he is ...sick."

Carroll nodded. "No is insult taken." Then he took a furious Jessie-Mae's hand to help her down the trail. She was near tears. "We can't leave! Tasha's off in the woods. She could break her neck in that ravine!"

Adam soothed her. "She's probably embarrassed. My secretary and I will find her. You guys just go home, and she'll be okay."

Carroll Jadwiga looked like he wanted to kill Adam, but with his crying wife on his arm, he just left.

Adam's first impulse was to run into the woods after Tasha, but that might get them both plunging off the cliff. He turned to his tall secretary. "Wynoma, I have to find her."

"This is not good."

He couldn't see his secretary's face with her standing in the shadows. "If you won't help me, I'll go myself!"

Finally, she started after Tasha with Adam following. Wynoma seemed to walk almost silently through the pine needles and darkness, but following her, Adam found himself crunching pinecones, tripping on roots, and getting hit in the face with branches. He was totally lost and didn't know what path Wynoma could be following, but finally, she stopped before a clearing's edge. Adam could hear river water rushing in the ravine beyond, and they both could hear Tasha's almost animal like sobbing.

Adam put up his hand to Wynoma. "I want to talk to her alone."

"You know what she is?"

"Yes."

"In transformative state–like a wolf--she could kill you, no matter how much she regretted it later."

Adam didn't care. "I'm going to talk to her."

"Talk, yes. You do anything more, her father will smell it and will rip you apart!"

"She's twenty-three, over the age of consent."

"Her kind lives by his laws."

That was a consideration, but ahead Adam could hear Tasha's uncontrollable sobbing. "Wynoma, please leave us."

Not looking too happy, Wynoma said, "If you return alone, keep the moon at your right shoulder as you climb. You will pick up the trail down from the temple, but you must remember Tasha is still promised to another!" Saying that Wynoma left. The branches didn't even seem to sway after her passage.

A rock slipped under his foot making racket, but Adam need not have worried about Tasha bolting off again, he found her lost in misery. Even blubbering away under pale moonlight Adam thought she still looked lovely.

He walked over and put a hand on her shoulder.

Wide-eyed, Tasha looked up at him.

"It's okay. I'm your lawyer—actually, I'm your father's lawyer–which is a good thing, then we don't have to worry about the ethics of a lawyer-client relationship, so maybe we could just talk as friends."

She spoke robotically. "I must marry Misha."

"Why? He doesn't exactly seem thrilled by the idea. Right now, he's running through my woods trying to keep from marrying you, and I don't think there is going to be much left of him if your father catches him. Or his father."

She looked forlorn.

"Misha should be overjoyed at the prospect of marrying you because any man in his right mind would be!"

"But he's not a man. And he'd rather stay a wolf than come to my bed." She dissolved back into tears.

"So he's a hairy idiot! You should be happy he's not marrying you!"

"They will force him," she said miserably.

"Are they forcing you? Because legally I can stop that!"

"They do not force me, but I don't want to be alone, and Misha is one of my kind." She looked directly into Adam's eyes, hers shining with tears. "You can't know."

"Your stepmother, she's human isn't she?"

"Yes." Tasha turned dismissive. "But Jessie-Mae is totally clueless. She thinks my father goes out at night on the full moons to pray to some Romania god."

"But they have had a happy marriage, haven't they?"

"Over nineteen years. But I wish a mate, who knows what I am, and one that understands me."

"A human might understand."

"My father did not want more of a family with Jessie-Mae. I want children."

"Jessie-Mae and your father can't produce children?"

"They might have been able to, others have. But Jessie-May had tied her tubes before she met my father."

This might be going his way. "Then you and I could..."

She sounded frustrated at his thickness. "Adam, as a mere human, you couldn't even survive seeing me transform!"

"See you become a werewolf? Bet I could."

"You will go mad if you watch me!" There was anger,

almost hatred in her face as she kicked off her shoes. Tasha began to pull off her leather bodice and ripped wedding skirt, throwing the elaborately embroidered satin to the ground. Stamping on it with her naked foot, as she stood in her white silk slip.

"Try me," Adam said.

"You can't..."

"Try me!"

She stared at him for a moment. Then she must have made some sort of decision, as Tasha began removing the rest of her clothes until she stood there naked in the moonlight. Breasts upturned with a strong, slender body, Adam wanted to touch her, caress her. Brunette haired Misha had turned into a black furred wolf, would the fiery-haired Tasha turn into a red wolf?

Looking like she hated him, Tasha sank down on her knees. Putting her two hands flat down on the mossy rocks before her, she closed her eyes and lowered her head in concentration.

Adam heard only the busy sounds of the woods peepers and the distant river.

Nothing, and then Adam saw a pinpoint of light, then several intense, tiny, bright burning lights. Starting at her shoulders, head, hands, then all over her. Tiny pinpoints of light that shined all along her whole body. The pinpoints grew brighter and then moved, seeming to rearrange themselves in some predetermined pattern, forming paws, tail, and fur.

Where Tasha's head and arms had once been, there was now pointed ears, a muzzle, and front paws. Adam was looking in the moonlight at a light-colored wolf, probably red, not as big as Misha but perhaps more muscular. A vicious looking wolf that now curled back its muzzle, barring deadly fangs, as Tasha began to growl deeply.

Adam found himself unable to move. He just stood there, knowing this creature was going to rip his throat out, but he was still fascinated by her beauty. A beauty that undoubtedly had to kill any human who saw her transform.

With her fangs and claws, he didn't have a chance of fighting Tasha off and paralyzed with fear, he couldn't move, but years of family court training kicked in. With a positive attitude, he could talk his way out of this, so he forced a tone of contempt. "That's it? My Uncle Jeremiah's Labrador, Lucifer, growls more viciously at me when I get near his food dish."

The wild wolf stopped growling. She just stood there staring at him.

He forced a confident smile. With his face in shadows, could she even see it? "Yeah. Transformation. It isn't everyday stuff, but it isn't something that is going to strike a human dead just seeing it. Sorry about that."

Giving an almost whimper, the she-wolf ran off into the darkly shadowed woods.

"Tasha!" Adam needed to talk with her. Needed her.

But she was gone.

He was alone.

Adam could stay by her clothing. He walked over and picked up the satin skirt, with its heavy embroidery, and he smelled sweet lilac. Tasha might come back for it, but she had left her street clothes in her car. He searched Tasha's ceremonial clothing, no pockets so no keys. Her jaguar was still parked in his driveway, probably unlocked with the keys inside. She would have to go back for it, even if she drove home naked.

Adam left her clothing into the clearing, then tried to find his way back. Yeah, Wynoma's 'keep the moon on your shoulder' didn't work so well when thick pine boughs above him kept blacking out the sky. Yet he managed to scramble and scrape himself back to the granite rocked temple clearing were the wedding was to have taken place.

In the distance, he could hear two wolves giving long, lonely howls, but not from the direction Tasha had taken. Slavek and Salveg must still be trying to corral the cowardly Misha?

Thank god Uncle Quentin had built his house so far from prying eyes and ears.

It took more falls and some false starts on dead-end trails before Adam could pick up the right pathway down to the clearing around his house. Carroll Jadwiga's truck was gone, and by now all the vehicles of the Wencelas clan were gone. Just Tasha's silver Jaguar was still parked in the lot.

Feeling a little like a sneak thief, Adam pulled open the driver's door. He felt around the driver's seat, behind the visor, under the passenger seat, until he finally found a set of keys. Yeah, Tasha would have to come back for them, so he slipped inside her car to wait.

At dawn, she did come back as a woman, dressed in her ruined wedding finery that was now covered in muddy pine needles. Tasha opened the driver's door to find a sleeping Adam curled up in her car.

He awoke with a start, stretching. "Hey, lady..."

She raised her head and crinkled her nose disdainfully. "You peed on my car."

"Not on it! Just over there in the bushes. I was afraid if I went back into the house, you might come back and leave before I got a chance to talk to you."

"Get out, please," she ordered coldly.

"Hey, are you honor bound to kill me because I saw you transform?"

"I should have."

"My Uncle Quentin knew your father and his partners were werewolves."

"If you say so."

"Look, if you marry Misha, it should only be after you dated around a bit, and see what the other guys or wolves have to offer. Is Misha the only eligible werewolf you know?"

"He has cousins, and there are the European families."

"Oleg was looking at you kinda of hungry like."

She sounded surprised. "He's never said anything."

"Maybe between your father and Slavek, he was afraid."

Tasha seemed to think about it. "I think Misha really likes my younger cousin, Luna."

"But?"

"She's not inheriting the van lines," she said in a resigned manner.

"You know I've scheduled a talk with your father and Slavek. There are a lot of ways of cementing business relationships that don't entail sacrificing the next generation." He got out of the car and stood next to her.

Tasha looked deeply into his eyes. "Misha would not marry me. Adam, do you wish me? You can't lie to me—I will smell it."

Adam looked back into those amber eyes and just felt himself melting. She reached out, and they started to passionately kiss.

"Undress me," she said.

Adam looked at the cold, wet grassed ground. It would be so much more comfortable if they went upstairs to his apartment and soft bed, but he was afraid that if they slowed down, she would change her mind. He started pulling off her wedding bodice while she pulled at his pants.

His offices and the farmhouses were out of sight of the road, but if Wynoma looked out her windows or her father drove back, they'd be seen. It didn't matter. They were down on the hard ground, rolling on the dewy grass.

Finding Tasha a virgin, he tried to go slower, but she was like an animal, wanting more and more of him.

The sun was well up before they were dressing again when her father's massive truck pulled into the driveway.

Nostrils flaring, Carroll stared at his daughter to Adam. "He ruined you!"

"Papa, please. Don't do this! I want him alive." Tasha was begging. "Let us talk!"

"Mr. Jadwiga—you want me to marry her?" Adam

babbled. "I'll be happy to! Today! My uncle's a judge–Jere could marry us!"

Adam was facing Carroll on the left, with Tasha to his right. Even she seemed to stay out of her father's range and be afraid of Carroll as he stripped off his clothing. God, if Tasha at five foot nine inches transformed into that big a wolf, what a monster Carroll was going to be. Adam tried again, "Mr. Jadwiga, your daughter is of legal age to make her own decisions..."

"Papa, I want him. Adam is mine! Don't do this!" Tasha pleaded desperately as she is pulling off her wedding outfit.

Her father bent over, his long hairy arms reaching the grass, and what humanity that had been in Carroll Jadwiga's face was rapidly draining from it. He was slipping into a vicious, ravaging beast before Adam's eyes. Should Adam run? He didn't figure he'd get far. He looked to Tasha, who was terrified and helpless, but as her father dropped to position to transform she did also.

In his mad transformation, would Carroll kill both Adam and his own daughter? Adam screamed, "Run, Tasha!"

The two werewolves ignored him.

But from behind Adam, came a firm and resolute voice. "You will do as your daughter says! You will leave here! Listen to her wishes and think before you come back!"

Both Tasha and Carroll were looking behind and slightly to the left side of Adam. He turned and saw a grim-faced Wynoma. In both hands, she balanced the substantial weight of Quentin's double-barreled .577 elephant gun. With her right index finger on the two triggers, she coldly informed Carroll. "You will leave now!"

Tasha looked anxiously at her father. He looked from Wynoma to Tasha, and then to Adam. His black eyes glinted in anger at Adam, but finally, he looked back at the gun and the uncompromising woman holding it.

They all held their breaths, and then Carroll straightened

his back and stood up again. Tasha, visibly relieved, was also rising.

Carroll looked at his daughter, his voice is gruff but not unkind. "I will listen, but we will not talk here."

His red-haired beauty nodded and gave a fast, relieved smile to Adam as she started pulling on her clothes. "It will be all right."

Dressed she went to her car, as Carroll got back in his truck.

Staying in his position, Adam felt like his knees were too weak to walk. Yhep, society needs laws, law theories, and law in practice, but sometimes--even Uncle Jeremiah would have had to admit--the winning argument may require judicious use of a double-barreled elephant gun, loaded with fragments from a silver platter.

Our Last Day of Embers

Mors venit avis alae nigra! Or 'death comes on the wings of blackbirds!' Adam Martin had that fragment of Latin in mind, as he returned from his early morning run. Crows were in the trees, hundreds of them. A massive flying force of inky-feathered combatants squawking threats from the large pines near Wynoma's cottage, while the opposing feathered legions perched in the twin oaks in front of his Queen Anne house. They did this crow war early every Spring, but this was June nineteenth?

Wearing a plaid shirt and jeans, Wynoma stood in the gardens around her house, her black hair was bound up in her usual bun above her head, making her seem even taller. It was early, so his law secretary hadn't changed into her usual uniform of white buttoned shirt and long black skirt. As he watched, Wynoma raised her bent arm up high, and a wild crow alighted on it. With her other hand, she fed him something. Raw flesh from those chickens she endlessly raised?

Adam started to walk over to her when he heard heavy tires crunching gravel on his dirt driveway. His late uncle's mansion was a quarter of a mile from a rural road and well screened by forest, so they didn't get many visitors. Who'd be coming here this early? Maybe a new client driving a truck?

A huge silver tour bus pulled around the bend, and hundreds of crows rose almost as one, flying off in every direction. In that sudden silence after their departure, the tour bus's diesel engine seemed even louder. No, the greater noise was coming from a second bus. It must have once been a school bus, but now the yellow was also painted with huge, blackbirds. Both buses just picked a piece of his lawn and parked across the drive from the other.

Adam wiped his forehead and walked over to the silver one. The former tour company's name had been sanded off its sides. With a hiss, the door folded back, and Adam saw a really muscled, dark-haired guy sitting in the driver's seat. He was young, with high cheeks, and his long, black hair was tied in a ponytail with a rawhide thong. Adam thought he saw a flash of lighter eyes, but the driver only looked ahead, then looked to look back into the bus, he was looking anywhere but at Adam.

Coming down the aisle was a smiling, curvy blonde. "Hello," she said in a low, seductive voice. "You're out early." On her neck, she wore a thunderbird beaded collar, and above her low cut, tight jeans, she wore a short, fringed leather vest that had been made to be worn over something like a blouse or bra but wasn't.

Adam smiled appreciatively but politely pointed out, "Miss, this is not a restaurant or a hotel. Actually, it's private property."

Her smile lost some of its confidence, and then she looked to the back of the bus. Adam couldn't see much through the black-glass passengers' windows, but he had the impression that there were only a few more people on board. Across the drive, through the clear glass of the ex-school bus, he saw a light-haired male driver, two or three large males, and two females, with the rear of the bus curtained off in a dark, yellow-starred fabric.

Suddenly, the blonde pulled back and slid into the front seat to make room, and the driver sat at attention, as a tall, muscular male filled the front. Of course, Adam was looking up at him, but this guy must be six foot five or more. He had raven black hair, reddish skin, and true Native American features, except for his pale, almost white irises. Now he started down at Adam with a look of contempt.

"As I was explaining, this is not a rest stop," Adam started in a friendly tone.

The man ignored that, demanding arrogantly, "Where is Wynoma Poxcow?"

Wynoma? Adam automatically looked beyond the buses to her two-story house, as his secretary was sedately walking towards them.

Following Adam's eyes in a predatory fashion, this male saw her and climbed down from his bus. He wore a faded, blue-velvet Navajo shirt, cargo pants, and around his thick, muscular neck hung necklaces of polished stone beads. He stood on the ground, not walking to her, forcing Wynoma to come to him.

"Dear sister." He smiled, showing a full set of yellowed teeth with wolf-like canines.

Wynoma reached them, stopping just out of range of this guy's mighty arms. She said nothing, just crossed her arms over her chest.

"Is this your brother?" Adam asked.

She still said nothing. The male turned again to Adam. "She never mentioned me? I'm Tsoai Poxcow, and I've come to visit my sister for awhile." As an afterthought, he added in a demanding tone. "You are?"

"Adam Martin, Quentin Martin's great-nephew and the owner of this property." It would have been polite to put out his hand to shake, but Adam found he didn't want to touch this arrogant male. He pointedly looked at the two buses. "How long do you plan to stay?"

Again Tsoai ignored him, looking at his sister. "Soon, my time comes!" It was less of a statement than some sort of avowal.

Wynoma still said nothing.

Adam had sixteen rooms in the three-floored main house, Wynoma had her two-story farmstead, there was also the tenant farmer's cottage, and one other empty guest cabin on the property over by the lake. Should he offer shelter to this motley looking tribe? Adam looked at Wynoma.

She had an unreadable, stone face as usual, but no, he could sense--anger. A rage that was as white-hot as it was helpless.

Tsoai looked back to his driver. "Josh, we'll be here for awhile." Then with a sneering smile to his sister, Tsoai climbed back into the bus, as his driver hissed the door closed right in Adam's face.

Saying nothing to Adam, Wynoma walked back to her house.

Adam did the short jog to his porch, got himself a coffee from the kitchen, then came out again, and watched as this ragged clan set up a couple of pop-up tents for the propane stoves and tables. Not just planning to picnic, they then set up five tents of khaki green that looked like surplus officers tents from WWII.

He didn't feel like offering a hook up to his outside water faucet, but that didn't seem to matter when two of the males unrolled a double hose extension. With Adam standing there, they hooked up to his outdoor water line without bothering to ask permission. Wynoma's porch would have been slightly closer, but they seemed to be staying away from her.

Adam saw Tsoai and five strong looking males. Five with black hair, one with light golden hair, all six had strong Indian features. Thinking if anything showed up missing, he might need to provide the police with some sort of descriptions, Adam went upstairs and got out his long-distance lens. From his bedroom window, he started photographing each of his uninvited guests and their bus license plates.

When Adam clicked the first snapshot, Wynoma's brother was facing away from him, but Tsoai instantly turned, staring upwards and focusing directly on the window Adam stood behind. At that distance, even with the long range lens, Adam had trouble making his visitors out but, apparently, like his alleged sister, Tsoai Poxcow had phenomenal hearing.

Feeling like a peeping Tom, Adam lowered his camera. Then had to remind himself that this was his property, and he would photograph what ever or whoever he wished. And if Tsoai didn't like it, maybe he might just pack up his bus gypsies and leave.

The next morning, it seemed most of the camp chores

were being done by the seven or eight women. While the men all seemed Native American, Adam noted that bus ladies came in all skin colors and flavors: Oriental, Black, American Indian, and Scandinavian Blonde, all young and shapely. Each one seemed to be waiting for Tsoai to put his great arm around them and draw them close, which he obligingly did for Adam's camera, a la Manson clan style.

Adam returned to his law office downstairs. The phone was ringing unanswered, for the first time during business hours since he took over, Wynoma was not at her desk off the foyer to the start the morning. He answered the phone. "The law firm of Adam Martin."

"Adam?"

That lovely, soft voice instantly gave him an alluring vision of cascading, dark-red hair and honey colored eyes. "Tasha?"

"I just wanted to call you, it's been awhile." She sounded happier than he had ever heard her.

"How are things going?" Was Tasha marrying that boob from her arranged marriage? Was she finding others of her own kind, as Adam had advised her to while wanting to cut his tongue out?

"Things are very good. Pappa and the Wenceslases are working well with the new company set-up you arranged, and Misha is courting my cousin, Luna."

Adam laughed. "She'll probably be too much for him."

Tasha joined in laughing, and then said a bit shyly, "We'll be buying new vans for Silver Wolf soon. I'll be in St. Louis for the trade show."

She'd be coming? "Do you need a lawyer? I mean, just as counsel or something?"

"I thought you decided I shouldn't be a client if we were going to be...friends."

"Yeah, I'm your father's lawyer. Not yours."

"But I'll need an escort to the banquet. Silver Wolf

would pay for your time?"

"No! No pay. I'll do it for free." He was delighted. "When are you coming in? I'll take you to dinner the first night, no, I'll pick you up at the airport."

"June twenty-third."

That soon? "How long are you staying?"

"I have the hotel room for a week. Maybe I'll stay longer."

"Want to stay at my house? It would save money."

She hesitated, then said, "Maybe after the show, I'd like that. I'll e-mail you my itinerary."

There was one big problem. "Tasha, is your father going to know about this?"

She hesitated, and then said, "He is not pleased that you are not of our kind, but Papa's sorry he tried to kill you..."

Okay, so they were making progress. Adam rang off feeling like the world was his, Tasha was coming to stay with him! But what the hell was he going to do with the cult day-camp on his front lawn?

On his evening run past Wynoma's cottage, Adam heard sounds. Not really voices, more animalistic growls of anger or pain. Those sounds suddenly ceased, as he stepped on to her front porch. Before he could knock, the door opened inwardly, and Wynoma stood there. Her face impassive as usual, but to Adam's anger, he saw a darker patch on her high cheek as if she had been slapped--hard!

Wynoma didn't invite him in. In fact, she was blocking his entrance, but Adam just gave her a big smile saying, "Desperately need to use your bathroom."

She still stood blocking his way, but her massive brother had come up from behind. If he had caused the bruise on her cheek, he got the worst of it with bleeding claw marks down the side of his face.

Tsoai smiled as he said, "Wynoma, let your little friend in."

She looked back at Adam but didn't move.

Tsoai continued, "My sister was just bleeding her chickens. You know that we drink the blood, don't you?"

Adam faked a casual smile. "Yes, that gives Wynoma her nutrients and leaves plenty of chicken meat for me." Well truthfully, he hadn't known, but he did now.

Reluctantly, Wynoma backed away from the door, letting Adam walk in.

Ignoring Adam, Tsoai turned to sister. "The Day of Embers approaches..."

"As it does every year." She looked at Adam. "There's a bathroom behind the kitchen."

Since Tsoai made no move to unblock the hallway, Adam just changed direction and went through the wide arch to the left parlor. Adam realized he'd never been in this house before. There were no carpets, just wide, age polished oak floorboards, and a small spinning wheel in the front room, with a ball of black wool on the spindle. Also, there were few well-stuffed chairs, that looked like they were cast off from another residence, standing opposite a large rocking chair. And in the corner was set a thick, twisted branch. Actually, a tree trunk with a heavy base, that Adam realized must have been set up for a perch.

But a perch for what? It would have supported an eagle, easily or possibly two or three eagles. Maybe it was for a monkey? The window next to it was fully open, with its cream lace curtains blowing inwards. Had her pet escaped?

As he expected, the front parlor gave way to an open pair of pocket doors leading to the dining room where a ten person table was set with cream-colored damask linen and two, tall wine glasses. Adam found a side door through the butler's pantry that led into a large, country kitchen.

The house was probably built in the 1840's. The refrigerator and stove looked like they came from the 1950's, but the sink faucet looked the early 1900s. From his uncle, Wynoma had inherited tenancy for life, but technically, Adam owned this house. Was he responsible for keeping the fixtures up to date? Didn't he pay her enough to afford something better? What did he pay her–she kept the books.

He should at least pretend to go to the bathroom. Adam looked around and found a back door off the kitchen. It opened to a dark hallway, which was a rough boarded shed addition to the house. He opened the unpainted door to his left, and the high, dusty windows let in slanting sunlight. Adam realized he was in some sort of woodshed. One speckled brown hen, no three, had been tied by their legs and hung upside down with their feathered wings flopped to their sides.

First, their heads had been chopped off, Adam could see the ax and heads on the stump block by the outer door. These chickens were hung from the rafters so their blood could drip into three pails, as he stood there the scarlet drops made little splashing noises. Now, Adam had been around farms all his life, and he well knew how those bacon and beef burgers got to his table, but still, walking into this shed kind of made him feel a little sick or maybe ashamed as if he was violating a close friend's privacy.

Retreating back to the hallway, he found the bathroom with its cheery white daisies on yellow background tiles. He flushed the toilet to make it sound good, then he splashed cold water on his face. The clean yellow towels had been hand embroidered with more yellow-centered daisies that Adam had often seen Wynoma working on while she waited for the phone to ring in his office. There was a plastic yellow flower on the soap hand-pump and a white wooden medicine cabinet with a silvered mirror crackled from age. As he dried his hands, Adam listened. If brother and sister had been fighting, they weren't going to do it in front of him. Good.

When Adam came out, Wynoma was in her kitchen lifting slightly scorched, round loaves of homemade buttermilk bread out of her stove. One of those he expected would appear in his kitchen for breakfast tomorrow.

"Where is your brother?"

"Tsoai left." Her voice held its usual neutral tone.

"He hit you." It was wasn't a question, just a statement of fact.

"Mr. Martin," she started formally...

He was getting angry. "I'm not 'Mister' anything to you! Since I've inherited Quentin's law practice, you've treated me more like a backward nephew than a boss. It's 'Adam,' and I may be your employer, but I also think I'm the closest thing you've got to a friend. If your brother is hurting you, I'm not letting him, and his cult groupies stay here!"

She looked at him, her face showing heavy lines of strain. "You will make him leave?" Her voice didn't sound like she believed that possible.

"Yes, mam." He continued, with the strength of generations of Martins who had been lawyers and judges. "I will ask him politely to leave. If he doesn't, this my land and this is your house. I will get an order of eviction from the courts. I will show it to him, and if he doesn't go, I will call the cops. If Missouri cops can't enforce a court order, they'll get the National Guard out here. If necessary, my Aunt's a Federal judge. Tsoai and his friends will go!"

Wynoma stared at him, with that impassive face. "My brother once was attacked by a bear, with only his bare hands Tsoai broke its neck."

She waited for that ghastly image to sink in. Adam thought about it, and then calmly questioned, "Did it have black fur or white?"

Wynoma seemed perplexed. "Why does that matter?"

"White fur indicates a polar bear, which is a lot stronger and more vicious than a smaller black bear."

"It was a Grizzly," she finished grimly.

Adam gave her that. "They're mean...but I'd match my uncle Judge Jeremiah and his growling Labradors against your brother and his bully boys any day."

She looked tired. "Please don't bring the authorities into this."

"Can you get him to leave?"

"My brother is dying," she said quietly.

That took Adam back. "A doctor..."

"Couldn't help him."

"Paracelsus? For a few centuries old alchemist, he's still a pretty good pharmacist?"

"My brother will outlive you, even with Paracelsus' potions extending your life. Tsoai may outlive me, but my brother needs to be worshiped, he feeds on it, and he isn't anymore."

"What about that entourage of nouveau-hippies?"

"They aren't enough for Tsoai." Wynoma looked to the shed. "I'm bleeding several chickens, the blood will clot soon and unpleasantly thicken." She walked to the shed, was gone awhile, and then came back with a large, cut glass decanter of dark red liquid. Adam followed her into the dining room.

There on the cream damask cloth were still the tall glasses. She must have been expecting Tsoai to stay. Wynoma poured a deep ruby glass for herself, and then looked at Adam. "Would you like...?"

"I'd prefer wine."

Wynoma actually smiled. She left and returned with a dusty bottle that she handed to him with an opener. Then after first looking out her closed windows towards the buses, she sat at the head of her table and started drinking. Taking long sips of blood seemed to relax her a bit, as Adam pulled off the bottle's lead seal and dug the opener into the dry cork.

Absentmindedly with her fingers, Wynoma wiped a touch of blood off her lips, saying, "Tsoai can't face the fact that this world has grown beyond him."

Seeing her casually drink blood caused Adam's stomach to contract uncomfortably, but if he was going to mediate this situation, he needed to be stronger! He poured the thinner, purplish wine for himself. Drinking its warmth helped settle him. "If your brother can not accept his lot in life, neither of us can help him."

Seeming a bit surprised, perhaps gratified that he could accept her ways, Wynoma drained her glass of blood, then poured herself another. As she started to take a sip, she winced touching her cheek. "Tsoai does things without thinking. Maybe if you left and stayed with one of your cousins, he and I could work this out."

"Your brother is a major fruitcake! I'm not leaving you alone with him and his nutty hangers-on." But why was she trying to get him out of here? "Is he using me as leverage to force you to do something?"

"He won't dare hurt you." She spoke like a mother bear protecting a threatened cub. "I have put a protection on your house. But those ones he influences, they might do something stupid..."

Back in his own house, Adam headed for the books. Uncle Quentin had amassed the largest library of esoteric knowledge he'd ever heard of, with bookshelves in every room. The volumes upstairs in the master bedroom were probably his best shot.

Adam started taking out the necromancers chronicles, spell books, Medieval bestiaries—many of them in handwritten on parchment or in foreign languages. He hefted one dark book with a very faded-gold lettered title 'The Secrets of Being' or was that 'Beings'? The book was in Latin bound in age darkened leather.

As he studied it, Adam noticed there was a faint marking on the front cover that made him look closer. It was in the leather, not painted on, and he turned the book sides-ways it looked like a stylized ram's head and seemed at an odd angle to decorate the binding. He looked closer. It wasn't painted on or impressed on the leather, but it rather looked like a faded tattoo.

Feeling creeped out, Adam put that book down. Reading all of this would take months, no years, and most of the counter activities he had found depended on identifying what sort of spirit or being he was dealing with. Tall, ageless, pale-eyed Wynoma Poxcow claimed to be a Cherokee, but Paracelsus had laughed at that, saying because of vanity, ladies reduced their age. The Cherokees were originally an Eastern people forced west; still what if she and Tsoai were of an older tribe? Or were these blood drinking tall ones something entirely different?

With the exception of Wynoma, Paracelsus was the most learned person he knew by several centuries, but the alchemist was so grateful for Adam straightening out his affairs that he was forever brewing up those horrendous 'life extension' potions. Adam was due one about now, and if he drank it, he would be hallucinating for a day, and have that disgusting taste of some rare earth metal in his mouth for a week. Adam dialed the alchemist, but Paracelsus didn't answer.

Tsoai said something about the 'Day of Embers,' but in Quentin's books, Adam couldn't find a North American Indian tradition associated with 'Day of Embers.' He Googled it on his laptop and came up with a Roman Catholic tradition of four, three-day periods considered especially favorable times for the ordination of priests. The Roman Church was famous for co-opting pagan sacred rites, so Day of Embers was probably an older, western European tradition.

Adam glanced at the time. How late do Gorgons stay up? He put in a call to Madame Alexis Ceto in Greece. Someone who has lived for centuries should know something about how things worked.

"Geia sas!" Came a husky, sultry voice.

"Madame Alexis, it's Adam Martin."

"Oh, Adam, my darling boy!" She just about purred. "It is so good to hear from you. When are you coming to my island? I'll send my jet!"

He wanted off that subject. "How is your niece?"

She gave a warm, rich laugh. "You are such a matchmaker! Dr. Ravi has been here three times already–vastly interested in studying the snakes of my island, of course." She laughed deeply again. "He puts great blushes in my precious Dia's cheeks. They say nothing, but I think soon I will invite you to a wedding."

That's good news. "Listen, there is something called the Days of Embers. I know what it means in the Roman Catholic Church, but is it a survival from older Pagan worship?"

"But, of course, the Days of Embers are four days a year, that corresponded to the solstices and the equinoxes."

"Druid?"

She laughed. "Even I am not that old, dear Adam. But yes, probably the solstices were observed as an important marker in the Druidic calendar."

"That makes it Western European, but I'm coming across it in the context of North American Indians rituals. Possibly pre-Columbian."

"Because they tell you Columbus or the Vikings discovered the Americas, you actually believe them? Adam, how foolish of you."

"Then the religious observations might have crossed over?"

"Certainly. A being that has wings and flies doesn't have to stay tethered to Mount Olympus."

This was going to be harder. "Madame Alexis, do you know of some sort of universal protection against harm?"

Hearing the seriousness in his tone, her voice too became sober. "What are you dealing with, Adam?"

"I don't really know."

"You saved my precious niece, if you are in need, I will come. My little ones bite well!"

"No, this is going to be over shortly, but thank you." Just her offer of help centered him a bit.

Going back upstairs, Adam didn't turn on the bedroom

lights so he could walk to the windows unsilhouetted. Outside by the buses, he could see campfires burning, they reminded him of a painting of some Civil War battlefield under siege. There were some lights in the tour bus, but the window shades were lowered, and there were no lights in the school bus or Wynoma's house.

Adam should rest, but he felt afraid for his secretary. It was more than just her brother's physical size and anger, there was an aura of ancient evil and vicious destruction about Tsoai. And in all the time Adam had known her, he had never before seen Wynoma as helpless.

When Adam had been threatened by Tasha's father, Wynoma had confronted him with an elephant gun loaded with fragments of silver. Silver, salt, and garlic were the traditional protections against evil. He didn't have any garlic, but in the pantry, Adam had a fifty-pound sack of coarse salt for the winter's ice.

He went downstairs to his dining room where he opened the top drawer of a heavy, black walnut sideboard that was carved with hunting scenes. Its many drawers held several magnificent collections of silverware. In the top drawer, he picked up a dining knife that looked antique, maybe Eighteenth century? It was heavy as hell. Could it be the real stuff, not plated, was it actually solid silver?

When he inherited this house, before he tired of it, Adam had started cataloging each of his treasures. He remembered this set as being covered with black tarnish, but now it was polished to a gleaming glow. Did Wynoma polish these when the office work was slow? Getting a pillowcase, he threw the priceless silver knives, spoons, and forks in, hoping the cloth didn't rip from the silvers' weight.

He left by his kitchen door, finding the combined load of the salt and silver an awkward haul. Outside it was silent, no peepers, and no birds rustling in the trees, all he heard was the crackle of the bussers' untended fires Still, it looked like his unwanted guests were all asleep.

Skulking about he felt like a thief, but, hell, this was his property! Adam walked over to the house Wynoma lived in, and he put down the salt bag. Gauging a rough circle around her house, every three feet or so, he stuck one of the silver knives or spoons or forks into the ground until he had completed an entire ring of protection around Wynoma. Then he ripped open the salt bag, planning to rewalk the circle, dribbling salt over it.

"Don't," said a quiet voice near him.

Adam startled, turned, and in the moonlight saw Wynoma. "I was..." What was his explanation for this crazy expedition?

She was looking toward the buses. "Come inside."

Adam followed her up on to the porch, still carrying that fifty-pound sack of coarse salt. Behind the dark door, she turned up the wick on a kerosene lamp, and it gave a yellow, dancing light to a small, shadowed area. Wynoma was wearing an old-fashioned, floor length, white flannel nightgown. Her hair was unbound and trailed down below her waist as she cautioned, "Please don't put salt out, it will kill my flowers." The lamp flickered as she carried it through the wide arch into the parlor.

He followed. "Don't you have electricity? I mean you do, you've got a refrigerator in the kitchen."

"I minimize its use," said Wynoma, "I find it prickly on my skin and its jittery movement disturbs my rest, so only the kitchen area is wired."

That bothered Adam. "Do my office computers and lights hurt you?"

"No, I do not sleep in your mansion." She sat in her black rocker.

Adam seated himself in a chair opposite her. "Your brother and his friends have got to go."

Oversized, the rocker looked as if it had been made for her, she said nothing, just rocked slowly.

Adam continued. "Your brother spoke of the Day of

Embers? That's the summer solstice on June twenty-first?"

"It can be any of the four lodge posts of the sun." She seemed to be listening to something from the porch that he couldn't hear.

"What does he want you to do?" demanded Adam firmly.

Before she could answer, the front the door swung open with a force that slammed it against the wall. Eyes angry, Tsoai strode in closely followed by his bus driver who carried a large woven basket. "My sister, your little friend comes to you late!"

Wynoma's eyes widened, and her voice shook with anger as she said, "You dare cross my threshold uninvited?!"

"Your friend has dropped something." Tsoai turned to the bus driver. "Return it to him!"

Josh turned over his basket, dumping the silverware out on to her floor. Knives, forks, and spoons clattered as they fell, every piece that Adam had planted in the yard now bounced on her floorboards. Tsoai had to jump back to keep some of it from landing on his boot. He glared at his sister. "Tell your little friend to be more careful!"

At that, Tsoai turned and walked out with his driver following him.

Wynoma waited until they were gone before she rose and closed her front door. Turning to him, her control was back, and she spoke quietly, "I know you are trying to help, Adam, but don't do anything like that again. Now go back to your bed."

She walked out of the room, leaving him. Adam noted two things: Wynoma had polished his silver and could, therefore, touch it, but Tsoai did not touch the silver, he had his driver do it.

Awaking shortly after dawn, Adam heard activity. Sounds of digging. He looked outside his bedroom window and in a field to the left, several of Tsoai's males were using a post hole digger and shovels. Soon they were struggling to raise a pole, about the thickness of a telephone pole that looked twenty feet high when it was sunk in the pit.

All of Tsoai's females were out in the field. Watching? No. As soon as the pole went up, a rope was looped around it, and then a fifteen-foot line was knotted to the loop. The boot shod women used that line to measure a perfect circle as they stomped the grass around the pole.

Adam headed over to Wynoma's, to find her drinking her breakfast blood.

"What does he want from you?" he asked. She said nothing. Adam tried to sound as stern as he could. "Answer the question, please!"

"It is not your affair," Wynoma spoke with a deadened voice.

"My secretary's getting beat up. Her brother and his personal army are building whatever on my front lawn–but that's not my business? What is that thing going to be? A teepee? A sweat lodge?"

"It is a dance circle."

Adam faked delight. "We're having a party? Am I invited?"

"Have you heard of the Ghost Dance?"

Adam had to think about that. "Are we talking about the nineteenth century? A religious revival that led to the massacre of some Blackfoot Indians?"

"Lakota Sioux in1870."

"Okay." He waited.

"After the buffalo were destroyed, when the Western Indians were being squeezed on to reservations, they were starving, and they turned to a ritual that was called the 'Ghost Dance.' The Lakota Indian Agent felt he was losing control, so he panicked, called in the military, and that resulted in a massacre of hundreds."

Adam was struggling to understand. "The Ghost dance was only a religious movement. A social gathering, right?"

Wynoma looked into his eyes. "No, it was more. The

whites translated the name as 'Ghost Dance,' but it actually was the 'Spirit Dance.' The Indians knew they had transgressed, turning away from She-Who-Creates. They suffered under the white man, so they thought that if they made the proper obeisance if they danced and prayed, the earth would be renewed. They danced for forgiveness, believing their dead loved ones would walk again, and the thundering buffalo herds that sustained them would return, bringing food and peace to the land."

"That was fantasy," Adam said.

"No. If the chosen ones do the proper Spirit Dance, it can reorder the world. Bring back another time." Wynoma stopped, not looking at him again. "But it would be a mistake to do. It is wrong to change what has been grown. It would upset the proper balance."

"But your brother wants you to dance?"

She only looked at the dark carmine dregs in her wine glass.

Adam pressed. "Are you one of the chosen? Can you bring back the Indians' world?"

"I will not," Wynoma said finally, her face more closed than he had ever seen it.

"Who is stronger–you or your brother?"

That impassive, Easter Island Moai like face almost looked frightened. "In speaking to the ancient ones in the past, they would listen to my voice, not Tsoai's. But," she sighed, "he has grown stronger."

She hadn't really answered his question, but he had the distinct feeling that she didn't know the answer herself.

Back in his office, he finally got Paracelsus on the phone. The alchemist blathered on. "Adam, I've got your latest potion. It's almost spoiled so I may have to brew another for you. That is a terrible bother, you must come here at once to pick it up!"

"First, I need your help. You once told me that Wynoma

is not a Cherokee, that she was something else, something older. What exactly is she?"

There was a silence on the line, then Paracelsus seemed to speak reluctantly, "Dear boy, you and Quentin have been very good to me, but I've made promises, given my word...one can't..."

Adam was being blocked by the confidentiality of ancient friendship? "Her brother is here."

Paracelsus' voice lost it's whining, straying qualities, as he focused sharply. "Which one?"

"Tsoai."

"That one." He didn't sound happy. "It is rare for one to live so long and still hate so deeply..."

"Tsoai's beating her up! He's got a bunch of hangers-on, and he is trying to force Wynoma to perform the Spirit Dance on the Day of Embers."

"That's coming up, isn't?" He asked vaguely.

"It's today, Paracelsus!"

"She can't do the dance!"

"Why not? I mean it can't really bring back herds of buffalo–can it? In the middle St. Louis?"

"Well, there won't be a St. Louis or a United States."

"What?"

"The Ghost Dance, dear boy. When time is inverted and turned back on itself, when the Indian dead rise and the buffaloes return, the whites will no longer be."

"Are you saying that if Wynoma dances, that you and I and every other white is going to disappear from North America? What's happens to the mixed bloods? What happens to Europe and China?"

Paracelsus voice came over as annoyed. "Don't try to work out the convoluted mechanics! **The dance must not be done!**"

"Why?"

"Having the power and understanding its ramifications

are two totally different things! Tsoai and Wynoma think that they can just neatly twist time around. Well, it won't happen that way! Yes, Archimedes was right when he said 'give me a place to stand on, and with a lever, I will move the earth.' You can throw this planet across the solar system, but our world will be destroyed–for all of us!"

"Who is going to tell that to Tsoai?"

Paracelsus was quiet for a long time. "He's got total contempt for me–for anyone." He was silent again, then said, "Wynoma is very powerful..."

"Wynoma's afraid of him."

"Has she summoned Ursus and Wind?"

"Who?"

"Her elder brother and sister, assuming they still exist on this world."

"How do you go about summoning them?"

"Ask Wynoma, but if young Tsoai has grown in power and has allies to feed him, he might be able to overcome all three of them. My dear boy, we may have a problem!"

"Whatever species or creature Tsoai is—there must be something that can hurt, stop, or kill him?"

More silence on the line. "I don't know of anything you or I could manage." His voice changed back to fussy annoyance. "And do come pick up your potion. I'm sure I'm getting closer to your proper formula."

It seemed stupid to drink that poisonous potion to extend a life that might end tonight. Adam headed outside to the lovely sight of one Tsoai's men peeing on his apple tree. With the circle around the central post tramped down, the woman with their bright neck scarves or beading neck throat pieces lounged in front of the buses, waiting. For what?

Adam found Wynoma on her knees, working in her garden as she weeded her herbs. "Would you like chicken dumplings or fried chicken Friday?" She asked.

"Does it matter? Am I going to be here after tonight?

Paracelsus says if you do the Spirit Dance, you guys are going to crash this world!"

As she started to stand up, he offered his hand to help rise. As he did, Adam noticed a roundish stone about the size of big pumpkin in her garden. It was moss topped, but was some sort of sculpture, that he moved closer to see. It was a chubby-faced baby's head, carved in gray stone in Olmec fashion. The squinting, angry face seemed strangely familiar, and suddenly Adam had one of those 'feeling-knowing' moments. "That's Tsoai as a child?"

Wynoma nodded. "Our Brother Ursus carved it."

"Ursus–the Great Bear? Is he still alive?"

"Yes."

"Can he help you with Tsoai? What about your sister, Wind?"

She looked so beaten. "I have sent messengers, but they have not answered." Wynoma looked to the sky. Heavy, gray clouds were massing overhead as a group of five crows were flying into the trees beyond the clearing.

Adam had to push her. "You've got to do something! Is there anything... " He shouldn't say 'kill.' "That can stop Tsoai?"

Wynoma turned and walked toward her front door. Frustrated at being ignored, he just followed as Wynoma carried her cutting basket into the front parlor. He was about to say something when they both became aware of movement in the corner of the room.

The heavy twisted branch was still there, but now standing on it was the biggest raven Adam had ever seen. It looking more like an eagle. The giant bird appeared to be carved from obsidian and perched untethered near that fully opened window. The raven had only one good, light-colored eye, while the other seemed to be damaged shut.

Did Wynoma's rigidly held body relax a little when she saw the bird? As Adam watched she walked to the huge raven.

It cocked its head to look at her, and they both stood silently for a moment, then Wynoma turned back to him saying, "A storm is coming. A very powerful one."

"You want me to stay inside?"

She looked to the raven, who seemed to stare back at her. "No, I don't think it matters. You may come at sunset tonight. That is when Tsoai wants his Spirit Dance."

"Tonight is the twentieth. Day of Embers is tomorrow.

She smiled tightly. "The old religions start the next day at sunset."

They weren't ready. "Can you hold it off?"

"No." She turned away, carrying her basket of herbs toward the kitchen.

Knowing he get no more explanation, Adam turned to leave. On her rocker next to her sewing basket, was a mound of white doeskin which he walked to and picked up. He held the sleeve of a dress, worn soft with age and tied with small purple shells and beaten metal horn bells. There was a bone needle stuck where Wynoma was mending the fringed hem. Her gown for the Spirit Dance?

So tonight would be a Day of Embers. Day of the End? Outside her house, he heard sounds of wood chopping, people cursing, with all their racket, the bus clan apparently didn't seem to care about alerting anyone.

One of the men was digging a pit, just out of range of the ring around the pole. Others-- men, even the women, were carrying branches, brush, and logs. Chopping wood. By the time Adam finished a tasteless lunch, there were two more pits being dug, and the first one was already set up with a tall teepee of logs and chopped up two by six's waiting for a bonfire.

By three p.m., they had completed four fire pits, and Adam realized, they were all placed at roughly the four cardinal points of the compass, at equal distance from the central post. At four p.m. they started lighting them or trying to ignite the thick wood without proper kindling. Finally, some fool came out and poured gas on the wood, making flames that shot two stories high as blue smoke billowed out. With the drought, lighting sparking fires wasn't such a great idea, and Wynoma was right about a storm coming in, the wind was picking up.

Adam checked the weather report on his TV. Yesterday the prediction was for sunny weather today, but now it seemed something big was rolling in. Even the five p.m. weather man sounded surprised.

Back on his office desk, he looked down. The Redferns' wills needed to be finished, but why the hell should he bother if the world was ending? There was Tasha's e-mail with her flight times, and Adam printing it out. He was so close seeing her. Adam wanted to call and tell her to fly to Europe and safety instead, but somehow he didn't think that would help.

While he was standing there looking out his front window, the phone rang.

"Adam." The voice of Madame Terri, but it was not her usual radiance or even her childish, confused voice. "Adam, something's happening."

He held his breath and tried to sound neutral. "What do you feel?"

"The dogs are restless. Thurston won't leave my lap, and Houdini growls at the door."

"There's a storm coming." Adam tried to sound calm.

"It wasn't supposed to rain," she said in a frightened voice.

"Yeah, the meteorologists missed this one."

"Adam, my mother was a psychic and my grandmother too. When I was a child, they started training me to read the cards. I've been reading Tarot for over sixty years, but this morning, when I laid out the cards, I don't see anything. It's like there isn't going to be anything ahead?"

"Yeah." That's pretty much what Adam expected.

"Maybe there is something wrong with me...?"

"No. It's not you! Do your guides tell you if there is

anything I can do to change things?"

Again she sounded very frightened. "I'm not getting anything."

"Okay." He had to sound confident. "Things will be fine. Now I want you to stay inside, snuggle with the dogs. And you know those really rich birthday chocolates that I gave you–the expensive ones? The ones you said you were just eating one at a time–splurge! Eat'em all! You'll feel a lot better."

He only picked at his chili dinner. Hearing the wind outside, he restlessly walked to the Game Room and looked up at Quentin's portrait. "You left me the house and your practice, but it looks like I'm the Martin who just lost the world."

Call Uncle Jeremiah? Explain there was this Indian named Tsoai, who was going to try to subvert time and probably would wind up nullifying them all? Wynoma and her kin were not in the judge's jurisdiction.

But what Jeremiah would have told him was that a counsel must present the best case he can, trust in the basic fairness of the court, and then stand up beside his client when judgment was pronounced.

Adam went upstairs, showered, took out his best, blue suit and red silk tie that Aunt Jereusila had given him when he went to law school. He searched for and found his grandfather's gold cufflinks that Uncle Jere had given him for his graduation party, and one last thing, he went back downstairs to his office and picked up the printout of Tasha's itinerary. This he lovingly folded and tucked into his inside jacket pocket.

One-half hour from sunset, he walked outside to his porch. Not that he could tell sunset was coming as an overcast sky covered the sun, with just touches of redness on the western clouds. God, that wind had picked up, and as the trees branches swayed, Adam saw crows, hundreds of them, thousands of them, all sitting in the branches of his oaks and in Wynoma's pines. But now all the birds were silent, just perching there and watching.

A strong wind was coming from the Northeast. He thought about going back and getting a raincoat. Didn't seem worth it. Tsoai's four bonfires were burning strongly, but the wind was flaring them giving off great sparks that flew toward the trees, the buses, and meadows. Where were Tsoai and his tribe?

Then Adam saw Tsoai and only two others. Two males had followed him, then moved off to squat cross-legged on the ground about thirty feet from the dance pole. They had leather topped drums, and soon they were using their hands to pound out a steady beat into the wind's howling.

Tsoai walked to the circle stamped around the post. He stood in front of the Western fire wearing a bright green velvet shirt over his dark pants, and he carried a huge staff, topped with a horned animal skull, and blowing black-tipped eagle feathers. He stood spread legged and waiting, his long hair whipping in the wind.

Adam started walking. He stopped ten feet from Wynoma's porch when her door opened. Under the porch light, Wynoma came out her raven hair long, with just a thin, cloth threaded hair-braid in front of each ear. She wore the pale-white deer skin gown with it's trimming of purple and white shell beads. Her feet were bare with just one yellow feathered ankle bracelet as she walked down the porch towards him.

A man followed her, fully as tall and muscular as Tsoai, his hair was as long as Wynoma's and birch-bark white. Ursus? He was bare-chested with tanned buckskins pants, and on the edges, Adam could see trimmings of iridescent green and black feathers. Ursus carried a heavy staff, topped with a turquoise inlaid human skull. Adam noted Ursus' left eye was pale, pale lavender, and he wore an eyepatch over the other eye.

Saying nothing, brother and sister lined up and walked forward together. Adam just inserted himself on the right side of Wynoma as they walked to the circle. From the left, past the buses on his driveway, came another figure. A woman, a shade shorter then Wynoma, she had the same ageless face, but streaks of white ran in her long black hair. Wind?

Wynoma and her brother stopped and waited for their sister to join them. As she got closer, Adam could see she was wearing some sort of primitive dress that was belted at the waist and woven with stylized bird and snake motifs that looked like an Aztec design. She too had the tanned skin and light orchid eyes of Wynoma's kin.

For a moment, they looked at each other but didn't speak. This sister joined the line beside the elder brother, and they all started walking forward.

Adam found himself almost having to do a double step to keep up. These people didn't appear to hurry, but their long legs covered ground. The steady drums beats could barely be heard over the wind's howl and the fires' hiss and crackling. Smoke made Adam's eyes tear.

They were forty feet from the pole when Wynoma reached out a hand and touched Adam's arm, saying softly, "Stay here."

He wanted to argue but didn't, as the other three moved on.

They split when they reached the circle, with Wind walking in a stately fashion to the Southern fire, while Wynoma walked to the Eastern one, and her elder brother took up his position at the Northern blaze.

They all waited, as at first the wind lessened, then it seemed to howl even stronger.

Adam didn't see them saying anything and they didn't even look at each other. He had an unpleasant feeling of electricity shooting about his body, as tremendous energy seemed to be building up. The hairs on his skin rose, and he could smell copper in the air.

Tsoai looked from the central pole to his brother and sisters. He seemed to be trying to mentally overcome them. Wynoma had closed her eyes, her body was swaying, not from the wind, but more with the beat of the heart drums. Tsoai was winning.

Then in unison, elder brother, sister, and Wynoma suddenly bent their heads down.

Tsoai screamed as if in terrible pain—shaking his fist to the sky!

A white flash with a resounding crack and Adam found himself on the ground. He thought someone had hit him, but he didn't know where the blow came from. Adam struggled to rise, trying to breathe back the air knocked out of his lungs.

In the center of the circle, the post was on fire. It must have been struck by lightning! Adam looked at Wynoma and was relieved to see that even with her bare feet on the earth, she still stood, and the rest looked okay too.

Except for Tsoai. He was screaming something that Adam couldn't understand, and his body was bent, as if in severe pain, yet Tsoai still shook his fists in helpless rage at the sky. Glaring in turn at the other three before him, he threw down his eagle-feather trimmed staff and limped away.

The other three just watched him, then Wynoma's elder sister and brother turned and walked into the darkness toward Wynoma's house.

What the hell happened? Something big Adam knew. But what? Adam hurried to Wynoma. She looked her perfect and calm self, but he noticed her hands were shaking slightly. Following his eyes, she carefully folded them in front of her.

He asked, "What just happened? You guys saved the world?"

"It will rain heavily soon. You should go indoors."

"Is this it? Or is Tsoai going to keep squatting on my doorstep?"

"He will leave."

"Will he come back?"

Wynoma looked down at him sounding exhausted. "I don't know."

"But we'll be better prepared for him the next time, right?"

"Perhaps."

She started to turn away, but Adam had to ask. "Okay, this saving the world business, did I help you? Or hinder you?"

That great rocky face finally smiled. "You did exactly what I expected." Saying that she turned and walked away on silent, bare feet.

The next morning, Adam woke at dawn, to hear the bus diesel loudly warming up. Half behind his window curtain, he watched them leave, the silver tour bus first.

He walked out down to his porch. The circle still had it's blackened, lightening shattered pole and he had four fire pits to fill in. The bus people had apparently never heard of *'leave no trace behind.'* His front yard was now a garbage dump filled with crushed cups, food wrappers, beer cans, and wet cardboard boxes. They'd also left stacks of full trash bags, and by the sewage stink, before they left, they must have emptied their tour bus's toilet tank into his meadow.

Oh, hell. At least they were gone so he could get this place cleaned up for Tasha's visit. Adam had gotten work gloves and a heavy garbage bag, and he was trying to pick up a soaked cardboard box when he heard a firm voice behind him.

"You forgot to stop by Paracelsus's for your potion." Wynoma was standing there, with a rake and more garbage bags. She was dressed in work jeans, but her hair was neatly bunned above her head.

The way his day was going that figured. "You know, that's just what I was planning for today, go right out and pick up that life extension potion from Paracelsus. Top of my list, in fact, right after I'm done here, I'm going to his place."

She reached into the pocket of her jeans. "Fortunately," Wynoma pulled out a vial, with bright red liquid. "He dropped by with it."

Adam could smell the vial's fox urine stench, even

across the open field of sewage, and his stomach wrenched at the thought of drinking it. Oh, shit. Well, at least things were back to normal.

The End

If you liked this book, please put a comment on your favorite social media, so that we both can both enjoy more of Adam Martin's adventures. Lynn

FOR OTHER BOOKS CHECK
www.lynnmarron.com
FOR PURCHASING INFORMATION

The following are published in print and e-book editions:

MYSTERY WITH A TOUCH OF WITCHCRAFT AND ROMANCE:

THE SEAPORT PSYCHICS' MURDER

When their Old Craft worshiping mother dies of stab wounds on Beltane, her young triplets are separated for seventeen years. Raised without knowledge of their witchcraft heritage, Holly Corey returns to Mystic, the Connecticut Seaport of her birth. Reunited with her two brothers, her immediate goal is turning 'Witch House' into a viable Bed and Breakfast to keep the three of them together; that is until she meets Sgt. Travinski, the handsome policeman, who is determinedly pursuing both Holly (for love) and her brother Frost (for murder).

GRACE FARRINGTON'S OYSTER RIVER GENETIC RESEARCH MYSTERIES:

ORR: THE NOBEL PRIZE MURDER

While working at Oyster River Research, Grace Farrington is passed over for this year's Nobel Prize, and then the DNA pioneer finds herself accused of murdering the man whole stole her first shot at the Nobel. With the formidable mental powers that Grace normally uses to unravel complex genetic puzzles, she is forced to solve a triple murder. In her efforts she is helped or sometimes hindered by her eclectic group of friends: a psychic Viking named Freya; an old money patron, who seems more interested in Grace's body then her body of work; a hot-tempered research assistant who can't stop punching, and a very politically incorrect marine biologist who wants her on the back of his bike when he goes midnight partying with his motorcycle gang.

CENTAUR WARRIOR ADVENTURES:

CENTAURESSES OF THE SILVER DRAGON

The Regiment follows the hoof prints of Jace, a ruggedly handsome centaur of Clydesdale proportions. Winning on their last field, but betrayed by treacherous princes, these sword-wielding mercenaries are outlawed. Now as he hunts a patron to keep his band together, he must hide a worsening leg wound, knowing a challenge to his leadership will end in death!

Stumbling on to a dying bazaar, this legendary fighter finds a patron in the stunningly beautiful Silver Star, a tall, gray centauress with sea foam white hair, luxurious tail, and ominous cloven hoofs. Star promises a vast treasure if the Regiment frees her rich mines from a rampaging dragon. But there are problems: Jace does not believe in dragons, and the lady has not told him of her real enemies, the deadly Scarlur.

With the free-ranging lifestyle of centaur society Jace has always had many lovers, but none truly have touched his heart, since he was forced to slay Ginger on the battlefield. Yet now Silver Star, this skilled healer and intriguing fast running she, awakens old desires within him. Beyond just mounting Silver Star, he must possess her! Even if her kin forbid their love and his warriors fear this silver siren is leading them all to their deaths!